THE COLLECTION

TOPSIDE PRESS

NEW YORK

THE COLLECTION

EDITED BY
TOM LÉGER
& RILEY MACLEOD

Léger, Tom & MacLeod, Riley C.

The Collection: Short Fiction From The Transgender Vanguard / ed. Tom Léger and Riley MacLeod

ISBN   978-0-9832422-0-8 (hardcover)
ISBN   978-0-9832422-1-5 (paperback)
ISBN   978-0-9832422-2-2 (ebook)
LCCN   2012940833

10 9 8 7 6 5 4 3 2 1

Cover and interior design by Julie Blair

This book is dedicated to the writing teachers who set the bar higher.

ACKNOWLEDGEMENTS

A volume of this magnitude would not be possible without the support of the dozens upon dozens of people who helped us during the two years leading up to its publication, including Vani Natarajan and Seth Carlson, who performed our copy editing and Katie Liederman, who coordinated our publicity efforts. Red Durkin, in addition to contributing to the book itself, devoted hundreds of hours of work in both community outreach during the submissions process and in the months leading up to publication. Her support as a friend and as an artist made this final product possible in the form it exists today. Additionally, Sarah Schulman and the generosity with which she has honestly shared her wisdom, experience and talent is the reason we were sure that vision we had for Topside could, and should, be realized.

Encouragement and support came from Zoë Holmes, Jay Kotowski, Matt Brim, Sarah Green, Taylor Black, Elizabeth Koke, Amber Dawn, Zoe Whittall, Cris Beam, Cristy C. Road, Annie Danger, Dylan Scholinski, Rachel Pollack, Jack Radish, T

Cooper, Scott Turner Schofield, Morty Diamond and Bodies of Work Magazine, Bevin Branlandingham, Jason Lydon and the volunteers at Black and Pink, T.T. Jax at the Lambda Literary Foundation, the Barnard College Library and the Barnard Center for Research on Women, and the many people who stepped up to share information about this project with their communities around the globe.

Special thanks also should be extended to Tom's MFA cohort, Beth Bigler, Wallace Wilhoit Jr., Karen Terrey, Jean Ann Wertz, Matthew Quick, and Kalela Williams, a source of strength and inspiration for many years.

Additionally, without the technical and artistic dedication of Julie Blair, we would never have even been able to consider embarking on this adventure. We will be forever in her debt.

//

Finally, our early supporters made *The Collection* possible by taking a chance on a not-yet-published book from a brand new, unproven publishing venture and so—on behalf of our team, all of our authors, and the readers of this book over the coming years—we would like to thank The 2110 Centre for Gender Advocacy, Adison, Ailsa Craig, Alex Holding, Alex K., Alice Kalafarski, Anders Zanichkowsky, Andrea Zanin, Andreia Blue, Annette Kirby, Ash Brown, Audacia Ray, Beth Gibbons, Bex Kat-Herder, Brynn Cassidy West, Callan Molinari, Candace Gittens, Christopher C Hamann, *in honor of* CeCe McDonald, Claire Cramer, Comrade Alita, Connor Raymond, Cory, Dana Biscotti Myskowski, Daniello Cacace, Delaney Manders, Devon S, Diana Cage & Max Crandall, DJC, DS from PGH, E. Steven Fried, Elle Rose Bemis, Ellen Shull, Emily Dix Thomas, Eric and Alejandra, Erin Bunny Burrows, Everett Maroon, Frances Jean, Gabriel Faith, Hayden Mills, HB Lozito, Heather Flescher, Jack Florey, Jane AlphaMale, Jayden Sparke, Jean Harris, Jeannette Montgomery, Jeff Brody, Jen Richards, Jeri Morgan, Jessica Hayes, Jessica Reardon Smith, Jessie Lee, Joey Alison Sayers, John Berdrow,

Julia Williams, JXB, Kacey Skye Musick, Karen Fredrickson, Kirstin Cronn-Mills, Kythryne Aisling, L. Sean Hubbard, L. Wheaton, Lee King, Lilith Graye, Lucy Grey D, Marcy Wehling, Marja Erwin, Matthew K. Watson, Matthew Stewart, Maxime Vallée, Melody J Proebstel, Michael Rosenthal, Mik Kinkead, Miriam and Joe Slipowitz, Monica Rodriguez, Morgan H. Goode, Morgan M Page, Mym Johnson, Naomi Clark, Nic Bravo, Nico Vitti, Noach Dzmura, Oliver Haimson, Omer Elad, Pam Park, Peter Finlon, Rachel Casiano Hernandez, Ray Drew, Rebekah Bassen, Rev. Cindy Bourgeois, Rice-Aron Library of Marlboro College, Ronan & Tobi, Roy Pérez, Sam Everett Byrd, Sarah Laing, Sea Parsons, Rabbi Sharon Kleinbaum, Shawn Syms, Smoove, Susan H Linden, Syl & George, Talya, Tara Durkin Rochford, Ted Kerr, Tess Yardney, Tessa Maria LaLonde, Tey Meadow, Theo Czerevko, Tobaron Waxman, Tyrone Boucher, Vani Natarajan, Wesley Flash, Wyatt Riot, and Zoey Leigh Peterson.

THE COLLECTION

INTRODUCTION

When we began this project, we didn't really know what the resulting book would look like. In the hundreds of submissions we read, even we were surprised to see a dozen different genres full of narratives we never imagined. As we read and re-read each story in the process of making a lot of difficult decisions, the very fact that we had these kinds of choices to make helped us understand that our dream of revising the landscape of trans literature could be realized.

We also found that our initial suspicions were correct: that there are hundreds if not thousands of talented writers interested in the same narratives we are, and that there are many writers capable of producing the kinds of stories other trans people and their allies want to read. In the end, we had to judiciously select only a small fraction of the work, and we have still ended up producing a book nearly 400 pages in length. (If we had included all the works we wanted to, the volume would have become unwieldy to print, sell, or read.)

These stories range in stylistic expression from experimental narratives to speculative fiction to close-to-the-bone realism. There are love stories, adventure stories, family stories, stories about class and racism and sexism and politics. Stories about bodies, real, imagined, and desired; about relationships beginning, ending, changing, and shifting; stories about moving to new towns and coming back to hometowns as a new person; stories about natural disasters; stories about the end of the world. Stories about all of these things together. Stories about other things entirely.

Thematically, the authors included here tackle everything from the exciting lives of demon catchers to the mundanity of shopping at farmers' markets. However, each author casts a trans character as the principal actor in their own life, as an agent of their own destiny. Those destinies runs the gamut—from trans superheroes understanding what it means to be superheroines, to couples deciding whether or not to live together as the Hadron Collider powers up, to coming home, to winning a prize at a local fair. But each story has a trans character growing, changing, and making a difference in the world, rather than letting the world happen to them.

The stories are very different, but they each share a similarity: each story sees a trans character as the protagonist, rather than comic relief or an incidental character for a cis-gendered protagonist to use as a tool toward self-revelation. We sought stories that tread new ground in trans fiction by exploring the emotional and imaginative impact of trans people's real lives. As the fiction in this volume begins to inspire artists and thinkers to take trans art to its next iteration, we hope that more authors will begin to consider what else trans characters are capable of, where else they can go, and who else they can be.

The last two years of our artistic lives have been focused on the book you hold in your hands. To us, this work was worth it because we know first-hand that literature, like all art, is a transformational tool that contributes significantly to improving the lives of the people who interact with it. We hope that these stories make your life better, either by showing you something new, or by showing you something familiar in a new way or from a new voice.

Above all, we think that you find the stories that follow enjoyable, inspiring, and thought-provoking. Even as this book goes to print, we, have been anxiously asking ourselves "what's next?" We don't know. We hope you tell us.

TOM LÉGER & RILEY MACLEOD, EDITORS
NEW YORK CITY
OCTOBER 2012

I MET A GIRL NAMED BAT WHO MET JEFFREY PALMER

Imogen Binnie

We could have the Jeffrey Palmer conversation, but it would be a waste of time. Here's how it would go: I'd want to talk about what he wrote, what he took from Alan Watts and what he rejected, how he was almost on the same page as his contemporary Eckhart Tolle, but where the fissures were and why—why they used such different language. I'd want to talk about his correspondence with Ken Wilber. If you were still with me, I might show you the tattoo on my bicep from a letter he wrote to Wilber when Wilber was already ignoring him: *quantification is both an over- and under-simplification of something so simple and complex as the self.* If you were keeping up, I might explain that as much as I find Palmer's work to be true and effective, I don't know if he really understood what Ken Wilber was doing—but you wouldn't be following me.

I could tell you about what Palmer thought about Daniel Quinn, Noah Levine, Sun Tzu, Yogananda—Rhonda Byrne. I'd want to tell you about how the beauty of Palmer's writing is how self-evident it is, how little interpretability there is, that that is the point. But your eyes would already have glazed over. You wouldn't want to hear about his influences, who he influenced, or why.

Completely disinterested in content or context, you'd be like "Man, webcam meditations, though. It just seems like such a silly waste of time. I sure couldn't ever waste so much time on that." And I'd be like, I know. You and everybody else. That's not interesting, that's what everybody who only knows him from that stupid *Vice* article from two years ago says.

So when I want to talk about Palmer, I do it on the internet. It's retro but I post on two message boards: a discussion board about his work and a board for trans women under thirty. Last December—almost a year ago now, when I was fucking that boy Charles, when my hair was red and I used to wear that awful green eyeshadow—there was a little convergence where a conversation about Palmer came up on the message board for trans women. And like most times you hear his name, it came up as a joke; in a thread about philosophy somebody was like "Jeffrey Palmer, LULZ." I didn't want to out myself as someone who actually appreciates his writing—someone who actually does the work everybody else thinks is so funny—so I just neutrally mentioned that I'd read some of him. And this girl Bat was like, "Oh, I met that weirdo once!"

Obviously you can't just be like, "OMFG YOU MET JEFFREY PALMER: SWOON." You'd just get kicked off the internet, or worse. I think I posted something like, "Oh cool." Still neutral, like neither endorsing him nor disowning him. But I threw up a little.

I checked out her profile and she was in New York, too. I threw up some more, but I didn't really do anything, because while I did want to hear more, I was nervous that I would've sounded at best kind of uncool and at worst like a wingnut cultist if I'd asked directly, and I couldn't bring myself to ask about him in a mocking way.

I didn't do anything about it for a couple days. I remember almost writing private messages to her a couple times, but feeling embarrassed at my phrasing, or at seeming all eager, or at caring at all. So I went to work. I chopped wood, carried water. When I had shifts at the coffee shop at night, I did my webcam meditations in the morning, and when I worked in the morning, I did them at night. I was feeling really uncentered, though, and I couldn't get it out of my head that there was a girl in this town—a girl I could meet—who'd met Palmer.

Then one night I let Charles sleep over because he'd said he'd make me coffee in the morning, which was a change of pace. I'm the one who spends all day every day making coffee, and it had made me laugh. I mean, I liked Charles okay, but we were definitely not in love. For one thing, he didn't really have a sense of humor, but more importantly he kind of dismissed my affection for the oughties—he thought the Animal Collective poster over my bed, my primary instance of décor, was just a picture of some ugly blobs, and he wouldn't even listen to the playlists I made for him—but I was fucking him because he was hot and didn't have weird shit around my body, not because we were emotionally compatible. He was an unimposing guy, only a little taller than me, but he was so lean. He had these small, muscular shoulders, and when he fucked me, he would lose himself so completely that I'd lose track of my body, too. He's the only person I've ever had sex like that with.

I mean, when we weren't fucking, he would talk about computer things, and his new headphones, the album he had apparently been working on for a long time, bands from now, all this stuff I didn't care about. I tried to be interested but the interest wasn't there. We would have made a terrible couple.

So anyway I remember very clearly that night he stayed at my house, we slept all tangled up, and then I woke up that morning with the idea firmly in place that I was going to e-mail this girl.

I kicked him out without letting him make coffee. I wasn't mean. He was very sweet, and he even kissed me goodbye. I made myself a coffee, sat at the computer, and wrote a super direct message:

> *Hey, I actually am kind of interested in Jeffrey Palmer,*
> *what was he like?*

She didn't respond for almost a month. This was back when I was wearing that Strokes shirt every day. That month disappeared into Brooklyn, and then I got a short e-mail from her. She was like:

> *yeah totes, I dunno, what do you wanna know?*
> *—Bat*

She signed the e-mail, "Bat."

////////

This is how I imagine Brooklyn in 2008: there was an American Apparel on every corner. This was before American Apparel became the big store at the end of every mall in America, back when it was still cool—before Dov Charney became governor of California and sold the company to Target.

Everybody was wearing American Apparel, tight skinny jeans and tank tops that were sort of oversized, so they draped across tiny rib cages like ancient Roman tunics almost. Everybody was in their early or mid-twenties. Bedford Avenue was always so crowded with people of all races and both genders that there were people walking in the street, slowing down traffic, even in the middle of the night. It was like a 24-hour 4th of July barbecue. Everyone was holding a can of Pabst with beads of water dripping down the sides and everyone was tall, very thin, and had long hair, even the boys. The girls' hair was longer though. Some people would be wearing headbands.

Sexually it was a total free-for-all: boys kissing boys, girls kissing boys, girls kissing girls, boys kissing boys and girls at the same time, bodies squirming together along the sidewalk like the sweatiest gay disco in the seventies. Total humidity.

Everyone was a graphic designer and everyone was in a band and every band made dreamy, swoony music with lots of reverb and echo and vague distortion. You'd go see them at the Trash Bar or Southpaw or the McCarren Park Pool or go into Manhattan and see them at CBGB's.

You'd make out with your boyfriend, who was the singer of the second-to-last band of the night, in the men's bathroom. They'd just have performed and he'd be sweaty, his hair damp, the hollow under his clavicles, and he'd reach his arm around and pull you close and grab your ass and your breath might catch and you'd feel his cock, hard in his tight jeans, so maybe you'd suck him off, right there, even though there was no lock on the door.

Everybody had those iPods that were like four inches long and two inches deep. Most people had the little white earbuds but some people—your boyfriend—would have big, oversized headphones that kept out the world around them. Sometimes he'd wear oversized, slouchy hoodies.

So on any night of the week, since everybody freelanced, everybody would stay up all night doing coke at somebody's beautiful converted loft either in Williamsburg or out in Bushwick somewhere, making out or watching Wes Anderson movies or listening to the new Ariel Pink album or talking about Jonathan Safran Foer or Dave Eggers' new book and smoking cigarettes and talking, sprawled across black leather couches.

The boys all had permanent stubble that was usually just long enough to be soft, but sometimes it was short and rough and it scraped your face when you kissed them.

Everyone was a spaced-out kind of happy, and everyone had enough money, and everyone was pretty, and everyone read books, and all the boys had such thick eyelashes that they looked like they were wearing mascara, and all the girls were the kind of tough that boys can't even be.

////////

After I got Bat's e-mail, I did some math. Palmer died in 2011, so if she met him, she must've been at least fifteen or sixteen in 2010, right? Maybe younger but probably not. So that would make her, like, thirty-five or forty right now. She was probably older. It didn't matter. I was just already thinking, I am going to meet this woman.

The main reason I was already thinking I wanted to meet her was that she had met Palmer, and I wanted to pump her for everything I could get about him. But another reason is that Jeffrey Palmer lived out his last two decades in Brooklyn. He was one of the original gentrifiers, back in the early nineties, who came to Brooklyn from Manhattan, back when people still wanted to live in Manhattan. I didn't think somebody who was in her thirties or older would be posting on that message board—and come to think of it, nobody over thirty even should have been posting there, which was my first hint that maybe Bat wasn't one hundred percent together, although maybe she'd been posting there since she was under thirty and got grandfathered in—which meant that most likely she'd met Palmer in Brooklyn in the early oughties. Which in turn meant that she'd probably lived in Brooklyn back then, and it seems like everybody else who was there then has either gotten old and boring and gotten over all the androgyny and danger, or else they've moved away and don't talk about it.

I wanted to hear firsthand what it was like in halcyon Camelot.

The more I thought about it, the more I threw up. I got all twisted up with nerves over talking about Palmer, and about meeting an internet person in real life, and even about owning up to my obsession with that time period. I shook it off, though, and sent her exactly the message I wanted to send her:

Can I interview you about him? Is it okay if I record it?

If I record it.

I should know by now that it's never as bad as you think it's going to be to out yourself—as anything—but I was surprised that I felt relief on sending it. It was out of my hands. Letting go of it, pushing back against attachment, erasing—of course it was a relief.

I drink a lot of coffee, but I usually just either drink it at work for free or steal it from work and bring it home. I can't afford to go out to other coffee shops; it's why Charles and I didn't go on dates. I couldn't afford my half. I mean, I still can't, I still live in the apartment I was living in then. I'm making a little more an hour at the coffee shop than I was back then, so I'm still just scraping by. But I live in Brooklyn.

You know my life story: when I was little, my parents let me wear girl clothes all I wanted. Even to school. At school, by first grade, I was getting enough shit from other kids that I stopped and convinced myself I was over it. Toward the end of high school I admitted to myself and then to everyone else that I wasn't over it at all and started wearing girl clothes again. Changed my name. Got on hormones. Moved to New York. It's the same life story you've heard from a million trans women. It's pretty much everybody's story, although I guess some of us don't move here. The only real difference in my story is that for a long time I was super resentful about the years I'd spent trying to be a boy—I was drinking a lot, having bad-news sex with jerks, doing too much coke, whatever, 'til at twenty I found

Palmer's book *The Ephemeral Now* on the kitchen table of a boy whose name I don't even remember. I took it, read it, and started letting things go.

So I feel like I owe Palmer pretty much whatever agency I have in my own life. I would've stayed in that town, married and childless, 'til I died, if I hadn't learned to let go of the resentment I had toward a bunch of five-year-olds I'd been in first grade with, the twelve-year-olds (boys and girls, both kinds of lunch tables) who ostracized me so effectively in junior high, and all the boys in high school I had desperate, secret crushes on.

I'm not mad at being broke. I'm not mad at being trans. I'm not mad at pretty much anything, and it's not because I actively try not to be mad—it's because I actively try to own, confront, and let go of that anger. It's not complicated.

So that's why I decided to spend eight dollars on a coffee at the Verb with this girl I'd met on the internet. Nobody really knows much about Palmer, because his writings were all published posthumously, and I doubted I'd ever have another chance like this.

In retrospect, of course, there are reasons he kept his personal life so personal, and the fact that I wanted so badly to know more about him only shows how far I still had to go in terms of spiritual growth. I'm not mad at my younger self about it, though.

I met her at the Verb, that café on Bedford Avenue in Williamsburg that's been around since forever, right next to the Ikea. It feels true that it's been there for decades: the wood's all old and dark and chipped, and even though I know that lightbulbs go out instead of just getting dimmer, it feels like the lightbulbs haven't been changed in forty years. When I walked in, Interpol was playing on the speakers in the corners of the room, and I was like, why do I work at the stupid coffee shop by my house instead of here? It would probably start to feel like hokey nostalgia-town eventually, but still. I bought a coffee, got a table, and started recording sound.

When she walked in the door, I knew this was the woman I was here to see. She looked normal enough, just tired. Her hair was long and dark and cut in these very shaggy layers, limp enough that it might as well not have been a haircut at all, the way it hung. She was wearing an old white tank top, skinny jeans, these cowboy boots that looked ancient, and a short suede jacket; basically, she looked like me on a good day, when I'm really into my outfit, feeling like I've got a modern version of a Cat Power thing going on, except instead of 28 and vegan, if I was sixty and didn't really take care of myself. Which made me feel tired.

"Buy me a coffee, doll?" she asked, walking straight up to my table and sitting down.

"Uh, sure," I said, immediately off-balance because I'd budgeted for one coffee, and the eight bucks for hers was going to come out of next week's food money.

Once in a lifetime opportunity, I remember telling myself. Let it go.

So I bought her a coffee, which she immediately started drinking, even though it was way too hot. I was like, are you so skinny because you don't eat? Do you think coffee is food? But I had that feeling like I was in the presence of such an unknown quantity that I didn't want to say anything to make her freak out or hate me or leave and not tell me about Palmer, so I just tried to be cool.

I know I shouldn't have recorded it. Or, at worst, I should have listened to the recording once when I got home, meditated on it, and deleted everything. But I didn't. I still have it.

"So hey," she said. "You're like, a JP nut, right?"

"Kinda," I said. "I guess."

"That's cool," she said. "I remember after he died, when kids were first starting to read him, I was like, that fuckin weirdo? Seriously? but I guess people get something from it or whatever, so I shouldn't talk shit."

"Why do you think he was a weirdo?"

"Oh my god, that fucker lived in this VHS tape castle in his own private kingdom of like... Wait okay."

You can't hear it on the tape, but I swear to god here she drank the entire cup of coffee. I still couldn't even sip mine because it was too hot. I remember thinking, this is a weird conversation, and being kind of bummed out that she hadn't introduced herself, that we hadn't hit it off—that I already knew on some level that she wasn't going to tell me anything that would mean anything to me, spiritually.

I already knew that this was a mistake, that I shouldn't have been recording.

"Okay," she said. "So around like 2008 I was friends with that guy Pete Malkowitz?"

She paused for me to acknowledge that I knew who Pete Malkowitz was, but I had no idea.

"He was in that band The Fourth Joke?"

Blank look.

"They had a song on one of the *Twilight* prequels' soundtracks," she said, moving on. "That was their big moment. Pete knew everybody at all the clubs and he'd get us into shows for free, so we'd go see bands like every night back when he was still around. Anyway Pete was friends with this girl Melissa and one night he was like, you've gotta meet Melissa, so while I was at Pete's place off Manhattan and like Metropolitan one night, this girl Melissa buzzes up and he lets her in and I'm like, fuck you Pete, you just want me to meet this bitch 'cause she's trans too? But he's like whatever man, he's so fucked up on I don't even know what that you can't even be mad at him.

"So this girl comes in, and she's nice, kinda shy, doesn't want any coke, doesn't want any weed, just kinda hangs out and drinks—y'know not a small amount of beer—and then, like, hours later we find out that Pete went up to the roof and fell asleep, but we didn't know that right then. Suddenly it's just the two of us in the room.

"I'm like, so how do you know Pete, and I don't even remember what she said. Who cares? We start talking, and all she wants to talk about is trans stuff, and I was kinda skeezy at the time, I was kinda like whatever, like maybe I'm gonna play it off like maybe I'm not trans, but eventually it gets boring just listening to her stutter and hesitate and not say anything, and all I've been able to think of the whole time is like, if you get to pick your own name, why pick something so fucking boring like Melissa? I mean why not pick something cool?"

"Like Bat," I say. On the recording I sound bewildered; I think by this point I've parsed most of it out, but at the time you can hear in my voice how alien the dynamic she's describing is to me.

"So I ask her and she's like, I don't know, somebody told me that you have to pick something incongruous so nobody will think twice about it. I snorted and hit the fucking bong, I was like, whatever. I remember I was healing this—" She showed me a big faded blob of ink on her forearm. "—and I was trying not to scratch it, I was like, whatever, darlin'. Then the night kind of blurs and then I guess that's how we became friends."

"Uh-huh," I said.

"So yeah anyway turns out my first impression was wrong, she was actually pretty cool, she let me crash on her couch for a couple months after I got fired from Capone's. She was really funny, too, you just had to drag it out of her. Uh, she died. But maybe like a month after that night at Pete's—he died too, actually—I was at her place and she was like, I've got to go pick up this coat or something I left at my friend's house, I'll be back in an hour or two. But I was like, Whatever, I'm not doing anything and I've got an unlimited Metrocard I found—I don't know how long it's good for, but I might as well take advantage. I'll come.

"I guess in retrospect she didn't really want me to come but back in the day I could be kinda pushy and like, god knows how she knew Pete, and I didn't know any other friends she had, but I figured I was being a good friend if I came along. I was prioritizing that shit, being a good friend. So like, I went with her way the fuck out to like Mapleton, or Dyker Heights or some shit, where you can smell the ocean, and this guy lived in a house. Like a detached house, not an apartment, he had the whole thing."

183 93rd Street.

"So we go in, and she's like, I'll be right out, like she expects me to wait outside, but it was early in the spring and I'm kind of chilly so I'm like nah, I'll come in, and inside the house, like the whole place—from top to bottom—every wall is like a bookcase full of VHS tapes. It's seriously like something out of an early scene in a David Cronenberg movie, where it's not totally freaky yet, just kind of weird you know? Just like setting the mood?"

"Sure," I said.

"So okay like whatever, the only thing in this house is VHS tapes, there's no couches or tables or fucking room on the walls to hang anything. I pick one up but Melissa slaps my hand and I'm like, Okay, sorry, and we go up the rickety stairs right inside the front door—they've been painted white so many times you can feel your feet sticking to them, like inside an old church or something—up to the second floor where it turns out he's in this bedroom, on the bed, filming himself, talking into one of those old-timey camcorders."

He was doing webcam meditations.

"I'm like, This whole house is a dusty pile of old tapes when the whole world runs on Netflix and DVD's and shit, and you're filming yourself with a video camera from 1984 the size of a fucking dog? I don't say anything, though. Melissa's like Hey, and dude turns the camera to her, keeps filming, he's like, hey, all pimply face and fat belly and shit."

Which matches the couple of pictures of him that we've got. At this point I'm basically salivating and hanging on every vulgar word she says.

"He's like, Hey, your jacket's under the bed, which makes sense that it would have to be hidden because it's not a fucking VHS tape and obviously all that's allowed in his house is VHS tapes and VHS recorders and, like, this guy himself. So she gets her jacket out from under the bed. He doesn't even get out of his bed; he's wearing this old black t-shirt with a hole at the seam of one sleeve, he looks pretty gross actually. Like his hair's all greasy and he's kind of pimply. Melissa's like, Thanks, she digs her jacket out, and we go downstairs and leave."

"That's it?" I ask.

"Yeah, pretty much," Bat says. "Well I mean, y'know, I found out about his shit later. After he died and they started publishing his books and stuff Melissa was like, Dude, Bat, remember that guy? You met him once, and I was like Who, Video McCamcorder? She was like, Yeah, and explained about how his work was actually kind of important, and how he was recording on videotapes 'cause they were analogue so they couldn't get leaked the way an album or a movie does, and how he took a magnet to them right before he died, fuckin' dumbass."

"Why was he a dumbass?" You can hear defensiveness in my voice.

"I dunno, man," she says, leaning back, away from my microphone. "I mean for one thing, videotapes, they're not fuckin' digital. You can't erase something analogue with a fucking magnet, even a huge fucking giant magnet like the one homeboy used. Some deep thinker, doesn't know the difference between analogue and digital. Plus: spilling your guts, watching yourself spill your guts, then erasing it? Wingnut shit, man. I don't even get what his quote-unquote philosophy was supposed to be—that all things pass? Big fucking insight."

The conversation pretty much ends here because I got too pissed off to keep being nice to her. I asked if she'd ever read him, and she said she hadn't, and I was like so where the fuck do you get off talking shit about shit you don't know shit about, and then it pretty much goes downhill. We're not friends. Who cares.

///////

Because this is what Brooklyn is like now: it sucks.

///////

After that conversation, I remember riding home thinking about it. Thinking: of course you should let this go. And I mean, I knew Palmer wasn't the most physically attractive guy, that's one of the first things he had to figure out a way to work through, to overcome, to accept and leave behind. He wrote about it. It was hard to hear about it from somebody else, though, especially in such indelicate terms. And to hear the house he inherited from his mother, where he did his most vital work, where he had the epiphany about furniture and clothing and clutter and people and emotions and clearing out clarity, to hear it described in such stark terms... by the time I got home I'd of course integrated it into an opportunity to let an idol go, to kill a Buddha, but I was still throwing up a little in anticipation of doing a webcam meditation about it. Maybe a long one. Maybe an important one.

I was thinking about Bat, too, though. How did a person get like that? I could sort of understand the relationship between her and Melissa—like, this was back when trans people were supposed to go "deep stealth" and it was awkward to know another trans person and nobody ever mentored anybody else and being trans was totally stigmatized and people called each other "GG's" and "t-girls" and "trannies" and "autogynephiliacs." But why be so obnoxious?

Cocaine?

I've done my share of cocaine, and it didn't stop me from looking for a piece of serenity. And why was she so judgmental? Was it leftover pain from transitioning back in the Stone Age when you still had to get a psychologist to write a letter that said you weren't crazy, even though they all thought you *were* crazy, and then you had to carry that letter with you everywhere? I know that back in the day you even had to pay for hormones, so only rich trans people even got to transition.

I don't know, man, I still don't. I try to have empathy but seriously: fuck those damaged goods. No room for that in my life, even if it's in a context of respecting elders. Fuck a pointlessly moochy and judgmental elder.

The first thing I did when I got home, though, was look up VHS tapes. Turns out Bat was wrong: they occupied this weird grey area between analogue and digital. Like the information they communicated was digital in that it was zeroes and ones, but the tape, the medium itself, degraded from magnetic contact with the VHS player every time they were read. They communicated their digital information in an analogue way. So knowing she was wrong about something, I didn't want to believe anything Bat said. But everything else was spot on: the description of 183 93rd, the quantity of videos, the attention to his video recorder instead of the people in the room with him; these all fit with what we know about Palmer. She wasn't making it up.

I sat down at my desk, turned on my computer, turned on the video recorder, and I started talking. I explained about how meeting Bat had been an impulse I understood from the beginning to be selfish and counterproductive, but as a human being with flaws I hadn't been able to resist. I talked about how she probably *had* met Palmer, and how she was probably a jerk the whole time; that being trans, or having met Palmer, or having lived in Brooklyn in 2008, or having probably seen all the best bands—none of this made her anything other than herself. And who she was wasn't me, and who she was didn't have anything to teach me.

I digressed: of course there was something for her to teach me. There was a lot to learn from her about idolatry and euphemisms and hero worship and how age doesn't necessarily do anything good to you. I talked about how maybe Jeffrey Palmer wasn't attractive but that didn't matter. I remember talking about how Charles actually was attractive, one of those thoughts that bubbles up and then you let it go. I finished by talking about how in a macro sense of course none of this mattered, and in a micro sense it was all an opportunity to learn and grow and strengthen and let go.

I watched the video once and then erased it. Then Charles came over.

SAVING
• Carter Sickels

"Dean, you okay?"

I realize the engine is still running and turn the key. "Yeah."

Jillian still looks a little woozy. I had to pull over for her a couple of times after we left the highway. This is her first time in Kentucky.

"Finally." She opens the door. "Fresh air."

We left Brooklyn early this morning, and now the mountains throw long shadows. I hesitate, then get out, as Jillian strides across the overgrown lawn, marveling at the trees, commenting on the loud cacophony of crickets and spring peepers, carrying herself like she's never wanted to be in any other body. Her skirt rides up, revealing long muscular legs. Her hair is thick and red. She looks beautiful, and out of place.

My grandmother's house is a little one-story clapboard hidden in the hills behind a fortress of maples and oaks. The paint is dingy gray, sloughing away like old skin. A dented GE washer sits on the front porch. Before I go in, I take my time walking around the yard. Jillian does the same, framing her hands around her face like she's looking through a camera. A dense web of kudzu has swallowed the hen house. At the edge of the woods rests a heap of aluminum cans, old tires, and discarded appliances. From here I can hear Sugar Creek, which cuts through the lower woods. When I was a kid, my grandmother and I fished for catfish and trout, but after the coal company started stripping above us, the water turned the color of Tang and most of the fish died. A pillowcase still droops from the clothesline, as if my grandmother had been hanging clothes one day and then vanished into air. I feel like I've come back to bury her, but she's not dead: she is in a nursing home, where I put her.

I push open the door, step into the musty, warm, familiar smell. It is eerily quiet. My grandmother usually had the TV and radio going at the same time. The house is dark and gloomy except for a few drizzles of sunlight. I flip the overhead switch and look at what I'm faced with. Boxes of old medical bills and Sunday circulars, tin cans with the labels scrubbed off, piles of clothes and fabric. Empty mayonnaise jars, plastic ketchup and dish soap bottles. Stacks of newspapers, yellowed church bulletins.

"You were right, she is a hoarder." Jillian picks up a framed picture of me. I'm seven or eight, wearing a ruffled dress, a yellow bow in my hair. "I can't wait to start filming."

When I first asked Jillian to come with me, she didn't want to leave the city, but then she started seeing it as a filming opportunity. "Back to your roots," she said. "Trans guy in Appalachia."

Suddenly I feel embarrassed, her seeing where I grew up. I light a cigarette, she looks at me with disappointment. Smoking on testosterone increases the risk of high blood pressure. I've been smoking since I was fourteen. When I started injections last year, I recorded the changes in a notebook—weight gain, body hair, muscle mass—and Jillian took pictures. But after a while, the changes became too subtle, or maybe we both stopped noticing. Everyday I look at myself in the mirror, wonder if this is the real me.

"God, it's stuffy in here. I need a shower." Jillian lifts her wild mane off her neck, puts one hand on her hip. "You grow up without running water?"

"Funny."

When she smiles the lines around her mouth pop out. Jillian is almost forty, six years older than me. She's got a horsey face and a yoga-trained body, and she's flirtatious and loud; when she walks into a room, people look at her, draw close. Only I get to see her in the mornings, her eyes puffy, her brow grainy with creases and lines.

While she showers, I walk through the house. Last year when I moved Grandma into a nursing home, I felt too overwhelmed to deal with the house, so I just left it stuffed with all her crap and hoped no one would break in. The coal company wants to buy the land. I told them it's not for sale. Back in Brooklyn, I started dreaming about fixing the place up. It will be Jillian's and my vacation house. She'll work on films, I'll plant a garden, our New Yorker friends will visit for long weekends. We'll have barbecues, sun ourselves at the swimming hole, read under the shade trees.

My grandmother's room looks exactly the way I remember: chenille bedspread, wallpaper printed with tiny roses, a dresser cluttered with ceramic animals and miniature teapots, and framed pictures of family, including her husband. My grandfather died before I was born. He was a deep miner and a drinker, and one day he was discovered by the creek, his skull cracked. He'd gotten drunk, fell on a pile of rocks. My grandmother never remarried or even showed interest in another man, at least as far as I know. I moved in with her after my mother died. I was eight years old. My grandmother wasn't affectionate, but she raised me and always thought I'd come back one day to take care of her.

In the walk-in closet, her faded dresses drape from the wire hangers like the skins of animals, the coats and blouses moth-eaten and old as the bones of this house. Bulging boxes of scrapbooks, photo albums, and loose pictures are stacked next to my grandmother's thick-soled brogans and a pair of navy blue church shoes. I take out a handful of snapshots, shuffle until I find one of my parents. My dad in fatigues, slim and handsome in a weaselly way. My mother in a blue cutout dress, her thick hair falling below her shoulders. She's leaning against him, her face open and smiling. I don't remember them ever looking this happy.

"Find something?"

Jillian is standing naked in the doorway. Her ropey wet hair is a tangled nest, her skin pale and freckled and smooth. A Japanese-style tattoo of a pink budded tree stretches across her ribs. Her heavy breasts hang downward, the large pale nipples like a pair of closed eyes.

For the first time in weeks, she reaches for me.

"Not here," I say, stepping out of my grandmother's closet.

Back in the front room, Jillian slips into a t-shirt and underwear. I've missed my chance. She is thinking about her film again, studying the room. Jillian's work is experimental, and I usually don't understand it. She has shot me hundreds of times, but there is still so much she doesn't know.

She asks about the history of the house, about my grandmother's collections of junk. I don't know where to start. Grandma was always a pack rat, but it wasn't until after I moved away that she started to save so much. I push open the window by the sofa, blow a line of dead flies off the sill. They scatter like ashes.

I tell her it's my turn to shower. "We can talk about all that stuff later," I say.

In the steamy bathroom, I strip and wipe a clean circle on the mirror. My eyes are milky brown, like my father's. My face is more square now, also like his. My hair is short and spiky, and stubble peppers my chin. It is strange to think that I am here and that my grandmother is not. It is strange to think that my lover is on the other side of the wall. I hear her moving things around. I flex my muscles, clench my jaw, admiring the angles. This is what I used to dream about, years before I had language for any of this. My chest is flat and scarred, the nipples numb. After the surgery, nasty blue and yellow bruises made it look as if I'd taken a beating. I remember how it felt the first time I could run my hands down my chest without feeling the rise and knots of soft flesh, how that nothingness, that hardness, thrilled me.

//////

Exhausted, we collapse on my bed. Grandma never took down the posters from my youth—Madonna, Depeche Mode, and INXS—now yellowed, curling at the edges. I turn off the light, and when I reach for Jillian, she doesn't move. It's been like this for a while.

"Dean," she says sleepily.

"Yeah?"

"Tomorrow you promise to talk about your parents? For the film?"

I haven't told Jillian much about my family, about my childhood. This has always been a sore point. Jillian wants to know everything. Transparency, she says. Trust, she says. I was an only child, didn't have many friends. Grandma and I did not need to talk about what was in our hearts, we weren't that kind.

"Okay."

Soon, she is sleeping. She breathes open-mouthed like a child. I lie here for a long time, wide awake, trying to make myself little. Jillian takes up most of the twin bed. I finally get up and fish a couple of blankets out of the cedar chest and make up the couch. But I still can't sleep. Can't stop thinking about what I'll say to my grandmother. Can't stop thinking of my parents, their fuzzy faces materializing like Polaroids behind my eyes. It's all the stuff in here, I think, it's suffocating me.

I slip on shorts and sneakers and head out to the creek, breathing in the country air. The silver moon leads the way. This was who I used to be, a country kid who loved the woods. Not boy nor girl, just a kid. People think that the decision to transition is something you've always known, or that one day you experience a single earth-shattering epiphany. Maybe for some it's like that, but for me, for so long, I've both known and not known; I've had experiences that led me here, took me away, and brought me back, a tide I can't predict. Something rustles in the brush, probably a coon. The warm air smells clean and woody. This is my home, I say. But the words, spoken aloud, sound empty.

In the bright daylight everything about Perry looks worse. Burned out storefronts, rows of old coal camp houses pressed close to the road. I start to drive through quickly, but Jillian asks me to slow down. Jillian grew up in the rich suburbs of Long Island, a train ride away from the city. We met at a mutual friend's birthday party in Williamsburg. She pulled me onto the dance floor, pushed her hips against mine. She told me I was handsome, her voice low in my ear.

"What did you do for fun around here?" She's wearing big sunglasses, and her hair is piled on top of her head like a stack of flower petals.

"I don't know," I say. "What did you do?"

"Hung out in the East Village, and went to clubs."

"No clubs here. People had parties in the woods."

"You're such a country boy." She says, "It's sexy."

I glance over to see if she's kidding, the glasses make it hard to see her expression. "I just mean, you know, it's so different from how I grew up." She adds, "More real."

What I see are poor people and falling apart homes and hardscrabble lives and junker cars on blocks. Families that go back for generations, and keep going, sprawling with cousins, half-siblings, step-kids. But not my family, whittled down to just me and my grandmother. A tight, closed-off circle we will die out. I drive by a duplex where a girl I used to have a crush on lived, and then to where my parents' house once stood, now rubble.

"Do you miss your parents?" she asks.

"I try not to think about them very much."

We pass the diner where my grandmother used to work. Jillian wants to eat breakfast there, but it would be too complicated. "I might see people I know."

I continue on Route 12, taking us out of Perry and toward Murphy, where my grandmother now lives. It's a bigger town, feels safer-I don't know anyone here. On the way Jillian asks me questions about my parents, trying to open me up. The digging makes her happy. She's won awards for her films, shown them in art galleries.

I exhale a stream of smoke, remembering how my mother's hair fell out after the chemo. "My dad was only nice to my mom after she got sick," I say.

"He felt guilty." Jillian clears her throat and hesitates like she's just thought of this question but I know she's been wondering. "Did he hit you, too?"

Earlier, when I admitted that my father sometimes hit my mom, Jillian's face cracked with interest, and I quickly backpedaled, downplaying it. She wanted to know why I'd hid something that big from her. "I wasn't hiding anything, I just don't like to talk about it," I said.

Now I say, "He never paid much attention to me. After she died, he spent even more time on the road." My father was a long-haul truck driver. Whenever he'd first get back from a trip, things were good, but they never stayed that way for long.

"My parents would sit in the kitchen and eat doughnuts, listen to the radio. He'd tell stories about what he saw on the road, sometimes he played checkers with me," I tell Jillian, remembering how when he laughed, which was rare, his eyes crinkled, his thin moustache jumped.

"He didn't know what to do with me, so he gave me to my grandma," I explain.

"You were twenty-one when he died?"

"Twenty." Willowy and athletic, with shoulder length hair and slender hips. "I was away at college when my grandmother called with the news," I say. "He had a heart attack on the road. A few days before, I had just had sex with a girl for the first time." At the funeral I couldn't stop thinking about her, I remember, her hot breath on my face, the way she'd bucked against my hands. "I don't think I could have ever come out to him. . . as anything," I add.

"You came out to your grandma though. As a lesbian."

"A long time ago. She was cooking soup beans. She stopped what she was doing and said, To each his own. Then she kept right on stirring. We never talked about it again."

I pull into the nursing home parking lot.

"What do you think she'll say when she sees you now?"

"I don't know."

Last year the sheriff called to tell me that my grandmother had taken to wandering. She'd stolen the neighbor's mail, driven his pickup across the county line. I had sensed from our phone conversations that she'd grown forgetful and nervous, but I didn't know how bad it was. I'd just started hormones and there was nothing noticeably different about me; some saw me as male, others as female. I booked a round trip flight, didn't stay long. After several doctor appointments and meetings with nursing home staff, I signed the papers. She didn't fight me. Half the time, she didn't know who I was.

Before we get out of the car, Jillian takes off her glasses and looks at me with clear blue eyes. "I'm glad you brought me here."

"For your film," I say.

"No, not just that." She reaches for my hand. "It means something, you sharing so much. I know it's not easy." Her long fingers curve over mine like ribs of a small animal. "Telling me all this, it's good for you, too. Don't you think?"

"Yeah, maybe." I add, "I'm glad you're here."

Her smile is big and loose, and gives me the extra encouragement I need to go inside. Before we walk through the doors, Jillian asks if I'm sure I'm okay with her filming, and I tell her it's fine. She carries the camera under her arm like a pocketbook, and I suddenly wish I'd brought something to give to my grandmother, flowers or a cake. I try not to look at the old people parked in wheelchairs, slobbering, sleeping, staring, and I walk up empty-handed to the woman at the desk and tell her that I'm Gertrude Pearson's grandson. She doesn't bat an eye. Jillian and I pass as a straight couple, no problem, a thin, delicate boy and his sexy girlfriend. Sometimes I still feel nervous inside my skin, wondering how people see me, what they think. Jillian says I worry too much: "Just be yourself."

Outside room 12, I take a deep breath. I've played this scene in my head over and over, but I don't know how I'm going to explain to my grandmother who I am. It's not like I've radically changed. My clothes, hair, all of that is the same. For years I've been presenting as male. But my voice is deeper, and the hair on my arms and legs is dark and thick. I debated whether to shave my sideburns, but left them, the faint soul patch, too.

There are two beds, two beat up TV's. The roommate is not here. My grandmother sits in a pale green armchair staring at her palms as if she's reading her fortune.

"Hi," I say.

She looks up, thinner than I've ever seen her, an emaciated elf with long ears and a nose two sizes too big for her face. Gigantic glasses slide down the bridge. She wears a pink terrycloth robe and fuzzy slippers, clown shoes.

I go to her, kiss her forehead. "How are you?"

She looks at Jillian, then back at me. "Is that the new nurse?"

Jillian's lost her big smile and she seems nervous now, like she's afraid to get too close. I wonder if all this is too much at once. The junk in Grandma's house, the dilapidated town, the stink of the nursing home. All this decay. But then she recovers and steps toward my grandmother with her hand outstretched, and I think about the way she used to smother my hands and face in kisses when we first started dating. Jillian's face is tender and kind. My grandmother doesn't take her hand though, and Jillian drops it to her side.

"I'm Jillian," she says loudly. "Dean has told me so much about you."

The blank expression on my grandmother's face doesn't change.

"Grandma," I say, moving closer to her.

As I do that, Jillian quietly lifts her camera. "Pretend I'm not here," she instructs.

I put my face in front of my grandmother's. "Do you know who I am?"

Her eyes narrow. She purses her thin lips, then opens her mouth. "Last night a man come in here through the window and tried to rape me," she says.

Everything inside me locks together and then explodes into pieces in a matter of seconds. "Grandma, that's not true."

She smacks her lips. She's wearing new-looking false teeth that are straight and white. "Yesterday they strangled that girl."

"Grandma."

She shakes her head, impatient. "You don't know what goes on around here."

"What are you talking about?"

She's quiet, then mumbles under her breath, "My Jell-O."

"Wait, what you said about that man."

"I'm hungry."

I take a deep breath. "Grandma, do you know who I am?"

She lifts her gnarled hand, brushes my face. The skin of her hand is shiny like bone, the wrinkles like the ridges on a shell. I wait, my heart pounding.

"I'm your granddaughter," I say because I don't know how else to do this. "I'm Anne."

She spots Jillian's camera. "What's that thing she's got?" She looks alarmed. "What is she trying to do?"

Jillian lowers the camera, nervous again, like a kid caught stealing candy. My grandmother glares at her, then orders Jillian to bring her a bowl of Jell-O. She says to me, "These people, they don't know what real work is."

I sit behind the wheel, shaky and sick. "I shouldn't have put her in there."

"The place isn't that bad."

"I could have come out to stay with her. I'm all she has."

"You can't live here."

I swallow hard and close my eyes, feel Jillian's hand on the back of my neck.

"What if there's some guy really hurting her?"

Jillian softens her tone. "Dean, she's confused, delusional. Maybe she's getting mixed up with things that happened in the past."

I open my eyes and start to ask what she means, but stop as her hand falls away. I turn the key, the engine rattles, starts.

"You look so sad," Jillian says.

"I'm fine."

"Don't think I'm fucked up." She stops. "I'd really like to film you."

"Doing what?"

"Nothing, just be yourself."

I'm quiet and can feel her waiting, worried about what I'm thinking of her. Then I tell her to go ahead. I drive back to my grandmother's, the wheel pulsing in my hands, the camera on me, a weird monster eye. Everything rushes past. I don't see any of it.

The next several days go by quickly. I put in few hours of work, but without internet service, I can't do much. Our cell phones don't work either. New York is far away. Jillian spends the days behind her camera, filming me, filming the house. I spend the days organizing and cleaning, still thinking about how I can fix it up. Wondering if I should move my grandmother back here where she belongs. She wouldn't recognize the place now. I'm only throwing out what's clearly junk, but still, that's a lot. The rooms are beginning to open up, to feel brighter.

The closest neighbor, Paul, lives on the other side of the hill. He comes by each day to complain about something, and he offers to haul my grandmother's junk to the landfill for free. He's some relation to the old guy that used to live there, and he has no idea about me: he assumes that Jillian is the granddaughter, that I'm her husband.

"New York," he says with disgust. "Why in the hell would you want to live there?" Paul is in his late 50s and can't talk for too long without breaking into a heavy smoker's cough.

We stand outside by his pickup. When Jillian walks by, waving, he winks at her. Then he says to me, "Watch out for that one." He hasn't said much to Jillian, but he's always polite. She says he leers.

"I don't like him," she says. "I'm not straight. That's not who I am."

"We've got to be safe," I tell her. "We can't be raging queers out here."

Jillian has dated trans guys and non-trans guys and women, and she told me early on, "All of my relationships are queer, doesn't matter if I'm with a guy or not."

Now she says, "It's fucked up."

Still, we fall into a kind of routine and move easily around each other like the married couple Paul imagines us to be. I tell myself this is who I am-there's no hiding anymore. I pretend this is where we live, that we are happy.

Tonight Jillian volunteers to make dinner. I'm on the front porch, looking through my old sketchbooks that I found in the back of the hall closet. The pages are soft, velvety. I used to draw all the time when I was a kid. I flip the page to a leggy princess with rhinestones in her hair, then a boy pirate with quick fists and the power to turn invisible. There are also a lot of strange animals that fill the pages, mythological deer and horses and owls.

I can see Jillian through the window at the kitchen counter, her back to me. She moves quickly, with purpose. Chopping, tossing. My grandmother used to can in the summers, steaming up the kitchen. She'd warn me to stay away from the hot mason jars. She always seemed old to me, her hands bent and gnarled, her back hunched.

She still doesn't know who I am, although she seems to be getting more used to me. One of the nurses thought I was Anne's brother, and I let her believe it; another called me by my old name, and I didn't deny it. Jillian comes with me in the mornings to film. They're growing more at ease around each other, even though my grandmother still thinks that Jillian is a nurse and orders her around. Sometimes in the afternoons I go back alone, and we sit and look at each other. Grandma always has a horror story, someone hitting her or trying to shoot her. I asked the nurses about it and they looked at me with pity. "Oh, you poor thing. Nobody's hurting her."

We eat outside, swatting at mosquitoes. Lightning bugs hover, and the bushes look like they've been sprinkled with glitter.

Jillian needs more material. "What are your most vivid memories of your parents?" she asks.

When I think of my mother, I see her crying or cowering from my father. Nothing was ever right—the food she cooked for him, the house she cleaned for him. I know this is what Jillian means when she says "material." Jillian's parents give us tickets for the opera, and over dinner, they discuss the Whitney Biennial. Everyone in the family goes to therapy, they're always telling each other what they feel.

"What about good memories? Did you ever go on vacations or anything?" she presses.

I start to say no, then remember. "Once we went camping in the Smoky Mountains." Jillian wants more, how did the trip make me feel? "My mom fried bacon over the fire and sang country songs, and my dad, he seemed at peace, for once," I say. "We all slept in a tent together. I never wanted to leave."

"What was it like when he was on the road, when it was just you and your mom?"

I remember her looking out windows, staring at the phone, always waiting for him, always sad. "She missed him," I say. "How fucked up is that?"

"Do you think your grandma knew about how he treated her?"

"I think so. At church she used to ask the congregation to guide her lost son."

"Is she scary religious?"

"Everyone down here is religious. Grandma is a good Christian lady, but she's also superstitious, and I don't know, spiritual. Everything counts. Animals, trees. Everything's connected, the dead and living."

"So she's Buddhist. In a way."

"In a way."

I don't want to talk anymore. I set down my bowl of pasta salad and lean toward her, and push my lips against hers, force her mouth open with my tongue. I move my hand under her shirt, but she does not soften to my touch. The noise of the crickets is a hum inside of me, my heart trying to get out.

Jillian pulls back; we untangle.

"Maybe we should go out. What do people do? Honkeytonking?"

"You want to?"

"Maybe tomorrow." She picks up a sketchbook, thumbs the pages. "You had a wild imagination."

"Grandma used to tell me stories."

At first, after my dad left me with her, my grandmother didn't know what to do with me. I stayed out of her way, the way I was used to doing with adults. Then one night after supper she called me out to the front porch. She was sipping homemade wine that she got from old man Ruffy up at the head of the holler. After a couple of jelly glasses, she started telling me about ghosts, about the creatures that walked the hills. "I know you sense them out there," she said, "just like I do."

"I want to use these sketches in the film." Jillian flutters the pages.

"I don't know."

"Come on. These will be great. They tell a story."

"What story?"

"Your story." She pauses dramatically. "Dean." The way she says my name scares me.

"What?"

The pause again, but then she shakes her head. "Oh, nothing. I'm just tired." She stands and stretches. "I'm going in, I'm beat."

I crack another beer and wonder if she's missing the city. Jillian's friends are artists and queers, and she's always taking me to openings and parties and films. I don't have many of my own friends. I moved to the city to escape the isolation of my childhood, but it followed me, a disease in my bones. Grandma encouraged me to go off to college. "Live your life," she ordered. I just kept going and going, a wind blowing me north, rarely came back to see her.

I've been spending the nights on the couch. We haven't said much about this. Jillian asked if anything was wrong and I said no, and she said, "The bed really is too small for two people," and I agreed. Now I lie here staring up at the ceiling and thinking of my mother on the couch. Whenever my dad was on the road, she would just lie there, forget to make supper. She didn't put on makeup, didn't do her hair. I would comb it out for her, and she'd absently pat my hand and call me a good girl. She'd tell me stories about how they met, how he swept her off her feet, saved her. I never learned from what. When she got sick, her hair falling out, her breasts cut off, my father became desperate, hugging and kissing her, and finally, she was happy. Happy and light, rising to heaven.

I can't sleep. I go in the kitchen and watch moths flutter wildly against the screens trying to get to the light. After another beer, I walk past the couch and go into my childhood room. I can't tell if Jillian's sleeping or not. I put my hand on her hip, waiting, my heart beating fast. Jillian sighs, shifts away. I start to get up, but then she changes direction and moves against me, her ass pushed against my hips. When I move my hand between her legs I feel her wetness and she moans. I want her to feel all of me. I hold down her wrists with my hands and press my flat chest against her, and we stare at each other in the dark, and I am waiting. I am waiting for her to tell me what is wrong. She gives me a sad little smile; I loosen my grip.

"He tried to kill me last night."

Rain pelts the only window, which does not open and looks out onto a parking lot. The light from the lamp next to the bed is a sickly yellow.

"He's after me."

"Who?"

"There are things," my grandmother says. "Things you wouldn't understand."

I hold her hand until the anger in her face subsides. I've shaved off my sideburns and soul patch. I've shown her photographs of my parents, herself, me, her parents, her dead brother, her dead husband. I've played the music she used to listen to, like Patsy Cline, Hank Williams. Nothing works, nothing pulls her back into herself.

"Remember that time you caught a snapping turtle when we were fishing? Remember?" I try again. "Grandma, I'm your son's kid. You remember your son? Do you remember Charlie?"

"You're going to be late for school," she says, suddenly perking up. Then, nothing more.

Before leaving, I ask to see the director. The receptionist picks up the phone and in about fifteen minutes, he's next to me, a chubby, balding man in khakis and a baby blue golf shirt.

"I'm Gertrude Pearson's grandkid. From New York."

"Right, um, Anne," he stumbles.

"It's Dean."

"Dean." He is still smiling but his nose crinkles.

I tell him what she's been saying, that I'm thinking of moving her out of here, maybe someone is hurting her. He rests his hand on my arm, then looks nervous and removes it.

"It's the dementia. People get confused, hallucinate."

"Why would she say those things?"

"She's getting it from the TV, probably. The nightly news, TV shows. Could also be her medication. We'll talk to her doctor about it." He pauses, thinking. "Or maybe she's remembering something from her past and mixing it up."

"No," I say. "I don't think—"

"I know you're worried, but I promise you, she gets the best possible care." He lowers his voice like he's telling me something nobody else should know. "I promise, we're taking good care of your grandma."

////////

When I wake up, I don't know where I am. I sit up, my heart racing. Then I see all the boxes, the mantle cluttered with pictures and figurines. I reach for my cigarettes, and the dream slowly comes back, my mother standing over me, clumps of hair falling out. Jesus. I've gone years without thinking about her or my father, but now that I'm here with Jillian, everything is stirred up. I stretch, look down at my naked body. Touch the scars on my chest. After my mother had the mastectomy, she refused to wear the falsies that my father bought for her. Her chest was flat like mine.

In the kitchen I find a note from Jillian: *Went to town, be back soon.*

After I shower, I swab my skin with alcohol, draw in the testosterone. I do this once every two weeks. There is not this single moment that you transition, Clark Kent ducking into the phone booth. It's not a magic pill, you don't go instantly from girl to boy. There is not a clear start or end. It's ongoing. The way you dress, the name you choose. If you have surgeries or not. Hormones or not. There is no easy path, no before or after. You're the same, and yet more yourself. More the person you imagine yourself to be.

When I met Jillian, only a few people knew me as Dean. But Jillian introduced me to everyone by my chosen name. When she talked about me, she used male pronouns, like there was nothing strange about it. I remember how right the "he" sounded, how everything else melted away, and this part of me, so hidden and protected, was finally seen. She's been with me every twist and turn of my transition, but now that I'm here, at last growing comfortable with who I am, I'm scared she's not.

The needle sinks into my flesh, a shot of sweetened pain. I am a project, I think, that will never be finished.

Someone is knocking at the front door. I pull up my underwear, zip my jeans, grab a shirt to hide the scars.

Through the window, I see a fraction of a person. I open the door, and Paul greets me. "Hey, how you doing?"

"Good. You?"

"Alrighty." He pulls at the bill of his hat, which says, *Sit Down and Shut Up.* Paul is a big guy, over six feet. His belly hangs over his jeans. He's got a craggy face, a head of thick dark hair.

"I just come by to see if you needed me to haul anything."

"Uh, not today. Maybe tomorrow."

He stands there lingering at the door, so I ask him if he wants any coffee.

"I could use a cup. Thank you." He follows me into the kitchen. "Where's the little lady?"

"Oh, she went into town."

"You better keep an eye on that one."

I laugh uneasily, wait for the coffee to brew. Paul coughs for a long time, his face turning red and sweaty. Then he catches his breath, looks at me.

"I'm heading to town too. Got to take care of some paper work." He shakes out a cigarette. "Care if I smoke?"

I tell him I don't mind and he offers me a cigarette and I take it. He mentions the paper work again, like he's waiting for me to ask. So I do.

"The ex wife." He makes a sour face. "Goddamn trying to clean me out. This house that Thomas left me, it's about all I got left."

He tells me that they got divorced a year ago. "Women." He shakes his head. "*Women.*"

Paul blows on his coffee, drinks it black. I don't say anything, and he keeps talking.

"She was messing with one of my buddies. I wanted to kill the both of them, but then he got throwed in jail for drunk driving. She moved out, served me with papers." He looks at my hand. "Thought you said you was married, I don't see no ring."

"Oh, well, we're not really married yet. We're engaged."

I sip my coffee, trying to act like this is normal, the two of us hanging out.

"You best think twice before you get married," he says. "You best think twice."

If Jillian wasn't with me, Paul probably wouldn't be such a friendly neighbor. He would peg me as a queer, an effeminate New Yorker. Jillian is what he recognizes: she gives me hetero credibility. Paul goes on about his ex-wife and women in general, and I just sit there, feeling ashamed, listening to his rant. Jillian would be disappointed. I'm a coward.

He takes a long drag on his cigarette. "For a goddamn year she was running around on me. I was too damn pussywhipped to see it."

He shifts his long legs. He has no idea who I am. For so many years I tried to ignore my feelings. I was scared for a lot of reasons. But one of the biggest ones was that I would turn out to be like him, the one who taught me what it meant to be a man.

"I better get back to work," I say. "I'm trying to get a lot of stuff packed up."

"You think y'all are going to stay?"

"I don't know."

"You thinking of selling?"

"Thinking about it," I admit.

"Well, I wouldn't blame you none."

Then he reaches out, catching me off guard, and we shake hands. Something crosses his face, just a subtle twitch.

"Catch you later," he says.

I drag boxes out of the back room. One is as light as a carton of eggs. Inside I find folded clothes in plastic, like evidence from a crime scene. Little clothes. My clothes. Tiny t-shirts and shorts and dresses, ruffled socks and shoes the size of my hands. I hold them up in front of the mirror and wonder how I ever fit into them. My grandmother was glad I'd been born a girl. "The female's got a harder lot than the man, but we're better for the earth." She didn't say much about the men in her life. Her husband, father, son. They only caused her pain.

When I hear Jillian come in, I set the clothes aside, thinking she'll want to use them for the film. She's in the kitchen, putting away groceries.

"What's all this?"

"Stuff to grill, and liquor. I thought we could make margaritas." She's wearing short-shorts and a t-shirt that dips into a V at her breasts. "I got some good shots of the place where your parents used to live. I'll show you later, if you want."

I tell her about Paul coming by.

"He was ranting about his ex wife."

"I'm glad I wasn't here." Jillian takes peppers and onions and mushrooms out of a bag. "I think it'll feel good getting back to New York. Don't you?"

I nod, but I'm afraid of returning, what will happen to us. Jillian was the first person to see me for who I was. Now I don't know what she sees.

"I'm going to the nursing home," I say. "Did you leave the keys in the car?"

"Wait. Do you have to go now? I was thinking we could have a few drinks. Talk."

I've told her too much, I think. She's stripping me down, turning everything inside out.

"More recording?" I ask.

"No, just talking." Her smile is small, forced. "About us."

She looks tired. I see crow's feet around her eyes, a few new lines hugging her lips. The light coming from the windows shines on her face and glints on a single silver strand of hair. Her face is open and sad, and wanting too much.

"Please, Dean," she says.

"Later," I tell her, "when I get back."

Her face clouds as I give her a peck on the mouth, taste her waxy lipstick.

Instead of going to the nursing home, I turn on a back road that leads to the cemetery. My grandmother used to take me to visit my mother's grave, but I never knew what I was supposed to do or say. I take a few wrong turns, then find the headstones planted at the bottom of a hill. There are no flowers. The day is bright, hurts my eyes. Many of the headstones are flanked by little American flags, framed pictures, plastic flowers. I wonder if I should take Jillian here for the film. My chest feels heavy, like it's sprouted phantom breasts. After I first got my surgery, there were nights I'd wake up panicked, swearing that I could feel my breasts growing back, and I'd have to touch my chest over and over.

I sit down in front of my parents' graves, but just like when I was a kid, I don't know what to do or say. The cemetery is butted up against a forest, and a crow caws. My grandmother used to say that some spirits never rest. Her husband was one of them. My father, too. Now I know what she means. He's still out there, stumbling through the forest, tripping over tree roots. But not my mother, her soul is at peace. She's not here in the ground but in a big nest somewhere, high in a tree, protecting a clutch of tiny blue eggs. Hidden from my father. Hidden from me. Before I go, I pull up the weeds, revealing my parents' names, the dates that they lived and died.

//////////

Jillian has started the grill, and she stabs the vegetables through the skewers. By the time I finish my first drink, she is on her third. Her cheeks are red, her laugh too loud. She puts her hand on my crotch, and a hotness shoots up to my chest. Then she pulls back. Studies me.

"What?"

Her eyes flick past me, toward the house. "Have you decided what you're going to do about this place?"

The junk pile is still there at the edge of the yard, the washer sits on the porch. The paint is peeling away, the roof caving in. Fixing it up is not going to bring her back, and none of our friends will visit, I know that. It will always be a separate part of my life, the part that is the deepest and oldest.

"I don't know," I say.

The blackened vegetable bits on my plate look like pieces of bone. My mouth tastes charred. I start to ask what she thinks I should do, but a loud rumbling blasts from the driveway; both of us jump.

Paul climbs out of his pickup. "How y'all doing?"

I offer him a drink, but he's on the wagon. He asks me if I want him to take a load of junk to the landfill.

"I thought you were coming by tomorrow."

"Shit, you're right, I forgot." He rubs his face, leaning in. "I didn't sign those damn papers," he talks low. "She ain't gonna get another cent from me."

Jillian grabs our plates. "I'm going to wash up, honey," she says in a fake polite voice, but her face is hateful.

Paul doubles over in a coughing fit, then sits in Jillian's chair. He takes a deep breath, wipes his eyes.

"I kind of gotta get in there, Paul. We're, you know, talking."

He grins, thinking we're on the same page at last. "Don't let her boss you."

I start to laugh, but then I don't. I wonder if Jillian can hear us from the house. "It's not like that," I say. "We've just got things to figure out."

Paul's eyes crinkle, like he's going to cry. His face is splotchy from too many years of drink, his hands tremble. He's just a lonely old man, heartsick. "Things are gonna be all right," he says. "You go in there. Everything's going to be all right."

Jillian's at the table, resting her forehead against her fist, her hair falling around her. I can't see her face.

I slowly pull out a chair, careful with my movements, as if I'm carrying loose eggs. She finally looks up, tears in her eyes.

"I don't know how much you want to know."

I want to know all of it and none of it, but I stay quiet for a while.

"Someone I know?" I finally ask.

"No."

"Tell me."

She says he's a guy who has a studio in the same building that she does. He's an artist, like her. I hear her words but can't look at her.

"How long?"

"A few months," she says quietly.

I'm staring at the scratched table, my hands clasped together so hard that the knuckles whiten. Everything feels speedy and wild, my heart beating too fast, my mind racing. My face throbs with heat, like I'm standing too close to a fire. I clench my teeth and squeeze my hands tighter, trying to stop this thing that's growing inside me, this rage that fills my throat like bile, that spreads through my body burning me.

"Is he trans?" My voice sounds too loud, strange, an echo.

"Dean," she says. "You know that doesn't matter."

"It matters," I say, but I don't know if it does. I just want something that will make me understand, a clear answer, a reason.

"I knew you would think that, that's why I couldn't tell you, I knew you wouldn't understand. Would you look at me? Listen. It's not like he's some straight dude. We're still queer."

The *we* slices through me, and I don't want to look at her but I do. She is still weepy, but when she talks about him there is a light in her eyes. My face is burning. I let go of my hands. Words are thick in my throat; I force them out like I'm spitting teeth.

"You love him?"

She doesn't answer, and I want to hit her, I want to hit her the way my father hit my mother. All this rage that's been inside me all my life, waiting. I force myself to flatten my hand against the table. She rests her hand on top of mine. I clench my other hand into a fist, dig it into my leg.

"I wanted to give this another chance," she says. "I thought coming here would do that."

"You just wanted to make a goddamn film."

"That's not true, that's not the only reason. I wanted to feel closer to you, to fix things." She shakes her head. "It's not working, Dean."

Her hand on mine is warm and beating like a heart. Finally, something snaps, movement returns. I get up and go outside, leave Jillian crying at the table. The air is stagnant, covers the yard like a sheet of plastic.

At the creek a school of tadpoles dart behind a rock. The gnats are thick; sweat rolls down my neck. My father stood over my mother when she was on her deathbed, cried like a baby, but it was too late. I crouch down like I'm going to be sick, but nothing will come out. My hands press into the damp dirt. All these months have been a lie. This trip, a lie. A dull thumping rises from my chest to my skull. She doesn't love me anymore—she didn't say that, but she didn't have to. I've known for months now, just couldn't admit it. Maybe I don't love her anymore either. I loved her because she knew me, but maybe that's not enough.

I take a deep breath, walk back. Early evening light slants across the house.

"Where are you going?"

"Town," I say.

"I'm coming with."

I don't tell her yes or no. She gets in, and I shift into gear, the tires grinding dirt and gravel. I've never spent much time on the road, but my father trucked thousands of miles, all of it blurring by like the years, gone. I punch in the lighter on the dash, hold the red circle to my cigarette.

Jillian tells me she didn't mean for it to happen, she wasn't expecting it. Things sometimes just happen, she says. "I felt terrible, all this time. He did too, he really did, Dean." She explains that they have a lot in common. He grew up near the city too. He makes paintings. He goes to therapy. They talk. She feeds me details that I don't want. The sun is going down, turning the sky a dusky, depressing blue. I drive faster, and as soon as I get cell service, I make the call to the coal company.

"What was that about?" Jillian asks.

"Nothing." When I look over at her the rage returns. I feel sick with it. I look at Jillian and I see her with a cock in her mouth, I see her waking up in the mornings with her soft puffy eyes, I see her laughing in his arms.

I speed up. Something shifts in the road. I don't swerve fast enough and there is a loud, sickening thud.

"Stop," Jillian yells. "You hit something."

I pull over and look in the rearview and see a dark lump. Jillian scrambles out, and I chase after her. I pull up short. It's a puppy, a mutt. Chocolate brown with floppy ears. Positioned weirdly on its side, shuddering. Blood seeps from underneath it, and its hind legs look tangled, like the roots of a gnarled plant.

"Oh, God," Jillian kneels next to it. "Dean."

I touch the dog's velvety head and it bares its teeth, whimpers, and then is still. Its belly is limp and I can't tell if it's alive or dead. It's not much bigger than the length of my forearm.

"We have to find its owners," Jillian says.

There are no houses, only an empty field, a patch of dying woods. A burlap bag is tangled in the high weeds. "Someone dumped it," I say.

Jillian is on her knees, like she's going to give the dog mouth-to-mouth, and I run back to the car and get a blanket out of the trunk, drape it over the dog, leaving its head exposed. I'm crouched next to Jillian. I can smell my own sweat, the blood of the dog, the expensive product that Jillian uses to tame her curls. No other cars drive past. Swallows or bats sweep across the field. I reach out and touch the dog through the blanket. Its body is still.

I stand and take a deep breath, and Jillian stays crouched, her shoulders hunched like an old woman's. "Come on, it's dead," I say, reaching for her.

She knocks my hand away, then suddenly jumps up and rushes at me, punching my chest, smacking me.

"Look what you did," she yells.

I grab her wrists. She tries to break free, but I won't let go. Her breath is ragged, cheeks flushed, the way she looks when we fuck. Her face crumples and there are tears in her eyes. "I'm sorry," she says. "It's not your fault, I'm sorry." I tell her I'm sorry, too. I let go and she wraps her arms around me and we stand there in the fading daylight, our hearts pounding against each other, until a truck rumbles by blaring its horn.

When I pick the dog up, still wrapped in the blanket, blood drips through onto my hands. It's heavier than I expected, like a sack of oranges. I carry the body into the field and set it under a tree. Jillian watches from the side of the road, arms crossed over her chest, hair lit up by the setting sun. I feel like I should say something, a prayer, or a goodbye, but I don't have any more words.

///////

There are specks of blood on my palms. I shove my hands in my pockets. This man Jillian loves, he's not afraid of himself, not afraid of what he comes from.

"Hi, Grandma."

But she is looking at Jillian, sunglasses perched on her head, t-shirt clinging to her breasts. Grandma says, "Sara." My mother. "I'm so glad you're here."

Jillian doesn't look at all surprised. It's the first time she's come in here without her camera and she walks over to my grandmother and cups her face in her hands and pretends to be my mother. "So am I," she says.

"No. Tell her who you really are. Jillian, tell her. Grandma, this isn't Sara."

My grandmother isn't listening. She touches the hand on her face, then holds it in hers. Jillian and my grandmother holding hands. "Honey, are you okay?"

"I'm fine," Jillian says. "I'm okay, I promise."

My grandmother looks at me. "Charlie."

"No, no. I'm not Charlie," I say. "And this is not Sara."

My grandmother just smiles. At my father's funeral she did not shed a tear, but she said, as we left the cemetery, "I tried to raise him right." She knew there was something in him that was wrong, just like something was wrong in her husband. But wasn't something also wrong in my mother? One time my father was punching her, and when I ran over to put myself between them, my mother pushed me away. I always told myself that she was protecting me. But she didn't even look at me. She rubbed her jaw and gathered herself, and then she followed him into the bedroom and locked the door behind her. The violence haunts me, just like it does my grandmother. My father's blood is in me, so is my mother's.

"Charlie?"

"Grandma, no. It's me. Your grandchild. Sara and Charlie's kid. I go by Dean now. I used to be Anne."

"Anne's gone," she says. "Who's Anne?"

My grandmother blinks wildly like she's woken up from a long dream. She can't stop talking. She's not saying anything about anyone hurting her—she's just repeating names and dates and little bits of memories, nothing bad. She calls me Charlie, her son, she calls me John, her husband. Him, a man she rarely spoke of, but I know that he is the one who is after her now. Like father, like son. She goes on and on, calling me the names of the dead, these men who beat their women, and I am afraid to say a word. I'm afraid to meet Jillian's eyes. I want to apologize to my grandmother, how sorry I am for leaving her. Grandma leans in closer to me, I smell her rotted breath. My grandmother who kept a room for me all these years, waiting on me to come back home.

Jillian and I sit by Sugar Creek, not touching. The mountains and trees hide the stars, but there is still enough light to see each other.

I tell her about the box of baby clothes. "You want to use them for your film?"

"I think I've got enough."

"You're finished?"

"Yeah."

She tells me she will go back to New York tomorrow. She already bought a plane ticket. She twists her hair with her finger, curling it even more. She's got so much of it, whenever we had sex it used to get stuck in her mouth, stuck in mine.

"What do you think the film's going to be like?"

"You know, it'll be like my other stuff. It's not traditional."

I know what she means—that once she pieces it together, the story of my father's death and my mother's death, my grandmother's fears about her husband killing her, and all the beautiful and sad shots of the mountains, the house, my grandmother's junk, my flat chest, the pictures of my mother who lost her breasts, the baby pictures of me, none of it will add up, there will not be an easy story. I will not recognize myself.

Now here I am, leaving what I know. I got rid of what my grandmother was saving and put her in a nursing home and now I'm selling her land. She used to hang my drawings on the refrigerator. The princess was her favorite, but I liked the one with the angry fists, the invisible one.

"Dean, I wasn't just here for the film," Jillian says.

I think how things could have turned out differently. If I hadn't hit the dog, we could have taken him home with us, I think, to our house in the mountains, and everything would be fine.

"If I had just stopped a second sooner," I say. "The dog."

Jillian doesn't reply. Tomorrow she will go, and in a week or two, I will leave too, and no one will be here, except Paul, bitter and lonely, and all these old ghosts wandering the woods. When I come back to visit, my grandmother won't know who I am.

The peepers, impossible to see, grow louder. They're all around us. I thought Jillian was the first one who ever saw me, but that's not true. For a few seconds the noise suddenly stops. Silence reverberates. Then there's a single chirp and they all join in. My grandmother taught me to look at what was hidden, to see what was right in front of my eyes.

This afternoon, before I left, I promised her nobody would ever hurt her again. She reached out her old claw hand and cupped my face.

"You're a good boy," she said. "A real good boy."

TO THE NEW WORLD
• *Ryka Aoki*

Dammit—I thought Asian hair was supposed to be easy!

Millie Wong was on the verge of tears. *Tangled and frizzy... shouldn't it be long and straight?* She yanked at her brush. Maybe it was some hidden genetic female thing: her sister had perfect hair, and her mother, too. *You're so stupid! You don't even pass to your own hair! You clumsy tranny freak...*

A sharp pain as several strands of her hair snapped brought her back to reality. *Okay, okay, calm down. Come on, Millie, deep breaths. You slept with wet hair, that's all. Deep breaths. No yelling today. Breathe. Think of Grandma.*

Millie steadied herself, took smaller strands of hair, and brushed gently from the ends. When she was done, she repeated the process with her straightening iron. Feathers of steam floated off the iron, leaving her hair like shimmering ribbons. *Thank goodness.* She peeked at the clock and shook her head.

Getting ready was bad enough on any Sunday morning, but this was her grandmother's birthday.

For Millie, her grandmother's birthday was not just remembering her passing. It was her most important family gathering, even if it was just between her and her grandmother's picture on her kitchen table. Back when she was Victor, Millie had been her favorite grandson. Of course, Millie had no idea how her grandmother would have reacted to her transition—she probably would have been horrified. But one could always imagine otherwise, and besides, since her death two years ago, she was the only person in her family that Millie could love without fear of getting disowned.

And today, Millie was going to the farmers' market to find something for her Grandmother. Something special.

She peeked outside and frowned. It was another stupid LA winter day—not enough drizzle to call rain, but enough to spoil all the work she had put into her hair. But there it was, so she sighed and grabbed her purse. She trudged past the greasy Thai restaurant to the crosswalk, where a tow truck stopped to let her pass. The driver nodded as she hurried across the street.

And Millie Wong smiled for the first time all day.

You see, that truck—that driver—would have *never* stopped for Victor. It's not easy, almost getting run over by cars and trucks pretending not to see you, or not even trying to disguise that they don't care. That's how it was for Victor Wong. A nondescript Asian boy, he was an afterthought. A non-thought. It wasn't so much being hated, it was being invisible. It was going to the mall and having the store salespeople help the next customer. It was waiting too long to get a table at a restaurant. But for Millie: cars would stop. Doors would open. People would smile—even flirt sometimes.

Millie knew about objectification. You don't grow up being Asian and *not* hear all sorts of things about why Suzie Wong and *Memoirs of a Geisha* were racist or sexist rubbish. But after a life of being ignored, was it wrong to like people being *nice* to you?

//////////

By the time Millie wandered down Sunset to Ivar and turned into the farmers' market the skies had cleared, and a clean offshore wind mixed with the familiar smells of car exhaust and blended with fruits, vegetables, and sweaty patchouli. Almost instinctively, Millie studied other women—how they were walking and speaking. Her parents lost their accents by mimicking the TV and radio; one of Millie's main reasons for listening to KPFK was to practice "Nina Totenberg, NPR News, Washington." But nothing was better than watching people live, catching snippets of conversation that conveyed gender, ethnicity, even social standing:

"I'd *like* a mocha *latte* with *soy* milk."
"What's a *good* recipe for Hun*garian* peppers?"

Listening to conversations swirl around her, she purchased two heirloom tomatoes, which were strangely available, even this out of season. But it wasn't a great day at the market; the produce was pretty sketchy, and she tried not to judge the sorry excuse for fresh basil. *We're not in San Gabriel. We're in Hollywood, and it's organic. It's organic.*

And then she saw it: a poofy loaf of sweet bread, made with milk and sugar and butter. It was soft, like a steamed bun. Her grandmother had loved that sort of bread, especially towards the end when she couldn't chew very well. Putting the loaf into her bag and preparing to pay, Millie remembered the hospital room. She remembered pulling off small bits of steamed bun and feeding them to her grandmother with fragrant, lukewarm tea.

Suddenly a loud voice brought her back to Hollywood.

"Yo, Millie, what up?"

Her name was Sierra, and to Millie, she looked it. She seemed as tall and solid as a mountain, with snowcap eyes that rarely blinked. She was one of those dykes that didn't just want to take back the night—she wanted to grab and throttle it. When Millie first met Sierra she was a loud voice from above complaining about the excessive sweetness of Fuji apples. Millie was awestruck. How could she be so loud and yet so completely female? Sierra had laughed when Millie first asked this—she said Asian women were like those little *beep beep* horns on a Prius. "Sure, they're cute, but the big truck crowding your lane ain't gonna move. You gotta sound like you *mean* it!" Sierra had said. And whatever it was, Sierra meant it.

Millie had never been exactly comfortable with Sierra's blanket take on Asians—she knew some pretty obnoxious Asian women—but she had been happy to make a new friend. Sierra warmed to Millie quickly over afternoons of homemade scones and political protests, and she infused Millie with opinions on nuclear power, on meat, and on patriarchy and stuff.

Then, during one conversation about "Why penises?", Millie decided to confess that she was trans.

Sierra stopped, and Millie wondered if she was going to get up and walk away. Then Sierra busted out laughing.

"I knew there was something about you. I mean I couldn't tell, really—I mean you're beautiful, but something was different... *shit!*" Millie started laughing, too, and then came all the usual Trans 101 questions, which Millie tried her best to answer. Sierra listened, and then pronounced Millie was okay, because she didn't feel that male energy come off of her. This made Millie happy and safe, especially since Sierra was pretty buff: not someone she wanted to see mad.

But from then on, it wasn't the same. Oh, Sierra was still just as friendly as ever, but Millie could sense the difference. Sierra started treating Millie less like possible dating material and more like a younger brother-sister. She was happy to tell Millie what it meant to be a socially and politically responsible woman, but also made it clear that, with trannies, there was always male privilege to root out. "You can't go out alone at night, or walk into any old sports bar without fear anymore, you know!" Coming from Asian parents who taught her to avoid large groups of drunken white men, Millie had actually never *been* to a sports bar, but she nodded and listened, careful not to interrupt her friend.

Today, Sierra focused on the bread in Millie's bag. "So you're still supporting the dairy industry, eh?"

Millie trembled. She had been caught with the non-vegan bread. Of course it wasn't vegan. It was her grandmother's favorite type of American bread, but if it wasn't, Millie probably wouldn't have gotten it, because she was thinking about becoming vegan. She really *was* sad that she had been born with male privilege, and maybe by being vegan, in some way she could be closer to the woman she wanted to be. A caring woman. A strong woman. A *vegan* woman.

"It's my grandmother's birthday, and it was her favorite," she finally ventured.

But Sierra continued, "Patriarchy is patriarchy. Do you know that dairy cows end up in McDonald's hamburgers? They're genetically engineered to produce milk, but once their production falls, they're just killed. It's worse than what happens to beef cattle, in some ways. I mean, it's like the Tibetan women—they have nothing but their stories and weaving, but the men in the Chinese government want to take that away from them, too."

Millie knew better than to interrupt. Though she wondered what Tibetan women had to do with dairy cattle and the loaf of bread, she knew that Sierra was active on so many fronts that sometimes she made connections which might seem impenetrable to others. Plus, any argument on her part would surely trigger accusations of male privilege, and, in this case, of possible connections with the Chinese government.

Millie nodded to Sierra and put the sweet loaf back.

As they walked away, Sierra gushed about this great spa just outside Palm Springs with an authentic Japanese Zen garden. Millie mentioned she might like to go, but Sierra said no, it's a women-only space. "You know, *women* women—but I thought you might appreciate the Zen part, being Asian and all. Very feng shui."

Again Millie nodded. She tried not to dwell on women-only spaces, or why someone would mention a Japanese Zen garden in the same breath as feng shui. She remembered that she had made the mistake of talking about Asian issues to Sierra before. Sierra had told her that "men are men: Chinese men and Japanese men both abused women, like those women in World War II. Oh, that was Korea? Whatever. It's all the same oppression." Millie had thought about her grandmother escaping Vietnam in a rusty, rotting boat, and she had wondered if it really was the same. And today was her birthday.

"Hey, you okay?" Sierra's words shook her out of her thoughts. "That women-only stuff didn't bug you, did it?"

"Uh-uh."

"You can tell me. I know all about tranny issues. I'm still friends with you, right?"

Millie tried to smile, but it wouldn't come this time. Sierra noticed and put her arm around her. "Listen doll: I've been there. I know what it's like. One of my girlfriends went and transitioned on me once," she said.

Millie looked up at her, surprised.

"Yeah, it was rough. One day she was she, then the next day—I don't know. I was confused, I'll tell you what. Of course I made sure that everyone knew that James had been Rebecca, and that she—I mean he—I mean *I*—was still a dyke. I didn't want people thinking I went straight. No way am I going to be straight..." Sierra's voice seemed to tremble before she caught herself. "James was so mad! But what could I do? I mean, hey, it's okay if she wants to go be a guy or something, but don't push that on me."

"Maybe you just weren't meant for each other," Millie offered.

"Yeah, no shit. James was great, though," Sierra blinked, coughed, and tried to turn it into a chuckle. "Trans women. What's up with that?"

Millie didn't know what to say. She didn't even think of correcting her on trans men. Instead, before she could stop herself, she blurted, "Well I think *you're* great." Then, wondering why she said that, she fidgeted and added, "I have to go home now. Get back to my grandmother."

Sierra didn't seem to notice. "Cool beans! I'd like to meet her one day—she sounds like a great woman. I gotta run anyway. Call me later, okay? Ciao!"

Sierra winked and turned away, then stopped. Suddenly she spun around and hugged Millie like she was made of clouds. She gave an awkward half-smile, a little wave, and was off.

Millie stood there waiting for the city to stop spinning. She considered going back to get the bread, but she wasn't sure about male privilege and about what to do if Sierra came back. So she took her heirloom tomatoes, along with some rather nice parsnips, and walked home. As she walked home, Millie again noticed the politeness of the drivers. She didn't need Sierra to tell her about fetishizing Asian women, but all Victor had ever gotten were sneers and indifference. It never seemed like much of a privilege. Was it wrong to feel good about being nodded at? About having a door opened? About having a car stop? Didn't they also stop for her grandmother? The same grandmother who would have been killed in Vietnam?

In the kitchen, Millie took her shoes off and studied her picture of Grandma. She retrieved the vegetables from her shopping bag, noticing that they looked a little smaller and tougher than they had at the market. Tomatoes... parsnips. *Parsnips?* Gazing at them, Millie suddenly started to cry.

You stupid! It's Grandma's birthday, and you didn't even bring home the sweet bread! She had bought tomatoes and parsnips; Grandma didn't even know what parsnips were.

Oh Grandma! Only three years ago, they were strolling through San Gabriel, looking for cheap groceries and steamed pork buns. Grandma would tell stories about Vietnam, about coming to this wonderful country after the blood and the pirates, about being so crowded aboard the boat that she could only sit because there wasn't enough space to lie down. Millie looked at the parsnips. She tried to imagine what Grandma would say, not just about her transition, but about this whole vegan business and how it somehow related to womanhood. Heck, what would she say about the farmers' market, when at the Ranch 99 the vegetables were half the price and twice as fresh?

And then, Millie stopped. In a daze, she opened her freezer and dug around. The two pork buns she found there weren't from providence; they were from being Asian and having a freezer full of ethnic food. She paused, full of trepidation about backsliding to meat, about oppression and male privilege and Sierra. But, with Grandma's picture looking right at her, she put the buns in the microwave.

Of course, the buns weren't from her grandmother—*that* would have been weird—but from her last visit to her parents. "Victor, why is your hair so long?" they had asked. "Who's going to marry you like that?" She had been waiting for the right time to tell them, knowing that it might never come. She was still waiting.

The microwave beeped, and Millie hesitated before opening it. She put a bun in front of Grandma's picture awkwardly, then took the other one and bit. The scalding pork filling burned her tongue, but instead of bringing tears, the pain brought memories. There was a rush of spices and aromas and tastes, a rush of family and faces and sounds. She remembered moon cakes and pork buns and screaming kids and beating her cousins at poker late into the night. Violin from Suzuki and math from Kumon. Smuggling bags of dried cuttlefish into the movie theater, and Costco beef jerky into Disneyland. She remembered all these things, and so much more.

If I come out to the family, I'll lose everything. But it's more than that. I don't want my family to be laughed at, for all my mother's friends to see her and say, "Look, there's the one with the freak for a son." Yet, I can never go back to living a lie.

Suddenly, Millie realized something in a way that she never had before.

Once, in the hospital, Millie had told Grandma that she was very brave to have left home for America. To her surprise, Grandma had started laughing. It reminded Millie of when she was little and had seen her first steamed crab. She had screamed that a big red spider had crawled into the cooking pot. "Brave? No, not brave. You do because you have to. Oh, you give things up, but maybe you find new things, too. I left so much family behind," Grandma had said. "They called me crazy. But they couldn't leave, and I couldn't stay. Of course I miss home, but look at my life here! We didn't have Ranch 99 in Vietnam, you know!"

As Millie remembered Grandma's laugh, she started to cry again, but it wasn't from sorrow. She felt new a new connection with her grandmother and with the rest of her family as she saw her own life and identity, for the first time, as an immigrant. It didn't matter whether the distance was measured in miles or communities, it was still a long and violent journey. It was still full of people who would call you brave, people who would call you crazy, and people who would never call you again.

Brave? No, not brave. You do because you have to.

Millie looked at the parsnips, seeming sad and out-of-place on the countertop. She thought about Sierra, and about her other friends, too: gay, queer, trans, Goths, poets—friends who sometimes just didn't understand, but who really meant well. *Oh, you give things up, but maybe you find new things, too.*

She held up her bun, flipped her hair from her eyes, and nodded to Grandma.

To the New World!

She chuckled as she imagined Sierra's reaction to her and her pork buns. Then she took another bite, and stopped thinking altogether. When she was done she smiled, sighed, and decided that she might call Sierra in a while, maybe get some coffee. Yes, she'd like that. Sierra seemed like she needed to talk—besides, maybe Millie could tell her the difference between trans women and trans men. Maybe one day she might even ask Sierra out shopping at Ranch 99—who was to say?

With a practicality that would have made Grandma smile, Millie covered the other bun and put it in on the kitchen counter, not in the freezer. The pork bun had kept well, all this time, but once thawed and warm and steaming, it was best a thing to be experienced as soon as possible, like life itself, even as doubts, accusations, and misunderstandings fade when faced with something real.

THE CAFÉ

- *R. Drew*

One of the great mundane tragedies of Sam's life on any particular day was his inability to remove the blackened, dried crust of coffee grounds that clung uncompromisingly to the laminate floor of the café. The crust was always there, always hiding, delighting in its own immortality and mocking Sam's best mopping efforts. The little hardened blobs hid under trash cans, perfectly in a shadow cast behind the leg of the prep table, just underneath the bakery case. Sam counted his triumphs of the day by how many pieces of food and coffee grounds and dirt and lipstick and milk foam and overall schmutz he could scrub clean from a dish, a mug, the floor, or the counter. Nothing pleased him more than a clean surface. The crusty spots irked him, to say the least.

Having been a barista for five years, Sam realized a long time ago that cafés are the most amazingly banal places that have ever come into existence. The café reminded him of a cross between a vending machine and an elevator. Not just any elevator, though—the glass ones at the mall that allow an audience to view your holy ascension to the big white retail store in the sky. At the café, the door opens and a customer gets in to purchase a few calorie-laden beverages or snacks and an opportunity for small talk, in a slightly claustrophobic space that plays hackneyed singer/songwriter selections on a miserable, mind-numbing loop.

The door popped open and it was a corpse—at least that's what Sam called them. Shitty coffee shops are always full of corpses, ghastly skeletons with ashen skin and wrinkles and croaky voices who smell of sweet perfumey sweat and stale cigarettes and want a small regular coffee with cream and sugar.

The particular corpse who had just walked in to the café was very unusual, however. She looked dead, as all corpses do, but instead of the typical grayish-green dull sheen that was the standard hue, her skin was a striking milk white. Her dark green eyes and coal-black eye shadow reminded him of a baby doll, with widened unblinking eyes and a fixed, goofy smile. Her lips never smiled, though; they always remained pursed in a slight frown and caked in dark mauve lipstick. She was rarely in, but when she was, she just made Sam plain uncomfortable. She spoke her orders in a direct, low tone that Sam could barely hear. However, he dare not ask her to repeat herself. Sam realized that maybe she really wasn't just a corpse after all, but some fallen angel of sorts. He nicknamed her Jewel.

Corpses (and fallen angels) weren't the only types of customers who come into the café. There were also the stroller moms, with their awkward and misshapen baby carts that always took up too much space and looked starkly uncomfortable in the cramped café. Sam knew for sure that when he and his girlfriend had a kid he was going to take it everywhere in one of those baby backpack things. He especially hated the stroller moms because they always left crumbs and crayons and mugs with dried milk foam and half-drunk cups of room temperature chocolate milk. Sam always knew that when a stroller mom was finally done joggling her caravan out of the store, there was always going to be something to go wipe up. Wiping up after the stroller moms irked Sam at first, but he did admire the grand clean surface he was able to recreate when it was all over.

He hadn't seen any stroller moms in a while, thank God. He'd seen a few corpses, of course, but that was normal. However lately he had mostly just seen the students. There were always lots of students. They were tiresome and indistinguishable from one another, like ants. They all had huge, horrendous books that all said the same exhausting things. They all either studied law or medicine and Sam only ever vended them tea or coffee. Then they just sat all day, still as statues, reading into eternity. They were so motionless that sometimes they looked like museum pieces. Sometimes they threw their notes in the trash and Sam retrieved them, but they never made any sense and seemed incredibly boring anyway.

There was only one student who didn't completely unnerve Sam. His name was Linc and he studied film. Instead of tedious books and silent statue poses, Linc was all fidgety and wore big headphones and read small books about writer's block. Linc was short, with small skinny limbs. He had caramel skin and cropped brown hair, big chocolate drop eyes and facial features that were round and curvy, like tree trunks or rivers. Sam knew that he was different from the other customers, because all the corpses and stroller moms and students and whoever else came in always had sharp, angular features that caught glare.

Sam usually wanted to ignore the customers, but Linc was someone he actually wanted to talk to. Since Linc had started coming to the café, he was frequently joined by a group of trans and queer friends. The group was all short haircuts, tattoos and glasses with cut-off short-shorts, testosterone-meets-curves and talk about queerness and race and class. Sam wondered how he could break in to the circle. He floated around them while he wiped the tables. He peeked at them from the sink while he bent over, washing his boss's baking pans, the Velcro from his makeshift binder cutting into his sides like tiny pen knives. Sam took great care to get all the crusty baked-on nuggets from the crevices of the baking dishes. He *hated* when his coworkers didn't get all the crusty spots.

All his coworkers at the café knew Sam was trans. He had told them all, and they all processed and accepted the information, in one way or another. The only spectacular thing that happened was that for no particular reason his boss stopped calling him Sam and started calling him Tony. His boss never, not once, called him "she," though. So some days he was Tony.

The customers always got it wrong, though. Sam knew it was his voice. It lilted into an angelic, high-pitched, "May I help you?" every time the door popped open. His height didn't do much for him either. At just over five foot, he peered, elfin-like, over the tea jars atop the bakery case at the customers. The stroller moms were the worst about the whole thing. They were always trying to teach their obtuse little wiggleworm toddlers to do something polite before they would stuff them with brownie.

"Say thank you to the nice lady."

The little dumpling would just stare at him, confused and blank, not sure whom to thank. Sam honored the sense of truth and understanding the child had provided him. The stroller mom mouthed a rushed, apologetic "thank you" and rolled her SUV off to park it clumsily against the cream and sugar stand.

Sam hated working Tuesday evenings more than anything else, ever. Tuesdays were the slowest, most unbearable, most boring day of the week. The only customers who ever came in that day were the students, and they were all as quiet as church mice. It was also the night before weekly garbage collection, and all the big trash cans out back were guaranteed to be all full except one. Depositing the day's trash after closing in a giant trash can that was only used once a week, for one bag of trash, annoyed Sam greatly for some reason.

However, the worst thing of all about Tuesday evenings was working with The Louse. The Louse was skinny and pale with pimply skin and wretched yellow-green teeth. He looked like a corpse but was too talkative to be one. The Louse very much enjoyed hearing his own voice, and bulldozed conversations into parking lots. He had a greasy smile and a loud, machine gun laugh that was often aimed at someone else's expense.

The Louse worked one evening a week: Tuesday. Everything about The Louse utterly disgusted Sam. He took off his shoes to adjust his socks or picked his nose hairs in the bathroom then washed his hands in the dishwater. He chugged Coca Cola or murky iced coffees that looked like old toilet water. He talked about shit stains and anal sex and milk teats and the shoe store he used to work at. He made fun of men dressed as women and never got Sam's pronoun right. He had an intolerable habit of saying "Excuse me, dear" when passing behind Sam.

Sam studied The Louse closely when he could. As horrid as The Louse was, Sam sometimes felt a greedy envy burn through him when he thought about his God-given male body. Sam coveted glances at his emaciated, flat chest, always covered by a loose, faded t-shirt. Sam frowned at his own lumpy, awkward chest that was smushed, hidden and aching behind his binder. When The Louse was around, Sam had a hard time distinguishing what was real. The Louse joyously abolished what little male identity he had. On Tuesdays he was simply a ghost. His Tuesday life was nothing more than The Louse and the silent students and the trash cans and the damn coffee grounds that never came off the floor.

This particular Tuesday, however, was shaping up differently already. The Louse had been late because he missed the train downtown. He burst through the door with his sunglasses on and his book bag hanging loosely off his bony shoulder. He never looked at anyone when he came in. He bounded down the steps to the basement to drop off his bag, and Sam waited, in a heightened anxiety state, for him to come back up so he could become a ghost. The Louse returned and walked straight-backed to the cash register.

As it usually went, Sam and The Louse tossed and turned and eventually drifted into their obligatory small talk. Rarely, but just often enough, The Louse would stop the chitchat dead when any customers came in the café. The Louse would then fold his hands over the tea jars atop the bakery case and ask, "How we doing this evening?" If the customers were female-bodied, he would always add a compulsory "ladies, Miss, or Ma'am" to the end of the sentence. The customer would offer up their languid and unconcerned volley of "Good, how are you?" back to The Louse and he would always respond the same: "Wonderful, wonderful."

The first customer to come in that particular Tuesday was Linc. Sam's eyes widened and his back straightened as soon as Linc walked in. Sam hid his face behind the espresso machine and eyed The Louse as he hovered over the tea jars, watching Linc and waiting for the precise moment to release his overly polite and gendered greeting into the ether. Sam watched his dried, nicotine-stained lips part.

"How we doing this evening, *Miss?*"

The question hung heavy in front of Linc. Sam felt his ribs suck in and his torso muscles tense as he held his breath. His chest and neck turned scarlet with embarrassment, and he lowered his eyes, not daring to look at Linc. All of a sudden he felt like a perpetrator, like he had been The Louse's accomplice in the dehumanizing act of misgendering his transgender brethren.

Linc fielded the question with humility and his own sense of cool vagueness. The Louse gleefully and ignorantly made him a tea, and Linc disappeared to the empty dining room next door. Sam exhaled and felt a momentary flood of hopelessness and sadness fill his small frame. It made his bones feel liquid and weak.

Sam had become the ghost. The Louse permeated the café, the street, the entire universe with his totalitarian courtesy. Sam shrunk weakly into a blurry, faint outline of the misshapen man-woman creature that he was.

He turned and bent low over the sinks, sloshing the mugs around in the gray water that looked like an overcast sky with vomit floating in it. The Louse perched himself on the prep table and settled into a book of facts about salt. The Louse liked to spend just enough time researching frivolous topics that he could appear smart in any conversation. In fact, The Louse truly loved nothing more than to orally defecate superfluous amounts of useless information just for the sake of permeating the universe.

The Louse had a particular penchant for using Sam as conversational target practice. He would go on about his theories of money as representation, the Renaissance period, fables about bugs, and being American. He made Sam question himself if he even knew anything at all. Sam wondered if knowledge was important to ghosts.

Sam hoped that maybe customers would save him, but The Louse talked loudly and domineeringly to them and pulled them into his collective, making sure Sam knew his place.

"How *we* doing tonight, *gentlemen?*"

There was only one customer who Sam thought could resist The Louse's clutches and prove that Sam wasn't a ghost. Sam's name for him was David the Prophet. He was a thin, mysterious black man with sweet eyes and shaky hands and long dreadlocks. David the Prophet traveled the city in specific patterns, only going to specific restaurants and stores on specific days. At night he wrote in a journal addressed to God. He studied religion

69

intensely at the University until he ran out of money and decided he wanted to live in a condo, so he reconciled his future to becoming a therapist.

David the Prophet had disappeared altogether lately, and Sam didn't even think about him on this particular Tuesday. Sam had conceded to an evening of nonexistence and that was that, so when David the Prophet entered the café, it caught Sam and even The Louse by surprise. David the Prophet accounted for his recent disappearance by explaining that he had fallen in love with a barista at a new café that had opened and then mysteriously closed a month later. Other than that, he simply admitted that he'd been around, but the café made him feel claustrophobic so he avoided it. He also made note that he was being treated by various doctors for low blood pressure.

Nevertheless, Sam was relieved to see him. The Louse delighted in his appearance as well. Any opportunity to parade his worthless collection of irrelevant, paltry knowledge absolutely tickled The Louse to death.

David the Prophet gently hovered over the counter, a solemn totem pole in the rolling sea of stroller moms and student statues. Sam extinguished the coffee stains from the counter, one by one, with his bar rag and engaged in a pious conversation with David the Prophet about their lives' journeys. Sam watched gleefully as The Louse waited on dry, middle-aged, soul-sucking businesswomen. The moment and the conversation and David the Prophet was all his. He shone with existence, brighter than the stainless steel counter he had just wiped to holy immaculateness.

As soon as the last soul-sucker left, The Louse toddled over to Sam and David the Prophet in a two-foot grand promenade of righteousness from the cash register to the end of the bar.

"Thought I'd scared you off, David. Too many deep thoughts." The Louse boomed with a toady grin.

David the Prophet's mouth moved slowly into his trademark binding smile. His teeth always wanted to burst through, but his lips hung tightly over them while the corners of his mouth turned up coyly.

The Loused continued. "I was rethinking my theory of quantum physics—quantum mechanics, as you said—and I found something that proved my theory precisely: *childbirth.*"

The Louse launched into his self-affirming pageant show of extravagant and delusional genius that was probably homophobic. Sam didn't know what the two of them were talking about and felt transparent. The Louse had stolen David the Prophet and any chance he had to feel real on a Tuesday. His heart would have sunk, but his binder held it tautly in place, and it just continued struggling to beat against his bound chest.

Sam fixed his attention on removing any spots he could find on any counters, floors, cabinets, fridges, or cases. He decided that he would dedicate the rest of his nonexistence to creating a divine cleanliness that was pure and sublime. His eternal plan was disrupted, of course, by customers.

The customers who flowed in this Tuesday were not the predictable babbling brook of facile, mundane tea-drinking students that he was used to on Tuesday evenings. In fact, this particular evening provided him a reckless and unpredictable stream of customers who were the ones he always hoped to avoid. He had never seen so many unusual customers at once. It overwhelmed him and he didn't quite know what to do.

It happened because of the rain. It had been raining for almost a week straight. The clouds had sporadically burst open and poured out buckets of water, and then quickly sewed themselves back up. The sky had become violently unstable, and a storm was always lingering somewhere, even on a sunny day. The rain had been driving Sam crazy lately. Periods of lightness and darkness shifted unpredictably all day. He could not exist in day or night for very long and the capriciousness of the environment was making Sam feel volatile and deeply unsettled.

That particular Tuesday the air had been uncomfortable and humid, and the smell of rain clung to the slow-moving breeze. The leaves of the trees turned up and begged for a shower of the cool wetness. All day, business people warily looked up at the sky and scurried quickly from Office A to Office B, umbrellas tucked tightly under their arms.

///////

The rain didn't come until early evening. The storm hastily pushed nighttime into the sky, and a sweeping, dark moodiness saturated the city. The sky finally cracked and blasted a torrent of liquid chaos into the streets. Even The Louse and David the Prophet grew momentarily quiet as the three of them stared out the big window at the ruthless cascade of water. The Louse eventually steered David the Prophet back into his ministry of propaganda and Sam watched the raindrops bounce off the sidewalk.

Sam remembered a dream he had where a big storm came and created a flood. The flood caused the kitchen of his father's house to sway and rock violently, then break off and be swept away in the current, with him and his father still inside. Sam imagined the dining room on the other side of the wall rocking and breaking apart from the café. He imagined floating down the city streets in the dining room with the customers.

The door popped open and it was Jewel. As she shook out her black umbrella and avoided eye contact with Sam, he felt his stomach tighten. Sam looked beyond Jewel at the viciousness of the storm and thought it odd that she appeared out of it. He wished The Louse would come wait on her, but he was pounding out a solid shit house of useless information for David the Prophet to dwell in. Her overall darkness made him feel anxious and small. He desperately wanted to do something to make Jewel less dreary. He tried to imagine what it would look like if she smiled. She existed in a deep, black murk and Sam wanted to lift her from it. He wanted to wash the shadowy makeup from her eyes and tilt her face into the sunlight. But there was no sunlight anyway, so he just stayed away. He felt trapped and lost in the dismal, rainy valley of her and The Louse.

She stepped to the counter and ordered a tea in her low, demanding tone. Sam quickly rang her up and turned to prepare the drink. The Louse, taking sudden, unsolicited control of the situation, asked, "Have you been taken care of, Miss?" Jewel rested her dark angel eyes on Sam and said quietly and pointedly, "*She* is taking care of me."

"Wonderful, wonderful," The Louse replied.

Sam felt a little pinprick in his heart and a tiny stream of blood coursed out of it, weakening him. He knew there was no hope of telling Jewel he wasn't a girl. The light of his truth could not penetrate her gloomy existence. He was afraid to tell her; he was afraid of her in general. He handed her the tea, and she left for the dining room to wait out the storm.

As soon as Jewel rounded the corner into the dining room, the door popped open again. It was a customer that Sam hadn't seen in ages: The Hermit. Sam had to keep his mouth from nearly gaping open at the sight of seeing The Hermit emerge from the rain. He looked like something that had crawled out of the backwoods after chainsawing a camp full of girl scouts to pieces. He was wearing his bright orange puffy coat with his blue, rotten backpack strapped across his chest. His thin gray hair was streaked and matted to his large forehead and he stood, dripping and staring, saying nothing. He didn't bother to wipe his boxy, silver wireframe glasses.

"A chamomile tea, iced." The Hermit said flatly.

Sam felt discomfort tingle through his body. He wished desperately there was some way to communicate a bit of small talk to The Hermit. For some reason, that's all Sam ever wanted to do; it would make him feel so much better. He had tried once and The Hermit had just said "thank you" and walked away.

The Hermit always said "thank you" the same way. There was never any emotion in his tone, but Sam thought his voice sounded younger when he said it.

Sam was sure The Hermit didn't see him as any particular gender. The Hermit was self-contained within his big orange coat and never let any words or thoughts out that weren't perfectly suitable and concise. It bothered Sam deeply that he couldn't break The Hermit's exterior.

The Louse was yammering about abortion as population control. David the Prophet was listening with lips pursed. Jewel and Linc and The Hermit were anchoring the dining room to earth. Sam was watching the rain and feeling dreary. There was nothing but the rain and The Louse's hatred of women and the morose acoustic music to fill his brain.

The door popped open and it was a corpse. Sam gripped the stainless steel counter to keep steady. He wanted to go home.

The corpse wanted her coffee with cream and sugar. However unlike the other corpses, whose eyes were dead, her eyes were brown pools of swarthy, dark sadness. He felt that the coffee meant something more to her than just a forced habit—like it was the only warmth she ever received. He felt sorry for her and poured the coffee with great, delicate care. He began to feel burdened by the weight of her melancholy. She seemed accustomed to the strain of her sorrowful energy and Sam felt helpless.

She kept her limbs close to her body as she searched through her small, neat purse for her money. Sam noticed her hair was more orderly than most corpses and he sensed that everything she owned was always kept neat and put away, even her own thoughts. She paid for the coffee, said "Thank you, *Miss*," and joined the refugees in the dining room.

When the last "s" in "Miss" hissed from the corpse's dismal mouth, Sam felt a deep, dark exhaustion settle over him. He began to wonder if he was going to make it through the shift. The Louse was chattering about death and subatomic particles separating in your brain. His words started to become incoherent and Sam wondered if his subatomic particles were leaving his brain. He felt defeated and empty. He wished to be swept away in the rain; he wanted a natural and violent force greater and stronger than humanity to dictate his existence for once.

It was then that the door popped open and the old couple came in. Sam thought about hiding under the counter. Sam *rarely* saw old people at coffee shops, but when he did, he always thought they seemed out of place. Seeing them made him feel heartsick. The old couple shook their umbrellas and smiled kindly at him. Old people love to talk about the weather. They love to talk about anything. Sam felt his neck hairs raise as he anticipated the presence of The Louse lurking toward the cash register, coming to suffocate the old couple with his incessant prattling. To Sam's surprise, The Louse was too busy feasting, spider-like, on his prey of David the Prophet. Sam was alone with the old couple.

They stood, dripping and grinning like two shaggy, wet dogs. There was a warmth about them that Sam couldn't resist. Sam knew for certain that when people got old, the texture of them weathered into either softness or roughness. They either feel worn and smooth like old stones or wise, round mountains, or rough like coarse, splintery wood or metal that's scabby and rusted. He examined the old couple's hands and saw smooth, nubby softness. The rain slowed behind them. Everything slowed with old people.

Old people always thought Sam was a girl. In some ways, he wasn't sure how to be male around them. He felt that male interactions with old people rested so heavily on being a nice young man. Sam only had a few months experience being a nice young man, but almost thirty years of being a nice young woman. He desperately did not want to upset the old couple by failing to be a nice young man. He awkwardly settled somewhere in between. The old couple tried to engage Sam in how terrible the weather was, but Sam started to feel his subatomic brain particles separating and he barely managed to give them the right change.

"What's your name, dear?" The soft old person said to Sam.

Sam tried to keep from jumping over the bakery case and running away. He stared at the old couple and his voice involuntarily chirped sweetly, "Sam." He forced a smile, hoping they would go away.

"Oh! Short for Samantha?" Sam sensed The Louse's ears perk and felt David the Prophet staring stonily ahead.

"Something like that," Sam mumbled, and he imagined himself spontaneously combusting.

The Louse returned to consuming David the Prophet, but Sam knew he was growing bored with his intellectual plaything. Sam knew that he was next. Sam waited for The Louse to sink his fangs into him and drain the last lifeblood that was quietly forcing itself through his tired, restricted heart. The only escape was to go wipe the dining room, but he knew the dining room hadn't floated away, and all the peculiar customers were still in there.

The storm had settled into a light, steady rain, and the sun had come back out. Bright rays shone through the watery air and made everything twinkle like thousands of tiny, brilliant crystals. Sam moved slowly and carefully past the swampy quicksand of The Louse. He grabbed the sanitizer bottle and rag, took a deep breath, and floated toward the dining room. It was just then that Sam, The Louse, and David the Prophet heard a loud clatter in the dining room.

Sam moved to the door frame and saw The Hermit sitting helplessly with his iced chamomile spilled out on the table, soaking his newspaper and used Splenda packets.

"Sorry," The Hermit said lifelessly.

Sam rhythmically began wiping the mess. The Louse stood in the door frame next to David the Prophet and stared at him, his arms folded over his chest. Jewel peered speculatively at Sam over the book she was reading. Linc glanced up from his laptop then continued working. The corpse sat numbly, her bony fingers wrapped around the warm coffee mug. The old couple stared and watched Sam, worried about the situation. The Hermit sat and gazed vacantly as Sam cleaned up after him. Sam usually delighted in creating clean surfaces, but he could feel his confidence waning. The acoustic song faded and the album ended on the stereo system, rendering the café silent.

Sam began to feel nauseated and a little unreal. He noticed that the paintings on the walls of the room were all crooked. The Louse came and stood behind him to inspect the mess.

The dining room stared at him as he cleaned for The Hermit. He was unsure of the gender of his cleaning. He felt like a woman, with his delicate, curvy body entrenched by the two expectant men. His small hands wiped the table, and he could not erase the experience of cleaning up after someone from his being. It felt glaringly obvious that he had never sat and waited for anyone to clean up after him. His hands moved over the tables the way they did after holiday dinners, while the men sat in the other room.

He could see the old couple wanted to help or take over in some way. They were getting anxious and their lips kept opening then closing. Finally, the old person burst with, "Samantha, you missed a spot." The Louse left out a sniffy, rapid-fire snicker. "You missed a spot, *Samantha*," he joked with a twisted sneer.

It was just then that Sam experienced his subatomic brain cells start to completely leave his body and he felt himself begin to die, when Linc looked up from his work and spoke loudly and clearly, "His name is Sam."

The Louse's sneer turned into a sour frown. The old people eyed Sam sympathetically. Jewel pretended to be reading. The corpse clung desperately to the last bit of warmth in her coffee cup. The Hermit sat, completely unfazed, still waiting for Sam to finish wiping up the mess. David the Prophet stared solemnly at the whole scene.

They all knew. Something had changed, but yet nothing had. Sam felt a surge of energy that lifted him. The wild, joyful notion of leaving the café flooded his mind and consumed his being. He set the rag down, felt himself float lightly into the street.

He stepped out into the sunlight that was rainy and confused, but happy, and started walking home. He heard a man's voice singing loudly and exuberantly. As he got closer, he saw a thin, hungry man in a ragged sweater and soiled corduroy pants, his long dreadlocks matted and gray. His arms were stretched wide open to the sky, and he sang into the sun and rain.

"You've got to step out into the light... Hallelujah, Hallelujah."

The man didn't notice Sam, and he was grateful. He smiled at him and continued walking home.

BLACK HOLES

• *RJ Edwards*

You have butterflies on your skin, welcoming me in.

"What do you think it would feel like to die in a black hole?" Joey asked, then immediately added, "Not being morbid."

Kant laughed. He had a loud belly laugh that made the bare bedroom feel full and bright. The mattress they were lying on had no bed frame, and, at the moment, no sheets. The only set not being used as makeshift curtains were drying in the basement. The only decorations on the walls were a handful of postcards. One was from Joey, one was from a high school friend living in Argentina, and two were from no one at all. Kant bought them himself, because he liked them.

Joey turned zer head to give Kant a wildly serious glare. When his laughs subsided, Kant said, "It probably feels like dying."

Joey sat up. "But what kind of dying? You know, maybe it would crush you, or maybe you would suffocate."

"Jo! This *is* morbid," Kant said.

"What if it didn't kill you?" Joey went on. "When I was kid, I thought black holes just brought you to other places. New worlds. That's what they did in TV. Or maybe the worlds that pass through them change."

Joey was too embarrassed to tell Kant why ze had a sudden morbid interest in black holes. Kant always seemed completely open to telling Joey any strange, spiritual, or superstitious thought that ran through his head. He told his roommate those things, too. He talked about them with people he bummed cigarettes from at the bus stop, if it was the right sort of day. Joey was still practically a stranger when Kant opened up to zer about his kinks.

They had met by chance three times. The first time, they were introduced to each other by a mutual friend at a birthday party. Then they sat together at the transmasculine spectrum support group that neither of them ever attended again. After running into each other at the Eric Carle picture book art museum, they decided to make a real, intentional appointment to spend time together. They met up one week later in a café called The Purple Kitty for brunch.

"Is it a latex thing?" Joey asked.

"No, it's not latex, and it's not just balloons," Kant replied, digging the side of his fork into his eggs Benedict. It had a crab cake in the middle instead of a slice of ham, and the menu called it Kitty's Seafood Delight. Kant had a knife but neglected to use it even once. "It's more specific than that."

"I don't know what you mean," Joey said. Ze had worked hard to get good at saying that. It used to be a terrifying thing for zer to admit.

"It's—I think it's the moment that they pop." Kant said, bringing a big gooey forkful to his mouth.

"I hate that noise," Joey said. Ze had finished zer modest plate of a single egg over hard with wheat toast and sat with zer hands folded on zer lap. Ze looked around at all the cat-themed photographs, paintings, clocks and trinkets littering the walls. There was one blue porcelain kitten with a white tip at the end of its tail on a shelf in the corner of the room, facing the wall.

"It's not the noise," Kant said tentatively, as if he was going to launch into a delicate explanation, but then smiled and shook his head. "I don't think I can explain it. But it just fills me up with heat. People just have those things, you know?"

"Yeah," Joey said.

"Do you?" Kant asked.

"Do I what?"

"Have one of those things?"

Across the Atlantic Ocean and underground, Jean-Michel Gregory was speaking to Dr. Benedicta Goeppert about the end of the universe. She felt very strongly about the nature of existence being cyclical, that all matter would eventually return to the state that stimulated the beginning of the universe as we know it. Long after humans were extinct and our sun was dead, expanding space would shrink until it was conducive to a Big Bang and everything that ever was would be again in its earliest, most basic form. Gregory wanted to know whether or not it would lead to another planet like ours, with creatures like ours, with he and Dr. Goeppert there, having this conversation again. She told him that this cycle would happen an infinite number of times, and since they were currently proving that this conversation was already a possible outcome, yes, someday, they would have this chat again. Gregory wasn't so sure. He told Dr. Goeppert that he felt the same way about the end of the universe that he did about God: he could never know for certain, so venturing guesses felt arrogant.

Dr. Benedicta Goeppert smiled at Gregory with a tight, pained smile that made him regret whatever he had just said. She excused herself, saying she had a lot more work to do before she went home. They were actually going *home* soon—they had been working on-site at the collider in Switzerland for a few weeks now. She would finally go to her home in Berlin and see her sister and her nephew, and he would go to his home in Lyon and see his wife, Anna, and their two daughters, Nadene and Anne. He was looking forward to it, but he already knew it would be very difficult going back. He had fallen in love with Dr. Goeppert during the third day they worked together. That was the day that a miscalculation about the placement of a magnet committed by someone they had never met and would never meet set them nearly a month behind where they were supposed to be. Gregory had glanced over at Dr. Goeppert, and he could see that she was flushed and trying very hard not to cry from frustration, and at once he felt it all. Her angst, his angst over her angst, a need to keep her safe and close to him, a need to run his fingers through her dark hair. He felt sweat, blood, idealism and dopamine. He loved her, oh, very much.

You know that I could kiss you forever and ever?

Joey had started writing bad love poems on any spare bit of paper ze found in Kant's apartment. Receipts, grocery lists, junk mail envelopes. Ze put them right back where they were before, and ze remained unsure if Kant accidentally threw them in the trash until he quoted them back to zer. On top of the polka-dot sheets that had been in the dryer the night before, Joey ran zer hands over Kant's bare shoulder.

"They say hi," Kant said with a tired smile, referring to the tattoo there. "Welcoming committee. Welcome inside, Joey."

He had gotten the ink when he was eighteen, before he started transitioning, before he even thought about being a boy. It was a very pretty cluster of black, orange, and yellow butterflies. Kant only started to get questions about what the butterflies meant when he was twenty four, after he started passing as a man and his chest surgery scars had healed. They drew attention any time he wore tank tops or went topless at the beach (or, more often, at the little swimming holes he and his friends found while exploring the woods of western Massachusetts). Before transition he had very much enjoyed trying to explain what the tattoo meant. On the rare occasion someone asked, he used to talk about growth, rebirth, and not changing, but becoming something you already are. Now that someone asked pretty much any time the tattoo was visible, he just said that it was pretty. He didn't like that people needed a justification for him to put something beautiful on his body.

"Can I stay this time?" Joey asked.

"You can stay as long as you'd like," Kant said. He shifted in the dark and kissed Joey's neck, then across to zer shoulder.

"Can I live here?" Joey asked. "I'll live right here, in the bed. I can come in and out of the window. I won't make any noise."

"Jo, what are you talking about?"

"I want to live with you, Kant. I hate going home all the time. I hate being alone in my apartment. It's making me nuts."

"We'll get you a cat," Kant assured zer, pressing his mouth on zer skin again.

"I'm allergic," Joey said, but Kant's kisses were trailing down onto zer chest. If he heard zer, he pretended he hadn't.

On July nineteenth, Jean-Michel Gregory was one of the last people to leave. He was unsure if he was even allowed to be alone inside the thing, but he took advantage of the quiet time in this underground city. The endless walls of metal began to seem less harsh and more majestic as he wandered undisturbed. It must have been past midnight. Everyone lost track of time pretty easily down in the Large Hadron Collider. He lay down on his back. The floor was cold, and he closed his eyes and imagined everything as it would be soon, bright and humming, full of possibility. He flushed with pride just thinking about it, even though he had no role in its inception and only a small role in its construction. He thought about Benedicta, about her tense smile. He hadn't seen her since their end-of-the-world talk. He knew she was probably busy, just as busy as he was, but it still made him nervous. He wasn't sure if he'd see her again after they went home. He wasn't anticipating making love to her on the floor next to a piece of the particle accelerator, but the thought of never getting to say goodbye filled him with a deep, cold loneliness.

"Eight, nine..." Kant counted. Joey was lying on zer back, and Kant gently pulled back zer lips to inspect zer teeth. "You know you have a funny wisdom tooth back here?"

"Yesh," Joey mumbled. Kant released zer lips and ze swallowed some saliva. "I know."

"It's almost sideways," Kant said. "Why didn't you get it pulled?"

"Because there's only one," Joey replied. "My dentist didn't think it was a big deal. I like being a mutant."

Kant smiled. "Do you want to get brunch?"

Joey breathed deeply. "Yeah, okay. How late are they open? Can I trim my hair first?"

"Sure, whatever. It's barely eight."

Joey cut zer own hair, so ze was in a state of constant trimming and adjustments. Ze stepped into Kant's bathroom and regarded zer reflection. Zer hair was currently in what ze thought of as its Safe For Work state, meaning that none of it was shaved or dyed, and the asymmetry came off as trendy instead of jarring. Zer summer job had ended a week and a half ago, however, and ze could use a change. Ze pulled open the cabinet behind the mirror and pulled out a pair of scissors. Ze grabbed a handful of wavy brown hair and chopped it off.

When ze closed the cabinet to take a look in the mirror, ze found light dancing in zer peripheral vision. Suddenly disoriented,

Joey sat down on the toilet and closed zer eyes. When ze opened them, the phenomenon was still happening. It seemed like the trick of light ze used to experience as a child, when ze could see tiny micro-organisms floating on the surface of zer eyes. These, however, moved much more swiftly, and were distinctly opaque and silver. It was just as likely a new trick of light, but Joey was consumed with anxiety. The complete foreignness of the sensation made zer feel like these were tiny silver slices in the universe. Reality seemed punctured, and these were fragments of something else leaking out.

Eventually both the phenomena and the anxiety subsided. Still seated, Joey opened the cabinet underneath the sink and pulled out Kant's razor.

"Buzzcuts all around, then," Ze said to zerself.

He saw her as soon as he walked in. Dr. Benedicta Goeppert was wearing a bright green dress with white buttons down the front. It wasn't the kind of thing he thought she would wear at all, but he was thoroughly charmed. He reminded himself that he didn't actually know her that well, that he was a ridiculous human being with a ridiculous fantasy life. He crossed the floor of well-dressed scientists and engineers sipping wine and stopped just before reaching her. Suddenly self-conscious about how he would greet her, he turned to a nearby table of food and pretended to consider its contents. She approached him and touched his arm, which thrilled him briefly. They talked about what they had done between leaving the collider and this reception. Then she asked a question that surprised him: Have you received any hate mail?

He gave a flustered no and asked if she knew of some enemy he had made. She told him about all the press around the world that the Large Hadron Collider was getting as the first run approached. She told him that some people thought they might create tiny black holes and effectively destroy the world.

He laughed at the suggestion, and asked if she had received anything. She said she had: one letter. She did not laugh.

After some drinks, they wandered out of the ballroom and down one of the halls of the hotel hosting the event. Dr. Goeppert went into a restroom and asked Gregory to wait for her. He leaned against the wall next to the door and let his mind wander. He thought about his wife, and wondered if Dr. Goeppert was right and if there was some incarnation of the universe in which he never met and married Anna. He loved Anna very much, but he thought that if he had never met her, tonight would be the night he would make love to Benedicta for the first time. In some other incarnation of existence she would come out of the bathroom and kiss him and ask him to stay here in the hotel with her tonight. When they were at the front desk, they would pretend they were married. They would hold hands like newlyweds, and in the morning they would plan to move here to Geneva together. If she was right, if the universe was born and died infinite times, then it had already happened, or it would happen, someday.

This time, she came out of the bathroom, walked straight to him, and put her hand in his. She looked up and asked him, using his first name: Jean-Michel, will I ever see you again after tonight?

He told her that she would, of course. They did not kiss this time.

I love your hips like mine, I love your body and I love my
body less alone. Your body draws me into my body, because
I know your body so well, and I know it to be beautiful.

When Joey finally emerged from the bathroom, head freshly shorn, Kant jumped.

"Wow," he said, "I was wondering what was taking you so long."

They went back to The Purple Kitty. Joey still had bits of hair scattered all over zer shoulders. They were especially noticeable against the kelly green of zer current t-shirt, the same one ze had worn to Kant's place the evening before. Joey had worn brown and black pretty much exclusively until ze dropped out of college.

"Joey," Kant started hesitantly, tracing a line on his cup of coffee with his index finger, "Have you been okay lately?"

"Is this because I shaved my head?" Joey asked.

"Of course not," Kant said. "It just seems like you've been... somewhere else lately."

Joey adjusted zer fork and knife nervously. "I want to move in with you."

"Is that really all?" Kant said. "Because we talked about that, and I thought..."

He trailed off. The first time they had talked about it had actually gone alright, but Kant's current roommate, Ariana, was opposed.

"But she doesn't like me," Joey said.

"She likes you. She just doesn't want to live with you. Or live with me *and* you. It's different. She wants her space."

"Why don't we move somewhere else?" Joey asked.

"And leave Ariana to pay the rent on her own? Or fill my room with a stranger?"

"Yeah," Joey said with an uncharacteristic firmness.

Kant paused, then said, "No."

His French toast and zer eggs came, and they both ate quietly for a while. Kant reached for the powdered sugar and picked up the conversation again.

"Just give her a while, alright?"

Joey felt a fluttering in zer chest. "September tenth," ze said.

"What?"

"Kant, that's all I can do." Zer throat grew dry and ze felt humiliated.

"That's five days. That's so random," Kant said indignantly.

"It's the... okay, *listen*," Joey said. Starting by demanding attention that way made zer feel like what ze was going to say was less ridiculous. "That's the day they're turning on the Large Hadron Collider. And I—I don't think the world is going to end, necessarily, but I feel like—there's no way we can know what it's going to do. And what the world is going to be afterwards."

"This is why you've been so weird lately." Kant said in disbelief. "A science experiment in Europe?"

"Don't make it sound stupid." Joey said quietly. "I just—I need to know that I'm—that I'm worth this much to you. That I can spend my days and nights with you even if your roommate will be annoyed or resentful. That you can deal with something so, so fucking small, because I'm worth it. Before September tenth. Because, yeah, I'm scared."

Kant thought, then said, "I've known Ariana for years."

"Right," Joey said. Ze got up and fiddled with zer wallet.

"Jo, come on. I'm sorry. It's not stupid."

"Prove it." Joey put a ten dollar bill on the table and walked away.

You have butterflies on your skin, welcoming me in;
I can't tell your skin from mine, but that's just fine.

On September tenth, when the Large Hadron Collider was awake and circulating proton beams for the first time underground in Switzerland, Jean-Michel Gregory was in France, tucking his youngest daughter, Anne, into bed. His older girl, Nadene, was also in bed, but sat up typing. An open laptop rested on the white cotton of her nightgown, and she tried in vain to find her father's name mentioned somewhere in news about the collider. Jean-Michel walked up behind his wife, who was standing on the small balcony outside their bedroom, and gently kissed her shoulder. He told her he loved her.

In Germany, Dr. Benedicta Goeppert was talking to her mother on the phone. She told her about the reception in Geneva without mentioning Jean-Michel at all.

And in the United States, in Joey's one-room efficiency apartment, the phone was not ringing. It had not rung. Ze listened to sad songs and looked online for a new job. The sun set, and Joey's melancholy soundtrack began to repeat itself. Ze turned it off and started searching for a new world.

OTHER WOMEN

• Casey Plett

My mom picked me up fresh off the red-eye and we went for donuts. It was the day before Christmas Eve. I told her all the fun parts about living in Portland, and she listened and hummed and marched her way through a Tim Hortons dozen. When I asked her about life at the hospital, she said well, thanks for asking. It's just fine. I was silent for a bit so she would know I wanted to hear more, and then she told me a story about how another nurse had misheard a 99 code and went pinballing through the hospital halls to find a patient not at death's door, as she had thought, but sitting with her newborn grandchild. That's funny, I said. Yeah, she said, running a hand through her wispy hair.

She didn't say anything about gender the whole day, which was nice of her. It was my first time home in Winnipeg since I asked everyone to call me Sophie, about six months ago, after I moved away last January. I wanted my visit to be a Christmas the same as any other. Mom's been trying to call me Sophie, but it's hard for her.

She left to work a shift around two and I called Megan. Dude, where the fuck have you been! She said.

Putting in mom time, I said.

Gayyyyy! She said. Megan says that a lot, though she's slept with more women than I have.

Dude, she said. I moved to Corydon, I live by the Blue Cactus now. It's great. I never have to worry about driving drunk. Meet me at my place though. I gotta return some bottles. If you wanna help me?

Megan always asks me to run errands or do housework and stuff with her, which I like. I like that hanging out doesn't have to mean coffee or dinner or drinks or some bullshit. We met in Grade 9 math and bonded over stuff like Philip Roth and Papa Roach, and we hung out for the first time when she asked me if I wanted to come over and help make dinner for her great-aunt. That was ten years ago.

When I got to her building, she was already outside, carrying bags of bottles to her car. I rush-hugged her and she dropped the bags and we teetered back and forth on the sidewalk with our boots creaking on the snow like rocking chairs. You look so good, she said. You look so good. Thank you, I said. You do too, you really do. Merry Motherfucking Christmas. She pulled me tighter and released.

Megan looked the same, actually, though I've always thought she looked amazing. Thicket of blueberry-blue hair. Water-green eyes the shape of grapes. Still refused to wear a coat appropriate for living in the middle of Canada, layered on padded hoodies instead.

We went upstairs to bag the rest of her bottles and take a shot of rum before heading out. It's my roommate's, she said, I need to get another bottle for him when we're out. Remind me.

Right before we left she said, Okay, sorry, I have to ask. Do they look like man-boobs or are they real girl-looking boobs? I didn't want to answer. I'm only a year on hormones but even though I'm a B-cup, I'm also six foot and they still seem small. They do look like girl boobs if you see them under clothing though, so I said do you wanna—? And she said yes before I could finish. I felt like a dopey teenager flashing her, but I feel like a dopey teenager a lot lately.

She nodded in this approving way. They're girl boobs, she said. Nice. Shit. I want to take pills to grow my boobs. I said sell you mine. Five bucks each. She slapped me around the middle and said you're such a fucking pusher! She laughed at herself. Then there was a key in the door and I had to straighten my bra. A short guy walked in with snow stuck to one side of his curly hair and his U of M parka.

Hey Mark, Megan said. This is Sophie. We drank the last of your rum. I'm getting another bottle now though.

Oh cool, he said, in a high, lilting voice. Hi, I'm Mark, he said.

Sophie, I said. I stuck out my hand and he shook it awkwardly. I made a note to pay attention to whether men and women shook hands with each other. All these new social cues were confusing.

You fall down? Megan asked, nodding to the snow on his side. Yeah, he said. These three big guys came up to me and told me to give them my parka, so I started running. I tripped after about two blocks. I don't think they tried to chase me though.

Yay Winnipeg, I said. Yeah whatever, Megan said. Let's go.

You got a girlfriend in the States yet? Megan asked in the car. No. You got a boy?

No. Boys don't like me. I said that couldn't be true, that she was beautiful, and she said well thank you, in that way you might tell a guy on the street that you've got no change on you, sorry, so sorry.

Megan and I never dated, but we did have sex once, my first year of university, when we were really high. We just pretended it hadn't happened in the morning. She said good luck on your midterm, and I said have fun at work, and she kissed me on the neck and left. Then I tried to fall back asleep in her bed, but I couldn't, so I got dressed, took one of her shirts, and left. I wish I hadn't lost the shirt, this stretchy bright green thing. I wonder how it'd look on me now that I have boobs.

Your heat not work? I asked Megan. It was thirty below outside and it didn't feel much different inside her car.

's a piece of shit. Takes a while.

Blech.

Eh.

HOLY FUCK! She screamed and braked. *SHIT!* We were in an intersection, and a red sedan on the cross street had braked too late for driving on snow and ice and was skidding sideways into our path. *OH SHIT* I yelled and then the sedan's back door collided with the front right corner of Megan's car. We slammed forward in our seats and stopped and there was a terrible mass clank of bottles in the trunk.

You okay? Megan said immediately.

Yeah, I said.

Good. She got out of the car. *YOU FUCKIN' BRAIN DAMAGED OR SOMETHING* she yelled. The driver was an old man with a red toque sliding off his head, staring slack-jawed at Megan.

She strode over to the car and he got out and straightened his toque and said he was very sorry, oh shoot, he was very, very sorry, and Megan said yeah, you better be. Then all business-like she said come on, let's get out of the road and do the insurance. Can your car go?

He said he thought it could and we skittered over to a side street. He sounded like a nice guy. We actually buddied up to him by the end. There wasn't much damage anyway since we'd both been going twenty clicks on impact. Just some dents. The guy shook our hands and said he was so sorry he caused such a nice guy and gal a hard day. Megan grunted and didn't say anything and then he left. It's petty, but I wish she had. Just said something like actually, we're both nice gals. Nothing nasty. Instead she looked at me and rolled her eyes. Then we checked the bottles. Only one had broke.

I don't know why I can't just say for myself, "Actually, I'm not a guy." I get this awful image of being like a little kid saying *Look, no, I'm reaaaally a girl. I promise. I super promise!* I wanted someone else to step up and say, You're wrong buddy-o, that there is a chick, she's no man and you should get your eyes checked.

Winter coats make it hard to see my new body shape, too, I guess. I used to love that about winter.

By the way, said Megan, picking up on my mood. I know this is kind of random, but I really like how your freckles have come out now.

Thanks, I said, blushing. That was nice to hear.

We returned Megan's bottles then went to the Blue Cactus and got hammered. After a couple hours Megan got a text and said Shit! I need to get rum for Mark.

Where'd you meet that kid anyway? I slurred.

Friend of a friend. Why?

Never seen him around before.

Yeah, I don't really know much about him, actually, she said. I've only lived with him like two months. And he doesn't talk that much. She threw back the rest of her Blue Hurricane. He's from the country. We gotta start walking.

Fuuuuck, I said. I shot the last of the vodka soda I'd just ordered. Thatta girl, she said.

Mark! Megan said, throwing back the front door.

Maaaaaaaark! I said, following her with the liquor bag.

M-A-A-A-A-A-A-A-RK! We both sang together, on a third, then a fifth. Old joke. We used to sneak up and surprise people in high school like that. Mark looked up from the cello he'd been playing. There was a pipe full of ash and an Altoids tin on the table and his eyes looked like Superballs floating in tomato soup.

Got your rum, roomie! Megan said. I gave the bag to her and she slammed it onto the table.

Oh cool. Thanks, he said. What're you ladies up to? He enunciated his words in a way that made him sound almost but not quite British.

We shrugged. I gotta get home in a bit, I said. There's no fuckin' way you could drive, is there, I said to Megan.

She laughed and said I don't think I could read.

Okay, I said. I did want to get home before my mom did. I didn't like the thought of her coming back to an empty house on my first day. I still had a couple hours though. Megan put on *Eternal Sunshine of the Spotless Mind* and Mark packed a bowl for him and me from weed out of the Altoids tin. It cool if we smoke? I said to Megan. She murmured sure. She used to smoke a lot but gave it up around a year ago.

Megan fell asleep in the first ten minutes of the flick and Mark and I started taking shots of the rum. We didn't speak through our respective hazes for most of the next two hours, expect to say things like holy shit and what the fuck. Neither of us had seen the movie.

When it ended, I had half an hour before my mom got home, so I tried to wake up Megan, but she just kept smacking her lips and turning over in her chair.

I gotta get home, I said.

She snort-laughed into a cushion. Are you kidding? I can't drive.

Dude! I said, more angrily than I meant to sound. I have to get home!

We'll die if I drive so that won't help you.

Megan! I said. Jesus Sophie, she said, her face not lifting up from the cushion. Just get Mark to do it. Her blue hair was covering her face and her outer hoodie was blue and she looked like an angry drunken Skittle. I told her this. She told me to blow myself.

Drive? Mark said. Sure.

No! It's okay, I said. I'll just call my mom. I went into the building hallway. I was disappointed. I liked being in Megan's car.

I called the hospital and they told me she was busy, but they'd tell her to call me back. I went back into the apartment and Megan was gone. Mark was playing his cello. I tilted my head in question and looked at the empty chair.

She went off to sleep, he said. Are you getting picked up?

She's gonna call me back, I said. I slouched against the wall. Walking had reawakened the booze and the weed and I was getting the spins. Hey, I'm sorry to bother you, I said, wincing. Like, I'm sorry, but can I steal the couch from you? I sank down the wall to the floor. I really need to lie down, I said.

Absolutely, he said. He picked up his cello. Go for it.

Thanks, I said. He disappeared down a hallway. I rolled over to the couch and slithered onto it from the floor.

I woke up to Mark tapping my arm. Sorry, he whispered, I just thought you might be glad to have these when you woke up. He was sitting cross-legged on the hardwood floor. Next to him was a thin pillow and a green and black blanket. Next to those was a large tumbler of ice water, and next to those were a bag of Old Dutch ketchup chips. Sorry, he said, seeing my eyes meet the chips, it was the only food I could find that you don't have to cook.

I laughed. Aw. You're nice, Mark.

He stuck his arms out and palms up in an aw-shucks gesture. Oh, I am not that nice, he said. You just gotta get to know me first. I said ah. I took the pillow and blanket and sat up covered. Then I drank all the ice water.

I'll get you some more, he said.

Aw no, it's okay, I said. I lay down again.

It's no biggie, he said, you are very welcome here. He came back with a refilled glass. I thanked him.

So what do you do, Mark? I said, looking at him sideways from the pillow. I liked saying his name. It sounded crisp.

I'm an engineer. Or that's what I study, at least. I'm a civil engineer, like the kind that designs bridges.

I know what a civil engineer is, I said. It came out meaner than I meant it to.

Oh cool, he said. Well, I am one of those, he said, unperturbed.

Well look at you, eh? I said, trying to sound nice. A pot-smoking, cello-playing, civil engineer.

He laughed, a quick, two-toned treble laugh, like the sound of getting a coin in old Super Mario Brothers games. *Ba-Ding! Ha-Ha!* Heya, he said, doing the aw-shucks gesture again. I try my best, honey. What do you do?

I am a master of the shipping and receiving arts, I said. Books specifically.

Oh cool. That makes sense.

It does?

Yeah, he said, I was wondering, because of your figure.

What?

Well from a distance you just look skinny, he said. And you are skinny, he said quickly.

This was a lie, I was one-ninety-five. But I appreciated the thought.

But really up close you can see your muscles, like, you're quite toned. But it's subtle. It's work strength, not gym strength. He paused, looking thoughtful.

You look really good, he said suddenly. You pull it off. You look tough and pretty.

I blushed. Thank you, I said softly.

He smiled and said, Just the truth.

Suddenly I really wanted to know if he was straight or not. I wasn't into men, but I wanted him to be into women. He burnt a hole through my gay-dar.

He did make me feel pretty though, regardless.

My mom called back. I took out my phone and it rubbed against the five o'clock shadow on the cleft of my chin. I stopped feeling pretty.

Hey, my mom said. We got a few patients in at the last minute that need a lot of documentation, so I'm going to be late coming home. Normally they wouldn't do this, of course, she said. But they don't have to pay me overtime because I have the next few days off. Anyway, so. Don't wait up for me before you go to sleep or anything.

Okay, I said. I tried to use as few words as possible. I'm at Megan's now, I said. Mark mimed asking if I wanted to sleep here, tilting his head towards his pressed-together hands, then pointing toward the couch.

Oh okay, Mom said, her voice characteristically blank. It was hard enough to suss out her feelings even when you weren't drunk and high. I wondered if she was mad. She didn't offer to give me a ride, so I guessed she didn't care if I came home or not.

I might just stay here, I said. If that's okay? I'm really sleepy.

That's fine, Mom said. We could go for lunch tomorrow if you'd like. I said that'd be great and then we hung up.

Thank you, I said to Mark.

Oh cool, yes, of course, he said. His eyes had contracted enough by now that I could see they were a deep brown. They'd looked so black before. Do you need anything? He said.

No, I'm fine, I said. Thanks. You're nice. I laid my head down. He got up and waved goofily. Goodnight, Sophie, he said.

Thanks for the hospitality! I yelled quietly as he closed his door, but I couldn't tell if he heard. I heard him stumble over something in his room and say *ow fuck* before his bed creaked with weight.

///////

Mom and I spent all of Christmas Eve together. We went to Earl's for lunch, then to the Forks to go ice-skating. I kept speeding up, and then I'd see I was losing her so I had to wait for her to catch up. You Americans are always trying to get ahead, she said. We laughed. I started sweating from all the exercise, so I opened my coat and let it fly around my arms, and the air felt deliciously cold.

We went to Robin's for donuts and coffee afterwards and that's when Mom asked me if I felt safe down in the States. I said mostly I did, why?

Well, it's America. She paused. And there's your new lifestyle.

Yeah, I know, I said.

She looked at me hard. I hope you do, she said. There are certainly a lot of—she paused—rude people out there.

Yeah, I know, I said. I'm alert, I promise. I've been fine. Portland's safe and it's really friendly to people like me. It's safer than here actually. I paused. Last night, we didn't go out or anything, we were inside. She said well, that's good to hear, and took a double chocolate and broke it in half.

It's not true. That everything's always friendly. I was at a bar a few weeks back and some guys threatened to throw a knife in my face. Someone yelled *fuckin' faggot* when I was walking home the other day. I moved to Portland partly on word that it was a queer-dripping liberal dream, but I wish I'd researched geographical specifics before I signed a lease on 104th and Powell. Honestly,

I just feel lucky no one's tried to punch me yet. Or stab me. But Mom doesn't need to hear any of that.

She took the trans thing pretty hard. It wasn't bad when I came out to her a couple years ago, admitted I wore dresses, told her I was just thinking about transitioning. She'd listened and frowned and said okay, well, I think you make a fantastic son, and I certainly hope you can learn to love yourself as a male.

So that was a relief. It was when I told her last year I was going on hormones that she said oh lord really softly, and then kept excusing herself to go to the bathroom till finally I said Mom, just bring the Kleenex box here, I know you're crying, it's okay! Just *please* can we talk about this? I don't know why that was so important, why I had to talk *right away* when she just wanted to go cry alone and process. There was a long silence and I asked her what she was thinking. All of the things I did wrong, she said. She didn't say much else because she was trying to think of something positive to say, because my mom doesn't know how to say hurtful things to people she loves. She finally said well, your acne will get better. Will it? I said. She said yup, cause you'll have to take spironolactone, and that's something they often use to treat acne.

It was hard after that. She stopped signing her e-mails "Love, Mom." Stopped going out in public with me. Those were rough months. Another reason I moved to the States is because I thought we might never be close again, and the idea of staying in Winnipeg with the ghost of her memories on every corner made me nuts. I vomited once, just a little in my mouth, alone in my living room, over the thought of losing her.

We got a lot closer after I moved, though. She even called me her daughter last month. That was really nice.

We spent the rest of the day at home. Read books, chatted. I helped her clean the bathroom. We were eating takeout for dinner when she asked me what I was wearing to church tomorrow.

Our family always met up at my grandparents' on Christmas morning for coffee and pastries before church. We've done it every year since they moved to the city, when I was five. My mom and I aren't religious, but we go to church on Christmas. Family.

When my mother was eighteen, she and my dad renounced the church and eloped to the city from a town south of here. Three years later they had me, and two months before that she booted my dad out of the house for reasons that neither of them will tell me. I don't see my dad that much. He lives in the B.C. Interior somewhere. He moves a lot.

Their families were Mennonites, not the kind so hardcore as to shun electricity and cities, Amish-style, but enough that apostasy was kind of a bridge-burner. My grandparents didn't talk to her again until I was born, and only then for my sake. They thought it was too terrible for a boy to grow up without a family. Those were my grandfather's words, anyway.

I told my mom I had this eggshell-colored dress I wanted to wear. Hm, my mom said.

Will that be okay? I asked.

Well, I don't think your clothes will be a problem, no, she said.

So, she said as we were driving the next morning, have you given any thought to how you're going to deal with the church crowd?

No, I said. I'd been more worried about my grandparents. I really loved seeing them. They'd half-raised me. Mom was always working and I was always at their house. I didn't know how they'd react to me. I e-mailed them months ago, asking them to call me *she* and they never said anything back. Mom says they haven't mentioned anything to her about it.

But the other churchgoers didn't cross my mind. Um, I said, maybe I'll just take the cue from Grandma and Grandpa? If they think anything should be different?

Well, she said, I'm not sure they'll know what the best course of action is.

We sat in silence for a while. Should I not sit with you guys or something? I asked.

Well, that would certainly take a load off their minds.

Sure! I said. No problem.

We pulled onto the street of their townhouse. My grandpa was shoveling snow on the driveway, a dot of a red parka floating on white in front of the beige row of houses. He waved to us with both free and shovel-clasped hands when he saw us.

Hello there, Lenora! He said to my mom when we got out of the car. He hugged her and then shook my ski-gloved hand and said hello, welcome! Glad to know you can still brave it up here even if you are an American now! We laughed and my mom tittered.

Inside, Grandma hugged us and said oh, it's always just so nice to see Lenora and her child! Mom and I both bobbed our heads and said you too!

They sat us down in the living room for coffee. My grandma said oh crumbs, I forgot the shortbread. My grandpa made to stand up and said I'll get it, and my grandma said no no, you sit here and visit, and then they both stood up at the same time.

Well, I guess now we're both on the hook, my grandpa said, and my grandma laughed and scratched the inch-long scraggle of hairs on his head and they walked into the kitchen. Don't worry! said my grandpa, I'll supervise her! and my grandma laughed again.

I've always liked my grandparents' house, drab as it is. It was cozy. I liked to lie on their burnt-orange couch and read by the window that looks onto the street.

We ate shortbread and drank coffee and visited. Grandma kept straightening the trays. I asked when the rest of the family was coming and Grandma said oh, Tim and Jeni and their kids are going to meet us at church and it turns out Helmut and Mary couldn't make it. They said the pipes had frozen out in Kleefeld this morning and they didn't think they should leave.

Oh darn, that's too bad, my mom said quickly.

Oh, I said.

It certainly is cold! said my grandfather.

It's nice they haven't called you by your old name, don't you think? My mom said as we drove to church. Yes, I said, it was nice. My old name, which I hate hearing, is Leon. I've started to get this weird visceral reaction every time I hear it. Or even see it on a piece of mail or something. Too many bad memories, I guess. Not of anything specific, just unhappiness. Boy body. All that. It is nice that they haven't called me Leon, but I hope I can hear Sophie soon. I'm just glad I'm still welcome in their home though. Means a lot.

Church was fun. I may not believe in God, but I like Christmas services. Everyone's in a good mood and the sermon's reflective and peaceful.

I sat in the back and brushed my hair in my face so my grandparents' friends wouldn't recognize me. Then I slipped out as soon as the service was done. One of the ushers gave me a funny look as I was putting on my coat, so I turned away from him. Then a thirty-ish woman making her way into the fellowship hall walked right by me and whispered I like your dress. I smiled at her, then went to sit out in the car. I turned on the radio and sang along to O Holy Night and Hark! The Herald Angels Sing while texting *Merry Christmas* to everyone in my contacts.

Megan texted back. *Merry Christmas you wild bitch, how's the fam?*

Theyre not bad, I said back. *Hows your dad?*

He's great, she said. *Mark is over he couldn't get home cause theres a big storm down by Winkler. Dad loves him. They might run away together.*

Ha awesome, I said. *Hey btw random q but is Mark straight or no? He threw my gaydar into a tizzy.*

idk, she said back. *Im curious too. Will try to ask him. He says Merry Christmas btw.*

Merry fuckin Christmas to him too!

My family came out after not too long. Thank you for waiting out here, my mom said, that was very considerate of you.

Back at my grandparents' house, I met up with my Aunt Jeni and Uncle Tim and their two kids, Bernie and Cheryl. Bernie, who's twelve, asked if I could do a puzzle with him. I said I'd do my best and he gave me a thumbs up and said well that's all I can ask.

We poured the pieces on the coffee table. Bernie connected all four sides in the time it took me to fit in ten pieces, so I decided to reform my position to one of moral support: Go for it, Bernie! Yeah, you can find that piece! You're Puzzle Player World Champion! He smiled and gave a thumbs up and scratched his dust print of a moustache.

I got a cup of coffee from the kitchen and waved to my mother and my aunt, chatting at the table. I looked out the window and saw my grandparents and uncle stepping out to play in the backyard with Cheryl, my younger cousin. She was squealing and my uncle started chasing her and making monster noises: GARRRGARRR *Ahhhh!*

I piled up a plate of shortbread for us. When I came back, Bernie had fit in what looked like another thirty pieces. I sipped my coffee and brushed crumbs from my dress and continued cheering. Then Bernie said hey, um, can I ask you a question?

Sure.

It's sort of a personal question, he said. You don't have to answer.

I grinned. Bernie was super, super polite. Sometimes I found it grating, but usually I just thought he was cute.

Why did you choose Sophie? He asked.

I smiled. That's totally okay to ask, Bern. I've just always liked the name, I said. I sipped my coffee and propped my chin on my hand. Read it somewhere a few years ago and it just seemed right. It's not much of a story.

Okay, he said. That's cool. Maybe other people don't think it's cool, but I do.

I grinned. Hey thanks, Bernie. Really, thanks.

You're welcome, he said. He fit in another puzzle piece. I think part of my head will always think of you as Leon though.

Oh, I said. I tamped down an urge to throw my mug through the window. Well, give it time, I said.

I don't know, he said. He asked for a sip of my coffee. I heard, belatedly, how sad the kid's tone was. He looked worried. I wondered what his parents might have told him.

Well, I said to Bernie, what if you thought of it this way: What if it's that I've always been Sophie on the inside, so actually I was never Leon all along, it just looked that way?

I saw his gears turning as he thought about this. Hm, he said. Wait, what?

Never mind.

Maybe it's just because I always liked your name, Bernie said. Then he said I like Leon in this next-to-inaudible voice. He was looking at the puzzle piece in his hand when he said it. It's like a romantic name, he mumbled. He saw my face and then he said but Sophie really is nice too. He gave a thumbs up.

I do like Sophie, I said, trying to smile.

Then he said, hey, so do you go on dates?

I knew he meant did I date boys or girls, but I didn't want to have that conversation now, or here, so I scooped up my phone and coffee and said, Hold on, and left the room. I walked into the garage where my Aunt Jeni smoked her du Mauriers. I do love my name. I read it in a book when I was fourteen and have never wanted to be called anything else since. I don't even remember the book. It's really not much of a story. I took my notebook and pen out of my bag and lit one of Jeni's cigarettes and wrote Sophie Sophie Sophie Sophie Sophie over and over, Sophie Sophie Sophie Sophie Sophie Sophie Sophie Sophie Sophie Sophie Sophie Sophie Sophie I was starting on the other side of the page when my mom and aunt opened the door and I looked up and saw them watching me smoking and writing on the cement garage floor in my eggshell dress. Oh, my mom said, and for a second she looked scared, and then a heaviness colored her face, like sandbags had dropped through her irises. Oh hey, my aunt said, I didn't know you smoked.

Dear Lord and Heavenly Father, my grandfather said, as we bowed our heads and took each other's hands before dinner. We come to you on this holy day, the birth of your son Jesus. We come gathered in thanks, hope, and gratitude. We are thankful that we have so much of our family here, that you have blessed us with their presence, and enabled us to sit down to the meal we are about to graciously receive. We are especially thankful you saw fit to guide up from America our grandson Leon—

No, Sophie, I said.

I know you're not supposed to interrupt prayer, but I couldn't help it. My grandmother took in a sharp breath and my mother said hey now in this quiet and angry voice and I said I'm sorry.

My grandfather paused, as if he were deciding whether to address me or not, then moved on to pray for somebody else. I opened my eyes and saw everybody else's were still shut, except for Bernie, who shut his eyes as soon as he saw I'd opened mine.

Lastly, my grandfather said as he finished, we thank you for this food and ask that you bless it to our bodies. Amen.

I leaned over and apologized to him as soon as we started eating and he just frowned and said well.

No one called me either Sophie or Leon for the rest of the day. The one indication that the whole thing had happened at all was when I went to grab a hair tie from my coat pocket and found a large, neatly folded slip of paper sticking out of my boots. It had my grandmother's handwriting on it: *Trust in the Lord with all your heart and lean not on your own understanding; in all your ways acknowledge him, and he will make your paths straight.—Proverbs 3:5–6.*

I folded the paper and stuck it in my bag. I didn't want my grandmother to see it in the trash but I didn't want my mom to see it either. The one time she'd gotten audibly squirrely about gender stuff in the last few months was when I mentioned to her that I'd gone to this march in Portland for trans rights. She made this exasperated noise and started giving me this big talk about brainwashing and cults and stuff like that. I got a little annoyed. I told her that just because a group of people gets together to make the world better it doesn't automatically make them a religion and she said Don't ever be too sure about that.

/////////

You need to stay here again tonight? Megan asked.

If you don't mind? I said. I'd rather not have to leave early, I wanna see everyone.

Of course, she said.

We were headed to a Boxing Day party at Tyler's, a friend of ours from high school. It was the one time I was going to see all our old friends, I was flying back to Portland the next day. Tyler was my only other close-ish friend besides Megan. We'd known each other since Grade 1. We stuck fingers in each other's ears in choir class.

Megan and I were pre-gaming in her living room with rum and Cokes. Cello music was coming from Mark's room. Thanks, I said. Then I sucked up a breath and said hey, do you know how Tyler or the rest will, like, react to me?

I don't know, she said instantly. They were kinda angry when you sent out that coming out e-mail months ago.

Angry? I said. Nobody responded to it except Tyler and he said he'd do his best, he didn't sound angry. Angry?

Don't worry about it, she said. I told Tyler that if anybody gave you shit tonight that I would fucking murder them.

I smiled at her. Really?

Of course! she said, sounding offended I might have expected less. Bitches gotta go through me before they get to you, she said. That's what I say.

Aw, I said, grinning.

Just feel it out, she said. They might be weird, but I think they just don't understand.

Nobody ever can understand, I said. I meant it in a simple, fact-stating way—of course they can't understand, no more than I can understand Tyler's taste for liver and onions—but Megan looked irritated when I said that. Yeah, that's a great attitude, she said.

I meant like, I don't get why people have to understand, I said.

Let's just go, she said.

I put on my coat and she layered on her hoodies and we walked down to her car, not speaking much. I started to get jittery. I checked my makeup and ran fingers through my hair. I thought about the awkward dinner my mom and I had had at Earl's a couple hours before. We talked for ten minutes about converting my old bedroom into her office, it was that kind of awkward. When we got the check she said so, I wasn't sure whether to say this or not but I think I will. You know that Uncle Helmut and Aunt Mary didn't actually have frozen pipes, right?

I put my hands around my Diet Coke. I did wonder, I said. Yeah.

They didn't, she said with finality. But it was nice of your grandparents to say that, I think. Wasn't it?

I guess so? I said.

Well, she said. I just think we had a really nice Christmas.

I think so too, I said.

We picked up a twelve-pack and got to Tyler's new place. He'd gotten a sweet job with MTS and had moved into this nice Victorian by himself out by Wolseley. The house was huge. Little window-laden turret and everything. Some girl we didn't recognize let us in and we went to the kitchen to drop off the beer.

This house is wild, Megan said. The kitchen had the oddities of a guy living by himself for the first time: Well-used microwave, cupboards empty except for boxes of granola bars. The fridge contents were beer, Kraft singles, milk, sliced turkey breast, three things of broccoli, and a jar of Cheese Whiz.

Tyler came into the kitchen as we were cracking beers. He'd cut his thin red hair so short it looked like someone had sprinkled powdered carrot on his head. He'd lost weight, too. Hey Leon! He said, smiling big. Damn good to see you! He shook my hand.

I hugged him and winced at the same time. Actually, I said, it's Sophie now.

Right right, he said jovially. So how're you? How's the U.S. of A.? Feel like a Yankee yet, eh?

Yew be quiet, I said in an exaggerated Southern accent. Ah own yew and yer mayple syrup drinkin' land.

Hello? Megan said, do I not fuckin' exist over here?

You bitch, Tyler said. They hugged. Tyler poured us shots. Cheers, he said. You'll always be a Canuck to us.

Cheers!

We drank. I looked into the living room. I didn't know a lot of other people at the party.

So how are you? I said. Hear you got a new job?

Yeah, he said. I work with Sam Wiebe, actually, remember him?

He gave you a swirlie once? Right?

Oh! I still give him shit for that. He's cool now, though. Never thought the guy'd turn out to be an engineer though, eh?

Yeah weird. Hey, you're looking good, man, I said. Different. I like the hair. He nodded and said thanks. There was an awkward silence so I said I mean, I know I look a little different too. Got some growth in the chest, hips are a little wider—

He laughed really loudly and awkwardly and looked around and then said, Hey, be cool, alright?

What? I blinked. He slapped me on the back. Megan had left to talk to someone else. Look, I'm cool, okay? He said. Just like, don't—he looked frustrated and trailed off. Don't be gross, he said.

Sorry, I said, I didn't think I was being—

Look, he said, I'm cool with you. Doing whatever, like, I don't get it, I mean, if this turns you on, whatever. But there are people here tonight who wanted to kick your ass, okay? I talked to them, they're cool, but just like, relax, be normal, it'll be fine. Okay?

Uh, okay, I stammered. I worried a lot about safety, but I didn't think it'd be here.

He said cool. Okay, sorry about that. Want another shot?

Sure, I said. I thought I saw some people down the hallway staring or pointing at me, but it might've been my imagination. I did finally recognize a few people. Old friends from high school. I waved, they waved, then I cheered Tyler. Someone in another room started yelling that the Jets were definitely coming back to Winnipeg, he'd just heard it on the way over. Everyone started whooping. I never even fucking liked hockey.

Megan found me in the corner of the kitchen about half an hour later, on my third shot and second beer, listening to a theatre kid named Jesse I'd avoided since high school talk about how the Boston Tea Party was an example of performance as protest. Megan interrupted him. Hey, she said. She raised her eyebrows. How you feeling?

Ummm.

You wanna go?

Maybe? I dunno. How're you doing?

We can go, she said, nodding.

Thank you.

I chugged the beer then found Tyler. He shook my hand and said hey, don't let us keep you, good luck down in the States.

Good luck in finding out what turns you on, I said. I meant it to sound like a joke, but it came out sounding mean. I decided I didn't regret it. Jerk, I added. We went outside and I lost my balance on the porch steps and fell-sat on the top stair. Then my butt slipped off from the ice and I clattered down to the sidewalk on my ass.

Way to go, Megan said, tightening the Velcro on her leather gloves. They looked so fancy contrasted with the four hoodies she had on.

Fuck him, I said.

You are hammered and you're a dick, she said. She hoisted me up and guided me to her car.

I'm not a dick, I'm a bitch, I said.

Stop it! she said. We were silent for the walk to her car and then for most of the drive back to her place until she said so you want to help me clean my kitchen?

Mark was re-watching *Eternal Sunshine* when we got in. This movie really got to me, he said later.

Megan put on the Yeah Yeah Yeahs. I did the dishes and the counters while Megan got the floor and Mark eviscerated the fridge. She and Mark started catching up to me with the rum. It was nice. We got in a groove. I started singing, and I realized my range had gotten higher from talking in my female voice. It's nice to hear you sing again, Megan said. Cool, yeah, you have a good voice, said Mark.

Aw, you guys, you're really sweet, I said. That's really, *really* sweet. I got emotional saying this. I hadn't sung in a long time.

I felt awkward after that so I said Do you have any beer? I'd been drinking water and was starting to feel less sloshed.

That rum was the last of the booze, Megan said.

Daaaaaamn, I said.

We kept cleaning and then Mark said hey, I'll be right back. He was gone for ten, fifteen, twenty minutes and then came back ruby-faced and holding a twelve-pack. I hugged him and told him he was my new best friend. Then I wrote "NEW BEST FRIEND: SOPHIE" on his arm with a Marks-A-Lot. He laughed for a long time after I did that. We finished cleaning and sat around their kitchen table, drinking and talking and bullshitting. Megan kept the music going. She and I bumped legs under the table and kept them there. Mark mentioned something about an ex-girlfriend while telling a story and I drenched myself in the pretty compliment all over again. After an hour Mark stood up and said goddamn I need to lie down, and wobbled off to his room.

Megan went to the living room, then came back with Mark's pipe and the Altoids tin. Haaaaa, she said. You wanna smoke a bowl?

You sure? I said. Megan was a serious pothead before she quit. Quarter-ounce-a-week serious. I once saw her make a bong with a Gatorade bottle.

She waved her hand. I'm fine, she said. I can cheat once for an old buddy. That's not bad, is it?

I wasn't sure if it was bad or not, but smoking sounded too fun so I said let's do it. She turned around to walk and crashed against the fridge. Ho shit, I'm hammered, she said. I laughed and helped her up, then fell against her.

We went to her room and got good and baked and watched *So You Think You Can Dance Canada*. Megan got two cans of ketchup-flavored Pringles from her closet. We were at the bottom of the first can when I started laughing every time the French judge said something.

Duuuuuuude, I've totally forgotten how the Québécois speak. I giggled. *Kay-bec-wahhhh.*

You! Megan said. You are a fucking Yank now! You're like George W. Bush with a machine gun, and, like, a baseball glove. Filled with apples.

Quiet, you! I said, almost laughing too hard to form words. I can send a fucking tank up here! I'll do it! Do you think I'm fucking joking!? She laughed so hard tiny triangles of Pringle landed on her blankets and she slapped me playfully and said shut the fuck up. Then she didn't take the hand away, she kept it resting on the skin of my stomach and started rubbing it, even as we both turned our heads back to the screen. You're so soft, she said. I put the tips of my fingers on her arm. She turned her head to face me. We kissed, not in a furious or hard way like the last time, but slow, savoring, slow enough that I could feel the glide of the white-soft hairs on her cheek. She slid her hand over my face and whispered you are so fuckin' pretty. I shivered and whispered thank you, thank you, God I missed you. I had missed her. She put one hand on my hip and the other on my shoulder, then seamlessly pushed me down into the mattress while sliding her right leg over mine. She sat up straddling me and her blue hair blended with the TV light, her head looked like it was bleeding blue, blue falling in disconnected rays down her shoulders and her white cotton shirt. She leaned down and kissed me harder, running her hands up and down the length of my sides, and then her fingers were hovering above my right nipple.

Can I? she asked softly.

Yes! I whispered.

She smiled pertly, lifting an eyebrow. Are you sure.

God please, Megan—

She twisted my nipple and my head hit the mattress and I cried *Hanh,* that noise resembling a goose honking. *Hanh.* Harder, I said, right before she put her hand over my mouth and said quiet. I strained against her with a fraction of my strength and felt all of her muscle push me down.

Then she twisted again. Harder? She said. Yeah?

Hanhhh—My voice came muffled through her fingers.

We were down to our underwear when I slid my hand past her belly button, into her panties, and she put her hand on mine and said here. Stop. She placed my hand by my side and then put her hand in my underwear and said mmm, I see this is still here.

Sometimes, I said timidly.

Hmmm, she whispered. She started touching me lightly, two fingers sliding up and down my atrophied penis. I whimpered. She was really good at this. I put my arm under her and kissed her neck.

After a minute or two, though, Megan started looking frustrated. She started jerking harder. She looked unhappy. Are you okay? I asked. She stopped, flinging her arm back to her side. So what's wrong, she said, do girls just not do it for you anymore?

What? I said. No, it felt really good. What do you mean?

It had felt good, but I knew what she meant, I hadn't even gotten half-mast. Hell, third-mast. That's been the deal for a while. Even when I orgasm on my own, which isn't often, it hasn't gotten all the way up in a long time.

No! I protested. It felt good, it felt really good, you're amazing, I said desperately.

I didn't feel anything from you, she said.

It's the estrogen, I said. It makes it really hard to get hard. It never happens like it used to anymore.

She looked really discouraged, then she raised her eyebrow and said well I guess I'll have to do something you haven't been used to in a while. She kissed me and then kissed my chin.

Oh, I said, and then I didn't want her touching that part of me, I hated how she talked about it. Like if my dick didn't seem happy then I couldn't be. I wanted to have my hand inside her, making her come, I wanted to sleep with her chest against my back, I wanted to lift her off of me and say *my penis isn't me*. Her kisses reached my belly button. She took my cock in her hands.

No, I said.

Shhhhhh, she said.

No, I said, more forcefully. She took it in her mouth and my head was on the mattress again. *Hanh.*

Then I said but. Just but, in this feeble voice. She reached a hand up and put a finger on my lips. It felt male and unnatural but my nerves had exploded in crossed wires of black pleasure and my dick inflated like it never had since estrogen entered my body. I moaned no, no, God, yes, no, fuck. My hands curled around her bedposts and I slid into my booze-and-pot haze, pressed further into her mattress and back, back into maleness, back into boyhood, I traveled years into the past and remembered Leon, saw his body again through my eyes, breathed in his throat and left quarter-moons in his palms, I grunted and groaned through his deep, rolling voice and said oh fuck, god I fuckin' love it.

Megan took her mouth off me and smiled and said yeah? Hmmmm. Yeah? I was ice pick hard now. A condom appeared in her hand, and she said Sophie, Sophie, oh my baby, Sophie.

And then I was back, Leon like a malevolent imp hovering on the bedpost. Exhumed but not gone. Oh, I said. No. No, I'm sorry Megan. No.

Shhh, she said. Sophie, I got you, baby.

No, I said. Stop.

Shhh, she said. I'm gonna take care of you.

Stop, I said. She put her mouth on my cock again. The crossed-wire pleasure surged and I sat up and scooted backwards. No! I said. Please! My mouth and eyes scrunched up. Please! I'm sorry! I can't.

She looked at me with bloodshot, frightened eyes. You can't? Did I—

I can't, I said. I'm sorry.

She bowed her head. I could only see her tangled blue hair. Then she looked up, hurt, furious. No, she said. I'm sorry, don't *worry*, I won't *bother* you again tonight. I think she was about to cry. She whacked ineffectively at the Pringles shards on the bed and yanked the blankets over her as she lay down.

I put my clothes on and sat on the floor, hugging my knees. Scattered tears slipped out of my eyes. I'd trusted Megan.

I sat there crying for a while, my head between my knees. After a bit I looked up at the empty space next to her on the bed. I was so tired but I couldn't get into bed because if I even accidentally touched her again I didn't know what I would do. I thought of the couch out in the blackness of the living room, and if she would bother to wake me up before she was gone.

Earlier that afternoon, Mom had gone out on an errand and I'd gone in her bathroom for cosmetic pads. Her old tape deck was on the counter. I leaned over and read the label through the window of the player: *Leon Choir Christmas 2001.*

I had a solo in that one. I hadn't sang for a long time—I was a bass and I got too self-conscious. My mom and Megan had both said, always, that they'd loved hearing me sing. They both came to that concert, when I was in Grade 10. The two of them sat in the third row and cheered when I had my solo and we all went out to Earl's afterward. Megan had just dyed her hair shiny-black and my mother started telling her how to keep the color in. And then Megan kept my mother laughing and she even ordered a few glasses of wine and Megan had to drive her home, the only time I've seen Mom need to call on a DD. They really got close that night. Megan kept asking about what I was like as a little boy and Mom told her I'd built forts behind the couch with blankets and pillows and laid down covered and cramped for hours, and I made patterns on my bedroom wall with boogers. Megan clapped and laughed and asked for more and somewhere in the night I stopped being embarrassed and propped my face up with my hands and elbows on the table and listened to the two of them go on in the booth, they moved on to talking about religion, piano lessons, tampons versus pads. I drank glass after glass of Dr. Pepper and listened to them bust each other up. It was like watching the daughter and mother neither of them had. Or thought they didn't have. When Mom and I got home, her still tipsy, she said you've known Megan for a year now right? And I said yup, and she said I think she loves you.

Megan did love me. And I have always loved her. She was the only person in high school who knew I was a girl, and one night when I was sixteen and had called her at two in the morning, she said to me, Leon. Leon. One day everyone will call you Sophie. And I'm going to be so fucking proud of you when they do.

We never did want anything romantically from each other. The other time we had sex was just because we were high. But my mom always wanted us together. Megan was the only friend of mine she ever really trusted. Mom asked about her again today, at dinner. She asked if Megan had gotten the Safeway gift card she'd sent her for Christmas. Mom gives her one every year.

Eventually I got up and looked outside. An old woman was carefully plodding through a parking lot in heels, leaving twin stiletto and sole marks in the snow. We were two floors up but I could hear the crunch of her shoes. I looked through Megan's closet and took a bright stretchy purple shirt before leaving.

Mark? I said, tapping on the door. He opened it and a cloud of weed smoke blew out after him. Whoa, hot box galore, I said. He grinned sheepishly. Hi, he said.

Hi. Megan went to sleep so I came here, I said.

Oh cool, he said. His room was mostly bare. There was a poster of Ghost World beside his dresser and his cello was lying on the floor along with a few books and a pair of shoes. I bent down to look at his bookcase but only noticed a Studs Terkel collection before losing my balance. I fell onto the bed and burped.

Excuse me! I said, embarrassed. I looked down and saw the same green and black blanket he'd given me the other night. Mark, your blanket is awesome, I said.

Oh thanks, he said. He sat on his desk chair and smiled awkwardly.

The hell are you doing over there? I said, lying on my side, my face almost buried in the bed.

What? He asked, his face in a stupid hardened smile.

Come here, I said into the bed. He did and I sat up and took his face in my hands. I thought of the sluiced confidence with which Megan had gripped me and laid me down. Do you want to kiss me? I said brightly. We made out messily, wetly. I'd made out with boys a few times before I transitioned, but it was different now. I liked this more, the smoothness of my body melted into the roughness of his. I kissed him hard. He worked his hand up under my shirt. I realized I didn't know if Megan had told him. I hadn't wanted to ask. I never liked finding out that I didn't pass.

Hey, um, there's something you should know about me, I said.

I know, he said softly. It's okay. I think you're wonderful.

I'm sorry, I said, feeling stupid.

Don't be, he said, kissing me suddenly and ferociously. You. Are. So. Beautiful. Don't. Be. I thought he was going to rip through my teeth with how hard he was talking and kissing and I kissed him harder and said thank you thank you thank you thank you and took off his shirt. I felt for his dick and he stuttered, seized up, moaned. It felt nice to hold, it felt nice to worry about somebody else's dick. He started getting hard and holy shit Jesus, he was big, like really big.

God, you've got the fucking Chrysler Building down there, I said. He blushed and smiled and said well thank you. I kissed him and gave an extra hard tug and he gasped.

Soon all the clothes were off again. He reached into my underwear and I pushed his hand away.

No? He said.

I stopped stroking and rested my hand on the tip of his foreskin. No, I said firmly.

Oh, he said, looking sad. Okay. I just—

No, I said. No. No. No.

He looked sadder. I'm sorry, he said.

Well, I said. Maybe. I started stroking in fits and starts. Maybe, I said, maybe it depends (stroke) on how hard (stroke) you can fuck me (stroke). So (stroke). We'll just have to see (stroke) how much of a (pause, stroke) man you are, and we'll (stroke) see (stroke) what I can be for you. He convulsed and kissed me and pulled down my underwear.

I didn't care that I hated the words I was saying, and I didn't care that I was lying and that I would never let him near my dick. I refused to give up what I thought was my power and I didn't care what I had to do to keep it. I wanted him to split me open. I reached onto the floor to grab Megan's condom out of my pants, then I kissed his cock and unrolled the rubber. I took his shoulder and guided him to a standing position, then said lube? He said oh wait! He wheeled around to open a dresser drawer, his wrapped penis boomeranging with him, and came up with a small full bottle from a brown paper bag. I smiled and bent over his bed, then found out that didn't work. I was too tall and the bed was too short. It only came up to my knees. I looked at him and laughed. Your bed sucks, I said. He looked concerned. Desk? He asked. I turned around and swept everything off. Notebooks and sheet music and Wunderbar wrappers swirled over his floor as I bent over. I heard him lube up and felt him pushing his dick around the inside of my cheeks, trying to get inside.

For some reason, it only struck me then how short he was; I had at least six inches on him. In my head, I saw this short skinny boy fitting his huge wang into this tall girl's behind and it seemed pathetic but in this lovely, wonderful way. I put my head down so my hair brushed the desk and giggled to myself really softly.

Then he got in. I gasped, a deep, shuddering, guttural gasp. I thought it sounded really male and I worried about it fleetingly but I don't think Mark heard it. I breathed hard and groaned. It felt so painfully, jarringly good. I gripped the corners of his desk and moaned yes, oh God, pull my hair. What? He said. Pull my motherfucking hair! I said. He gathered a handful and drew his arm back. I gasped again, face toward the ceiling. For a few minutes I did nothing but concentrate on him inside me on the bottom and pulling me on top, saying Mark, Mark, God you feel so good. I felt only him and the coolness of the desk on my hips and I didn't think or feel anything else.

Then I started to get sore. He was really going for it.

Hey, slower, I whispered, and I think he really tried, for a minute or two, at least.

GREENHORN

- *K. Tait Jarboe*

The last time I visited the ghost town, I appeared at the edge of the road on the far side of a dusty field. The town began on the other side, starting with the train station, then the hotel, the church, the bars, the theater and the restaurant, then the houses and workshops and municipal buildings beyond that. The day was warm and gray, and the air felt heavy with the anticipation of rain. I couldn't remember the last time it had been so humid there. Maybe it was the first time in years; I wouldn't know.

Sorry, now I'm talking about the weather, but I just don't want to take anything for granted.

The field was full of hundreds of little black birds. I bolted towards them, hollering war cries and stretching out my arms in case I might take flight alongside their scattering, lightweight little bodies. It's like they all knew where and how to reconvene in the sky. They swooped in unison over the train station, cutting the daylight like a sharp black pen, and perched on the church steeple. There are nests upon nests accumulated in the bell tower. I won't even tell you how it smells. So maybe I *will* take a few things for granted.

The important thing was that it made me notice the train station. There were lights in the building, and then there were more of them. It was a rare thing, but I had seen it before. The town wasn't dead, after all—it was haunted. There's a difference. Sometimes haunted things wake up: they repeat themselves, like an amnesiac with obsessive compulsive disorder. But sometimes, they know they've been gone, and they have these impossible insights. They'll offer them, buried in their twisted, obfuscating sense of humor. "To be or not to be" is an old cocktail party joke for a ghost. The lights in the hotel came on, too, then the marquee at the movie theater. There must have been a real crowd that day. I started into a run, towards the illuminated buildings. I thought that this time I finally knew something they didn't.

Oh, and I want you to know that I am not trying to be inaccessible by using words like "obfuscating," I'm just trying to say exactly what I mean. The most accessible languages I can think of are the five thousand advertisements I see on a daily basis living in the city, and that scares the crap out of me. Sorry, I'm just worried about being, you know, "called out." But, like, whatever.

When I basically dropped out of college, I had to fill out this goldenrod form. There were boxes on the form for "medical leave" or "psychological leave." I checked off "medical leave" and wrote "mononucleosis" underneath it with a precision that was probably conspicuous. The real reason was that I had made a disaster out of that chance to reinvent myself that everybody says college is good for, and I wanted to hide out in extended childhood until the clouds of shame lifted of their own accord. I think only liberal arts students really get to reinvent themselves. In brochures for their colleges, friends of various racial markers walk across grassy quads and smile, clutching important texts. Maybe that was my problem: I went to a technical school without any flora.

Still, there are not yet diagnostic criteria for generalized disastrous personality. I knew better than to tell them I was messy in my head. And when I say messy, I don't exactly mean that I was crazy, and I'm probably offending the psychologically-challenged by implying a negative connotation to crazy. It's really difficult for me to not turn this into a tangent about words and violence. I think I will inevitably get to that, though. So, when I say messy, I mean that I was introverted, neuro-atypical, gender dysphoric, and accidentally visiting another dimension. All of those things are still true, but they were then, too. As a combination, according to my experience, these things can make the magic of friendship with peers elusive, and the adventures of young adulthood vicarious through solitary marathons of BBC shows and cartoons intended for grade-schoolers.

I did know two people from college, and I ruined everything with both of them the same way, which was with sex and my personality. One of them was Carlos, who will no longer make eye contact with me. The other was Kate, who disappeared after losing her on-campus housing because she told the school psychologist about her cutting. I guess this kind of thing happens all the time, probably because the school doesn't want anything messy and permanent associated with their brand. The school is just a company, which has legal personhood, which scares the crap out of me. I missed Kate a lot at the time (I either "know better" or have stopped caring now). But all it takes is that psychological leave and then poof, gone, like ghosts in a ghost town.

Man, queers really like supernatural metaphor. I wish I was making some kind of Jenny Boylan point but, legit: I hang out with ghosts.

Here's something actually scary: the administration building of my former college was made of so much concrete that it inhibited all emotions except heavy paranoia about atomic warfare. The one dorm was a converted office building, and since it was not designed for living, all of the sounds and smells that occurred within were public events. It was a school for people who wanted to become engineers, designers, or anything involving measurement. Margins, distances, times, statistics, demographics. I used to hate the futility of reducing life and the world into words and numbers, but now I feel like, I dunno, just because we use something to hurt doesn't mean it has to be a weapon.

My favorite first year class turned out to be an English elective about fantasy novels. We talked about the idea that all of the evil in the world could be contained in one very bad person who could be defeated through the power of friendship.

I feel like if there is a God, he might be a ponytail nerd.

After I took my "leave of absence", I called my mother. I have to do this regularly or she will email me asking me why I haven't. I have nothing against it; I just don't like feeling like I have to. I rehearse every conversation, inevitably winning her over to my perspective on everything, but then in actuality we just have awkward double monologues. But it's a great opportunity to say exactly what I mean, because she will only process about one to ten percent of it. When I turn on my radio and tune it to static, one to ten percent of what I'm hearing is radiation left over from the Big Bang. That is exactly what a conversation with my mother is like.

"I'm taking some time off from school," I said, talking at her.

"Your Oma told me the same story three times this afternoon and then we drove to the doctor and waited an hour to be told everything was the same," she said, talking at me.

"Did you know *they* is a legitimate, singular gender-neutral pronoun?"

"Opa is starting to fade, too, but he's just as angry as ever. Angry and confused."

"I think I'd really like it if everyone referred to me with gender-neutral pronouns. But I guess they are not really neutral if they are my gender. Still, that would be great."

Radio silence.

"What the hell are you talking about?"

I tried using the right language. Certain words had become like great, big, delicious Rice Krispies of identity, puffed up with affirmative power from all the social justice blogs I had been reading.

So, I told her outright exactly what it was.

More radio silence. I pictured her making that face like there was sand in her eye. I realized that some of those words maybe lacked impact if the person I was talking to did not also frequent the same websites.

"Are you depressed?"

"I don't think so."

"You're probably just depressed. Don't worry, honey, you're a beautiful girl. When are you coming by to visit? I could use some help with Oma."

And that was that. Maybe I should have cried. I expected, at worst and at least, the kind of rejection that involves acknowledging what the conflict is even about. I wanted very badly to fight and then reconcile after dire circumstances. Maybe I'd save her from drowning in a river and she'd see how she hadn't lost a daughter, she'd gained an opportunity to make the extended family uncomfortable on Thanksgiving. Cue rain. Music swells.

Why do I always expect everything around me to change when I do?

"I'll come by in a few days, Mom. Leave me something to cook and I'll take care of dinner."

"Wonderful. We're all looking forward to seeing you!"

Oma and Opa had moved into my old bedroom in my mother's apartment. We called them that because they had been living in Germany when my mother and my uncle were born, even though they were Uzbek. Opa had done something for the CIA in the sixties, and that's when they came to the United States. He wasn't much for conversation, unless you count body language. He used to beat up Oma and Mom, but not my uncle, who now lives in Colorado and conveniently avoids having to deal with his parents in their decline.

My mom has a strong sense of duty to her family, even though they are the way that they are. I've only seen her lose her temper twice at her parents. She lost it at Oma during a serious conversation about why she stayed with Opa, and Oma said, "Wives do not leave their husbands." See, my father left my mother when she was pregnant with me, and nobody holds it against him. I'm afraid to tell my mother that I don't even hold it against him. If he was that upset by my existence, I'm not really interested in knowing him.

My mom gets sad and quiet when she sees those "Take time to be a dad" posters all over the city. I feel meta-guilt because when I see them I think, "Ugh, no, please don't."

Then there's the one other time I saw my mother lose her temper. I was little and just learning to hold pencils and forks and the like, and I had been left-handed. I was staying with my grandparents for a few days, and Opa hit me on the left hand with the metal part of his belt every time I tried to use it. When my mom came to pick me up and saw my bruised hand, she started yelling at Opa, who hit her. Then, I think for the first time, she hit him back. She told him that if he ever touched me, or her, or Oma again, she would kill him. I think she meant it. I think Opa thought she meant it too, because he continues to yell a lot, but he doesn't hit anyone anymore.

Still, I ended up right-handed.

When I first dropped out of college, it had been a daydream of mine to have my own apartment, because it seemed very liberating and mature. Then it occurred to me that I was unemployed. I got short of breath thinking about it and pulled out a bunch of hair, which is one of my embarrassing compulsions. Then, I thought about staying on my mother's living room sofa, Opa swirling around like a hurricane with Oma the silent, dutiful but foreboding eye. The next day I got a job working the night shift at the all-day supermarket and a cramped sublet with some benign stoners who kept dirty dishes in their bedrooms and left a film of bodily grease on everything they touched, but were otherwise unobtrusive.

My family is a small part of everything, but there's no homecoming revelations, and by the time you read this I will have already accepted myself, as well as the existence of alternate dimensions.

So, like, whatever. I'm over it.

After my first week of work, I came home one morning to an empty apartment. I crawled under my futon with a pillow and cocooned myself between the wooden frame and the musky swirls in my area rug. The floor seemed like a safe place, closer to something important. My area rug was clean, sort of, but it trapped all the smells that floated through the building, all the traces of transience and improvisation, of burnt cooking, deodorant soap, high fructose corn syrup, and salt. Always salt. I remembered going swimming in the Atlantic Ocean when I was small, accidentally swallowing the water and throwing up. I thought about being on Oma's lap at the dining room table in her old house, when she was still mobile, looking into her ornate silver box of these tiny, white crystals.

"They make anything taste like more of what it is," she'd said to me in Uzbek.

I put a handful into my mouth, thinking it would be just like sugar.

"No, no, no, my love!" she said.

I cried. The salt was going in my mouth and out my eyes.

I thought about tears, slugs, and mine shafts I'd seen in pictures that looked like throats into the Earth. I thought maybe I was falling asleep, lost in reverie. But I lifted my head and saw I was in a theater, an old-fashioned one that had been recently re-painted. I touched the seat I was sitting in. It felt too real to be a dream, but I was sure it must have been.

I mean, I was just lying on the floor, right?

But then I looked up again, and there she was: Patsy Cline, striding onto the stage. The back wall of the stage had been painted to look like rural crossroads. Bales of hay were arranged like bleachers in front of the painting, and on top of them sat these handsome, anonymous white people with great chins and cowboy hats covered in shimmering rhinestones. Patsy approached the microphone, this beautiful old-fashioned brick of an instrument, as if it were a natural thing to be standing in a cross-road. She wore her hat slightly to one side. Her eyes were soft and her lips were dark. She had this slight underbite. Her musicians appeared from the crowd behind her and burst into the opening chords of "Walkin' After Midnight."

Everything was sacred and stucco. I fell into a complete infatuation with her. It my was dream, after all.

Patsy finished the song, and the crowd in the theater, which I'd just noticed, went totally nuts with their applause. I looked back toward Patsy and saw Hawkshaw Hawkins and Cowboy Copas leading a giant blue ox out toward center stage.

Patsy tipped her hat. Then she mounted the ox and rode off into the painted sunset.

Hawkshaw started into "The Sunny Side of the Mountain."

Then I was back in my bedroom.

I felt like I must have been asleep for hours, but when I looked at my alarm clock, no time had passed at all. That's what made the least sense to me, especially because I felt totally refreshed. I checked the digital clock over the kitchen stove, and it told me the same thing.

Maybe this was just one of those weird things my body was going to do, I thought. Adjusting to the night shift.

I showered and changed into blue jeans and an oversized flannel shirt. I had a couple of pairs of shoes in my closet, mostly ratty second-hand sneakers, under a magazine cutout of Fluevogs I'd circled with hearts. But there in the corner was a dusty pair of cowboy boots I had only the faintest memory of owning. Had they been a gift? It didn't surprise me that they were there—I just couldn't remember how. They were seafoam green with light brown soles.

A First-Generation Yankee in Calamity Jane's Court. Okay, whatever. I put them on.

I decided to take advantage of my weird energy, so I went outside to wait for the bus. The bench at the bus stop was next to a massive lightbox advertisement for vodka, I think, with a luxurious image of a regulation hottie in a red catsuit. I couldn't figure out what these things had in common. Maybe I was being sold the future. In the future, everyone will wear catsuits. Maybe this vodka hadn't even been invented yet. Were there such things as facts about the future? What about history? Where does it go?

Shit, I was in a weird mood. I got off the bus in front of the comic and games shop and ran, literally, into Carlos and Kate, trying to board the same bus and smugly holding hands.

I made eye contact with Kate first.

She stopped short, surprised by the impact and then the recognition. She blurted out, "Oh fuck!"

Carlos burst into laughter, and then they pushed their way onto the bus. I slithered out and watched them through the window. Carlos peered out at me and gave me the finger.

I felt my face growing hot. I pulled at my hair. So much for my good day.

The sidewalk suddenly seemed expansive and naked. Everyone was surely looking at me now, everyone was watching and assessing, disgusted. I probably would have answered to the name Gregor Samsa at that moment. My head slumped, my shoulders rolled forward, I scuttled into the game shop.

I had frequented the tiny shop in high school, where it had been the venue for the table-top gaming club, *Twelve-Siders*. There was a fiberboard table in the middle of the store, populated with board games and scrawny boys on the cusp of puberty hunched over a game of *Cantrip: The Smattering*. One of the boys looked up at me and stared just long enough to make sure I remained uncomfortable. I started thumbing through *Preacher*.

"Olivia?" said a deep, tremulous voice from behind the front counter. I looked up and saw Nathan, the founding father of *Twelve-Siders*. I noticed that we now had the same unfortunate haircut; both of us were too round-faced and thick-haired to pull off a proper wedge. He'd gotten taller in the year since I'd last seen him, but he still had the same ruddy dry skin, thin lips, and massive hands. He was dressed in a worn-out black t-shirt and some cargo shorts that were probably a birthday present from his mom. He stood behind the counter and tapped his fingers nervously on the Plexiglas covering.

"Oh yeah?" I said.

"Yeah!" he smiled. "What's up?"

"I'm back from college."

My mom calls these kind of things my lies of omission.

"Me too! I'm here all summer... Uh, what's up?"

"You already asked me that." Then I actually *giggled.*

"I mean, what are you up to right now?"

"Nothing, I just finished... doing stuff. Looking at comics, you know."

"We have a punch card for those," he said, indicating the *Preacher* books. "If you buy the first, and then buy the rest within a month, you get a discount."

"Oh," I said, stepping towards the counter with the first volume. "Cool."

I wished our conversation was less boring to watch. I was going through this phase where I wanted other people to be entranced by everything that happened to me. I wanted to be a manic pixie ingenue. I don't even like boys that much, but I always kind of want them to like me. To look at me, but stop looking at me, to tell me I'm okay, but then tell me I don't need them to tell me I'm okay. It's kind of like carrying around a really heavy bag of stuff you convince yourself you need for your camping trip but never end up using, except the camping trip lasts your whole life and if you try to ditch the bag somebody writes "fucking dyke" on your face with a marker while you're sleeping.

I put the book on the counter and saw myself in the glass case behind Nathan. I looked like my grandfather with breasts, which I thought was sort of horrifying and sort of awesome at the same time. I tucked my arms across my stomach, though. That's something I'm still working on. I would eventually tape a piece of paper over the numbers on my scale that says "Just fine."

"Uh, so... you want to buy it?"

"I'm fine!" I snapped back into the conversation. "I mean, uh, yeah! Yeah, I'll get it."

"I'll give you my employee discount, but don't tell, okay?" Nathan whispered. I felt a little more at ease. "Hey, listen, I'm having Morgan, Stoian, and Seth over tonight. Wanna come over too?" He raised his singular eyebrow expectantly. I smelled something metallic and thought it might be me, so I fanned myself with the comic book.

"Yeah, uh, sure. I don't have work tonight so that's fine."

Morgan, Stoian, and Seth were the other primary members of *Twelve-Siders*. Morgan was a stout, chinless boy who chattered incessantly through most of the meetings, not leaving much airspace for anyone else to talk. Because of this I didn't know the other members quite as well. Nathan mostly talked about game-play and a few half-hearted comments about dating when provoked by Morgan, who made suggestive jokes at loud volumes. I remember there was one year where I made a private game of counting the number of varieties of Doritos he had between his teeth when he did this.

I had been "the girl." I wondered if I was going to try and explain that I wasn't that anymore. I didn't think they would get it. Morgan would be like, "Duh, so you're a lesbian."

In theory, being "the girl" wasn't the worst thing. It's not like there's anything wrong with being *a* girl. I just had these sensations, this uncertainty, about where my unhappiness came from and what I could call it. It was dysphoria, definitely, but I wonder if I've projected the history of it to feel more certain, more destined and infallible. Is it only true once I have medical vocabulary? I mean, what if I *haven't* always felt this way?

I guess I first noticed it when someone said, "Excuse me, miss," and I looked around to see who they were talking to. It's not inversion; it's just uncanny. I love that word. A mannequin in peripheral vision. Mistaking a stranger for a loved one. Being asked your gender and not knowing which is more absurd: the question or your inability to answer it.

Kate used to tell me that I had "internalized misogyny."

She had said, "if you're not looking to grow a beard or whatever, why can't you just be a different kind of woman?"

I yelled at her and cried, and then she threw a book at me.

"You're fucking crazy!"

"You're an asshole!"

"Oh please, don't try to manipulate me with your fucking martyrdom. Gimmie a break, 'genderqueer'! Awkward and bisexual doesn't mean you're another *gender*. Jesus, Olivia!"

I beat myself up about this possibility for a while. I eventually met a lot of other girl-assigned people who felt the way I did, but too many of them struck me as just kind of bananas (this coming from someone who claims to travel inter-dimensionally). Then I met this boy-assigned lesbian who told me the coolest thing:

"Right, and maybe I'm just such a straight boy and love women so much that I have to be one, too. A therapist told me that, you know."

"That's awful!"

"Yeah, maybe," she said, rolling her eyes. "But it could be true. And you know what I realized?"

"What?"

"Who cares if it is? So what? My brother hates our dad so much that he joined the army. I mean, like, at a certain point, who cares *why*? We're here, aren't we? Some of us are probably born this way, some of us decide it—why the fuck does it matter?"

After that conversation, I stopped worrying so much about who was bananas and found myself having a lot more fun.

I was on the bus home from the comic shop, and then I was sitting at a table in the front of a Western saloon. A man was sitting across from me, pouring tea into two small cups from a simple copper teapot while looking over some photographs he had laid out on the table in front of him.

"Ah, good," he said without looking up, "I hoped you might come again. I am your liaison for the course of any past, present, and future visits. How do you get here? You're a magician of some kind, I presume?"

"Excuse me?" I said.

The man was unnaturally handsome and gentle, decked out in the most flamboyant cowboy outfit I'd ever seen. It was made mostly of bright white leather with hideous tassels.

He nudged a cup of tea over towards me.

"Go on," he said. "It's Earl Grey, I hope it's to your taste."

Well okay, I thought. I took a sip and then stared back down into the cup. I could taste the spice of the tea, the heat; I could feel the cup between my lips. This was not a dream.

"Excuse me," I said. It wasn't just his politeness. I felt so natural and comfortable here. If it was real, I should have been alarmed, but instead I was as tranquil as I was lucid. "I have no idea what you're talking about."

The man nodded and looked at me with non-judgmental curiosity. "You didn't come on purpose?"

"I—No. I don't really know where this is, even."

"But you came to the concert."

"Uh..."

"Oh my, oh-my-oh-my-oh-my," he inhaled the entire phrase. "You're a special case! But how exciting! Allow me to introduce myself. The name is Mr. Jesse James."

He stood and held out his hand. I stood, shook it weakly, and then flopped back down.

"Jesse James," I repeated.

"Yes, ma'am."

"The... train-robbing, murdering gang leader?" I said it aloud without thinking. "From, uh, a hundred years ago?"

"Goodness no." He shook his head, amused. "I'm the *other* Jesse James."

I reached into my bag for my copy of *Preacher*.

"Older than that, too," he continued. "I am the myth of Jesse, the adventure dime novels, the cartoons and the trope." He beamed with pride.

"O...kay." I looked around. Mother Maybelle Carter came by our table with a plate of tiny sandwiches.

"You don't know, of course! But that's okay! There are so many worlds, so many places. Do you know how the formation of a new dimension occurs, uh... Miss... ?"

"Olivia," I said, wincing.

"Olivia. A beautiful thing happens in your world, where you're from! When a place becomes real enough, even if it has been made up, when a persona overtakes its person, it lifts off like a bubble and gleams in the fabric of the universe, twirling like a zealous ballerina!"

"I... see..."

Jesse sipped his tea and flushed slightly. I could tell he was genuinely excited, but self-conscious about being misunderstood.

"This place, this is one of many special little places, where myths live on well after their history has faded."

"Myths."

"We seem to have accumulated a strange amalgam of Americana here, don't you think?"

"Yeah," I said, helping myself to two tiny sandwiches at once. "So you're... ideas?"

Now he winced.

"We prefer the term ghost, if it's not too much trouble."

"I guess you're pretty self-aware for an... Yeah okay, whatever."

I empathized rather strongly with the request for self-identification, even if it didn't make a lot of sense to me. It still made more sense than whatever I had just come from.

It made more sense than feeling like a bug on the naked sidewalk. "Would you mind... calling me... like, something that isn't Miss?"

Jesse nodded as if the question were normal. It *should* be normal. "Mister, or perhaps *Mix?*" he suggested.

"What?" I sat up a little, intrigued.

"Oh, we have all kinds here. Your world has imagined ours in so many, many ways."

Being taken at face value was the most unbelievable thing I'd encountered thus far. I wasn't even aware I had been carrying that weight on my shoulders until it was lifted off. I actually felt lighter, a little giddy.

"So, like, if I wrote Grand Ol' Opry fanfiction..."

"If you believe it, on some level, yes," Jesse cut me off, embarrassed to know already know where I was taking that thought.

"Awesome," I said.

Jesse grinned and took my hand, rising from the table.

"Please, Mix Olivia, let me show you around."

Nathan picked me up from my apartment after he got out of work. We drove out past the university campus on the edge of town and into the affluent residential neighborhoods that lay beyond it. He pulled up to a driveway surrounded by gardens, and a side porch door into a three-level main house. We went in through the side door and through one of the living rooms and the kitchen. Nathan told me to wait there while he retrieved something from upstairs.

I waited in place for about eight seconds, then began to wander the massive rooms of the lower quarters of the house. They were brimming with mid-century maple and white pine furniture, a European parlor peppered with Chinese antiques and cabinets of glass apothecary bottles.

"Whoa," I said, poking my grubby fingers into an open curio in the second living room. It was filled with antique cameras and Muybridge prints of birds in flight.

"Oh, thank you," sang Nathan's mother, sailing in from the study in a sleeveless sundress and large silver jewelry. She was older than my mother, but slender, with a pinched face and short, curly hair. "My apologies, it's a mess right now."

It didn't look like a mess to me. It looked positively opulent. I wanted to sit down and sip tea with Jesse here, in hats with dead pheasants and fruit on them. He'd given me the grand tour of the ghost town, the denizens of which popped in and out of populace depending on the wills of the ghosts and the people who perpetuated them.

The grand staircase at the front of the house curled up each floor, tapering into the attic. The walls around it were embellished, like a crown, with framed photographs of Nathan's parents with recognizable politicians and celebrities. On the landing between the first and second floor was a fainting sofa underneath a circular, stained glass window.

I poked my head out of a regular window, peering out onto the back yard. The spearmint in the side garden had taken over most of it, so there was an ever-present sweet and herbal smell in the air that hung around the property.

Stoian's pistachio Subaru and Morgan's dirty black Jetta pulled into the driveway behind Nathan's car. I ran out to the driveway to meet them. Seth emerged from Stoian's passenger side in aviators and a heavy leather jacket that only emphasized his wiry frame.

"Oh. My. *God*. Olivia! You caught me riding in style."

Seth hugged me. Stoian nodded at me and sighed.

"Oh, hey!" Morgan tumbled out of his car, dropping his keys. He had gained weight and grown a soul patch. A massive digital SLR hung precariously around his neck.

"How are things, Morgan?"

"I've been working!" He held up the back of his digital camera, inviting me to take a look. It was full of modeling photos of petite white girls in heavy punk makeup and safety pins on their nipples. One was bending backwards and licking her red lips in apparent ecstasy, in front of an expansive white background with no horizon. There was something uncomfortably like a school portrait to the quality of the images.

"I did some photography at school," I said, handing him back the camera.

"Oh yeah? What do you shoot with?"

"Toy cameras that I make myself. Like out of cardboard and coffee cans and stuff."

"Oh," he laughed, "I thought you really meant you were a photographer. That stuff's so tedious!"

I laughed with him, for lack of a better response.

Nathan's mom cooked hamburgers on the grill outside, and we circled around a coffee table in the finished basement, settling in for board games as foreplay for the inevitable epoch of role-playing. Stoian grinned and pulled a bottle of coconut rum from his backpack.

"Finally traded in the diet soda, I see."

"Please, gentleman, we must move up in the world."

"Doesn't change the fact that I'm going to kick your butt at world domination," said Nathan, bringing us all mugs from the bookshelf and setting out a bunch of plastic pieces and a map board. He was the kind of adult man who still said "butt" instead of "ass."

"Roll to see if I'm getting drunk," Seth snorted, mocking all of us.

"Shut up, Seth," I laughed.

"Don't start with me, greenhorn," he winked at me, indicating my cowboy boots. "There ain't room enough in this town for the both of us."

I took them off and sat cross-legged on a pillow, wedging my mug between my knees.

The next morning, I slowly came into an awareness of where I was. It was cold. A window was open. I was on the sofa. My legs were covered in goosebumps and the short, prickly hairs on my thighs stood on end. I ached from the inside. I looked around and saw Nathan sleeping on top of his comforter, on the bed on the other end of the room. The other boys were scattered throughout the room, snoring softly, Stoian in what looked like a lazy yoga pose.

I stood up slowly and realized where the ache was coming from. I inhaled sharply. All my thoughts were foggy.

Quietly, I crept over to Nathan's bed and stood near it, looking at the blunt-edged reproduction of an antique sword hanging over him on the wall. The bed had no sheets on it besides the comforter. The headboard contained a small framed photo of Nathan receiving his Eagle Scout award. The walls of the room were sky blue, and when he was a baby, his mother had sewn three white pillows shaped like little clouds and hung them above the bed. They still hung there by their clear string, well cared-for and clean. It made the whole room feel like a cartoon sky.

I looked at Nathan and pictured him as a baby. It's very weird for me to think about people I know as babies.

He opened his eyes very slightly and let out a satisfied sigh.

"Good morning," he said, with a hint of sheepishness.

"Good morning?" I said. I meant to say something else, but paused. I saw something stuck to the side of his trash can, wrapped up in a tissue. "What happened last night?"

I could only remember being the first to fold from inebriation, falling asleep while the others sobered up, and their laughter and conversation sounding farther and farther away. I sort of already knew the answer, but something didn't add up.

Nathan made a little nervous sound with his throat.

"Alcohol makes people do... wacky things, I guess..." He closed his eyes.

"I guess..."

He was asleep again, or he looked like he was.

I turned and went upstairs to the kitchen for a glass of water, suddenly very concerned with things like water quality. My mind was attaching itself to a problem it could understand. Nathan's mother stood at the counter island in the middle of the room, cutting strawberries and tossing them into a large glass bowl. She looked up at me and gave me a polite but lengthy assessment, her eyes locked on me as I circumnavigated the room. She had a Mona Lisa smile, much different from the casual warmth I had seen on her face the day before. I felt a strange tingle of scrutiny and suddenly wondered how well sound traveled in the large, old house.

I missed the ghost town intensely.

Nathan drove me home in the afternoon, chattering with excitement about comic books, and future hamburger socials, and a girl named Sarah who was visiting him next month. In fact he was talking more than I could ever remember him doing. I responded with friendly feedback as if nothing were different, but intensely aware that we were alone in the capsule of the vehicle.

It didn't feel different, not yet. I still thought and felt in fog. The weather was nice. Nathan was still an Eagle Scout, and if something messed-up had happened, I thought, he couldn't possibly be an Eagle Scout. He was still my friend from high school. He taught me how to cook. He was nice to me. If anything were wrong, obviously it would be raining. Nothing was making any sense.

"Nate," I said softly, finally interrupting him. It took a few seconds to register that I'd spoken, and then he fell silent, smiling. "Did we, you know...?"

"Yeah, we did." He turned pink, glancing at me.

"But I..." I trailed off, still unsure what verb to apply.

His jaw twitched.

"I know," he interjected. "I've been dating Sarah. I wonder if there is a good way to tell her."

"Tell her what?" I pressed.

"That I cheated on her," he sighed. "Any ideas?"

There's this thing that time does when you are watching, say, a glass of water fall to the ground, about to break, but know you are helpless to stop it. Is it anticipation? If that was me, I was the water, about to become formless.

Nathan pulled his car up to my apartment building and went to hug me as I unbuckled my seatbelt. I stopped him, mostly because it was awkward to hug and unbuckle at the same time, but his touch triggered a second layer of resistance.

"Nate!" I said with a force that surprised both of us.

His jaw twitched again.

"Don't." I paused, then got out of the car and slammed the door.

Our eyes met for a brief, vulnerable moment. He saw something he hadn't been able to before, and I saw it, too. He understood something was messed up, despite the beautiful day. He shrank, crestfallen and panicked, and quickly pulled the car back into the road.

I put my things down in my room and called my mother out of habit.

"You're coming to make dinner tonight, right?" she asked.

"Yeah, I'm still doing that. I'm going to hang around here first, though. I need to... shower."

"How's work? Are you making enough?"

"I'm feeding myself. I haven't made any friends there or anything."

"Did you even try?" This question caught me off guard and annoyed me more than it should have.

"Um," I said. "Well sure."

"Well, what were you doing wrong, then?"

"What the hell? I'm not doing anything wrong, or right. I'm just going to work!"

"You should try asking other people about themselves. I know you seem to think everyone in the world is so mean, but I think you should give people a chance. Get off your high horse, you know?"

"Uh... have you been...?" I heard Opa in the background, swearing in Russian. There aren't a lot of great Uzbek curse words. "Actually, no, never mind. Thanks for the advice, Mom. I'll try that."

I slithered into the bathroom, locked the door, and ran the shower as hot as I could stand it. I stripped quickly and sat on the floor of the tub. I was covered in sweat and snot and dirt which washed away slowly in my melodramatic baptism. In movies, all sin is redeemed by symbolic falling water.

I peeked out from the shower curtain. It wasn't my own bathroom anymore. I was in one of the hotel suites. There was a knock at the door.

"Uh, yeah?" I shouted.

"It's Jesse."

"Um, come in." I decided that it was okay if ghosts saw me naked.

Jesse poked his head into the bathroom and fanned at the steam.

"Hoo-ee!" he said. "Nice to see you again. I got you a little something in my travels; I'll leave it on the dresser for you."

Then he shut the door and left. I wanted to be less excited about men being nice to me, seeing as it didn't seem to indicate anything else about their character. But I'd been thinking about what Jesse really meant about having all kinds here, why he was so quick to accommodate—or rather, *respect*—who I was. He wasn't really a man, either; just currently being imagined as one.

I laughed a little, despite myself.

The hotel was dark and stuffy, even in the middle of the day. There were thick, dusty drapes over the tall windows. I went to the dresser and found my boots there, laid out and polished, as well as a hideously kitschy yellow cotton cowboy shirt, jeans, and a little jewelry box. That part must have been the gift.

Inside was a pendant on a stiff, leather cord. It was the unmistakable cobalt-blue and white concentric circles of the *nasar*. My Oma and Opa had them all over their old house. They were a near-eastern thing, a protection amulet against the power of the evil eye. To me they were just part of the motif of my family, but this one was especially beautiful, different somehow. I put it on as I was getting dressed. The black pupil at the center shifted as though it were a spot of oil dancing over the surface of water. It was looking up at me.

"Oh! Well, hello there!" I said to it.

The eye swirled back to looking out at the world.

I put my hand on the dresser, admiring the mixed heritage of the furniture, the theatrical wallpaper, and the upholstery throughout the room. The building itself had a kind of naïve optimism. I thought about the paranoid concrete of school, the moldy cracking plaster of my apartment. Jesse reappeared in the room.

"Isn't it lovely?" he said. "American without being European. The elegant orphans of style."

I smiled and skipped over to him. He was so weird.

"The *nasar* looked at me!"

"Yes, it may do that... Ah, don't... mention to anyone that I gave that to you, though..."

I felt like I was back in the comic shop. I stiffened, fogging up again. Was he doing me special favors? Would I have to repay those favors, too?

"Listen, if it's valuable... I mean, it's *obviously* priceless, I don't have to—"

"No! No, it's yours. Just completely forget how you got it, okay? Really. If anyone asks, it's a family heirloom."

"Oh... okay," I practiced breathing. Just breathing. "I need to... tell you about something. Actually, I need to tell you about everything."

"Ah," he said, and pulled me close with a mad kind of enthusiasm. He whispered something strange to me. "Don't write letters, blow up bridges."

Ghosts, man.

I told him that I was worried about the real and the imaginary. I told him I felt like I was too fat to be taken seriously as androgynous, that I wanted to be some kind of dandy Robin Hood, a faggy freedom fighting fop in seafoam cowboy boots. I told him I wanted to go back to school in a Gothic castle with round stained glass windows and fainting sofas, with secret passageways that held clues to ancient mysteries and divine understanding. I wanted to further my education through the mastery of fairy magic, alien languages, and oil portraits that weathered sin for their subjects. I wanted no more people-corporations, only duchies and guilds and anarchists with angel wings who dwelt in trees and talked to rocks or whatever.

I started crying, and instead of comforting me, Jesse mirrored me. He cried too, and threw his head to the side the same way that I did. He didn't interrupt; he just kept listening and mirroring. So I kept going. How much of this had I been holding in? It was turning into a cross-dimensional psychotherapy session.

I told him about my family, and about how I thought violent habits were like some kind of tapestry that gets continuously woven as one generation passes their cruelty on to the next. I said even Penelope gets caught pulling threads out. What could I do?

I wanted to be strong but I had been reading too many internet forums and not actually interacting with other people enough. Well, interacting, but barely. Interfacing, like a bank machine.

"You're interacting with me," Jesse offered.

"I'm unloading like a dump truck on you." I wiped my eyes and sniffled.

"We don't see it like that here," he added. He fell silent again.

"I love this place," I said. "But it doesn't change, you know, what I see in the mirror, or the numbers on my bank statement, or make touching people any easier. I mean, who do I think I am? Like, everything I do is okay and subversive? I'm fucking awful."

Jesse stared at me.

I told him about Nathan.

Then I told him about Carlos, and how I used him to try to cure myself from the uncanniness. He didn't want me. We weren't even very good friends. But I "knew" from their own insistence that men would never resist an advance.

"I don't think so," he'd said.

"Please, you're a guy, there is no such thing as no."

I really said that. On some sick level I wanted it to be true, so that he could just be a man, which would mean I could just be a woman. And then it happened and then he never spoke to me again.

"Wasn't it, like, a joint effort though? I mean, he could have been more direct with his answer..." I trailed off. I heard myself, played back, and thought about Nathan, and thought about falling asleep drunk, and thought about trying harder not to, what, trust my friends? "But it's different," I said. "Like, he was awake, for one."

How could I be angry at Nathan, having done what I did?

I looked to Jesse for answers, but I was back in my bedroom, sitting on the futon.

My cell phone buzzed. It was a text from Nathan. It said, "Olivia, I'm so sorry. Is there any way I can prove that to you?"

Say the word, I thought, say why you're so sorry.

The *nasar* still hung around my neck. It looked up at me.

Magic is real, I thought, and he and I can't even form the sounds of our own guilt. Say the word, say what it is, what you did, what I did. But, he'd asked me a question, a stock question but one with dangerous allure.

I put the phone down and got up, pacing around the room and taking out my frustration on my cuticles, picking at them until they bled.

I tried not to spend a lot of time thinking about who I should be. I really did. I tried to spend more time thinking about what I wanted to be doing. For a long time, I think I resisted labels because I felt that surely *I* was more than words could hold, but then the only ones which stuck were the ones other people threw at me. The marker on the forehead at camp and all that. It's a dangerous thing that words describe ideas, but they create them, too. It might help if I just told people I was trapped in the wrong body, but I'm not. My body is trapped in the wrong world. I'm writing all of this down now, in the blind ambition that I may accidentally create a better one.

I was still angry, because every solution seemed counterproductive or absurd.

The pupil of the *nasar* spiraled around. Don't write letters, I thought, blow up bridges.

I picked up my phone and replied to Nathan's text.

"What you can do is tell everyone we know what you did and be really clear about it. Make sure they understand. Then I might believe you're sorry."

A few weeks later I found out from Seth that Nathan had done what I asked. Morgan hadn't seemed to care, and Stoian had some pointed words to say about my character. This was all in Seth's email.

"I know this whole thing is so messed up, Olivia," the email concluded, "but I also don't know you that well. So, I just wanted to say I'm here if you want to talk, but I don't want you to think it's because of pity that I think we could be better friends. I don't know where I'm going with this. If I were you, I wouldn't talk to any of us ever again."

The email did make me feel better, but I didn't respond to it. I just wasn't sure what I would say.

The *nasar* turned out to be useful, too; at least I think so. I seem to be able to visit the ghost town whenever I want to, instead of randomly, but there's no way I can tell if it's the necklace or something else. I eventually decided that Jesse's gift probably had to be a secret because he was my liaison, but he wanted me to know that he was also my friend. And it was probably stolen or something. I'm still learning. There's a lot to this time-space thing.

I saw Nathan one more time, by accident, when he came into my work as a customer. I saw him standing in the cereal aisle.

"Aw jeez," I said to my co-worker.

"Ex-boyfriend?" she asked.

"Yeah, kinda." I didn't want to get into it.

Approaching the registers, he finally noticed me. His jaw twitched and he went pale, just staring for a minute. I looked back at him. I had been dreading this. I thought I would be crippled by it, but he had no power over me. Maybe that was my protection from the evil eye, after all.

Nathan spun around and left without buying anything.

I thought about giving him the finger, but I didn't. Instead I put his abandoned groceries back on the shelf. I caught myself humming "The Sunny Side of the Mountain."

TAMMY FAYE

• A. Raymond Johnson

CeCe's key is stuck in the mailbox. She thinks about calling her landlord, then recalls the half dozen other times she thought about calling the landlord, only to forget the task as soon as she steps inside. She twists and jiggles and curses until her finger gets numb. The lock finally turns. Thankfully the box is not empty (it would have felt insulting after her hard work)—it's overflowing, even.

She pulls out the stack of mail and begins organizing on her way up the steps, putting the personal and interesting mail on top. Her eyes catch the corner of an ivory envelope, smaller than standard size used for bills and credit card offers, the mark of personal stationery. She double-checks it's intended for her. It is. The return address is in North Carolina and the first line is simply initials: *T.F.M.* The letters trigger nothing at first. CeCe stands in the foyer outside her door, forgetting to go all the way inside her apartment, when she puts it together. Tammy Faye Messner. No longer Tammy Faye Bakker, usually just Tammy Faye.

Tammy Faye changed her life.

Not in a Jesus way. Tammy Faye didn't talk to CeCe about Jesus. She didn't talk to her at all that January day two years ago. CeCe was coming out of an alley, trailing behind her brother and sister-in-law; they'd just parked the car and were heading to the only movie theater in the tiny ski resort town in Utah. They weren't there to ski, and neither were most of the people in the town that week: they were all in town to watch movies and be seen watching movies.

Tammy Faye was climbing into an oversized truck and slipped oh-so-delicately on the ice. She didn't fall, but she accelerated her pace in getting into the vehicle.

"Oopsy daisy!" she declared, then giggled as she sorted herself out. Tammy's escort did not react to the misstep while holding the door for her, would not even look directly at her. CeCe had been studying Tammy Faye's leopard print fur coat, its fluffy thickness that trailed down to her calves covered by black leggings. Her feet were housed in high-heeled black suede boots with matching fur trim. Then she saw the outfit wobble and disappear, heard the exclamation, and realized who was wearing the outfit she was admiring.

CeCe's brother and sister-in-law didn't notice Tammy Faye either, they kept walking. CeCe felt her presence before she even recognized who she was seeing. Her voice—even more distinctive than her trademark eye makeup—rang out in the air like a bell that summoned up vibrations in CeCe's gut. It announced her presence in the place, and that no matter how unlike the rest of the town Tammy Faye was in that moment, now matter how slippery that ice was, she'd keep herself together with animal prints and stilettos, and a self-effacing giggle. She saw in Tammy Faye what she wanted, what already was in her mind: unashamed of her glamour. In that moment, Tammy Faye revealed what CeCe would have to do for herself.

CeCe looks in the mirror every day now and unconsciously conjures up the memory of that feeling. That moment has been a talisman for CeCe, a passing microsecond in the middle of a week-long vacation in Utah that would prove to be the last time her brother was able to look her directly in the eye without fear or shame. The trip happened before she wrote a letter to her family informing them of her plans to transition, before her brother replied with a typed letter asking her not to send gifts to his about-to-be-born daughter (how presumptuous!), as she would have no place in her niece's life. There was no longer an opening in the family for the position of an uncle or an aunt, or maybe there was, but they wanted one and not the other. Certainly not someone who started as one and then 'changed their mind,' as he wrote.

She would be such a fabulous aunt, she thinks as she plucks out the individual chest hairs that still grow in sporadic but persistent spots around her nascent breasts. As she applies eye makeup and lip liner and gloss, she imagines playing dress up with her niece, Sammy, who would stand in a pair of CeCe's heels by the sink, wearing a feather boa (the lavender one) and she'd plead, "Do me! Do me!" CeCe would show her which colors of makeup would work best with her outfit, allow her to choose from the palette, then lightly brush her cheeks. They would later parade up and down the long hallway, CeCe snapping photos of their fashion show, then collect them into an album which would find itself into Sammy's luggage, so when she returned home to her drably dressed parents, she could find hope that at least one member of the family knows how to have fun with clothes and costumes.

(Her niece will think she's beautiful.)

CeCe doesn't wear costumes anymore. The first dresses were loud and sparkly and meant to be worn on stage while lip syncing, but she doesn't perform now. Unless of course you count every morning where we all stand in front of the closet and find the shirt that best turns us on to ourselves, the tie or dress that drapes properly, that will possibly bring about flattery and the desire of others. We all put on a costume, we all create our gender as a series of small decisions strung together, she'd discovered.

CeCe now dresses for everyday life. She is aware of every intention that moves her daily fashion choices. She selects a scarf and builds her look around the accessory, or she designs an outfit around a new eye shadow. She was never taught these procedures, discovered them through intuition and practice. It has always felt destined.

Destiny. Her friend's name when they performed at the cabaret together, before they both had money to start physically transitioning, before Destiny changed it legally to something feminine but dour. CeCe is a nickname that has stuck from that time as well, and it will continue to stick around, as it's linked to both the legal name she has and the next one she will occupy. CeCe stands on the bridge between two halves of her life, straddling the two genders.

Her search for her new name included saying every name in a baby book aloud—each night she selected a page at random and began the recitation, trying on each appellation to see if it fit, if the name matched her eyes as well as the smoky grey eyeliner. So many wonderful names (Veronica, Etienne, Maria) had to be tossed away because they simply weren't *her* names. When she found the right one, she expected Rumpelstiltskin to jump out from her dresser, wave his fists while stomping around and blowing steam out of his ears. She imagined the troll to look a little like her brother.

But no one appeared, even when she recited the name several more times, each time relaxing into the sound of the vowels, the cadence, the rhythm and the immediate recognition that this was her name. It just felt right.

She has not yet appeared in court, though she has chosen the outfit for that day. Her name is written on a piece of handmade paper, so thick and porous that the ball point pen tip pressed deep grooves which swallowed up the ink and she had to go back over the lines with a fountain pen. So thick that she felt she was painting on canvas, her own portrait, her name. Then she sealed it into a matching envelope and locked it in a bottom drawer where it remains until her court date.

CeCe doesn't tell anyone her real name, she doesn't even say it aloud to herself alone, though sometimes she will silently mouth the words while lying in bed, late at night, or upon waking in the morning. She will be anointed by a judge on her own day of reckoning, they will speak the name aloud and she will receive the baptism of the law and of the city with much gratitude and elation.

She wrote it down because sometimes she fears she'll forget, then the judge won't know it's her and the name will float in the courtroom above all their heads, never coming to rest on its owner.

Her niece's name, Sammy, is gender-neutral. Her sister-in-law loved the idea of boys' names for girls while her brother was not so keen on the trend. Clearly her sister-in-law won that argument. The topic came up during the Tammy Faye trip to Utah, four months before her sister-in-law became pregnant. They sat around the dining room table drinking whiskey and when her brother spoke, CeCe noticed he drapes his arm behind the back of the chair in the same way their father does.

Sometimes CeCe feels tempted to wish her niece will someday follow in her footsteps, perhaps there's a shared gene that plants the seed of misplaced gender in her, too. This would confirm her brother's worst fears that giving Sammy a boy's name will make her a boy. But CeCe would never wish the same pain she had onto another child, to grow up in a rigid, punishing household.

She knows she is supposed to feel proud of herself, but the pain makes it tricky. She's grown fond of the Sammy in her head and they haven't even met yet. The rejection stings certain places in her heart that she replaces with the pain of tweezers as she pulls the hairs out of her skin.

Electrolysis hurts worse than plucking or waxing. She know the hairs will continue to come back because she's not burning the follicles, but she can't stand the thought of killing anything on her body, even a tiny space in her pores. The pain of the electropulse, the tiny shock, is made worse when she imagines hearing the bursting of live cells in the hair follicles.

She doesn't tell her therapist about the tiny imaginary screams. She claims to pluck because she can save the money for surgery, that she is waiting until she's been on hormones for longer and for the hairs to continue softening on their own, even if that only happens to a small percentage of the hairs, depending on the person.

Electrolysis might be easier to contemplate after surgery, which doesn't frighten her a wit, even though it's further off in the future than the court date. CeCe usually pushes herself between her legs, tucks it into her panties, imagines her body without that phallus hanging between the lines of her thighs. She doesn't hate it like some other trans women talk about theirs. After all, it's not her penis's fault she's in this predicament *per se*. Sometimes she holds it lightly, sees how it feels it in her hand. It's always felt like it didn't belong to her, she was just taking care of something left to her. She thinks about renaming her sex, but nothing sounds right. Calling it a clit sounds just as foreign as calling it a penis or cock. Calling it her sex started as a joke to herself, it sounded so Victorian. Her last lover thought it sounded sexy, so it stuck.

She examines the rest of her body everyday since she began hormone treatments, fixating on every visible surface area. It's hard to notice the minor changes under such scrutiny, but she can't stand the thought of missing out on any moment.

She takes photos every week to also enjoy the gift of distance. Once a month she glues copies of the pictures into a book, writing the date it was taken underneath. She goes back to the beginning and examines the progression, resisting the temptation to flip quickly and animate herself.

In every picture there is something in her eyes and in the way she holds her body, how she stands. Her body changes around her posture. A trademark. It's her stance she first learned the night after seeing Tammy Faye getting into that truck. She stood in the bathroom for hours practicing. Tammy Faye's trademark is her eyelashes, but they actually vary. She has multiple pairs, in different styles, completely distinguishable from each other. Others claim they look the same, but not to Tammy, but not to CeCe who knows, who understands. It's not the eyes that make Tammy Faye fabulous. Her power is not on the outside. CeCe saw it through the clothes, through the stumble, through the voice. She wanted that power of consistency through transformation, the power of becoming and knowing.

Tammy Faye changed her life.

So two years later, CeCe wrote her a letter telling her about her search and what she found for herself, how seeing Tammy Faye helped her turn the corner. She sat down and wrote it in one take and sealed it into an envelope without rereading it, for fear she'd lose her momentum.

CeCe didn't tell anyone about writing it, fearing people would think her silly or star struck. She's sure Tammy Faye has gotten hundreds of letters from gay men and drag queens gushing about her influence, and she didn't want to be lumped into that slush pile. She surrounds herself with gay men and drag queens in real life, but CeCe felt it was important to make sure Tammy Faye understood this letter was different. She felt embarrassed that she wants that, so she told no one, not even her therapist.

And now CeCe is standing outside her front door on a Tuesday afternoon, holding a reply letter from Tammy Faye, seeing her name and address handwritten in sprawling cursive, and trying to remember exactly what she wrote in that initial letter.

She's finally inside the apartment and opens every other piece of mail first. Then she sits on the couch and tears open the envelope, pulling out a simple white note card with Tammy's name embossed on the outside in shiny silver. Inside is a short message written in the same handwriting as the outer envelope. Some letters are difficult to differentiate, they loop together and words blur together at points. CeCe reads the sentences three, four times, sounding out slowly the cryptic words.

> *Dear CeCe,*
> *Thank you for your thoughtful letter. You are truly blessed and you're in my prayers during your journey.*
> *Love,*
> *Tammy Faye.*

The comma is smeared, connecting with the *T* in the signature below. Tiny dots of ink are on the top half of the card from being folded down so quickly after writing.

CeCe is grinning, glowing. Her cheeks are almost sore, and she's not sure for how long she's been doing it. Perhaps since first unsealing the letter. The message is not especially personal in content, she notices right away, though the word "journey" certainly lends itself to interpretation. She pictures Tammy Faye sitting at a dining room table like CeCe's mother at Christmas time, organizing the holiday cards. Tammy Faye would take a notecard off the stack of blanks, write a message (probably the same words in nearly every card that day) push it into the envelope deftly with her long nails, then add it to the outbox pile. Perhaps someone else applies stamps and delivers them to the post office, she can't quite picture Tammy Faye walking down her driveway with a handful of mail, raising the red metal flag.

It probably wasn't written on a dining room table either, she continues thinking. Her letter never saw the inside Tammy Faye's home. It arrived at her office and Tammy Faye probably writes responses at her desk, everyday at 10am while drinking a second cup of coffee, right after posting her daily inspirational reading on her web site.

CeCe reads the words again.

She's in her prayers. She imagines Tammy Faye's conversation with God, the words of solemn prayer escaping her lips while she reads CeCe's letter. Tammy Faye sighs, clutches it to her breast and one of those famous pairs of eyelashes flutters while she prays to God to help CeCe, to be with her, to show her love. To show her she's beautiful.

CeCe gets overwhelmed with gratitude. Then embarrassed about it.

She hasn't prayed in years, hasn't been to church since she was 18, but during childhood she went religiously, so to speak. Every week, she sang in the choir. She loved the God in the words of the hymns, even when she didn't feel God anywhere else.

CeCe looks around her apartment to determine which wall faces east. This suddenly seems important, though she's never worshiped facing either the sun or Mecca. After a moment of hesitation she kneels onto the orange rug in the den next to the futon couch. She leans back slightly and sits down on her feet. Her breath slows.

She doesn't know how long she sits like this, she can't see the clock on the wall, but when her thighs start burning, she leans forward slowly, slowly, all the way until her forehead touches the ground, then she stretches and folds her arms under and around her head, like children putting their heads down on desks at school. Her body feels good on the ground, nothing strikes her as wrong or weird, and for one tiny second, CeCe thinks she might be praying. She might be asking God to bless Tammy Faye? No, she's praying for Tammy Faye to bless herself.

Her body tingles all over. Not God talking back—her arms and legs have started the pin prickling that indicates circulation has been slowed to various extremities, her limbs sprawled on the hardwood floor with no cushioning and at awkward angles.

She stands up quickly, in one fluid motion and shushing the self-conscious thoughts that have begun to creep around her thinking. The room is silent, offering no comment on her behavior.

CeCe walks down the hallway and turns on the bathroom lights. She picks up her tweezers. She stares at the reflection.

THE QUEER EXPERIMENT

• *Donna Ostrowsky*

**From the Diary of Jennifer Rottman,
March 29, 1922**

What you are about to read is the true story of the events that
led to my incarceration in this so-called "asylum." The police
are too dim to comprehend what actually happened, my doctors
too narrow-minded, and my former friends and colleagues too
invested in what pitiful shreds remain of my reputation. But
someone must share this curse of knowledge, and so I commit
the truth to these pages.

On a clear afternoon in late November, my good friend Professor
Wingate Peaslee called upon me in a most excitable state.

"Jenny," he panted, as he nearly slammed my office door
behind him. "I've come upon something. Something grand. It
will change everything!"

I begged him to sit, and called my secretary to take his coat
and bring him a mug of souchong. Once she had closed the door
primly behind her, Professor Peaslee continued.

"We'll be able to see it—*everything*—for the first time. See inside their minds, inside their very souls!"

I chuckled sweetly. "Wingate, you're a psychologist. Surely that has always been your goal?"

"No, no, you don't understand! I mean literally *see*, with our eyes! And not only that, but to hear, to smell, to taste, to feel, to experience everything *they* experience, *to inhabit their world!*"

I did not need to ask him about the "they" to which he referred. As a tenured professor of abnormal psychology, he had made the study and treatment of homosexuals his life's work. But what was this poppycock about "inhabiting their world"? Surely the homosexual inhabits the same world *we* do? If only I had clutched this naive assumption and held on for dear life! Perhaps, then, my mind would still be whole, and I would sleep peacefully. Instead, I pressed him.

"It all began a fortnight ago. I was at the library, searching for du Champ's translation of the Sumerian graffiti found in the ruined homosexual bathhouses of Lagash."

"Of course," I interjected, "for your researches into the proto-Babylonian 'loincloth code.'"

"Yes, quite," continued Peaslee. "Having some difficulty, I inquired with Professor Wilmarth, who directed me to the desired tome. As I sat in my plush leather chair in the dimly lit library, I found myself growing drowsy and drifted into a deep sleep. There I had the most wonderful, terrible dream: indescribable pinks and fuchsias swirled above a city of strange, glittery beings, all of whom laughed and twirled maniacally to the unnerving beat of an otherworldly music. Just as I began to explore this fantastic city, I was awoken by a great slamming, and I blinkingly beheld a package on the desk before me. I opened it, discovering to my horror that it was none other than the *Necronomicon*."

Here I shuddered. The *Necronomicon* has the dubious honor of being the prize of the university's occult collection—and the center of more than a few dark rumors surrounding deaths, early retirements, and brilliant minds gone insane.

"I opened the book to the page marked by its ribbon, which they say is made of human skin flensed from the flesh of its mad author. It took me a moment to realize what I was reading: a description of a machine used by the temple priests of Lagash to commune with an alien world, a world of strange, swirling colors and glittering beings and ungodly music!"

"Wingate," I chose my words carefully. "You are one of my oldest, dearest friends. But you are speaking *madness*."

"Am I? Then explain, Jennifer, when I showed Professor Wilmarth the passage, why did the color drain from his face? Why did he stammer that, though he had read that very copy of the *Necronomicon* dozens of times, *he had never seen that page before that night!?*"

I swallowed. Peaslee's story had pushed my scientific curiosity past the tipping point. I knew then that I was a helpless thrall of his mania.

"Why tell me?" I asked. "About your dream, about the *Necronomicon*, about the machine?"

"Because," he grinned, almost maliciously, "you're going to help me build it."

Constructing a working apparatus based on faded diagrams and incantations in a 6,000-year-old book turned out to be no easy task, even for me. Without hyperbole or braggadocio, I can say that I am the most talented engineer—mechanical *or* electrical—at the university. Unfortunately, the title on the bronze placard outside my office is less impressive: "Jennifer Rottman, *Associate* Professor, Engineering."

To be sure, my career has been hindered by my gender. A woman with mathematical and mechanical expertise is a rare bird in the halls of higher learning, and there are those that would see her caged. Even more of an impedance, however, were the dogged rumors surrounding my former laboratory assistant, Johanna Fryburg.

When I was granted my professorship, Johanna was my first and only choice for an assistant. A mechanical genius with almost supernatural dexterity, her attention to detail and inspiring work ethic were matched only by her beauty and grace. As partners, we had a chemistry that made the long hours of study and experimentation glide by like the silken ripples of her labcoat.

But our prodigious output—and our hours of intimacy—did not go unnoticed. Friends told me of murmurings of a homosexual affair. I ignored these, dismissing them as professional jealousy, until I found myself occupied with impure thoughts of Johanna; her lithe figure, snow-white skin, dark eyes, and the full, curly locks that cascaded down her neck. It was when I found myself almost kissing that perfect neck that I first sought out Professor Peaslee.

Wingate assured me that my urges were a fairly common form of hysteria experienced by unmarried women in stressful occupations. The cure was simple: dismiss Johanna, and redirect my lustful energies to my work.

Sure enough, with the object of temptation removed from my sight, the urges more or less disappeared. Occasionally I caught myself pining after one of the undergraduate co-eds, but a shake of my head, a sip of black coffee, and a flip through the latest journals were enough to purify myself. I did not spare Johanna a second thought until Peaslee approached me about his terrible machine.

From the outset, it was clear I would need a proper assistant. Wingate wouldn't do—he was a psychologist, not an engineer, with a poor constitution to boot. I needed someone young, strong, with capable hands—and discretion. Our experiment was to be unorthodox, and we did not want the harsh glare of peer scrutiny until we were ready to present our findings.

Johanna had been crushed by her dismissal. The poor girl had wept and promised me anything—if only I would take her back—and it was time to hold her to that promise. I approached her, made my offer, and she quickly consented to my stipulation of absolute silence regarding our unwholesome project.

Thenceforth, Wingate, Johanna and myself devoted every spare moment to study and experimentation in the abandoned barn we had purchased for our workshop. But try as we might, we could not transfigure the ancient words into a workable schematic, and we spent more than two weeks banging our heads against the proverbial wall.

All of that changed when, after an exhausting evening of fruitless labor, Peaslee went home to his wife, while Johanna and I—unencumbered by marital duties—decided the full moon and a fresh pot of coffee might be just the things to inspire a breakthrough. But the only thing the moonlight inspired, as it filtered through the rain-warped rafters and danced on Johanna's pale skin, was *lust*. And the coffee only made our hands tremble as we unfastened each other's clothing.

My mind was wracked with guilt, but my body was wracked with pleasure. As we cried out in mutual rapture, we were shocked to discover that our words took the shape of technical instructions. Quickly, we disengaged from each other and copied down the words we had screamed. We stayed up until dawn, engaging in acts of engineering and tribation not seen on earth in 6,000 years. When Peaslee saw our work the next day, he did not question us when we suggested that perhaps it would be best if we henceforth worked alone. A month later, the device was ready to test.

On a blustery evening in late December, we gathered in our fur overcoats, clipboards in hand, ready to embark on a sensory journey to the perverted mind of the homosexual. Had I known then the depths of horror to which I was to descend that night, I would have burned the whole blasted contraption along with the cursed barn that housed it.

At the stroke of midnight, I was given the honor of throwing the great switch. At first, none of us detected anything but a low humming. Then, an eerie, pinkish light began to emanate—not from the machine, but from the very air. Suddenly, Wingate cried out:

"My God—your skin! It's... twinkling. Yes, *glittering*, almost!"

Johanna and I looked at each other. Sure enough, our features melted into a bright, glittery silhouette. And that's when the barn faded from view.

Wingate, Johanna, and I were transported to a city of great, festive spires. As far as the eye could see it stretched, rainbow-colored edifices and streets of impossible design and gay aspect. The residents of the city twinkled like Johanna and myself, and rode blinding-white unicorns. Everything seemed to move to the rhythm of a wondrous music, and it was all I could do to restrain myself from joining the swirling crowds. Behind me, I could hear Wingate furiously jotting down notes. Then the shrieking began.

The unicorns reared. Their riders gestured towards Peaslee. We turned to him, and I heard a primal scream escape my lungs. Where my old friend had stood was a demon, a formless hellspawn too horrible to behold. Johanna fainted. I turned away, groping for the machine. Stumbling into it, I shoved my sturdy clipboard into its mighty gears. The humming died, the spires faded away, and the pinkish light disappeared from the firmament. I looked back at Peaslee. That's when I lost consciousness.

The doctors here say that I am delusional, that I have suffered an emotional breakdown over the murder of my old friend, of which they so adamantly accuse me. But I know they lie.

I pray every day for the hour when I am allowed to leave their interrogations and return to my solitary cell. There, at least, I do not have to gaze upon their faces. Oh God, their faces! For you see, that machine opened my eyes to the true and hideous form of the heterosexual.

I pray, now, for the companionship of one like myself, for Johanna. But she has not come to visit, and they will not tell me where she is. Last week a careless orderly dropped a newspaper into the wastebasket, and I was able to read it without being noticed. Inside was an account of that fateful night: when the police arrived at the barn, Peaslee was dead, gored in the chest with some sort of horn which was never found. I was unconscious, and Johanna was missing—as was the machine, which the doctors tell me never existed.

Why, then, did they find my clipboard, crushed—as if by gears?

TOMBOY OF THE WESTERN WORLD
• Terence Diamond

ONE.

The room is small, dark, and smells of feet. Giant toe jam encrusted, athlete's foot burning, haven't had clean socks in a week, feet.

Breathe through the mouth. No dressers. Clothes strewn everywhere and mixed up with *Ray's Pizza* boxes, plates, shoes and nail studded Doc Martens. A banged-up alarm clock displays 16:28. Telltale signs of a joint in progress, an ashtray with burnt papers and a few cigarette stubs. Need to get that going. Pull the ashtray over gingerly and sort through the debris. Perched on the lip, a nice fat roach. No light. *Oh, shit! Probably why the roach survived.*

Get up and rummage. Can't tell where I am. Street too quiet. Sky that blue-gray mid-winter dreary. Sixteen o'clock and twenty-eight minutes. Dress and leave, the coward's way out. Pocket the roach. All right. Black old man's thrift store pants. Shit-colored mens 50s shirt. Skinny tie. Black overcoat. Fruit boots from 14th street. Don't wake her. It'll be excuses and pleas to stay and have breakfast or something. Morning sex with a mouth that reeked. Gag. Open the door. Look down the corridor. Lights on one end. Sound of laughter and talk. Other end, a door. Creep on bare feet. Grab knob. Turn, door swings open.

Out on the white spotless tile. An antique table holds a vase of fresh cut flowers. Inhale. Green scent of suburban garden. Behind that a large, polished antique mirror. Shut door quietly. Pass the table. See reflection. Check it out. A bit worse for wear from the hangover. Handsome boy, is he. Stone Mulligan.

TWO.

Someone's beside me, shaking my shoulder. I open my eyes. It's Pussy. Her face two inches from mine, squinting through her cat lady glasses. I smell her scent for the first time, a mix of femme pungency and musk. There are mattresses on a floor occupied by sleeping bodies in couples, triples, groups.

"What are you doing?" She says.

"What happened?" I recoil from her.

"Wow, are you okay? Did you take something?" She sniffs my head. Like a dog. I push her away.

"Still want to party?" I look around, bleary eyed. There were no people left dancing. I am alone on the couch.

"I thought this *is* the party."

"It's a drag. Let's go to my place." She pulled me upright. My legs feel wobbly. "Christ, you're really trashed."

I have been more trashed than this. But the mind is working funny. I keep trying to remember something but it won't materialize. The single thought—a heavy, cast iron safe teetering on the edge of a windowsill. Impossibly, it maintains its balance and won't fall. The tender place between my legs is still engorged. I want to kiss her.

"Can I kiss you, Pussy Chick?" I say.

"Go ahead. Kiss me." She says defiantly. I lean toward her, eyes closed. She giggles. I pucker up and miss. I get her cheek.

"Nice try, Big Dog."

"What?"

"If I'm Pussy Chick, you're Big Dog." I like this.

"Okay, let's quit it. What's your name?"

"My stage name is Sarasvati Futura. I like the goddess and her mythology." She's chatty. "My real name is Sassafras. Like the tree".

I interrupt her. "Two names?" I am feeling very happy and stupid at this precise moment.

"My parents are hippies. They make their own MDMA. The side affects are toxic to the liver so they make it as organic as possible. They boil the sassafras leaf."

"You're really named after a drug?"

"No, I'm named after a tree." She picks up the pipe the couple had left on the table in front of me. She sniffs it. "Parents were hippies, what do you want?"

"My mother wanted a boy."

"Just like Pinocchio's dad." She grabbed my wrist. "Let's go."

What did she say? Pinocchio's dad?

"Are you coming home with me or not?" She interrupts my reverie. I lean toward her.

"Oh, not again." She pinches my nipple, hard. *Ow! What the fuck?*

"I don't kiss on the first date." She grabs my hand and leads me past the snorting, farting, whimpering bodies on the floor.

THREE.

She grips me by the wrist and drags me along Avenue C. I falter like a reluctant bridegroom. I know not to read too much into the physical contact. I know this chick is the type of female that feels free to hug, kiss, hold hands with, or embrace a total stranger. I've been deceived a few times by the easy intimacy. These broads never put out, I've learned. But sometimes they've got good drugs.

We tear down the avenue past groups of people huddling in doorways or on the corners. Not been this far east in the City. I hunch my shoulders. Ready for a fight. Shocked by the burned-out husks of buildings. The empty lots that look like miniature trash dumps. The wan lights illuminating each block. It's 3 am. The street is full of people. Shots ring out, hoarse voices shout in Spanish, threats to, *"yo te voy a matar, hombre!!"*

And then sirens, police cars, and fire trucks race up. Cops jump out, guns drawn, the junkie bloodstream of Avenue C getting its hourly speedball. The cops are useless against the drug pumping through the spiked vein of the city. I turn to stare.

"Let's keep moving!" commands Pussy Chick. I look at her. *Okay, she's knows her way around.*

We skitter around the corner of 13th street. I see windows above, ablaze with light. She fumbles around in her green leather handbag, uttering curses.

"Fucking, fuck, fuck, fuck." She turns her face up to the windows.

"X-Cessive!" No answer.

"X! Are you up there? X! *X!*"

A masculine, accented voice yells out in a mincing falsetto, "X, X??" in response to her plaintive appeals. Laughter follows from the same direction across the street in a boarded-up building. She looks over at me and sizes me up. "Bend over."

"What?" She points to the fire escape ladder.

"I can pull myself up by that if I can reach it."

"Up there? You'll fall on your head."

"You're such a pussy. I've done it a million times. Here—" She grabs me and bends me down.

"Get off of me, what the fuck are you doing?" I move away from her.

She laughs. "C'mon, you're a strong dude. I'm gonna straddle your shoulders—and hey, I'm not wearing panties. So bend down."

Well in that case. I comply. She puts a leg over my shoulder. Then the other. I can feel her wet pussy against my neck.

"Now, stand up straight." I slowly unbend. She is heavier than a child but once I straighten up I can balance her weight easily.

"This is great. Now move over under the ladder." She reaches up and pulls on it. It doesn't budge.

"Shit!" She pulls on it harder. Still nothing. Without warning she pulls herself up and stands on my shoulders like a trapeze artist. Her heels are digging into my neck muscles.

She shouts. She yells, "Get out of the way!" and grabs onto the lowest rung. I duck. She hangs there for a second. The ladder screams like a wounded creature and descends. She jumps clear. She turns, gets a good grip on the second rung and starts climbing. I stand there, astonished.

"What the hell are you waiting for?"

"Is it safe?" She scrambles back down and grabs my sleeve.

"You want safe? Go back to Jersey," she says snarling, and climbs up again. I grab a rung and hoist all 222 pounds of myself up the ladder. My knees shake when I stand upright on the first landing. Then the rest is easy—just climbing rusted-out stairs with jagged edges past the windows of folks that may or may not have a loaded gun at the ready for intruders. Easy unless you step the wrong way. We reach the top landing where there are lights and music pounding from a pair of windows. All I can see in there are bodies moving. Pussy Chick pulls up the window sash and angles a leg over the sill. The smell of B.O., hash, beer, men's cologne, some nasty food smells, and heat blast forth. The talk is loud and raucous with an undertone of the Sex Pistols. She ducks and puts in the rest of her body. She sticks her head out and looks at me. "Watch the radiator." She waits. "You coming or not?"

I follow her.

"Hey Sassy!" A very pretty henna-haired woman rushes over to her. I watch Pussy Chick and the woman embrace and kiss on the mouth. When they stop, Henna-Haired looks around and spots me.

"Oh, this is my date," Pussy Chick says.

"Yum. What's her name?"

"His. I don't know. We haven't been introduced."

Henna-Haired slips her arm inside mine.

"Okay, let me make the introductions. This is Sarasvati Futura, queen of the underworld. Sarasvati, this is—what did you say your name was?" She waits.

"Stone."

Pussy Chick shrugs. "His mother wanted a boy."

"Stone. I am Trixie. Trixie Forbidden Fruit. You can call me Trix."

"Uh, okay." My hostess holds her hand out to shake mine. I catch a whiff of something imperious about the gesture. I grip it hard and shake it.

"Nice to meet you, Stone."

"Yeah, okay. Samewise." This feels retarded. Pussy Chick grabs Trix by the elbow. I hear her say, loudly, over the noise.

"Now Trix. Let's get to the most important question of the moment. Where are the cocktails?"

Trix motions with her head. "There's 48's chilling in the bathtub."

"No, I mean real drinks."

"Oh, Sass. You and your affectations. There's cheap vodka in the freezer. But don't tell anyone."

"Olives?" Pussy Chick produces a martini glass from her green leather bag.

Pussy Chick walks away, that cute ass swaying in the tight miniskirt. That is the last I see of her.

Trixie turns to me and says, not unkindly, "You're on your own, dude." Like she knows Pussy Chick's ways.

I slump in the corner of the room on a soft, brown, Naugahyde love seat. It reminds me of the couch at home. I feel a lump rise in my throat. To stave off tears, I stare hard at the partiers for a while. A couple, next to me, are making out and emerge only to toke on a pipe. They offer it to me—kinda generous. I put it to my lips, inhaling deeply. Hold it in my lungs, nod thank you, pass it back. Exhale. The smoke has a strange taste. A thought flickers through my mind. *Oh, fuck what was that?* It seared my lungs.

Someone's reading something out loud in a snotty voice. I don't understand the words.

The people here are dressed in costumes of various styles. The ones in spacesuits and boots look like they walked out of a Jetsons cartoon. A lot of the women are dressed like vintage sex kittens, brandishing generous cleavage but touched with a hint of the dowdy. They dance to this loud crashing music, jumping up and down, their heads bobbing like inflatable toys in a pool. I'm fascinated as they slow down, their movements flow, simultaneously moving like waves and discrete particles. Alright, this is a good drug.

I run my hands over the Naugahyde, touching the grain, marveling at its authentic feel. The couple is mauling each other under their clothes. Pervy, I keep watching them out of the corner of my eye. I feel a swelling slowly in my crotch. My heart opens up as the couple fucks. I catch a glimpse of a large dildo and she has her legs wrapped around his middle. She moans. I listen but stare at the slow motion dancing of the crowd. A warm syrupy affection wells up for these strangers. I sink into the fake leather. It feels like home. My heart bursts.

FOUR.

"Don't walk away from me!" Caroline Ann screeches.

"I have to pee." I slip cleanly through a plywood door that leads to a dark corridor. The place is confusing, all these passageways. I can still hear the music as I grope my way in the dark. I come upon a door with light bleeding out its sides and bottom. Must be it. I open it. Standing there staring at herself in the mirror is the chick who ranted about fisting a pussy! The Emcee introduced her as some such hippie name I don't know how to pronounce. Stunned, I can't speak. So loud, sexy, and dirty-mouthed on stage, here she is, the leopard pants down around her knees, her ample tits in a push up bra exposed, smoking a joint on the toilet.

"Occupied!" she yells. I close the door abruptly. She stops me.

"Hey wait," she says, putting her hand on my arm. She turns her back to me.

"It's the fucking tenth time this happened. I get out of them to pee and the zipper gets stuck." I stand there, a bit confused, idle. She pulls the leopard catsuit up and inserts her arms. She waits.

"Are you deaf?" She says. I quickly close my fingers around the zipper and the zipper flaps and pull up. Hoping a few foot-pounds of pressure would do it. Doesn't move. It's really stuck. It's metal, an old-fashioned tongue and groove type. Eating up the fabric.

"It won't—" In a state of confusion, I pull down on the narrow metal tab again. I look at Pussy Chick's soft neck, the small downy hairs stirring slightly. I shiver. I peer down the slope of her neck to her breasts, rounded, generous. She turns and sees me looking. My face flushes. She notices and laughs. I feel my face redden and a tingle in my belly.

"Stop staring at my tits and fix it."

"I wasn't staring, it's busted. I can't do anything with it." She turns around abruptly, snarling. My eyes keep drifting to her tits. She sees me doing that!

"My god, you're useless. Who sent you?"

"Nobody did. I was looking for the toilet."

"You're not the intern? Oh, turds. I'm sorry." Her meanness melts away.

"No, I'm not an intern. Even if I was, you shouldn't talk to people that way."

She rolls her eyes at me. "Not from around here, are you?"

"No. So what?"

She pauses and looks at me for the first time.

"There's a party I'm going to later tonight. I'd like you to be my date. I'll be done by 2. Wait for me out front."

"Why should I?"

"Cause tomorrow you'll kick yourself if you don't."

She took off down the dark corridor, heels clacking on the wooden floor.

I look at the toilet and the sink and the shower with the shower curtain an incongruous frilly thing with the telltale sign of mildew. This is someone's home. I think. How do you let 100 strangers into your home that you know are going to drink and trip and fuck up the furniture and smoke cigarette that turn the ceiling all yellow. What kind of person does this? I look for evidence on the bathroom walls. The entire chamber is bright white—walls, curtains, toilet cover, rug, towels, and ceiling. The lighting is a fluorescent and incandescent mix but of very high voltage. I catch a look of myself in the mirror and see my newly shorn head, the down on my upper lip, my man's shirt. I feel shock. *No wonder these girls—ah, fuck that.*

I unbuckle my belt and unbutton the fly on my 501's, peel down my jeans and stand over the bowl. I shoot a warm stream of piss into the clean porcelain. It makes the sound of strong steady rain on a window. I feel a sexual tingle from my bladder. My anus contracts. I piss out the two beers I drank in quick succession while Caroline Ann tried to mindfuck me. I piss out all the women I'd fucked in the past year. I piss out my homelessness. I piss out my exile. I piss out my neediness, my confusion, my desire for things, my homesickness.

I piss out the pure crush of grief. Then, when I can't piss anymore, I bend and take a few small squares of tissue and wipe myself. Pull up the jeans, button the fly, buckle the belt. Run water over my hands in the sink, soap them with the thin sliver of brown-flecked blue soap, and stare in the mirror once more.

"This won't last." I say to the face in the mirror. I hear myself say this and wonder whose voice it is. But even more so, I can't tell if it is a threat or a consolation. Then, loud, rude, pounding on the door.

"Hey numb-nuts, you fucking someone in there?"

I throw open the door and see a small, compact man dressed in a white leisure suit, with a big pompadour hairstyle, looking like Tony Manero. He brushes past me and shuts the door. I stand in the dark corridor unsure where to go. Then the music. I recognize it. The Stiffs singing, "*We don't care what you say, fuck you!*" I walk in the direction of the music and chaos. Abruptly, the sound is cut off. Then I hear Pussy Chick begin her spiel again. The crowd screams. Her invitation resounds in my head.

FIVE.

The next performer steps up to the microphone. She is dressed in fake leopard capri pants and a tight, cleavage-revealing black sweater, and black studded platform boots. Her hair is bright punk pink, styled with razor blades. She wears black rhinestone studded cat lady glasses on her pert nose. The lights go down around her. She is brilliantly spotlighted. I have never seen anything like her before. Someone in the crowd screams, "Show us your pussy!"

"I am Sarasvati Futura and I come from the planet Clitoris." The crowd is really revved up. Some women are crawling on their bellies toward Sarasvati, their tongues licking everything in sight.

"I have a message from my people. I come in peace." More screams.

"I have to adjust my mind to receive the transmission." She

closes her eyes and sways. Then she begins to speak in a trance-like voice.

"Hurry up, hurry baby, to me. I feel my atoms colliding, moving faster and faster, condensing, falling into each other as they concentrate and I feel that thickening, oozing slough of molecules condensing and shaping and waiting for the spark—your spark, baby, your spark, the little girl actress with the nose job spark who wants my attention but won't give what's under your skirt—won't give me that juicy flesh and wetness and hot sweet honey. And I feel that pulsing, throbbing light under your skirt, honey. And I want that under thing that all the goddess of the fucking heavens call blessed. That thing, that essence, that purity of self, of woman, of womanhood, of the divine feminine expression. Give me that pussy, baby. I want to enter into the woman again, into your woman. My fist creeps up and you scream and I say 'I'm gonna fuck you like you've never been fucked in your life.' Your glistening honey runs over it as I ram it in and out of your pussy, and you ride my wild fist—my wild, fascist fist—until the walls of your thang collapse and quake and there is no more.

"I hold you after you come. You tell me how much you loved it. Could I kill you by fucking so hard? Could I kill *myself*? Would I let you fuck me like that? You better believe it!"

I shake my head and laugh. Twisted shit. Sarasvati Futura's arms reach above her head, eyes closed. She sways. Then the lights black out. The crowd goes wild. I shake my head. Caroline Ann is whistling loud taxi-summoning signals. The Pussy Chick is a rock star. Whatever the fuck that was, it sucked.

"She's so hot!" Caroline Ann screams.

"Got a mouth on her." I say.

"You're such a prude. When she trances it heals the whole world!"

"You're crazy."

"Why do you say that?"

"Like what she just said heals the planet? You're nuts!"

"You're a prude. And you need to get laid." Caroline Ann wrinkles her nose.

I kick the scummy floor. "You say so."

"I find self-repression very sexy." She runs her finger down my cheek.

"See, you *are* crazy." I duck and turn my back to her.

She whines, "Don't you want to go home with me?"

"For what?"

"I want to heal your wounds." More whining.

"What?"

"Someone hurt you real bad." Sounding like some kinda TV shrink.

"Even if they did, it's none of your business."

"I want to help you."

"You can't help me. You're crazier than I am. At least I have a reason for living on the street. You're doing it for fun."

"You like me but you're scared."

"Scared of *what?*"

"That you might like something that repulses you."

"Like what?"

"Like *this.*"

Caroline Ann grabs me by the neck and kisses me. I shoved her away.

"What the hell did you do that for?"

"I want to help you overcome your hang-ups."

"About what?"

"About sex with a woman."

"You think I've never had sex with a woman?"

"No."

I turned on my heel to find the bathroom. Bitch is crazy.

SIX.

Skirt pushed up around her midriff, her bra already up around her neck. Pussy Chick's on a stained mattress, legs apart. I am licking her soft black pussy. She is practically baying, shaking. Bucking her sweet ass and thighs.

"Oh, Stone, fuck me. Please. Please, fuck me. Stoooohhhnne!!!"

SEVEN.

Most weekends, Stone starts out at the dive bar on Friday night and then makes his way to the Upper East Side. He crawls through a few dyke hellholes and ends up back at the park by daybreak. There is a bar on Lex & 83rd named Lulu. There is a women's disco called the Red Desert on 3rd or second in the 60s. Stone meets a woman at LuLu one night and talks her into going to the Red Desert with him. Hears it is a cool place with lots of nice women. The lady tells Stone she is from Texas. A Librarian or something. Robert Lowell's biographer. Stone is not familiar with Robert Lowell so it makes no impression on him. The Librarian tells Stone she is married and has two children. That throws Stone. Stone asks how could The Librarian frequent lesbian bars if she was a mom. The Librarian says, why not. She likes women and there was nothing wrong with it. They head for the Red Desert.

Stone doesn't know the exact address but they find it, a joint where sweaty women congregate outside. There is a window display—a silhouette of two femmes with a palm tree behind them with real sand inside the glass, almost like an ant farm. The Librarian stands next to Stone as they stare at it. The Librarian says, "That's why they call it the Red Desert, because it has sand in the windows." They go inside. More drinks, The Librarian pays. Stone objects, but only faintly. Stone blew his cash for the night two bars ago. They dance—until The Librarian tires. Cruelly, Stone teases her.

"I have two babies," she says defensively. They start making out in the bar. She invites Stone back to her hotel. It's late, maybe 3 or 4am. They spill into a cab and get out a short distance from the club. A fancy ass hotel. She leads Stone to her room, a tiny cubicle dominated by the bed. Stone balks. Stone doesn't want to touch her. Stone doesn't feel attracted anymore, even in his alcoholic daze. But he was here. He needed a bed for the night. The Librarian looks at him funny. What's wrong, she says. Stone says nothing. The Librarian's looks hurt. Stone looks at her and all Stone see is someone's mom, not a dyke. Matronly, and in a dowdy dress for godsakes. Stone realizes he can't do it. Stone feels Irishmale guilty. All those drinks. He sits on the bed in silence.

Then she strokes his cheek. Stone closes his eyes. He thinks of Svati—Svati's legs-splayed abandon. The alcohol is wearing off. He feels his sadness well up. She leans into him and puts her arms around him. She kisses him on the mouth. He finds himself responding. She isn't his type but he doesn't protest. She pushes him down on the bed gently and runs her hands under his shirt. Her desperation and lust deepens his sadness. He feels his flesh respond while his mind rebels. She removes her dress and crawls around on him, kissing and licking him. He feels his own arousal. He feels the imprint of her garter belt hooks on his thigh. He reaches under her and feels her wetness gushing. She moans. She still wears her Librarian sensible pumps. She sits astride him, grinding her wetness onto his hand. She moves faster. He makes a fist and pushes it slowly into her. She resists at first. The knuckles push against her pelvic ridge. But then the fist passes into her wet hole and she cries. Stone's excitement overcomes his resistance. He pumps his fist into the Librarian, venting his grief and his loneliness. She comes and collapses on him. *Shit.*

"Have to go."

The Librarian asks him to spend the night. Stone says he can't. "Have to go home."

The Librarian says: "Okay. At least take a cab home."

Stone says, "Nah. I'll take the train."

The Librarian says, no. It's too late. The Librarian puts on her coat, takes Stone down to the lobby, through the lobby to the entrance. The front desk clerk pretends to not notice Stone's Doc Martens and green army jacket. He summons the doorman. The doorman hails a cab. Stone gets in, The Librarian hands the cabbie cash. The Librarian turns around reluctantly. Pokes her head back in. Stone kisses her on the cheek.

Where to? Says the cabbie. He speaks in a Brooklyn accent. The Librarian looks at Stone.

"Tompkins Square Park." Stone says. The Librarian looks askance at this. Stone reaches out and closes the door. She waves. The cab shoots along 75th Street.

Stone looks out at the quiet, dead city. The cabbie starts chatting.

"Staying in the hotel?"

"No."

"You know someone in the hotel."

"No. Just that lady."

"How come you're going from the Carlyle to that address in the middle of the night?"

"What do you care?" Stone says.

"Hey buddy, I ain't picked anyone up at the Carlyle before. I was just asking."

Silence. Stone's eyes close.

"You know it's where George Bush stayed when he was in town."

"Really?"

"Yeah. Have some respect. He was the best president we ever had."

"If you say so."

"What are you, a red?"

"No, but some of my friends are."

The guy looks back at him and snarls. "Hey, I fought in Desert Storm for you little shits! Okay? Take it easy!"

Stone didn't want to talk to this guy any more. He reminded him of the jerks his father's age back in Jersey. All "my country right and wrong", and if you don't feel that way then get out. Stone felt like he couldn't respond, he was outnumbered. And because he was still called a "she" they would laugh. What the fuck did she know?

They were pulling off the FDR onto Houston Street. A light rain had started. Stone didn't quite know where they were.

"What address?"

"The corner."

"The corner of what?"

"Tompkins Square. Any corner. I don't care."

"You gotta be kidding."

"No. Let me off there."

"You live in the park? Are you a bum?"

"No, asshole!" The cabbie snarls and stomps on the brake. He flies out of the cab and throws open the door on Stone's side.

"Out of my cab!"

"No! You were paid to drive me home."

"Get out, you piece of shit—before I beat your ass!!!" He grabs Stone by the arm and pulls him out. Stone sprawls on the street into a puddle. The cabbie spits in his direction, slams the door and jumps behind the wheel. He stomps on the gas and peels off.

"Fuck you, asshole!" Stone should have gotten his license number. His jeans are soaked at the knees. He lies there for a moment to make sure nothing's broken. Stone's still not used to the rudeness and hostility of New York street life. He wishes for a harder skin to deflect indignities like this. He feels deserving of the punishment, though. He looks up and feels the mist on his face. It feels soothing, like he's being cleansed after having sex with The Librarian mother-of-three. He looks toward the east, down Houston Street. A few rosy fingers of Dawn brighten the sky. The traffic builds up to its typical roar, the sound of an unruly surf. Stone hears an incongruous sound of birdsong. Probably from the half-choked trees along the FDR. Then like Thor's wrath, the sound of a jackhammer commences its merry business of tearing up the sidewalk. There are footsteps, and a hard-hatted guy in bright orange florescence nudges Stone's foot.

"Hey, buddy!" A wide-grinned face peers over him. Stone notices the U.S. flag pin on the front of his jacket. "You okay? Do you need an ambulance?"

Stone rolls over and gets up. "Nah, I'm okay."

Stone trudges west on Houston Street. He needs to get to the park. Gone too long and the others take your things. He turns North on Avenue A and continues up to the park. He enters the park and heads right for his stuff. Today may be a better day.

A ROMAN INCIDENT

- *Red Durkin*

An average human stomach can hold 10 pounds of food before it begins to tear—two standard sacks of potatoes. Unimaginable to most, but there are those who dare to dream bigger.

To Charlie's immediate left stood a man who had once eaten twenty-one pounds of grits in ten minutes. All along the table in front of her, clad in the same free t-shirt she wore, adventurous amateurs stood shoulder-to-shoulder with vetted professionals who made their living rushing down enough food to kill civilians. Charlie prayed that in ten short minutes she'd have earned a place in the fellowship of the latter. Icy terror filled her empty stomach. She could afford to lose some of her nerve, but none of her appetite. She closed her eyes and counted down from ten.

At zero, the world completely exploded. Lights flashed, buzzers blared, and a crowd of thousands, surging like a bore tide, crashed into the security gate. Their cacophonous excitement splashed onto the stage, along with waves of their beer. Charlie was face down in her fourth mouthful of chicken when Pavlovian reflex gave way to human awareness and she realized what was happening. The Hooters World Wing Eating Championship had begun. Her destiny was at the bottom of the pile of poultry parts in front of her. She couldn't afford to be reckless. Every wing had to be clean in order to count and so she quickly rendered each one to polished bone before moving on to the next. Behind her, a gorgeous girl in emphatically tight orange shorts held a scorecard above her head. The woman bounced and smiled and cheered, faking her enthusiasm the way Charlie imagined her mother had taught her.

In part of her heart, Charlie would always bear a hateful jealousy for women like this. She begrudged them their big, friendly breasts, their happily bulging hips, all the legible parts of their bodies that spoke '*woman*' in every language. Charlie's inscrutable frame would never carry that confident kind of currency and she scorned the pretty girls for their oblivious luck.

When she was nine, she'd posted a note on the fridge that said "Charlie is a girl and she needs new clothes. End of discussion." Some years earlier, to get out of an intervention, Charlie's father had declared that the words 'end of discussion' meant exactly that in the Eaglehorne household. It was family law. The phrase had been employed when she was twelve and demanded to go on hormones and most recently at seventeen when she declared her intention to become a professional speed eater.

One minute down, one bowl of wings eaten. Charlie's heart kicked like a mule. Anxiety throbbed in her temple. Her jaw stiffened too quickly. She knew that if she didn't calm down and steady her pace that she'd be lucky to finish at all, but she was operating on a level baser than prudence. It was the reptile part of her brain that was grabbing and chewing and swallowing. She couldn't hear the sloppy roar of the crowd or the grunting gluttony of the competition. Like the few other women on stage, she was pelted with the countless ugly words for "girl" that fly so easily from the mouths of angry drunken men. She blocked it out. She'd had practice.

Tears and snot gushed down her face. She was soaked in a marinade of sweat and Buffalo sauce. *Grab. Chew. Swallow.* Each spicy wing tasted more like Styrofoam, and her cheeks bulged with unchewed meat. Every bedraggled second took a lifetime to pass. It was beginning to feel like home.

She'd been raised by a pair of New England hippies who'd moved to Alabama because they liked the leaves in autumn and equated dirt roads with rustic honesty. The Eaglehornes settled in a truck-stop town outside of Montgomery called Hope Hull, which was an appropriate name for a place so utterly gutted of anything worth looking forward to. The "Charlie is a Girl" campaign had been one of the most successful political movements in its entire history. As a home-schooled hippy whelp growing up on the fringe of an outskirt town, she was practically invisible to anyone who didn't share their meals with her. Between her mother's home-style lopsided haircuts and her father's surprisingly successful approach to homeopathic endocrinology, those lucky enough to lay eyes on her were neither certain of nor curious about what they were looking at. Her parents claimed her as their daughter and, so long as you didn't have the audacity to dye your hair pink or the nerve to be dark skinned, Hope Hull's residents were a proudly credulous bunch.

Charlie suddenly realized she couldn't remember the last time she'd taken oxygen into her lungs. She wondered how long her animal mind had been screaming. All the pain and confusion she'd foisted on it was immediately hers to deal with again. Four more minutes had passed, four and a half more bowls. Fifty-five wings in all. The top half of her body was covered in gore. Her jaw glowed white-hot with pain, her esophagus burning with the sensation of being strangled from the inside out. She tried to swallow, but the blockage in her throat only shuffled in place. She snatched a cup of water from the table and gulped it down. The lump lurched mercifully. As it finally moved to take its rightful place in her stomach, she gasped a great mouthful of air and the agony all over her body began to register on an all too conscious level. Her fingers hurt.

She took another deep breath and closed her eyes. She forced herself to master the pain. She refused to go back to hustling arrogant rednecks at the off-ramp burger joints that composed Hope Hull's economy. At one time, those moments had been proud and meaningful victories. Now, they felt more like the glory-day nails in her inevitably mediocre coffin. She was willing to eat her way out of that shit-splat town, even if it killed her. She picked up another wing just in time to catch a blur of green glass in her periphery. The bottle cracked her just above the eye and everything went white in instant.

Charlie had been hit before, of course. By her mid-teens, she'd traded her bean-pole adolescent androgyny for a sexlessly amorphous obesity. To the idle and idiot youth of Hope Hull, Charlie was a chimera of cardinal social sins. She was fat, opinionated, and ineffably weird looking. She had the disturbing habit of reading for pleasure and her free-spirited, Yankee kin might as well have been Martians. The girls spit in her hair and laughed at her back. The boys called her a faggot because she confused them. They punched her, she punched back, and, slowly, they all learned how to fight. Her sole companion was a pig-nosed girl named LuLu, who brazenly forced the friendship to garner disapproval from her pig-faced family.

In fluttering flashes, the world began to focus. She'd staggered back from the table but was still in the competition. Precious seconds had been lost to semi-consciousness, and she warded off wary medics to keep from losing more. The red in her eye might well have been Buffalo sauce. Her throbbing head reminded her of home. She wanted to sleep. She needed to eat. She split the difference and looked around. Four minutes to go and only eight of the original twenty competitors still stood on the line. For the first time she could see that, just past the grits eater and a bloated man wearing novelty sunglasses, stood Sonya Thomas, *The Black Widow*. She was a svelte Korean-born woman who had managed a Burger King before becoming the second highest ranked gurgitator on Earth. She held a dozen world records and, according to the scoreboard, a chicken wing that would put her twenty-six points out of reach. Charlie's stomach suddenly felt like a much smaller place.

Somewhere outside of her body, she could see herself chewing again. She had never planned on beating Sonya Thomas, she had only prayed she wouldn't show up. Some people want to kill their idols, but Charlie didn't want a fight. She just wanted to get out of Alabama. A mechanical waltz settled over her body. *Grab. Chew. Swallow.* She struggled to distract herself from the replete pain and doubt welling up in her gut.

She thought back to home and the perpetual motion of her life as a Podunk pariah. In the dregs of her diffidence, she knew that she'd fed the beast, had let the hurt go deeper than skin and grown fatter, weirder, even meaner as a result. She'd craved the hard touch of a town that would never claim her as their own, never love her, never brag about her. Her hope had been shining through an ever-clenching pinhole, but in that lens she'd seen *The Widow* competing on television. Charlie recognized her kindred in strife, another misfit among rubes. She saw in Sonya Thomas a whisper of freedom, a liberty to dance on the edge of womanhood and thrive.

Charlie's training had started the spring she turned seventeen. Her parents met her intentions of becoming a major league eater with a skepticism bordering hostility. Seventeen years of semi-responsible parenting had severely moderated the Eaglehorne idea of acceptable life-goals. Really, they worried that their chronically unpopular daughter's plan to etch a living shoving food down her throat was a proposition in suicide. She'd had to declare the discussion ended more than once.

In fact, she'd never been further from death. Her regimen was modeled on what she could glean from her idol's sporadic television appearances and the Internet. It was surprisingly in step with the recommendations of modern medicine: eight hours of sleep a night, daily jogs, and a strict seventeen hundred calorie diet filled with fruits and vegetables. Of course, eating all that food at once isn't in many fitness manuals, to say nothing of her bi-weekly all-you-can-eat "workouts," but the overall improvement in Charlie's health was undeniable. By the fall, she'd lost seventy-eight pounds and gained the beauty and confidence of a girl who truly believes she has control over food. Her public enthusiasm of eating competitions did her few favors with her peers, but her reclaimed featherweight kilter and the off-brand hormones her father bought online had given her a peculiar prettiness that at least kept boys from throwing rocks at her. Her friendship remained a social pitfall Lulu alone was willing to risk.

With thirty seconds left, something was very wrong and getting worse. The eighty-three wings she'd somehow swallowed were now in open revolt. Terror tied a knot in her stomach, making her nausea feel all the more urgent. She'd eaten beyond her means. Charlie was going to throw up.

Her breath came in shallow gulps. She wobbled drunkenly as her strength began to break and she closed her eyes. Clammy certainty enveloped her. Vomiting was intractable and inevitable, but desperately needed to be stalled. If a drop of her sick touched the table before the clock ran out, she'd be disqualified. A great wave of adrenaline washed up the last bit of resolve she'd so jealously buried. It was immediately followed by the half-digested ambitions at the back of her throat.

Charlie's hands shot to her mouth. A gleeful explosion of pleasure roared out of the voyeuristic crowd. Her shoulders heaved as though she'd been shoved by an invisible hand and she teetered slightly forward. The drool in her mouth tasted like batteries. The mess in her guts came flooding out over her lips and into her waiting palms. She shuddered violently as she buckled and began to fall. The final buzzer screamed out over the chaos. The Championship was over. Charlie's world strobed into blackness and she collapsed unconscious into a pile of puke and victory.

In her hallucinations, Charlie watched the Big Bang spew forth and begin to eat itself. She perceived a cycle of consumption, the tidal glut of energy that crushed stars and digested the cosmos. At the center of each galaxy sat an endlessly hungry mouth, a black hole that bolted down creation and waited for the final buzzer of doomsday. Serenely, she recognized creation as an elaborate eating contest. The thought made her happy.

She woke up to the bright, white glow of tarp in the sunshine. Her head lay on a starched, sterile pillow, and a clear tube of saline dripped into a vein in the crook of her elbow. The ebullient bustle of post-competition commotion outside told her she'd been unconscious for only a few minutes, though she felt like she'd witnessed eternity. Sitting up drew the relieved attention of a kind-faced young medic on the other side of the tent. Her heart fluttered, her head throbbed and he urged her to lie back down. She'd almost died. It was time to rest.

In a photo finish, Charlie's vomit had stayed in her hands and off the table until just after the final buzzer. The rules were clear: she'd officially finished successfully. Charlie was awarded third place, just five wings shy of the grits guy. On the plastic stool next to her cot, paper-clipped to a five-hundred-dollar check and a handful of Hooters coupons, was a business card with the International Federation of Competitive Eaters logo on it. She grinned deliriously, belched and fell asleep.

AN EXQUISITE VULNERABILITY

• Cyd Nova

Allen thinks he has the clap again. He wakes up restless from the booze leaving his system—that ever present alarm clock—*you are sober now!* It is 7am and he has nothing to do except wonder how to get azithromycin without Sarah finding out. He doesn't quite trust his family physician to not slip the information out—the man is obviously a heavy drinker with loose lips. Everyone in the country club knew Allen was taking testosterone way before his voice even started its seesaw drop.

Last time this had happened, Allen had gone to the anonymous STI clinic. He'd sat there in the rows of orange metal seats wearing sunglasses and a fake moustache. All the night before he'd stayed up, anxious that people would recognize him, but when he walked in nobody interrupted their gaze—the entire room trapped in a visual standoff with the TV chained to the wall. The movie was *The Green Mile*. On the yellowing screen a mouse dashed out of big black hands, a man screamed while being fried to death. Those in the room waiting for their HIV test results gripped their call numbers tightly, beads of sweat traveling down their cheeks.

There had been something very pleasing to Allen about his visit to the clinic. Being treated as the common man. In exchange for his number a flat-faced nurse led him to a room and barked questions at him tonelessly. How many sex partners had he had? How many had he barebacked with? Had he ever exchanged sex for money? When asked that, a warm feeling of flattery settled into him. He knew that these were just routine questions from a form, but Allen was enticed by the mere insinuation that even a chubby, middle-aged trans man such as himself could be a hustler—like a vision into an alternate life he *could* have had. For that reason, when he counted out how many sex partners he had, he left out Sarah.

The experience was so thrilling that after he swallowed his handful of antibiotics he went straight back to the bathroom where he had pissed into a cup just moments earlier, and he sucked someone's dick next to the toilet bowl.

He had promised himself to put an end to his sexual exploits. He was a heterosexual man married to a woman, made famous by a public transition that would make exclusive rights to any baby photos that his union might produce worth six figures *at least*. He had worked damn hard to keep his transition classy, but this ridiculous hunger for cock was threatening to get in the way of everything. He was investigating selling movie rights. He was solidly booked for speaking engagements and book signing events. His busy life of appointments and appearances had not served to curb his sexual habits, however. On the road and away from L.A., he was free. Once his publicist had gone to sleep, there was nothing to stop him from going on Craigslist with the explicit goal of trolling for sex.

He got varying responses. Many men on the internet looking for FtM's were hoping for someone prepubescent-looking. Countless ads ran—looking for *young, hairless, and slender*—whereas Allen was fat and in the throes of his forties. But then Allen found the bear community. All of the homosexuals he'd grown up around had been loud, well-coifed men who fawned over him, called him honey, but with a cold, disinterested look in their eye all the while. Bears were different. Sweaty and pungent, they served as father figures so unlike his own weak, hippy, republican dad.

The first time post-transition that a man fucked Allen was when he had first begun writing his memoir. Sarah had started drinking again, and when she left, the house would feel like the hull of a ship. Allen was never very good at socializing. Growing up the offspring of publicly scrutinized parents had left him unable to let the smile of his mouth reach into his eyes. It was hard to transition into being a more honest you when all the people you knew were so staunchly plasticine in their affect.

He started reading the blogs of trans men in the real world. Twenty-year-old Midwestern boys with the faces of startled deer, one arm clenching the shoulder of their prom date. Muscle bound Texas men with sideshow "strongman" arms posing for crappy camera phones. The words and images were torrential. Trans men in China, Australia, Taiwan, Spain, and Brasil—all documenting their transition in painstaking detail. Top surgery websites, countless vlogs, the porn and gender theory, the political squabbles. It was all a bit overwhelming and more than just slightly nauseating.

Allen knew that his language was not that of the "queer community." He had planned on writing a simple, palatable book about *his journey* but now he'd been cursed with the knowledge that his narrative was destined for derision. Every night after studying the Internet, he would go back through his book and try and rephrase and tweak his story to make it less problematic. Eventually he realized that there was no way to change it. It wasn't merely the language that was the problem, but his own history. Overwhelmed and depressed, he hired a straight woman ghostwriter to turn it out.

He didn't tell anyone about his failure except his lawyer. He had rented an office in downtown L.A. and every morning around 10am he would 'go to work'. He ate candy bars, staring out the window. He walked around the park where businessmen took their lunches and tried to look stressed for time. After walking briskly back to the office at 12:45 he would open up the computer. There is only so much to stare at within the reaches of the Internet before one starts to look through dating websites.

Allen had not ever cheated on Sarah, up to now the thought hadn't even occurred to him. So it seemed innocent to look at gay websites—investigating the lifestyles of the homosexuals that he had so recently been trying to distance himself from. At first he looked at profiles, then he made his own, read the monosyllabic messages when they arrived in his mailbox, and jerked off in his office chair before closing the chat windows. Pretty soon he started replying and then, one day, ended up lying on the hardwood floor pointing his crotch towards the camera light of his laptop while a guy who bore an uncanny resemblance to the singer of Placebo commanded him to plow his own hole.

For months it never went anywhere from there. He would chat with guys, invite them over then sit paralysed, heart racing while his phone vibrated in his hand, never picking it up to let them in. Then one day, instead of the victim of flakery sending him abusive text messages, he received a message that said 'I understand that you are nervous, just meet me for coffee. We can see if we like each other before we do anything.'

Allen stared at the words for 5 minutes. Then the phone began to ring with the same number. He picked it up and talked to the guy for 30 seconds. He didn't go out to coffee with him, he just buzzed him in and stripped down to his shirt and underwear before he even opened the door. They fucked on the couch. The guy was bald and had a musky asshole. It felt exquisite to be held by someone with a similar body, solid and imperfect. The sex was awkward. Allen failed to pick up on the cues of immediate intimacy. Not to mention Sarah had never been the type to wear a strap-on, so Allen's dick-sucking skills were definitely subpar. It all went so quickly. In just twenty minutes he was alone again.

Then he was addicted. Even though intellectually the sex registered as too fast and regrettable, he fantasized about it constantly. So he hooked up with another guy. A guy in his late 50s with a dick that didn't quite stay hard, so instead fucked him with thick stubby fingers, pushing almost his whole wrist in. Soon after, a younger cub fellow who held Allen's head down on his dick till tears streamed down his face. He threatened to leave him tied up with the door open if Allen so much as began to bite him.

All the hours set aside for book-writing were dedicated to finding sex. It's not that Allen was gay—or so he told himself. It was the lure of sexual simplicity. Interactions that were completely compartmentalized, connections that were about giving and receiving then never speaking again. He felt a deep trust in these men, even after he got his first STI.

He knew he should have felt ashamed, but the mundanity of it all only made his secret life more tangible. However, in bed now, feeling a familiar itch and discomfort, he knew that this could not continue in the vein it had. It wasn't just an issue of having better boundaries around fucking with condoms. Now the pressure of the media was bearing down on his multiple lives. Talk shows always wanted Sarah to join him on set, since she was so much more adept at being in the limelight than he. The spectacle of a woman who loved a man without a penis was just as interesting as the transsexual himself. He could no longer disappear mentally and physically as he once had, especially now that he had recommitted to sobriety.

Had he not been famous this would be simple. Trans men dabbling with dick was so common as to be a trope. In the plebeian world he could have bought Sarah a copy of *The Ethical Slut* and they could have joined some manner of support group for the polyamorous. Instead his reality was about public consumability. Any public evidence of his infidelity with men would explode into derision. He would go from being a champion of masculinity overcoming prejudice to—in the eyes of middle America—a deranged, ugly straight woman.

How glorious it could be though. If it wasn't for the terror of consequence that vibrated through his blood, if he didn't feel under contract with all the mothers and prepubscents that wrote him tiresome fan letters, if he hadn't invested money in this false image of himself.

Allen falls asleep dreaming of the carnality of outing. Of unscripted futures, unregulated selves. Of an exquisite vulnerability of letting the whole machine tumble.

MASKS OF A SUPERHERO

- *Mikki Whitworth*

Annie sat watching the evening news with a glass of single malt scotch. Watching the news allowed her to feel connected to her city, since she had long since stopped being active in the community.

"Crime wave hits the city since the disappearance of Captain Macho," the newscaster reported. Annie's attention locked on the screen. Annie's heart sank upon hearing this. She was so caught up in the moment that she didn't hear her son and confidant enter the room.

"It isn't your fault," Donavan said.

"Like hell, it isn't," she snapped. She took a shot of her scotch, it burned her throat.

"You can't save the world."

"Not without you," she said.

The memories of herself as Captain Macho and Donavan working and fighting side-by-side rushed back to her.

"Look out!" Captain Macho shouted as a baseball sized meteor nearly struck his son. Donavan dodged the fast moving projectile.

"Keep your eyes on the prize," Donavan answered. The *prize* was a quarter-mile wide meteor jetting toward the city below. "I can handle the little stuff." Donavan pulled the baseball bat off his back and began knocking the projectiles out of the atmosphere.

Macho focused on the task at hand, but it was a struggle. Lately, the new hormones were causing him to worry more... He pushed away from the ground to fly toward the impending doom of the meteor. Major parts of the city would be lost if he couldn't move it. As the gap between him and the object shrank, his costume began to burn away. Yet his skin withstood the searing heat. He marveled at his own resilience.

Donavan had cleared the area of falling debris. He and the remaining crowd watched as Captain Macho connected with the fireball in the sky. For several seconds, the meteor kept falling toward the city. Then, it began to move: slowly at first, but soon it was rocketing away.

The city was safe. Donavan held his breath, waiting to see his father return victorious. But this time, Captain Macho did not return.

After about an hour, Donavan left the crowd. Recently, it had happened more and more often that Captain Macho wouldn't wave to the crowd before flying off. Donavan had been watching the changes, but he hadn't said anything. He hadn't been sure what to say.

As he entered the small apartment that they shared, Donovan could hear crying from the bathroom. The shower was running and, huddled in a corner, Annie sat with the remnants of the Captain Macho costume stuck to her skin. Her body was mostly male, but new breasts had begun to grow. Donavan grabbed a soft pink washcloth and helped Annie to her feet to wash the burnt clothing from her. "Maybe this is a sign."

"But the city needs me."

"It was fine before you started protecting it."

"Was it?"

"Yeah." Donavan turned the now cold shower off and wrapped a towel around Annie. "And it will be fine while you take care of yourself."

"I don't know *how* to take care of me," Annie sobbed softly.

"Well, it's time for you learn."

After she began her transition, Annie was amazed at how completely different she felt. At first, she sat locked in her apartment, drinking and wallowing in her loss. But she eventually realized she had to learn how to move from being Captain Macho into her new self. Now, after six months, she loved the woman in the mirror. She loved to look at herself and see a woman looking back. Some days, she would see Captain Macho in the mirror instead, blaming her for all of society's problems. On those days, she didn't love the new woman so much, but those days were slowly becoming more and more rare.

Recently, she had been hired at a small boutique as a saleswoman, a huge change from her previous identity as a reporter for the *Salt City Gazette*. She loved the pretty clothes, and the women who came into the store didn't act as if they knew she had been a man at one time. She possessed a new confidence that even Captain Macho would have envied. Now, she smiled at strangers on the street and didn't feel the need to watch for the next impending disaster. Captain Macho wore a mask, even out of costume. Annie didn't have to, there was no secret identity to hide.

Donavan met her at the store to take her to lunch. He was tall and blond. His blue eyes sparkled in the light as he saw how happy she was in her new life.

"So, how has your day been so far?" he asked.

"Wonderful. We got some new spring dresses in."

"You sound like such a girl." They both laughed at Donavan's quip. "And it looks good on you. I don't think I've ever seen you this happy."

"I don't know if I've ever *been* this happy."

Donavan smiled as he led his mother to a nearby café. "Want to sit outside?"

"Splendid."

The sun had emerged, and it warmed the air. Annie watched the crowds move past them on the sidewalk. She noticed a woman in stiletto heels saunter by in a short lacy skirt. She wondered idly if she could pull off a skirt like that.

Suddenly a man with dark glasses, dirty hair and an Army fatigue coat walked up to the stiletto-wearing woman and grabbed her purse. He shoved her to the ground and took off, racing past Annie and Donavan. Both of them tensed as if to jump into action. Before they could react, however, a police officer rushed by them in hot pursuit. Slowly, a little chagrined, they sank back into their seats.

"They don't need us to protect them," Annie said.

"Yeah. It looks like they have figured out how to take care of themselves."

"I miss it, some days."

"I don't. But then again, when I want to play hero I just grab my bat and go."

"Ah, my little hooligan," Annie sighed fondly.

"Oh, you know it isn't like that."

"Do I now?" she smiled.

"Do you?" he winked.

"I do. I raised a good boy."

On that note, they ordered a plate of goat milk cheeses and Italian aged meats. Annie drank a bottle of sparkling water and Donavan had a beer. She raised a disapproving eyebrow.

"Mom," he said (Annie loved it when he called her that), "I have the day off and it is after Noon."

"Don't make a habit of it. Your other job..."

"You taught me well."

Their lunches of vegetable lasagna were too hot to eat at first, so they lapsed into an awkward silence. They didn't always know what to talk about now that they no longer had to plan how to fight crime.

Annie's worries about the city and her own future lingered. Would she live out the rest of her life as a saleswoman? Was there something wrong with that, something less heroic or noble? Didn't the city *need* its hero—more importantly, did that hero *have* to be her? Why had she even *started* saving people in the first place?

///////

Twenty-five years earlier, when Annie was known as Charles Waghner, he had started his first newspaper job in Salt City after finishing college. He liked the work, but it didn't feel like enough. "What am I doing here?" he would ask the man in the mirror. "I need to be strong."

During those first years, Charles went to work and returned home at night to dress in his favorite women's clothing, which was soft and silky. He tried to deny his abilities to "go play dress-up," as he called it, but he knew that his nightly wardrobe changes were something that couldn't be ignored. So, he started dressing up in a different costume—the costume of a superhero. The costume of a strong, confident man who could always be counted on when things got tough.

At the time, it was about the crime and discrimination in the city too. He needed to stand up for those that couldn't do it themselves. He believed the world could be a better place if there was some kind of example for people to follow. The cliché, *"with great power comes great responsibility,"* continued taunting Charles until he did something about it. In doing so, he chose the name, Captain Macho.

One morning, he was driving down the mountain after a quiet picnic alone. He could have just flown up there and sat enjoying the view and the cooler air, but that seemed to be misusing his powers. Alone on top of the mountain, he had dared to slip off his bulky sweatshirt and change into a lacy woman's top, letting the breeze caress his bare skin. It had felt both freeing and terrifying, and it seemed like going out where someone could see him dressed like that was a braver act than anything his superhero alter ego did.

Near the tightest curve on the mountain road, he heard the sound of squealing tires and a crash as a bright red Volkswagen van hit the median and bounced back across the road into the guard rail. The van didn't stop. Charles slammed on his brakes and pulled off the road. He worried about the sound of a crying infant coming from the crash. Seeming to forget he could fly, he ran for the damaged guard rail and then began the treacherous climb down to the crumpled van fifty feet below. It looked like a ball of red foil, and a man and woman appeared to have been thrown through the windshield. They weren't breathing. He still heard the sound of a baby, but it was overwhelmed by the sound of approaching sirens. He pulled a door from the wreckage. In a baby seat in the middle of the van, untouched, screamed a baby boy. Two paramedics arrived at the site.

"Are you hurt?" the first medic asked.

"I just came down to help," Charles said. "I think his parents are dead."

"We have to get the two of you up to safety," the other medic said as he tried to help Charles with the baby. Charles didn't want to let him go. He knew he could take care of the baby, but he also knew that he had to act like a brave man in shock and not a superhero. He didn't want the medics finding out about his secret.

The baby screamed as the medics escorted them back to the road. Charles clutched the car seat to his chest. He still could not let the baby go.

"We need to take you to the hospital for a more thorough examination, sir," one of the medics said. Charles' blood ran cold as he remembered the women's top secreted under his sweatshirt.

"We're fine," he insisted.

"It's policy."

"We're fine," he snapped, too roughly. The baby began to cry. "Really. We'll... I'll just take him home. Don't you think he's been through enough?"

The medic looked at the two of them dubiously. Charles could feel his heart banging inside his shirt. He knew he could just fly away if he wanted, use his powers, but the thought of using one secret to conceal another made his head hurt.

From that day forward, he wore a mask. He didn't like the face in the mirror and he wanted things to change. So, if a building was on fire, he would run in. If a tornado appeared, he would fly through the eye of the storm to break it up. The more dangerous the event, the more likely he would risk his life. Meanwhile, he worked to adopt the baby from the car accident. The protective feelings that were directed at the city were even stronger for the orphaned baby boy.

The baby's dead parents had been raised in foster care together and married each other shortly after turning eighteen. Neither of them had any other family. Charles learned all this through his newspaper connections.

"What about—" Charles paused. "Do you know his name?"

"Donavan," the social worker explained. "Investigators found several papers in the van: marriage certificate, past due notices from many sources, and a birth certificate."

Charles considered this information. If Donavan didn't have any other family and the state was just going to put him into foster care, Charles wanted to raise him. Thus began a long process of becoming a foster parent to gain custody of the baby. Donavan was nearly two when Charles finally brought the toddler home as his own. Donavan had learned to walk but he still didn't speak. Sometimes Charles thought it was better that way. If the boy couldn't talk, he couldn't ask Charles questions, and he couldn't tell anyone about all of Captain Macho's masks.

Charles loved to watch twelve-year-old Donavan play baseball. He would sit with the mothers of Donovan's teammates, and sometimes he felt like he had more in common with these women than with their husbands.

As Donavan grew, Charles noticed that Donavan was faster and stronger than most of the children. On several occasions, Donavan would hit the baseball so far that none of the opposing team could even find it. The accuracy that Charles witnessed began to concern him. Donavan exhibited strength and acuity above that of normal kids.

When Donovan was a little older, Charles made the decision to bring him along on his rounds to protect Salt City. Charles felt the need to instill Donavan with the importance of helping others.

"Okay, I need you to listen," Charles explained. "Listen to the city and what it's telling you."

"I hear a siren," Donavan relayed. He could hear loud voices, music blaring from bars and car horns honking. In addition to the sounds, he could smell fires, gasoline and alcohol. "There is so much going on."

"You need to focus."

"I'm trying. There's so much noise, so many people in trouble..."

Then the sound of tires squealing caught his attention. He jumped to his feet. He stood very close to the edge of the building while Captain Macho sat watching the city. "They need help."

Captain Macho grabbed Donavan around his waist and took flight in the direction of the sound. They flew toward the mountains, and Captain Macho realized that they were the same mountains where Donavan's birth parents had died years earlier. He sat Donavan down and then ran toward the out-of-control vehicle. Donavan picked up a stone, threw it in the air, and then hit it with his baseball bat. The stone moved in a straight line toward one of the car's tires and turned it slightly to give Captain Macho more time to stop it.

Two young women sat inside the car—shaking, but uninjured. When the women were safely out of the car, the heroes flew away.

Spending time as a hero made Donavan more confident. He began to date. The girls who interested him were usually tall and blonde. Donovan kept his secret from them, and no matter how much time he spent with them, he always made sure to be home in time to patrol Salt City with Captain Macho.

Charles also changed over those years. Despite having Donovan, despite his necessary and exciting role as Captain Macho, he couldn't get the thoughts of being a woman out of his head. So he started to see a therapist, hoping she could help him make the thoughts stop.

"I don't understand," he explained to the therapist.

"I think you really do," the therapist pushed him.

"I... I want to be a woman," Charles sobbed, pressing his face into his hands. The therapist nodded sympathetically.

"That isn't impossible," she explained. "It's frightening, but you can do it. You just have to be brave."

Charles worked with his therapist every week. After months of therapy, he began to visit with other doctors. The doctors discussed the risks and side effects of starting sex hormones to feminize his body.

Keeping the secret of who he was began to strain his relationship with Donavan. Donavan had moved into a dorm room at Salt City University. While this gave Charles the privacy to transition, it also meant he only saw Donavan when there was an emergency of some sort for Captain Macho.

Eventually he made an excuse to spend some time with his son as parent and child. Charles drove Donavan home after a dinner where neither seemed to want to talk.

"You know I love you..." Charles began to shake with fear.

Donavan answered by taking his father's hand.

"I... I need to tell you something."

Donavan turned his head and furrowed his brow, worried.

Charles took a deep breath before speaking again. "I am a woman... stuck in this body."

Donavan stared at his father. He didn't have words but he squeezed the hand he held.

Donavan struggled with the changes that his father went through as he watched Charles become Annie. Even as Annie developed, she continued to fight crime and save people as Captain Macho.

Donavan thought he knew the difference between male and female. Genitalia defined gender, or so he thought. But university life had opened his view of the world of right and wrong. His experiences hadn't forced him to question this area of life, but after his father's revelation, he began to read about gender and gender identity. The reading only made him ask more questions. As the questions filled his mind, he would wander the campus. All of his senses focused on his own confusion. He didn't smell the aroma of the food coming from the various dining facilities. He didn't notice the colors of the flowers blooming. He even stopped listening for sounds of people in need of his skills.

"Are you okay?" asked a woman dressed in slacks and a loose blouse. She was the type of girl who would have normally caught his eye.

"Yeah."

"You seem distracted. I've seen you sit down here several times but not come in."

Donavan wasn't even sure where he was. He looked around. He sat on a concrete bench outside the "Counseling Center."

"We have people you can talk to... You don't have to be afraid."

"You work here?"

"Yeah." She smiled. "I sit at the front desk."

He hadn't even considered consciously talking to someone himself. He knew his father had someone to talk to, but he felt so very alone.

"I guess... I need help."

After the lunch with Donavan in the café, Annie noticed how much she missed her work as a hero. That nagging feeling about power and responsibility returned. So, she pulled the unused Captain Macho costume from her closet. She ran her fingers over the soft cloth, considering putting it on. But returning to a male persona felt inauthentic. Pulling a sketch pad from her desk, she began to draw a new costume.

Her shape had changed greatly; she was no longer mistaken for a man. The curves of her body transitioned from a "V" shape to an hourglass one, though it hadn't happened overnight. Her old costume didn't fit her anymore, physically or otherwise.

Three months after beginning to study the new uniform, she began to sew it, recycling all of her old costume material. The colors, purple and white, had always been her favorites. The new costume top was cut low enough to show off the cleavage that she had developed. The bottoms hugged her curves. She made a short skirt out of the cape. It clung to her body like a second skin. Finally, she purchased a pair of thigh-high purple boots with a slight heel.

Annie held the phone as Donavan's cell phone rang.

"Hi, Mom."

"Would you stop by tonight?"

"Sure. What's up?"

"Oh, nothing much. I just want to see you."

"Okay, be there in an hour or so."

While she waited for Donavan to arrive, Annie changed into her new costume. She kept only one thing from the old one: the mask. When she was finally dressed, she checked herself out in the mirror. Her red hair hung long over shoulders. The purple and white fabric made her looks soft but the tight fit of it highlighted her new form as well as her strength.

The doorbell snapped her out of her self-examination.

"I'm here." Donavan called out as he entered the small apartment. He noticed that Captain Macho's boots were sitting next to the dining room table. "When did you pull these out?"

"Pull what out?" she asked as she entered from the bathroom.

"The boots—" The words caught in Donavan's throat as he saw his mother's new attire. "Wow Mom! You look fantastic." Annie blushed as her son hugged her.

"Thank you."

"Are you coming out on patrol with me?"

"Yes."

STONES STAND STILL

• *Madison Lynn McEvilly*

Her silhouette was all I could see. Eyes less than a foot away—don't
see well—sensitive to light, new pills in me—her silhouette was
all. My fingers were tense and balled from gripping the edge of
the bed. Sheets covering our toes and nothing else. A Breather.
A Breather is what they call it.

I could feel her fingers. Tracing, grazing. Exploring. Close your
mute eyes and listen, feel. Her fingers' grace and trail slow to
a stop. I can't but she sees fine: long flesh scars form grids and
maps, pointing to pleasure and to absence. She stops.

"Is this okay?"

"They're..."

*Warm evening light, cold water, hydrogen peroxide, dogs barking
outside; no blood on the sheets I know what I'm doing.*

"... Okay."

Tracing again. No sight, only patterns and pictures and history. Lingering at the deep, circular one on my tits. Muscles tightening, new blood flowing, eyes open. We fuck and for a few moments, the scars fall off.

///////

When I was a kid I held my breath at night. I knew some things then. I knew that sleep is this thing where at one moment you are like awake or whatever and the next there is nothing. I knew there were dreams but dreams did not concern me. What concerned me was that moment when awake met asleep. The transformative event where consciousness turns to absence. Logic told me, it told me when you are awake you are alive because alive things move and not alive things don't move. Birds fly but stones, they stand still. So when I am awake I am alive because I move. But sleep was this thing where you are alive but then you don't do anything for seven hours until you have to pee and your brain turns back on.

///////

Grief is a simple thing. At once there is something and then there isn't. At times, this is crushing. At times not. At times the [ ] of another inspires the [   ] of the self. It is like that. It is like crying; crying in a very large room, without amplification.

///////

When I was a kid I learned some things. I learned that some things are alive and alive things die and some things are never alive to begin with. I thought, alive things can die and turn to objects but objects can't go alive all willy-nilly, that seems like kind of a bum deal. If I had my choice I would be an object so I wouldn't have to choose and I could sleep all day. Somebody told me death was like sleeping forever. I thought that seems like kind of a bum deal. What do you do then when your brain doesn't turn back on in the morning so you don't pee the bed? I'd better make sure I go pee first before I die or that would be embarrassing.

//////////

I remember lying in his bed, after what we called sex, when he stared, examined, moved over my entire body. Told me everything he was going to miss. Tracing fingers along my back, tailbone, those rises and dips, cock and asshole and perineum. I'm going to miss this, and this, and this. What is going to happen to this—*gentle bump at the crest of the ilium?* Sadness in his eyes, longing and sadness—*mourning.* My body was no longer a body, It was a piece of What Was. He held my cock in his hand and said this, oh this I am going to miss most and we laughed. But really, do you think you're going to?

//////////

When I was a kid I figured things out on my own. Logic told me, it said when you die it's kind of like sleeping. It said that sleeping is dying only you wake up in the morning so you can go to the bathroom in peace. I practiced sleep as best I could but I could only hold my breath for thirty seconds or so because I wasn't good enough at it yet. Kids get better at things after they become adults, I said, I'd get this down some day.

//////////

This is an act of cartography. What roads or rivers are thoroughfares, who was there or who wasn't. The elevation is telling. These marks, caressed like cherished tapestries, one thread over the other, adorning this body in texture and history, breathing and quiet as stone.

To the uninitiated reader I hand over a Key. This is North. This mark is a town; this one a city. One kilometer is seventeen years.

To read maps is an art. Lost too often, one learns to mark her way back to base with scars and scorches in the living earth. She returns and looks at what's left behind. She remembers. And she picks at the traces to make sure the pathways back home remain mapped in a bold, unapologetic atlas.

When I was a kid I held my breath at night. I knew some things then. I knew that sleep is this thing where at one moment you were awake or whatever and the next there is nothing. I knew there were dreams but dreams did not concern me.

TWO GIRLS
• *Alice Doyle*

Tony was the kind of person that you didn't need to know for very long before you realized that he should be receiving psychiatric attention. Not that it kept Rose from seducing him. It was obvious immediately that Tony knew how to fuck, that he knew everybody with the best drugs, that he could look longingly through dense cigarette smoke. He made it seem unique and vital even though it was the same contrived routine he had used on every other girl.

Rose met Tony in the dark. It was mid-August and the power had been out for a week. She first spied him visiting her neighbors, a gay couple with uncomfortably mismatched ages whose only meaningful communications were their frequent shouting matches. Tony told her that he came from Brooklyn but never why he'd landed in Mississippi or why he'd stayed. Everyone else who had somewhere safe to go had left town before Katrina. His voice was clear but so low, inaudible from across the room even with the entire city quiet around them. She would lean close to him, put her face near his and breathe in. She was only 19, and Tony smelled like soap. He called her *Baja Rosa* after a strawberry liqueur he loved and never tried to give her an orgasm. Rose was charmed by Tony.

The night that they met, he came to her window at four in the morning. Rose was sticky with sweat, her dark hair tucked behind her ears and stuck to her wet shoulders and throat. "*Rosa,*" he said. He had been thinking about her, he said he was *obsessed.* She wrapped her legs around his waist and he kissed her salty chest, told her he might be in love with her. When Rose laughed he pulled away, looked her in the eyes and insisted. She only pet his rough face, pulled him close again, unzipped his jeans. The nights often ended this way.

The last time they saw each other was just a few weeks later. Suddenly the city had power again and everyone was beginning to calculate the damage to the land and to their lives, and Tony told Rose they needed to talk. She'd just come from the beach where she had been collecting lost photos of families she hadn't known. She tried to remember where all the floating casinos had been before being pushed on land or destroyed, mentally organizing the buildings along the shore as she remembered them but not quite able to recognize their stripped frames well enough to identify them all. Tony sat at the top of her long bed, pulled her head to his lap and put his fingers in her salty hair.

"*Rosa,*" he said. He leaned close. "I'm going back to New York next week. Come with me." Rose closed her eyes and turned her face to his belly. "We can stay with my brother."

"What would I do in New York?" Tony's hand moved from her hair to her neck and she opened her eyes, watching his shirt pull and relax as his body moved beneath it. She imagined his face in New York, his clean smell. She tried to picture them together for more than an hour without his hands finding their way up her dress.

"Girls like you can make a lot of money." Tony leaned back. He could start dealing again, he knew a guy. If Rose was hooking it'd be easy.

Her eyes met his and she thought about the stack of sandy family photographs on her kitchen table. In one, a little girl was laid across a coffee-colored couch, her arms stretched above her toward something or someone Rose could not discern, blotted out by the sand and the water and replaced by faint pink swirls.

"I don't know."

He rested a hand on the top of his head.

"Guys love girls like you in New York." Tony was always trying to get Rose to talk to him about her body. He had decided that Rose was different only after her nervous insistence. He never called her a transsexual. He seemed to understand that she was intimidated by the whole complicated business of her body when he noticed that most of his touch elicited only a fearful shake, like an open hand rested forgetfully on the hot surface of the stove. When he fucked her he became unreserved, he begged, but Rose only blushed and pushed his hands away from between her legs. She distracted him, pulled him closer and deeper until he forgot whatever he had wanted. It always worked this way with Tony.

Rose lifted her head from Tony's lap and moved next to him, their backs against the headboard.

"I don't know if I could do that, Tony."

"You could." He put an arm around her and pulled her head back down. Rose remembered the empty beach and the grounded casinos, the girl in the photograph with eager little fingers. "It's easy. You love to fuck." Tony laughed, moved a hand under Rose's head to the front of his jeans and squeezed his dick. Rose sat up, she laughed. She tried to be the fun sort of girl who could pack a bag and move to New York with a man she'd just met. She shoved his shoulder playfully, gave him a coy look that felt unnatural. "It'll be good, *mami*. Just say yes." He put his hands behind his head and leaned back against the headboard. He closed his eyes, his mouth a sneaky smile. "I bought your ticket."

"Tony, you didn't."

"Mississippi's not for you, baby. I want you with me." Rose flushed. She imagined New York's dirty streets and Mississippi's dirty sand, and in her mind the stripped casinos began to click into place along the shore. *La Belle Eau* belonged near the pier. Down the street the unrecognizable shell of the Golden Swan had lit up an adult bookstore that was completely washed away by the water.

"I kinda like it here. I don't know if I'm ready for New York."

"You'll like it better there. They'll love you, *Rosa*. You can make so much money."

Rose moved to face him. "Have you seen the beach yet? Everything's been pushed around. It's crazy." Tony shrugged. Rose excused herself for water or soda or aspirin or anything that wasn't in her bedroom with Tony.

In the kitchen she held the photograph of the little girl up to the light. The girl's thin arm was an arrow, a pale mark that led to another pale mark, larger and populated only by the bent pink lines. She brought it close and moved it away again, she sat it back down on the countertop to study it from above. There was something in the swirls that she could still detect. Maybe a tall body, leaning.

"*Baja Rosa*, come back."

The tall body was a woman, she could see it now. She was bent at the waist, her face near the little girl's hands. Her expression was bleached by the sun and the water and scrubbed away by the sand, but Rose could finally see the edges of her body, the pink outline of her long wavy hair hanging loose like the girl's. Maybe it was her mother or her sister, a best friend. Maybe the little girl was an adult now and afraid. Tony was hard and Rose could hear the soft noise of his urgency moving closer from the bedroom. She studied the blank face in the photograph, searched for anything. She imagined the girl somewhere across town still reaching out and not knowing what for. Rose waited for Tony.

RUNAWAYS

· *Calvin Gimpelevich*

Travis woke to the *Star Wars* theme beeping off his cell phone. "Nike" flashed across the screen, right under the clock telling him to sleep for another hour. He rolled away and put a pillow over his head. The ringing stopped, letting sleep tug his mind back under, before she called again. And again.

"What?" he croaked.

"Hey hey, sleepy head. Time to get up."

"What do you want?"

"I need help with something. Meet me at the tracks."

He groaned. "I have work in, like, three hours, and I'm not leaving my bed."

"Come oooon," she whined. "I'll pay you with beer. It might be gone if we wait."

"Fine."

He hung up and thought about ditching. He let himself lie back for a full minute staring at the ceiling before forcing himself up and into the morning routine. Breakfast, energy drink, brushing teeth. He couldn't find his binder and had to dig through the piles of dirty laundry covering his floor, sniff-testing for a decent one. He pulled the tight compression shirt over the deflated breasts still hanging off his bulky frame. A trickle of chest hair ran through the cleft separating them. T-shirt, jeans. Fully dressed he could face the mirror and his morning debate over whether or not to shave the new beard. The hairs coming in looked like trimmed pubes. He kept it anyway.

He found his back tire flat (again) and pumped it up before rolling out and biking to the train tracks by Nike's house. Her car—a beat down white pick-up more rusted than not—perched half on the street and half on the rocks holding the tracks in place. Broken glass and flowers pushed up through the iron bars and wooden slats beneath her wheels. Nike sat in the truck bed, legs hanging off the depressed shelf and a cigarette between her lips.

He kicked the wheel.

"Hey! Watch the rims," she said. "This is a classy ride." Her Filipino accent clipped words down to the bone so they shot into sentences, machine gun style, before Travis could form a thought.

"What's so important you had to drag me out of bed for it, huh?"

"Awww. You don't want to see me? Too important to spend time with your friends?"

"That's right. I'm a busy man. Got money to earn, places to be." He pinched his t-shirt as though straightening suit lapels. The PBR logo warped as he pulled the fabric out.

"Pshh." She blew a cloud of smoke in his face. "Traitor."

"Fine. If you don't want help I'll be on my way."

"That's right," she said. "I don't need you."

He picked up his bike as though going to leave, then turned around and grabbed her legs.

"Ahhhh! No." She tried kicking away but he pulled her further. "I'll scream," she laughed.

He wrapped one arm around both her skinny legs, pinning them together, and scooped under her arms to support her back. In a moment she was airborne, cradled like a baby. In the next he had her hanging upside down from the ankles, hair brushing gravel.

"You win! You win!" Five foot three and a hundred pounds soaking wet, Nike looked, with her dyke-chic faux hawk and permanent grin, like a twelve year old boy. "I'll *let* you see what I found."

"Why thank you," he said, letting her down. "I'm so grateful you would lower yourself to show me whatever you fucking woke me up to see."

"Check it out." She ran ahead, pointing to a filthy hunk of metal balanced across the tarnished rails.

"It's junk." People left crap on the tracks all the time, anything they didn't want to pay the dump for or bother selling. He'd seen people camped out, drinking beer, waiting to see the incoming trains plow through and wreck shit.

"I need your big he-man muscles to carry it back."

He rolled his eyes. Everyone thought he was a macho man. "Because you're opening a junk shop?"

"Dude, it's a shell! A camper shell to put over the bed. They're, like, a thousand dollars. Or maybe even more!"

Ten minutes rubbing spit-soaked rags over the lump proved Nike right. The windows had been so covered in grime that he hadn't seen them. The back one had a round jagged hole, where broken pieces of glass still crumbled down.

"I already measured it," she said. "Totally the right size and everything."

Travis took one end and Nike grabbed the other. Crap rained down as they hauled it up, step by awkward step, over to the truck. Travis held the back aloft while Nike clambered up and guided the thing into place. She tightened it on with some old C-clamps and pushed the top back and forth to test stability. It wobbled.

"Beautiful!"

"Uh huh." Travis wiped his hands on his jeans. They left behind dark streaks of grime. "Work is gonna love this." He was assistant manager at a Starbucks downtown, where customers expect their baristas to be fast, clean, and happy happy happy.

"All you do is work," she pouted. "Bor-ring." Nike wrote code for a living at home. Flexible hours, flexible everything.

"Gotta save up for that surgery. Three more payments 'til my very own set of boob-free man-pecs."

And to quiet the voice his parents left him, where regular work is good and more work is better. *It means you're responsible, not a threat. Proving you can be a productive member of society, no matter what people think when you walk past them at night.*

"Very cool." Nike fist bumped him. "But what are you going to do afterwards?"

"Run topless on the beach. Pick up all the fine ladies. Slather on my scar cream."

"But with your life. What are you going to do with your life when you aren't saving up for anything?"

He knew this line. She'd been using it since high school, inspired by the hitch-hiking crust punks rolling through town. That's where they met, in school, Travis attached at the hip to Alice Walker, Octavia E. Butler, Toni Morrison, and bell hooks. He was in love with black feminism, and Nike wanted an excuse to blow the system, any system, up. They ditched class and planned demonstrations that never happened. When Travis moved north, Nike followed, ready to take Oregon by storm. But they got older and plans tapered out. Now he just wanted to settle into society, breast-less and conflict-free. Nike still wanted explosions.

"I don't know." He sat on the ground, back resting against a tire.

"I'll tell you what you're gonna do." Nike hopped down next to him. "We're going on a road trip."

He snorted.

"I have a shell now. We can sleep in the truck and fill the cab with food and go fucking anywhere we want. We could go to Texas and be in the rodeo. We could move to Portland or Canada or anywhere. We'll meet girls and smoke blunts, forget about work for a while."

"Yeah, what about your girlfriend?" he asked. "Is she gonna fit in the trunk?"

"Forget about her."

He whistled. "Like she'd let us forget about her."

"Don't worry about that. You worry too much."

They sat in silence for a moment, watching nothing go by. She scratched a little hole in the gravel, worrying it with her shoe.

"She's still tripping over her sister, huh?"

Nike shrugged. She picked one of the larger pebbles up and threw it at the fence, as hard as she could.

Nike and Maya: always fighting. Maya wanted Nike to get a better paying job, keep normal hours, be an adult. Nike missed being able to grab her girl and skip everything for a couple weeks to go camping and get blackout drunk. The more responsible Maya got, the more Nike turned into a sulking kid. Something had to give, and Travis thought it might be their relationship.

He dug into his pocket and looked at the cell phone display. "Fuck. I'm running late."

"I'll give you a ride," she said.

They wrestled Travis's bike inside the closed-up bed. They had to lay it sideways now. They shut the awkward hinged doors.

"You want us to sleep in that?"

"After I clean it up, Mr. Prissy. I'll wash it later."

"For our road trip?"

"For *the* trip to end all road trips. No girlfriends allowed."

"Well, shit." Travis scratched his head. "What am I gonna tell the five I've got hidden at home?"

"You tell them who's boss!" she shouted, pounding the wheel.

They drove to Starbucks and parked in a neighboring lot. Two men spotted Travis getting out of the car. Baseball caps, athletic shorts, crisp white socks pulled up to their calves, both thick with football muscles. They were the jocks from his high school nightmares, ready to haul him into dumpsters for being a queer.

"Hey faggot," one of them shouted. "Where you goin' with that kid? Off to show him your junk?" Crotch grab. "Fuckin' pervert."

Nike slammed her door shut and started towards them. Travis pulled her back. "Don't worry about it."

"Fuck that," she said. She flipped the guy off. "I will drown you in my pussy juice!"

They laughed and walked away.

"I'm gonna run them over," Nike fumed. "Assholes."

"Fuck 'em." He rolled his bike to a parking meter and hooked his lock through the frame. "I don't want any trouble."

"You can't put up with that."

"Don't have much choice," he said. "Thanks for the ride. I'll see you tonight."

He walked into work five minutes late, poured himself a cup of coffee, and tried to forget about those guys. Prayed none of them came to work that day. Last time they did, he had almost gotten fired. The same clique had camped in front of the register shouting "pedo" and "rapist" at him while he tried to ignore them and unclog the espresso machine. The manager threw them out, but he started watching Travis sideways. Another scene like that would finish him.

His heart pounded away, making him feel sick. The coffee shook in his hands. He wanted to puke. Or hide. Instead he tied the apron around his waist. Nike wanted him to fight back, but she didn't offer how.

He *was* a wuss. A pansy. A little black nerd. If he agreed that they were right, maybe they would just go away.

It had started weeks and weeks ago, when a girl accused him of exposing himself to her at the bar. Or maybe the trouble started when she didn't accuse him outright, but when she sent her posse of friends to throw him out instead. The trouble of staring down (up) six huge men, still in uniform from the evening's game, and wondering how to explain the beautiful irony of his not having a dick to flash.

Travis, Nike, and Maya were taking the night off—Travis from work, Nike from programming, and Maya from the sister who'd just moved in. They hit their local dive. Big, old TV's broadcasted the latest football scores, overlooking worn green felt and pool balls crashing into each other. Travis had to piss and that meant walking through the unlit yard filled with secret little corners for people to do their secret little business. Gropers and coke heads weren't uncommon.

He had passed the girl on his way back. Didn't touch her. But maybe someone else had? Grabbed her arm and put her hand on his naked cock the way she claimed? Or maybe she was psychotic and tripping back to some childhood trauma long buried in her brain? Or maybe she was a drunk bitch vying for attention, as Travis tried not to think, with all her friends staring him down, calling him a pervert, making it really hard to hold onto his sisterhood-is-powerful feminist ideals.

He hadn't known how to respond. It was like a Kafka comedy: no exit, no guilt. Should he flash them and risk the reaction? Call *her* a liar? As though her friends would take his word over hers? Both options were bad. He'd used a fake ID to get into the bar—at age twenty-five—because he was *that* paranoid about people knowing his given name. The gamble was in which tidbit the small-town gossip would blow through faster. He decided to keep his pants on.

Nike and Maya stood up for him, but it didn't help. And he couldn't help thinking that no one had ever accused Nike of something like that. It's the kind of thing that, drunk, she'd actually do. But no one would cause a fuss. He wondered if it was their skin, if black was scarier than Asian, but that didn't explain it all. He'd never gotten that kind of shit before hormone therapy. Butch dykes weren't a threat. An abomination, sure, bad example or ideology, but nothing to make people check their wallets at night.

The worst part was being able to relate. All those years working at the rape crisis center hardened his feelings towards men. He remembered the fear and tried to wrap that memory around this new idea of himself as a threat. They didn't mesh well. He didn't *feel* like the oppressor. Statistics hung in his mind: the seventy percent of queer murder victims who were people of color, the quadrupled poverty rates, the stories of police violence, the doctors refusing care. It all mashed into a big knot inside his chest, contracting around his heart and giving him panic attacks.

If he had actually flashed her, those guys would have kicked his ass. But the truth could have gotten him killed. Neither seemed good, so instead he ran away.

Orange sky met him after work. It was navy by the time he'd biked, shivering, back to the tracks and found the familiar house. Nike answered her door.

"You owe me beer."

"We don't have any. Go away." The door slammed shut. He pounded on it again. "What?"

"Liar." Travis forced himself past her and into the living room. Maya and her sister sat on the couch watching cartoons. The room was lit by TV glow, a modern bonfire for a sheet rock cave.

"Hey Travis," Maya waved. "You wanna grab me a drink too?"

Nike threw her hands up. "Now we'll never get rid of him. He just comes and drinks and drinks and makes eyes at my woman, pees in the sink—"

"Shhhh!" Cassie put a finger over her lips. "I'm watching."

"Sorry," Nike whispered and motioned Travis into the kitchen.

"How 'bout we shut the TV off after this episode?" Maya asked in the background. "You've been watching all day."

"But it's a marathoooon."

"Last episode. Got it?" Maya said with the kind of last-word steel you'd expect from a cop. Or a social worker. She had her eyes on CPS: pulling messed up kids from their houses and fielding calls from worried neighbors, teachers, whoever, getting the details of other people's shit shows.

Travis grabbed a six pack from the fridge and slouched into the couch for the last five minutes of cartoon madness. Nike perched on the armrest, opening bottles with her lighter. Cassie collected the caps and stacked them into a crooked tower on her knee.

"Can I try some?" Cassie asked, pointing to her sister's beer.

"No."

"Just a sip?"

"No."

"Why not?"

"Because I said so."

"Well, can I smell it?"

"Fine," Maya cracked. "But one sniff, that's all."

She held the bottle under her nose like a wine connoisseur and took a big whiff before giving it back. She picked up abandoned caps from the table and smelled them too, to compare.

"Is this a good beer?"

"Cassie, enough with the questions. You're not allowed to drink."

"Not even water?"

Maya shook her head, exasperated. Travis looked to Nike, who slit her finger across her throat.

"Come on."

She pulled him into the bathroom. The door was lighter than he expected and he accidentally slammed it. Living room conversation floated in unencumbered, Maya getting frustrated, then giving in and putting the cartoons back on. Travis closed the cheap toilet lid and sat down. It popped in under his weight. Nike rooted around in the cupboard under the sink. She pulled a bong from behind the pipes and chemicals and set it on the floor. A little more exploring found a prescription vial of weed. She unscrewed the child-proof lock and packed a bowl.

"I need a fucking break," she whispered.

"I know."

She lit the fresh greens and sucked an expert hit of smoke through the long glass neck. Her shoulders dropped on the exhale.

"Do I look mature enough for this shit?"

He laughed. "'Bout mature enough for seventh grade."

"Fuck you." She flipped him off with both hands. "I'm Asian."

"Just sayin'. I think even Cass looks older than you."

Nike snorted. "Probably."

Barely ten and it was already clear that she would hit puberty hard. There were hints in her eyes and the start of her curves and questions about everything teenagers hide from their parents. He could picture Cassie running after older boys with cars of their own, her big sister trying to warn her off. Torn between telling Cassie every dumb thing she had done in high school—all her regrets—and keeping secrets so as not to put ideas in the little one's head.

Maya *was* a bad girl, the kind Nike adored, playing fast and loose with drama. She had since reformed, and now she walked around with the tired grounded eyes that sex and social workers have. Nike's last girlfriend had left her credit score wrecked, fucked all of her friends, and left a burning case of the clap behind. She and Travis did the Planned Parenthood treatments together—Nike choosing to believe Travis's story where he waited until after they broke up to sleep with her ex. Responsible Maya seemed a godsend after that. The bills were paid on time, the fridge was stocked and the details were handled.

"What are you gonna do?" Travis asked.

She shrugged and took one more hit before passing the bong. Dilated pupils made for big black eyes, like a demon boy.

Travis helped, when he could, walking Cassie to school when Maya worked early shifts. It swelled his ego, being everything a man should be: protective and gallant and strong, scaring the bad guys away. Faking for both of them that nobody could fuck with him. But he couldn't do it full time. The aftertaste of being macho stripped too much protection away, and he feared the athletes walking in, humiliating him in front of the kid.

Cassie was getting ready for bed when they got out. She fought every step, wanting to stay up and talk. But tomorrow was a school day and Maya wasn't having it. She feared Cassie missing class, looking underfed, too tired, anything that might make a teacher take notice. She didn't have real custody; she was only holding onto Cassie until their dad got out of jail. Maya had too many arrests of her own, and if anyone realized Cassie was living without parents she might get sent across the country to live with a mother she never met. The stress made Maya rigid. She tried too hard to become the kind of structured parent neither of them ever had.

She was outside with a cigarette lit the moment Cassie dragged her feet into bed. Travis and Nike followed. The fog from their breath blended with smoke.

"How much longer?" Travis asked.

"We're going to court on Monday. He might get probation."

"What if he doesn't?"

Maya didn't answer.

"Hey, that's a good question," Nike said. "What happens if your dad stays in jail?"

"Then she stays here."

"Oh yeah? She just lives with us for, what, the next two or three years or whatever the going rate for possession is?" Her voice rose. "That sounds like a great idea."

"Nike—"

"No, really, we're totally set up to raise a teenager. What could possibly go wrong? I mean, fuck, let's just hold on 'til she turns eighteen—"

"God damn it." Maya slammed her drink down. "What do you want me to do? You want me to call her mom? The one who flew back to Chicago the minute Cassie popped out? Or how about a group home? That sounds like a great place to grow up. Just have another adult walk out of her life? Is that what you want?"

"I didn't sign up to be a parent."

"Neither did I!" She struggled to keep her volume down. "But I could use some fucking support from my girlfriend. Is that too much to ask?"

"Hey," Travis said. "Look." He pointed to the window where Cassie stood, wide-eyed and listening, in her pink Barbie pajamas.

"Fuck," Maya whispered. "We'll talk later," she shot at Nike before storming back inside. They heard her trying to calm Cassie down, to avoid questions she couldn't answer and get the kid back into bed.

"Let's get out of here," Nike said. "I wanna go on a drive."

She must have spent all day cleaning, because the whole truck shone more than Travis had ever seen. Even the shell looked good. She'd duct taped over the hole, a giant silver triangle on the back window. They got in the cab and she blasted music for the first half hour, chain smoking while they didn't talk.

"It isn't her fault," he finally said.

"Does that matter? Cass is going to be a crazy teenager."

Travis agreed. It was strange, the girl entering her first puberty and him exiting his second. He knew it would be hard for her, that it might swallow her whole. The real tragedy, he thought, is the ones who never make it out. Because deep inside no one thinks they'll survive—no one thinks that being a teenager will ever really end. Until one day they wake up and know they're out of it. That they don't have to put up with the abuse, or unrequited love, or hormones, or feeling like a loser anymore. Except for the ones who don't escape. The ones who overdose or run away too soon or manage some other permanent damage in the midst of it all.

He knew Cassie might not make it. The thought felt empty. He wished he could share his adult perspective, tell her that it ends and no one feels awkward and hurt forever. But she wouldn't listen. No one does. And she'd come out as fucked up as anyone else. He wasn't concerned with protecting her from that; everyone got traumatized, everyone had to heal. Wasn't that what made them human? She wouldn't be different just because he wanted it. Just because Maya tried so hard to be the shield.

Nike pulled off the road. They were next to a field, probably corn. Stars dusted the sky. She keyed off the engine and everything went still.

"Should I stay?" she asked.

"I wish I could tell you." He knew she hated big decisions. She'd consult her horoscope, her therapist, parents, friends, anything but tackle it alone. His little Peter Pan. "Are you happy there?"

"Not anymore."

"But you love her?"

She paused. "Yeah."

"Then I don't know." Travis liked Maya. She was tough but that wasn't all. There were fun parts, funny parts. She partied hard, took the reigns, confident everyone else would follow. And when she listened, all of her was there, taking it in. He used to be jealous. It seemed like she and Nike had something good.

"How could I leave her? Over her being a *saint*? I'd be a dick."

"Probably."

"Maybe I *am* a dick."

Travis thought he might be a dick too. If he wasn't trans he'd be the kind of guy everyone in town seemed to see in him. And if everyone saw it, it might be true. Maybe he was the kind of creeper forcing himself on drunk girls, then running from their friends. Or maybe not. He'd never know.

"Maya's too good for us," he said.

"She's too good for herself." Nike rolled down the window to spit. "We should run away. I'm sick of this town. I wanna go to Texas and wear a big hat."

Travis shook his head.

"Aw, come on. Why not? What the fuck do you have here? A crap job? People hating you? We could do better."

"I hear it's the same all over," he said.

"Bullshit."

"Dude, I'm just sick of giving up. All we *ever* do is run away. I'm sick of it." Nike slumped down further in her seat. "I mean, fuck, look at your girl. She's stepping up and handling shit. I work and hide and work. She's raising a *kid*."

"Yeah, well, I never asked to be a parent."

"I didn't ask to be scrawny and trans and surrounded by racist motherfuckers. You deal with what you've got."

"Easier for you to say," Nike spat back. "You're not living with them."

"You're right. I'm not."

From his seat, the sky looked so far away. He opened the door and stepped onto the field. It was cold and windy, and he realized he was standing in the sky with the stars instead of apart from them. He looked back at his friend.

"But I'm moving in. You've got room, you need the extra cash, and I can help with Cass." Saying it aloud calmed his nerves. His ball of tension started to give. The ground was muddy and his shoes sunk in. He could be part of the world instead of hiding from it.

"Time to grow up," he said.

TO DO LIST FOR MORNING
· *Stephen Ira*

1. BREAKFAST

Tell him you'll wake up properly once you've had coffee. Go downstairs. Move the carton of beans to the side of the kitchen cabinet; move the carton of nondairy creamer to the other. Reach for the teapot and run water from the filtered water faucet. Set the pot on the stove. Settle down at the small child's table that your father never gave away once you got big. Bite your lips. Realize you're bleeding; have a Nicorette.

Don't buzz him on your intercom to ask whether or not you can swallow Nicorette without adverse side effects—he won't know. When you're angry that he's ignorant, even though it's not important, do not swallow the gum anyway. It won't kill you, but you'll be nauseous.

Wait for the kettle to boil. Take it off the stove and pour the hot water into the mugs over the PG Tips tea bags. Now buzz him. Tell him the tea is nearly ready and just needs to brew. When he only answers drowsily, go back upstairs.

Stand in the bedroom door in your plaid boxers and your oversized t-shirt with the smiley pistachio on it. Your bed is only a mattress on the floor; you got rid of the frame when you were fifteen. Watch as he turns on your bed without waking. Watch the muscles in his back. Sit in the chair at your desk; roll over to him and nudge him with your knee. When he turns over, lean down, kiss his forehead and say, "We've still got time."

"I know we do," he'll say. Drag your fingers through his hair, which is matted, and tell him to brush it. Tell him you'll do it if he doesn't want to. Tell him you want to do it. Tell him the tea is ready, the shower is broken, the sausage is going bad because nobody eats it when he's not around to fry some, tell him anything that will make him come downstairs with you and have breakfast so that you can be two human beings in the world together.

Don't use the brush that snags his hair. You know which one it is. Use the one with the soft bristles that your mom used on you when you were more of a child than you are now. But you're still a child. You're a child with another child in your bed. You're a child with tea brewing downstairs. You're a child offering to brush another child's hair, cupping his chin in your hand, rubbing sleep from your eyes while you're watching him shift in the sheets like they're heavy and wet.

Ask: "You're not angry, are you?"

Ask: "You want to borrow my old pajamas to wear for breakfast?"

Ask: "You mad?"

The only reason he isn't answering is because he is mostly still asleep. Don't get all worked up over it. Later he'll tell you that he isn't angry, just tired. "You're exhausting," he will say. It will mean "you are beautiful," or "you are kind." Or you can *make* it mean that. You're the smart one here. You can make his words mean anything you want them to.

He'll emerge from your bed with the sheets falling off like a cape, as always twice as broad as you are. Rest against him for a minute. You deserve it.

Then hurry downstairs. You're young and he's young and time isn't on your side.

"This is PG Tips," he'll say with pleased surprise, but after a moment he'll add that it's bitter. He'll pull an acrobatic frown, cheeks turning down, eyes huge and sad. He's right, it's bitter. You like your tea bitter. Stand up to him about this. Do not tell him he is right. Do not tell him that you are sorry. Do not offer him Splenda, because he will laugh in your face. Laugh in his face instead. You like your tea bitter. There's no reason to be ashamed.

Offer him milk, cream, a saucer. Wrap your arms around his waist from behind while he squints into the cereal cabinet, deciding what he'll have. Watch the decision being made. Try to read into it some sort of depth. Try to believe you want him here because of what he unwittingly demonstrates when he says he can't choose between Rice Krispies and Cheerios. What he's showing you must be weltschmerz: *the knowledge that physical reality can never satisfy the demands of the mind.* Believe this.

Kiss the back of his neck. Maybe one day he will learn that it means you want him to kiss the back of yours. Toy with the hair on his face, which is too soft and wispy for stubble.

He'll sit on the child's chair with his cereal. You'll smear cream cheese on a bagel and sit on the table itself. You'll lean your legs on his knees and you'll send smiles through his face until he smiles back. You'll get cream cheese on your nose.

"Wanna lick it off?" you'll say, and he'll laugh and you won't have meant it as a joke, or not entirely, but you'll laugh along anyway.

He will fry the sausages, and as he does he will take one hand and touch the lobe of bone behind your ear. He'll pet the soft hair there with his thick fingers. Two of them are enough to cover the space between your neck and your ear, where your brain swims. If he touches your hair then it means something. And so you stay.

2. ACROBATICS

Just because you can climb onto the countertop and wrap your legs around his torso doesn't mean you should or that he wants you to.

So don't.

Put on the playlist you composed for him and let him talk to you about the girl. Like college and publishing, social justice and personal equilibrium, she's far away from both of you. Minnesota.

You will climb onto the countertop and wrap your legs around his torso as he's talking about the girl, who he says is unique, who he says he will never find somebody like. You will wonder why he sees no contradiction between the girl's existence and yours.

You will tell him she sounds wonderful, that you'd like to be friends with her but it might be awkward. A poem about her breaks off inside your head, the part of it he petted with two fingers as he fried the sausages.

Every time he says something absurd, you'll tell him with a laugh, "Well this is why we're friends."

He'll say: "There's this girl on the news who doesn't age. She's sixteen. She still looks like a toddler. Nobody knows why."

He'll say: "Not enough people have adventures anymore."

Tell him poems are like adventures and he'll tell you they aren't. Say maybe stories are. He'll tell you they aren't. He'll ask what you need to write a story. You don't need guns or rope or tents, his smile will seem to add. You don't need companions for the road. You don't need the equipment of adventure.

"Well," you'll say, and you'll bite a strip of skin off of your upper lip. "You need to know when and where you are. And what everybody in the story wants."

"If anybody knew what anybody wanted," he'll say, "we wouldn't have enough problems to make up stories."

"*You* need to know," you'll tell him. "The writer does. Not the people in it."

"Oh." And this will satisfy him.

Don't come back to the subject later. Let the marble kitchen take you in its shell. Relax against the curved sides. Pretend it's an egg. Pretend you're with him in some way that matters. Inside an egg, inside a story, inside your own house and not your parents' with his father coming.

You must watch him without letting him know you're watching. A little watching is all right; a little watching at the proper times. During the night, when you're not supposed to be doing the things that ordinary people do, things like eating breakfast, reading the paper, turning on the playlist that you made for your best friend.

Wrapping your legs around his torso is not as revolutionary an act as watching him shuffle across the room to the toaster. Nobody rubs against somebody else in that act, or if they do, it is without a goal. Watching requires less acrobatics than sitting above him, your hands in his hair, kissing his forehead with your legs wrapped around his torso.

Someone's going to have to decide what you are, and what that makes him when he dips his mouth down onto the nameless pink between your legs.

3. Repairing

Your speakers will be broken. You knew this before you suggested putting on the music he likes. He will hunker down before them and frown. "It's the flicky thing on the back of it," he'll say.

"This is why we're friends," you'll answer.

"Goddammit," he'll say, but not at you.

Say: "Like I said, why we're friends."

Do not try to fix the speakers yourselves. Do not call him a busybody. For god's sake do not touch him while he tries to work. Watch the telephone. It will buzz when his father pulls into the driveway. When his father does not, do not touch the lobe of bone behind his ear. When his father does, do not touch the lobe of bone behind his ear.

When his father finally walks to the door, open it. Smile, say hello cheerfully, calling out before you even get to the door. You don't know why his father doesn't ask you for an explanation. Don't worry where I am—I still don't. It's all right. I have dinner with them every so often. It isn't awkward, but it used to be. I used to focus on the saltshaker as though I were wondering whether to steal it or not, but I've since learned to meet eyes with eyes.

When he walks to the door with his shoes in his hand, laugh at him. Toy with the laces of the left one. Say something about the show at the Hollywood Bowl that you will know that his father attended last night. Say something about his father's girlfriend.

Say: "We all need girls like that!"

Say: "And the fireworks—god!"

Say: "We watched a bunch of *Seinfeld*, it was great."

Let him go without touching. Tell him you'll see him soon and he'll agree to it. "Why wouldn't he?" I say now, but I'm bitter and you aren't. Just your tea.

Stand in the doorway with the wind on your legs because you're still wearing your boxers. Listen to the shuffle of his feet as he leaves. He'll still be wearing your pajamas. He'll promise to return them at school, but he'll always forget. He'll never give them back. Don't call out again. Don't go back inside to write about it, just stand there and love him.

WINNING THE TIGER

• *Katherine Scott Nelson*

Thandie parked the car beneath the temporary floodlights, on the stomped-down and dying grass that covered the parking lot. Mile-high clouds waited behind the candy-colored tents and Ferris wheel. Ze tied the silver laces of hir knee-high boots and readjusted the hot pink striped leggings underneath hir white dress. The afternoon air smelled ripe for thunderstorms: hot, sultry, and still. We almost swam through it as we strolled down the fairway, arm in arm. Sweat formed on the back of my neck, under my black t-shirt, and ran between my breasts and soaked my binder.

I leaned into Thandie's shoulder, resting my cheek against hir wiry muscle. The sun glinted off the flecks of glitter that had fallen from hir eyelids and scattered across hir bare skin. I kept scanning the crowd—for downturned mouths, or beer-flushed faces, for anyone we might have to protect ourselves from. I wrapped my arm around Thandie's waist, and squeezed hir close.

We hit the food tents and loaded ourselves up with buttered ears of roasted corn, funnel cakes, cheese fries, and handmade strawberry ice cream with frozen heart-shaped slices buried inside. The woman at the ice cream booth took Thandie's order, and without looking too closely at me, asked "And for him?"

"It's *hir*," Thandie said as ze passed over a few bills. Danger swirled all around me. I squeezed Thandie's hand. Ze ignored me.

"Do I hear what?" the woman asked.

"Hir. Ze and hir. We're non-binary transgender people," Thandie instructed firmly.

The woman looked us both over. "Oh." She handed us two dripping ice cream cones. "Have a nice day, ma'am."

"It's *not—*" Thandie growled, but I tugged on hir arm and ze allowed me to lead hir away. We ate our ice cream cones next to the bandstand, catching the pink drips that ran between our fingers, and swallowing our bitterness with strawberries.

"You used a word I've never *heard* before!" Thandie fumed, imitating the woman's accent. "So I'm just going to call you whatever I want and tell myself I'm being nice!"

I thought of our date at the art museum, where we'd strolled through white hallways gazing at an unflinching parade of men and women, neatly defined male and female images, stretching back through eternity. "There isn't a place for us," I said.

"Because we're living under a five-thousand-year politicide." Thandie crunched on the rim of hir ice cream cone. "If people like us existed, it'd destroy the false biological basis on which patriarchy and male domination are founded."

I leaned my head against hir shoulder. "Come on Thandie, let's go in the arts and crafts tent. I'm roasting."

Beneath the hum of industrial fans, we wandered up and down rows of obscenely thick zucchini and pies sporting blue and red ribbons, admired intricate grandmotherly crochet patterns, and proclaimed that we could produce better paintings than that pedestrian suburban oil landscape with the ribbon mysteriously pinned to its frame. At one booth, Thandie plunked a black Stetson hat over my ears and nose. "It needs an ostrich feather," ze proclaimed. "Or two. Right there." Ze tapped the brim. The old gentleman selling the hats chuckled but kept a safe and cool distance from us.

As Thandie petted the tie-dyed scarves and rang all the handmade wind chimes, I watched people leading clusters of kids with Kool-Aid-dyed mouths, slender teenagers in damp shirts loping along the edges of the booths, and old folks lagging behind, secure at the ends of their predestined lives. We strolled past an old woman, fanning herself in a rocking chair, her legs bound in support hose. She gazed up at us, and her eyes were cloudy and supernaturally blue.

After that we hung around the animal sheds, where thick smells of must and shit floated around us. Goats climbed the bars of their stalls to stare at us and demand *whaaaat*. We petted their bony heads, their knobby horns, and echoed "What?" Prizewinning hogs lay in happy ruts of hay like half-deflated blimps, oblivious to us as we called them. The only other person in the barn was a man leaning over a gate at one end of a long aisle, fanning himself with a newspaper.

At one stall a row of tiny pink piglets ran to our feet, and Thandie squealed and reached through the chicken wire to stroke them.

"Yes!" ze cried. "Who is the cutest bacon ever? You are! Yes, you are!"

The man at the end of the aisle scowled at hir and spat on the ground. He shook his head as he turned away and stalked off behind the horse trailers. A hot rush of protective fury flashed inside me. I shook inside my tiny body, with my girl fists balled at my side.

"Oh, look at this!" Thandie hissed, gesturing for me to come kneel next to hir. One of the piglets had extended a tiny pink tongue and tasted the tip of hir finger. "Nice piggy," ze cooed. I offered the piglet the tip of my finger, and it coiled its soft lips around it and scraped my fingernail with its baby teeth. Thandie's hand brushed mine as ze caressed the piglet behind its ears. I held hir hand in mine.

We stayed in the animal sheds for a long time, meeting cows and having one-sided conversations with horses. By the time the long slats of light disappeared, and we grew hungry again, we were flush with childlike happiness. I thought about inviting Thandie to ride the Ferris wheel. I pictured the two of us clinging to each other as the lights and music rushed past, as we circled the earth in an infinite loop: rising and falling, falling and rising.

But outside, the wind had picked up, and the temperature had dropped. Dark clouds stormed low over the tents and flags, and people wrapped sweatshirts and raincoats around them as they hustled away. The wind whipped my loose shirt around my body, and my fingertips began to turn cold. To stay out of the wind, Thandie and I kept to the rows of carnival games lining the fairway.

"Let's win a ridiculous stuffed animal," Thandie said. "Like a bunny the size of a Saint Bernard."

But both of us were running low on cash, and most of the pink bunnies in top hats and nine-foot boa constrictors asked us to risk twenty bucks or more. We rejected the claw machine for its inherent unfairness. We also passed on the home-run simulation, as I brushed away memories of swinging away at softballs in my gym track suit while everyone else moved gracefully in buoyant and compliant bodies. The plastic ducks that shivered in a kiddie pool, bearing unknowable numbers on their bellies, were also too unfair—we knew never to rely on the luck of the draw. At the end of the fairway, we passed a shooting gallery with a ceiling full of realistic stuffed animals. Baby harp seals floated next to ostriches and chimpanzees. A tiger the size of a big dog bounced on the end of its hanger.

"Oh, tiger!" I cried.

The proprietor leaned over the counter and yelled to one of us, "How about it, sir? Win your girlfriend a tiger?"

Thandie turned to me, and smiled with more glee than I'd ever seen. Ze strutted up to the booth, slammed one hand on the worn wooden counter, and rooted through hir purse for a five. "Yeah, I'll win my partner a tiger. Hand it over."

He passed hir the pump-action shotgun and said "All right! Go for it!" but I thought I could hear fear in his voice underneath all that volume. He had been sweating, and he squeezed his hairy arms against his belly to disguise the half-moons of sweat under his armpits.

Thandie draped hir body across the counter, squeezing the butt of the shotgun against hir shoulder and rooting hir boot-heels to the dirt. "Haven't shot a gun in years," ze murmured as ze sighted along the barrel. Hir eyes shot to the proprietor. "Not since I was a kid. My daddy used to take me out to the woods, and he'd tell me, son, if you want to be a man in this world," ze trailed off.

He took another step back from hir.

"Like riding a bicycle, they say." Ze licked hir lips. The first drops of rain began to patter all around us. Thandie's body coiled tight, like one solid muscle, like a crowd preparing for a riot. The proprietor pressed himself against the wall of the tent as Thandie focused on the bulls-eye rushing back and forth above the line of lights. I placed my hand on hir shoulder blade. "Go," I whispered. Above us, the tiger swung in the balance. Thandie clicked off the safety.

A SHORT HISTORY OF MY GENDERS

• *MJ Kaufman*

My brother's fourth grade drag name is Henrietta. He and the kid next door kiss in the tree house hanging from the question mark while I sit in the tiny hole at the top. After school we walk to the store on the corner where we buy semi-colons for separating ourselves from ourselves while I mark his makeup in the tiny upstairs bathroom. I apply mascara leaning on the window-sill. I do it enough times to get really good.

He wears my purple skirt that spins like paper when you turn in a circle and my best pair of heels. One time we fool a whole dinner party. That's the same year I try not to eat; the same year my best friend's sister becomes her brother. The same year Dad gets sick. The same year I overhear the popular girl in the bathroom saying, I never expected a he/she from that family.

And it's not that much later that we switch and I start to borrow his clothes. Not that much later that we stay up late trying to invent a penis for my friend's brother; not that much later that I kiss my best friend on her bed and pretend not to like it. Not that much later that Dad is suddenly too sick to play catch and my brother abandons sports for a big ballet bag slung over his shoulder on two city buses a day.

While he gets big and strong lifting ballerinas up over his head I shave off all my hair and wear his big jeans all summer long. I get excited when people call me sir. I stand in front of bathrooms deciding which one is right for me today. I lead a workshop in a language I don't know very well at all on gender and identities and struggle and I have a hard time answering questions. I mentor a fourteen-year-old trans boy in poetry who tells me he envies boys' chests. At that time I don't understand.

I move to a new place and ride around with three other genderqueer kids, confusing a waiter who stumbles through some yes-ladies-I-mean-oh-sirmaam-sir's when handing over a coffee milkshake that tastes as deepdarksafe as my last home. We've just come from a poetry workshop that made us cry. Made that one girlboy kid I love so much sob on the bench outside while I slipped arms around her and reminded her how all feelings are forgivable. I was still shaking from an hour earlier when I stood before a group of strangers to spit about dressing my brother up as a girl. Spit some English-class-analyzable poem—a clean clear-metaphor/uses-devices-well-but-doesn't-tell-the-truth poem, and they knew and caught me for it and made me strip off all the layers. Made me unearth the scary shivering sentences that never made it into the poem in the first place for fear of being too explicit, or telling too much instead of showing. Whatever that means.

And all that unforgivable unapologetic showing needed closing/healing/safety, it needed milkshakes and midnight swims in the warm rocking ocean where all four of us girlboygirls could finally be just bodies loving bodies.

One Saturday morning walking to the farmers' market with my lover she tells me she needs to look like a man on the street. She hates binding her breasts. Hates having breasts, hates not passing. I press her. I ask her, but what do you feel like when you're naked in bed with me? Do you like your body then? She is quiet. Later she tells me she had a dream. Her mother brought home a bottle of medicine from the hospital for her. The doctor says she has to take it. The medicine is testosterone.

On Shabbat I remember to pray for enough space inside of me to hold all the darkness of the night and all the sunlight of the day. I pray for enough space for transformations as miraculous as the shift from day to night.

Later when that lover has changed his name and an ex-boyfriend has come out to me as a lesbian I go to visit my best friend's sister- turned-brother-turned-sister-again and she tells me about the blessing of having many names and using them all at once.

RAMONA'S DEMONS

• *Susan Jane Bigelow*

Of course they looked amazing. She had a tiny waist and blond hair that fell like waterfalls down her back. He had a quarterback's body and handsomely fine features barely hidden under a light peppering of delicate facial hair. I could have killed them both.

I sighed.

"Can you describe the object?" I asked. "I track by sense, but anything else you can tell me will be helpful."

They glanced at one another.

"You'll know it when you see it, ma'am," said the man, putting a slight emphasis on the last word that made me twitch.

I get it. According to my father, I'm "too ugly to be a girl." It's amazing, he says, that people don't just up and throw things at me in the street. My history is written in big block letters all over my face and body.

"Uh huh," I said. That was so very helpful.

"Sign," I said, shoving a piece of paper at them. They had matching pens, which somehow came out of her teeny little purse. Jerks. "You have the piece of the object?"

The woman handed me a little scrap of what felt like leather. My fingers felt like massive fat sausages next to her slender, dainty ones.

"All right," I said, tamping the usual jealousy and accompanying depression down. "I'll try to have something for you in a couple days."

"We appreciate it," she said, voice silky and seductive. I raised an eyebrow. "It's... very important to us."

The man smiled thinly. "Quite important."

"Right," I said again. "Thanks for coming. I'll call you when I have something."

Leslie popped her head in a moment later. "Go okay? You sign them?"

"Yeah," I sighed, waving the paper at her. She fairly burst into the office and grabbed it.

"Great!" she chirped with false good humor. "Better get on it, then." She gave me a quick little get-your-ass-to-work smile and vanished again.

I work for the Central Connecticut Supernatural Services Agency. No, I'm not a wizard. I have a tiny amount of magic ability left, inherited from my jackass father, and I use it to find things that are lost.

I don't get a ton of work. That's why Leslie, who has magic power coming out every orifice, is constantly on my case. She's made it clear that the only reason she took me on was because she owed me; she also had been making it increasingly clear that her debt was pretty much paid. I needed to bring in business, and fast.

So when the Gorgeous Twins showed up out of nowhere, asking after a lost object, she'd all but thrown them in my direction.

I spent a few minutes filling out the initial contact report, then checked my email again. Nothing but a message from Dori about Saturday.

Yes, I typed back, amused. *We're still on. Please wear your best hair and for fuck's sake, shave this time.* I sent it. That would piss her off. Sure enough, a few minutes later a long screed about how she had beautiful natural hair and had laser JUST THIS LAST WEEK and was way prettier than me arrived in my inbox. I was still giggling when Leslie stuck her head back in.

"Mona," she said, her good cheer evaporating fast. "Get. On it."

"Fine," I groaned, closing the browser window and hauling myself out of my chair. "I'm on it already."

My half-brother Al asked me once, if you can do magic, why don't you use it to make yourself into a *real* girl? After I told him to go screw, I answered that it doesn't work that way. Transformation is hard. I can whip you up a finding spell or something that hides a zit for an hour, but a real honest-to-crap permanent gender swap? No way. I couldn't do that even when I was at the height of my powers. Not even Leslie could manage it.

His response had been to punch me in the arm. You'd think he'd know at least a little more about magic or give a crap about his sister, but no. He'd much rather be a doofus. I told myself it was because *my* father was a magic demon killing machine, while *his* was a construction worker. He'd always hated that argument when we were kids; it was the wellspring of many black eyes and nut kicks.

Still, the little bits of magic I *could* manage these days were useful enough. Despite every nasty thing my father had said to me over the past two years, I was thankful to him for the power he'd passed on to me. I pulled my *Balay's Book of Common Incantations* from the shelf; it fell open to the page on finding spells.

I knelt down inside my engraved floor circle and tried to clear my head. The words were simple enough; they helped give form to my thoughts and shape whatever power I had into something I could use. The actual shaping, the *spell* part of the spell, was more difficult.

I spoke, I shaped. I held the piece of leather in my hand, feeding power into it, concentrating on speaking the words over and over.

Finally, after what seemed like an age, I felt a nagging little tug at the corner of my perception.

That way. That way. Come find me. Come find me.

All right. We were in business. I leapt up, grabbed my coat and sneakers, and headed off after the sense before it faded.

The cool autumn breeze felt great on my bare legs. I'd worn one of my better-looking dresses today, and as I tracked the *come find me* sense I walked with an extra little something in my step. I felt fantastic, right at home in the world and in my body, and I remembered why I'd done it all in the first place.

It was still worth it, even if estrogen had dried my magic up and my father constantly insulted and belittled me. I sighed. Back to work.

I sniffed the air, tasting the sense for distance as well as location. South and west. About ten miles. For this, I thought, I'd probably need the car. I wilted. I hated that car.

Ten minutes later my terrible old Plymouth Neon rattled and moaned out onto Franklin Ave., belching smoke and shaking like a leaf. It had been a gift from a grateful woman I'd saved from a demon, one of the few things I had left from those days. There was even a sword rack mounted in the back—empty now, of course.

I drove southwest towards Newington and New Britain, feeling every pothole and bump jar my bones. *Come find me. Come find me.*

I found myself in a residential neighborhood, following the sense like a bloodhound. I circled the quiet suburban streets, feeling the direction and intensity shift. There. I pulled into an elementary school parking lot and got out.

I recognized the place and ran a few fingertips idly through my long, tangled hair. This is where my half-brother and half-sister had gone. I'd been sent to a special school in Glastonbury; it had become painfully obvious in preschool that mixing a little kid with supernatural strength and magical abilities in with the other little boys and girls was a bad idea. My father had insisted I was special, too strong and too good for this place. And yet now here I was, walking through another one of my life's might-have-beens, searching for something.

School was in session, so I had to be careful. *If they ask, I'm a mom*, I thought, trying to fight down the old fears that a brigade of schoolmarm-y third-grade teachers would run out of the school, brandishing rulers, screaming "A man! *In a dress!* He's come to molest the children, hold him down while we call the cops!"

I shivered, all the jail horror stories I'd read online expanding into grisly detail by my overactive imagination. Maybe I should have worn more gender-neutral clothes.

I squared my shoulders and tried to act like I absolutely belonged there, that I had every reason for wandering around a playground during school hours. What I was looking for was here. The sense was strong, I could feel it pulling me in from the woods next to the baseball diamond. Yes. *Come find me!*

I ignored the gym class out on the diamond and gingerly picked my way into the woods, hunting for a trail or a way between the undergrowth. *Yes, please ignore the crazy lady in the nice dress wandering into the woods next to the school. No, please don't call the police! Ha ha, why would you need the police.*

Finally I got past the thick branches and bushes, finding myself among tall trees and fallen leaves. There. Ahead, very close now. I walked briskly forward as fast as I could go, thanking my foresight in bringing my sneakers along. Maybe I could find another way back to my car when this was done, I thought idly as I homed in on whatever this object was. Not bad for an hour or so's work, though. Maybe after this Leslie would leave me alone for a while. Maybe she'd even give a second thought to the idea I'd floated a few months back of us going out for a drink sometime. Oh, that would be nice.

I was so lost in happy possibilities that I almost missed it when the sense shifted. I stopped in my tracks, sensing the air, old battle reflexes triggered. No mistaking it. I'd been on a beeline for the object, and now it was behind me and to my right.

It was *moving*. Oh, wonderful. Maybe some damn squirrel had picked it up. I turned around and backtracked, and it moved again.

What I wouldn't have given for my old abilities. A *stock still* spell would have come in handy, I could have frozen whoever it was in place. Instead, all I could do was stifle a long string of swear words and creep slowly forward, masking my approach as much as I could. Easy... easy... closer...

I was right on top of it—I looked around, and spied a little hollow almost out of sight. I tensed my muscles, hoping to at least scare it into dropping the object, and *leapt* down. I landed with a "Ha!"

A little orange boy squeaked in alarm and curled into a little terrified ball in front of me; I shrieked in alarm and fell back onto my butt.

Okay, let's be clear. This boy was not tan-inna-can Jersey Shore orange. He was bright fucking pumpkin orange with green hair and fangs. He looked like an escapee from a Halloween cartoon. I wasn't expecting that.

All of my senses pointed right toward him.

"Oh!" I said, gingerly picking myself off the floor. This stained, ripped and covered-in-brambles dress was a goner, I noted ruefully. So much for the awesome high of ladyness for today. "I didn't—hey. Hi, kid. Uh. Sorry to scare you."

He scowled stubbornly, saying nothing. This was going well.

"Hey," I said, trying the direct approach. "You've got something, an object. You may have picked it up in the woods here. It might be made of leather– you'd know it if you had it. Do you, um, have anything like that?"

The *come find me* sense hovered all around him. He shook his head.

"I don't have time for this," I said. "I need that thing. My very attractive clients want it back."

His eyes widened and he started looking around like a deer getting ready to bolt.

I had a thought: a very, awful, horrible, should-have-seen-that-coming thought. I reached out and put my thumb on the kid's forehead.

A little *ping!* went off in my head, and the *come find me* was replaced by a jolly *Hey you found me! Good job, you sure worked hard.*

"Aw fuck," I said.

I sat on the ground, dress spread around my folded legs, bugs crawling into all kinds of places. Orange Kid still huddled in his hollow.

It could still be okay, I thought, trying to reason with my growing sense of dread. Maybe they're his parents. Maybe they're just friends! Ha, yes, friends who don't bother saying, Oh, and what you're looking for is a little green haired orange boy with fangs.

"Okay," I said. "So I was sent to find you. Can you tell me anything about the people who hired me? Are they your parents? Friends? They're two human-looking people, a man and a woman, both annoyingly attractive. The woman's a little blond girl, very thin and pretty, the man's tall and handsome with dark hair."

"No!" he cried, eyes wide. "Please don't take me to them!"

Welp, so much for the possibility of this not sucking.

"Okay, okay," I said, trying to be soothing. "Who are they?"

He looked around, scared.

"Demons," he whispered.

There are moments when the universe decides it's had enough of your nonsense and kicks you in the shins, hard. This was one of those.

"Demons, huh? Why they after you?" I asked, trying to keep things casual. The kid started to cry. "Aw, hey," I said, resisting the urge to scoop him up and hug him. "Hey, it's okay. They're not here, they can't hurt you." Demons have very little agency in this world—the danger's if they can drag you back to theirs. The only catch is that they're very strong, can look like anyone, and are nearly impossible to kill. Nearly.

"I'm not taking you to them," I stressed. "What did they want with you?"

He sniffled. "Dunno."

"My name's Mona. That's short for Ramona. What's your name?"

He sniffled some more. I stayed well out of range. "F-Fanatheene," he warbled.

"Right. Great. Fana... Fanatheene, nice to meet you." I extended a wary hand. He stayed put. "I promise. On my honor. I used to be a demon slayer, kid, and we demon slayers always keep our word. Okay?"

He gave my hand a dubious look, then crept forward and took it gingerly. His touch was dry and crisp, like old wood.

"Are you a boy or a girl?" he asked bluntly, wrinkling his nose at me. "Because you kind of smell like both."

Oh for— "I'm a girl, kid," I said, trying to remain cool. "So you can smell me, huh? Neat. What kind of little dude are you?"

The question was unfathomably rude—one didn't go around demanding "Whut arrrre yoooo" from every member of a non-human race one encountered. But I was feeling annoyed;

little kids aren't supposed to *say* it when they can smell the transgender wafting off of you.

One of his tears dropped onto the ground—and burned a hole in a leaf. Oh. That's what.

"You're an elemental spirit," I sighed. "Aren't you. No wonder they want you—they can feed on you for *years*." I checked myself as his eyes grew yet wider, and he started shivering. Good one, Mona! Let's terrify the preteen elemental spirit boy. Maybe he'll pee his pants and set the woods on fire. "Not that they, uh, will. Don't worry. I'll protect you, I know a lot about demons. Okay?"

"Okay," he said.

We drove north and east, back towards Hartford. We'd found another way out, but there wasn't any possible way of shielding the kid from the world beyond throwing a tarp over him. I had the brilliant idea of simply walking fast. The only people we'd seen had just looked away, minding their own business. I love living in Connecticut, where a solid wall of disgust keeps us all from interfering in one another's lives.

"So!" I said brightly. "Do you have a place around here? Family? Go to school?"

He shook his head.

"Came directly from the other side, huh," I said, dispirited. Well, that explained the clothes.

He nodded, still sniffling. Tears and snot hit the upholstery, which commenced sizzling and smoking. I rolled down a window and turned the air up.

"When? Did that just happen today?"

He shook his head but didn't explain. How long had he been here? And *why* had the demon couple decided to send me out looking for an *object*?

Unless...

I checked my rear-view mirror, then checked again. I turned right, then hung an unexpected left. No one was obviously following, except maybe... that green car? I swung the car around another corner. The car seemed to be gone.

Still, this was *very* strange.

The deal with demons is that they come here to find powerful souls to feed on. It's kind of their thing. They grab people they're interested in, then they open the gates back to the other side. Once they're back there, they can do what they want, like suck their lifeblood out with a demonic straw.

It was very, very rare for them to actually pull someone from the other side to *here* so they could capture him to bring back *there*.

Maybe they were getting smarter.

Or maybe they had no idea what they'd pulled through. I needed to know more. I needed to find a way to get rid of these demons and send the kid back where he came from.

I felt an all-too-familiar pang of nostalgia and worry. Three years ago, before everything, I would have just gone after them with my magic-encrusted sword in hand. Now?

I could almost hear my father's snide voice telling me that there was no way I could hack it against a demon as a girl, that I'd thrown my magic away and screwed everything up for myself permanently.

I had the sickening feeling he was right.

All I could do now was stash the orange kid in my apartment and call around to beg for help. Let's hear it for womanhood.

The South End's got some nice apartment buildings, but mine isn't one of them. I pulled into the lot and shut off the car. The kid looked more orange-and-green-and-fanged than ever. He even gave me a big toothy smile. "Is this your place?" he asked.

"Yeah," I said. There were a few people hanging around, neighborhood regulars. Like hey, that guy who's been in prison a lot, and those two dudes with the blog. Awesome. "Let's go," I said. "Just walk quickly and *don't* say anything to anyone."

"Why not?" he asked, picture of innocence.

"Just come on," I said. I ran around and opened up his door. He jumped out and looked around. The seat was full of smoking holes, but right now that wasn't even half of my worries. I took his hand. "Let's go," I said, grimacing as a little stab of pain lanced through my fingers. Apparently he'd wiped his nose on them. Painfully gross.

The two dudes with the blog whipped out their cameras immediately. "Guys!" I called. They had fun blog names like Horka Globb and Stanley Tool, but I didn't know what they were actually called. "Not now, okay?"

They filmed us as we approached. I glared.

"You put this on your site, and you're in deep shit," I said.

"Suuuure," said Horka.

"I mean it. This kid's on the run. Witness protection stuff. Please. Don't post it."

"Freedom of the *press*, dude," said Stanley.

"You're not the press," I snapped. "And don't call me *dude*."

He smirked.

"Tell you what," I said. "Here's twenty bucks. Just... wait a week or so to post it, okay? That's all I'm asking. For twenty big ones."

"Twenty entire beans?" laughed Horka.

"Twenty. Please. Go buy beers or something on me and forget it till next week."

They looked at one another and shrugged.

"Fine," said Horka.

"Deal," said Stanley.

"Thanks," I said, scooting the kid inside.

"So what kind of elemental are you?" I asked, rifling through my dusty pantry. Did I have any kid-friendly food in here? "Fire, right?"

"What's this?" he asked from just the wrong part of the room.

"Hey!" I said. "Stay out of there! That's, uh, not for kids!"

"Is this a *sword*?" he asked, sounding impressed. "It's *huuuuge*!"

Something crashed to the ground. I dropped what I was doing and raced into the living room, where the kid had the closet door open. One of my trophies, a cruelly-spiked helmet, had crashed to the ground next to him.

"Oh hell—I mean, heck! What happened, did you get hurt?" I demanded. I checked him over—he looked like nothing was currently oozing lighter fluid, so I assumed he was okay. "Stay out of that closet!" I instructed in my best imitation of a pissed-off mom. "For real! Not for kids." I gently shut the door.

"Is that *your* sword?" he asked, all enthusiasm.

"Maybe," I grumped. "Hey. I got Cheerios. Kids love Cheerios, right?"

He eyed me critically. "How could *you* even lift it? You don't look that strong."

"Are you hungry? Tired?" I said rapidly. "Need to go sleep for ten or eleven hours? Oh! I've got TV! And an Xbox! I think I even have some old games around here. You like games?"

He gave me a look.

"Okay, here it is," I said. "Ever played—"

But he already had the TV on and the Xbox started up. Apparently they had video games on the other side, now. He picked through my tiny shelf of games, picked out something suitably gory, and went to town. I fixed myself a bowl of Cheerios (stale!) and flopped onto the couch to think.

What was I even doing? I'd gone out on a simple find-and-fetch quest and now here I was with a young elemental spirit hanging around in my apartment, playing my Xbox and messing with my stuff. Now what? Oh, and my clients were demons. *Demons*.

I needed to give them some kind of excuse, stall for time. I thought up a few good ones as I hunted through my purse for my cell phone. Where was their number? Please tell me I'd written it down... ah.

I called them up and got voice mail. Their away message was creepily chirpy and upbeat. "Uh, hi," I said, trying really hard not to blurt out *You're some demons! Deeeeemons!* and ruin everything. "This is Ramona Kyle. I've had some luck but whatever it was *moved* before I could get there. I think someone picked it up." Yes. Better to weave some truth in there. "I'm going to have to try again, and it may take some time. I'll keep you posted on my progress. Bye." I hung up.

Okay. That got them off my tail for a while. I had some breathing room, though what I was supposed to do next was beyond me.

In times like these, there's really only one thing to do. I dialed my best friend's number, begging her to pick up.

"Dori!" I bellowed into the phone when she answered. "Cluck House! *Now.*"

The Cluck House is the worst restaurant in Hartford, and that's saying something. Still, it's also one of the cheapest, which is why Dori and I go there so often. Plus, they serve Hooker Beer, which is a real thing named for the city's founder. Dori about died when she first ordered it.

Dori was nearly six inches taller than me, but she had fantastic bone structure, gorgeous black hair and a very pretty smile. I'd met her in trans group five years ago when we were both going through transition. We'd bonded over making fun of everyone else there, and we had been close friends ever since.

The only thing that really bugged me about Dori was that she refused to accept my explanations of the supernatural side of my life. She just thought I was nuts.

Still, I needed to talk to someone, and Dori was it. I tore apart some greasy fried chicken and mumbled something about how work sucked.

"You think?" Dori said, mouth full of fries. "You complain about work every day."

"I know," I said. "But Dori. This is different."

"Uh huh," Dori said, waving it off. "Look, *my* day was about a million times worse. These people come into the library, right? And I'm just doing my thing and checking out books, but these *people*—"

"Dori! Listen," I said. "I went on a job to find this thing. But it turned out *not* to be a thing." I looked around. Nope, everyone here was terrifically ugly and probably non-demonic. Whew. "It turned out to be a kid. An *orange kid*, Dori. I have an orange kid back in my apartment playing Xbox *right now*."

She burst out laughing.

"I'm not kidding! Really. I shouldn't have left, I guess, but I needed to talk to you. Look—"

"Okay, okay!" Dori snorted. "So you gotta tell me, is he *orange* orange? Like what kind of orange are we talking about here? Spray-on tan orange?"

"Think candy corn," I said grimly. "Oh, and he has green hair. And fangs. And has flammable snot."

Dori didn't stop laughing for a full minute.

"This is serious!" I said when she finally came back to her senses. "I'll prove it. Look!"

I pulled out my phone. I'd snapped a blurry pic of the kid, and I showed to Dori. She took one look and started howling with glee.

"Hey!" I said.

"That kid! Oh! What! I don't!" Dori gasped. "He has tiny fangs! Oh God, Mona, this is the best thing ever."

"Will you *calm down*," I said, trying to make my face as deadly serious as I could. Eventually Dori's fit of mirth ebbed and I could talk again. "This is real. The kid's on the run from some demons, and I don't know what to do. You remember, right? The demon hunter thing I used to do?"

"Oh God, not this again," Dori said, rolling her eyes. "Mona, girl, you need *serious* help."

"It's real," I insisted. "I did it. I killed demons for a living back before I knew you. You've seen my sword!"

"You need to get yourself into some therapy, some real *non-gender* therapy, and fast," Dori said, pointing a piece of chicken at me for emphasis.

"I know, I know, you always say that. But what do you think I do all day? I work for a company called Central Connecticut Supernatural Services Agency!"

"I thought it was a psychic hotline," said Dori. "Like Miss Cleo!"

"I'm *not like Miss Cleo*," I said through clenched teeth. This was an old argument. Though, to be fair, we did have a psychic on staff. "I find things, I do finding spells. It works. I did a spell and went after what I thought was an object. But it wasn't. It was the *kid*. He says they're demons and they're after him, so I took him and hid him in my apartment."

"Demons are bad, right?"

"Yes!" I said, letting my frustration show.

"So whatcha gonna do?"

"I don't know," I said heavily. "That's what I needed you for. I left them a message saying I was working on things, but I don't know how long they'll buy it for."

"Didn't you say you were a demon killer or something?" Dori asked.

"Before, yeah."

"Well, why don't you *kill the damn demons*? There, problem solved. Can I tell my story now?"

"I—you really—*look*," I seethed. "I *told* you. I can't do that anymore. I don't have that power."

"Why?"

"Because I'm a *girl* now! That's boy magic!"

"There's boy and girl magic?" Dori asked, confused. "That sounds sexist."

"*I* don't know, I didn't make the rules! But the whole thing with demon slaying is that I have to enchant a weapon or it doesn't work on them, and I need..." I looked around again, embarrassed. "I need testosterone to do it."

"What?" Dori made a face. "Ew! Oh, God, Mona, *please* tell me you don't jizz on the sword."

"I don't jizz on it!" I bellowed, a little too loudly. Snickers erupted here and there. I lowered my voice. "It's *blood* magic. It needs blood. And if the blood doesn't have the right amount of T in it, it doesn't work."

"Says who?" asked Dori, stealing one of my pieces of chicken. I was so annoyed that I let her.

"My dad said. He told me when I transitioned that the magic wouldn't work anymore if I took hormones."

Dori gave me a look. "Your *dad* told you. I know I believe every single thing my parents told me," she sneered.

And suddenly I realized exactly what had happened.

I gave Dori an excuse and left the restaurant to call my father. "*You* did this!" I snarled. "You *hexed* me, didn't you!"

"Robbie—"

"*Ramona*," I corrected him, furious. "Two years, Dad!"

"Uh huh," he said, clearly not caring in the least. "I have to call you back."

"*Don't you hang up on me*," I snarled.

"Kid, I can't—"

"You lied! About my magic, you've been lying to me this whole time!"

"Oh," he said. "Right. That."

"Dad!"

"You have to understand, I was mad at you for doing the transgender thing, and worrying your mother so much." he said. "It was a tough time for me."

"What. Did. You. Do." I seethed.

"What do you think? I put a blocking spell on you."

I could barely breathe. *How dare he?* "Take it off, now!"

After a long pause, he sighed, irritated. "No. I don't think so."

"You can't be serious! Dad, I can barely get work! I need that magic! You had no right to take it from me!"

"Look," he replied matter-of-factly, "You've made your choices. If you're out there doing that kind of magic, that reflects on this family, and that reflects on me. You can do whatever you want, but there are going to be consequences."

"Please, that's such bullshit!" I snapped, trying not to burst into tears.

Ever since I was a little kid, my father had been my idol. He taught me everything I knew about magic and hunting demons. I wanted to grow up to be just like him, and for a while it looked like I had. I remembered how proud of me he'd been.

"Dad," I said urgently, "I have some demons after me, I have a kid I need to protect. I can't fight them without my magic!"

"Oh?" His voice took on a haughty tone. "You can't handle demons. Maybe I should come help out with that."

"I don't want your help! Just un-hex me! Now!"

He didn't say anything.

"I still have friends and co-workers," I said. "I'm not powerless. It's completely unethical to lock my powers away because you don't like what I've done with my life! What about the other demon hunters? What about *Mom?* If you won't help me out, *they will.*"

"Fine," he sighed. "You get killed, your problem..." He said a few words in French, the language he used for spells, and I felt a sudden surge of power.

Yes. Oh, God, yes.

It felt good. It felt like home. It also felt disturbingly like being my despised old self again. My skin crawled a little as I rejoiced.

"So, there you go," he said, sounding surly.

"Good!" I said, ending the call. "You jackass!" I added as an afterthought.

What was wrong with me, I wondered as I pulled into my apartment complex's parking lot.

My own father had cursed me! I'd let him steal away two years of my working life. I'd have to think up some way to deal with him later. Maybe I'd tell Mom anyway. She'd make his life hell.

The blog guys were standing around like they always did. They were filming a pile of mattresses that had accumulated on the sidewalk.

"Hey," Stanley Tool said. "Your orange kid left!"

My eyes bugged out. "What?"

"With a hot girl and a dude," he said. "Like an hour ago."

"You're shitting me," I said.

"Nope," he replied. "Got it on film. Wanna see?"

I peered at the screen as he loaded up the relevant clip. Sure enough, there they were. My demons. They had the kid, and he looked like he was crying up a hysterical storm.

"Fuck," I said.

"Is that bad?" Stanley asked.

"Real bad," I confirmed.

I bolted upstairs. The apartment smelled like smoke and struggle. The carpet was badly singed, and pieces of the couch and chairs were still technically on fire. I grabbed a water bottle and dumped the contents onto the still-smoking furniture.

"Damn it," I said. "Damn!"

They'd used me to get to the kid. They couldn't do it on their own, so they sent me after him, knowing I'd drag him back to my apartment.

It figured.

What could I do? I didn't even know where they'd gone!

Although... I still had the scrap of leathery stuff. (What *was* that, I wondered queasily. Never mind, better not to know.) I could track them.

Perfect. Now all I needed was something to kill demons with.

I opened up my closet door. There, in all its glory: what was left of my battle gear and trophies. The sword had been my calling card—people knew me as the little guy with the big-ass sword. I grabbed it by the hilt and lifted it down in an easy arc, only to lurch forward and crash to the ground under its weight.

"Stupid girl muscles," I muttered, shaking the pain off of my hands. "Ow."

Clearly that wasn't going to work. I have to admit, I was a little relieved. The flood of power had disturbed me enough, I didn't want to haul that sword around like a dude either.

But what could I use? I'd sold all my other weapons during those dark months when I was desperate for food, rent, and hormones. I didn't even have a dagger or my old crossbow.

My smart-ass brother used to ask why we didn't use guns. The reason is that the heat of the explosion of the bullet in the chamber messes up the enchantment, somehow. I don't know why. Of course, it had been my dad who told me that, so maybe it was bullshit, too. In any case, I didn't own a gun.

I did have a drawer full of dinner knives, though. I rifled through the kitchen, trying to find something I could use.

"Ah!" I said, drawing out a big carving knife. "Now we're talking." I whipped it around experimentally, practicing a few stab and slice moves. Muscle memory took over, and I tried a certain long, low slicing move.

My boobs kind of got in the way. Well, that was new. Not that move, then. Maybe I'd buy a smaller sword when this was all over.

What was I *doing*? I stopped dead, listening to myself breathe for a brief moment. How dare my father steal this part of me away! Two years, wasted—or were they? It felt intoxicating, this rush of power, but it felt awful, too. Did I even *want* to go back into this world? It wasn't actually being a boy again, so why did it feel like it?

Why couldn't anyone just accept all of me as I was—magic, trans, and all the rest?

I couldn't process it all.

I had no time even to think, I just had to act. I pushed all the conflicting emotions aside, trying to remember what to do.

The weapon needed blood magic to work on the demon. I wasn't dumb enough to slice open my hand, not right before going into a fight, but I could take a thin slice of my leg. I gritted my teeth and ran the knife's edge down the smooth surface.

"Ow!" I complained, like I always did. Blood magic is best done without anyone else around to make fun of you when you whine in pain. My father...

No. Focus. I went to my thankfully un-singed, built-in magic circle and started chanting. This one, I didn't need the book for. I knew it by heart, even now.

> *Blood and bone*
> *Stop and start*
> *Hand and eye*
> *Mind and heart*
> *Fire and ash*
> *Cold and hot*
> *One to another—*
> *Demon, rot!*

I felt an invisible hand reach inside me and *grab* something. I gasped, willing myself to endure. Then, a moment later, it passed. The knife's blade shone a dull red.

Done.

Next, the finding spell. I ran through it, trying to ignore the blood running down my leg. Maybe I should have brought a band aid into the circle. Too late now.

I waited. Then, from the north... *Come find me. This way. Come find me.*

North. Of course. They were almost certainly in the most demon-plagued town in the entire state: Windsor.

The old car strained and groaned as I tried to get it up to highway speed. I-91's evening traffic whizzed by, horns honking and fingers extended.

"GO FASTER," I commanded. It didn't listen. Maybe I could magic up a better engine for this damn thing.

Come find me. Come find me.

I got off the interstate and tried to figure out where the sense was coming from. I had this awful feeling that it was on the move. Closer now, though. Right. Straight ahead. Here! No, turn around, next street over—*yes*.

A baseball field? Attached to a retirement home? Well, only in Windsor. Some demons make weird real-estate choices when they make it big.

I can do this, I thought, nerves on fire. I could still handle demons, no matter what my father said.

I got out of the car, making sure my knife was secure in its makeshift sheath, and scanned the area. Demons were everywhere here; they looked like anybody else. They congregated here for all kinds of reasons, but mostly because the barrier between here and the other side was thinner in this town.

There they were, on the pitcher's mound. The kid was crying again, his tears steaming in the evening air. They were busy doing something—probably preparing to transport themselves back to the other side. Passers-by wandered past, eerily paying no attention. Demons. Damn them.

Why the pitcher's mound? Well, in this case, the "mound" was just a chalk circle. Magic likes circles. So there you go.

"Hey!" I called, launching into a run. "Stop!"

Their heads picked up as they saw me barreling toward them in full Leeroy Jenkins mode.

The woman's face warped into a cruel fanged sneer. The man held the boy close, clenched in his incredibly strong grip, and continued his preparations. Their forms rippled and shimmered, betraying the demon behind the glamours.

I was going to get exactly one shot before they realized I wasn't just a random low-level magic user. I concentrated on the nearer of the two: the smaller, which had been the woman.

"You can't be serious," she started to say as I whipped out the knife. She brought up a hand to block me—but it was too late. A second later, she was on the ground. Her body shivered and contorted, her eyes widened in utter shock, and then the body faded away as death took her back to the other side.

I didn't have time to react to the sudden, gut-wrenching violence. I could only turn shakily to the next target. The other demon roared in anger, releasing the boy.

"Run!" I said to the kid, dropping into a ready stance. He ran.

The other demon, his true form revealed, snarled at me. He was *huge*, seven feet tall at the very least, and bright red.

"Hey!" I said brightly. "Fall colors, red and orange!"

"Shut up," he snarled, swiping at me. I fell back instinctively—he barely missed me. "You! You're a demon hunter!"

"Yeah!" I said, concentrating on staying out of range. The blade of my knife pulsed red. I just needed to nick him, and his power would start ebbing. "I am!"

"You? Little gender-confused human fool! How dare you!" he howled, lunging again. Again, I danced away. His head came tantalizingly close.

Here's where I would have leaned in and shoved my enormous broadsword home. Well, I was going to have to find a new way to fight. Er, soon.

He laughed and lunged again, lightning fast, this time connecting with my shoulder. Blood poured liberally from three parallel gashes.

"That shirt was *new!*" I raged.

"It looked silly on you anyway!" roared the demon. He laughed again, closing his eyes for a brief instance.

I took my moment and struck, slashing him on his leg. Bright demon blood welled up, and he staggered back in surprise.

"They don't tell you about this part," I said softly, standing over the suddenly powerless demon with my knife in hand. "I just need to make contact, and you're done."

"I don't believe it," he wheezed. "Defeated by a tr—"

I drove the knife home. A few seconds later, he was nothing more than a patch of sunlight on the ground. The baseball diamond was suddenly still, leaving me alone with the bloody knife.

I fought back tears and nausea. They were demons, demons, I told myself. How had I ever been able to do this without losing my mind, before? Was I really so callous in the past?

A sound threw me out of my reverie. I looked around and gasped. A dozen forms had gathered around the edge of the field.

Other demons. They watched, impassive. I stood up and waited for them to make a move.

A long moment passed. The wind rustled the leaves in the sun-topped trees; gold and red floated gently to the ground.

Then, one by one, they turned and vanished back to wherever they came. I let go the breath I'd been holding, counting my blessings.

I searched the field; the orange kid was hiding in the dugout.

"Come on," I said. "Let's get out of here before more of them come back. This town is bad news after dark."

He took my hand, and we walked slowly back to the car. In the right light, maybe we could have been mother and son. I looked back at the retirement home and caught a glimpse of an ancient face peering out after us. She smiled and waved.

I raised my hand in salute.

The kid sat in my apartment's circle as I checked through books, trying to find the spell I needed.

"What's your dad's name again? Is it 'Faeleoush' or 'Falalalourn'?"

"Fantharoush," he said.

"Oh. Okay. I think I found that one." I spelled it. "Is that right?"

The kid shrugged, smiling a fangy little smile up at me.

I'd just got off the phone with Leslie. She wasn't pleased with the loss of the second half of the fee, but she was intrigued by the return of my magical abilities. She informed me that she had more work I might be able to do, now. I wasn't sure how I felt about it. My stronger magic still didn't feel quite like me anymore.

Curses, I was reminded, work better when the cursed one likes the effect.

Still, that was a problem for another day. I sighed and went over the lines. "Okay. Ready?"

"Ready!"

I stepped in and sprinkled dust around the circle. "Fantharoush, Fantharoush, summon, summon, portal, portal, voice, voice. Come and talk, come and speak. Behold our presence, breach the barrier. Fantharoush, Fantharoush!"

I waited.

Then, a shimmering dot appeared on the wall next to the bookcase, growing larger until it was the size of the nearby TV. A giant, bald orange head poked through.

"Fanatheene!" bellowed the big fire demon. "Where have you *been*? And who are *you*?" He fixed me with a most uncomfortable glare.

"Papa!" little Fana-whatever said. "I was taken by demons and lost and in the woods but this lady came to help me! She brought me back to her apartment but they found me and she killed them and it was soooo cool but now *I want to go home!*"

The fire elemental studied me. "This is true?"

"Yes," I said. "They took him. He got away from them, luckily, and they came to me looking for help."

"Hmm!" said the fire elemental. "Well done, then! Thank you, thank you for saving my son. Boy, come to me!"

The little orange dude gave me a kiss on my cheek and vanished with an audible *pop*, back to the other side.

I rubbed my face where his lips had been. Well, maybe the spittle had singed away some hair, I told myself.

The fire elemental studied at me. "I know you. You were a demon hunter long ago."

"Y-yes," I said, shocked. "How did—?"

"Your father and I are acquainted."

Oh, fantastic. I braced myself.

"He does not see the good in it, but I approve of those who undertake unorthodox journeys," he boomed. "Why, I myself was born a water elemental."

My eyes bugged. "Really?"

He nodded. "Really. So. In gratitude, I shall grant you a boon—the one thing in the world you need the most."

"Oh! Really? But—"

"No," he said, cutting me off. "Not that. Something else. Something you don't want to admit you lack. Thank you again, Ramona. Be well, and follow the path that is right for you."

With that, he vanished back into his world. I sighed. The apartment felt empty, even more so than usual.

I changed into something less blood-covered and wandered through the empty rooms. I called up Dori.

"Hey," I said. "I figured out the demon thing." She started yelling at me about running out on her. "Sorry. Hey, you were right about my dad. So help me, I'm never going to speak to him again."

"About time!" she said. "So, what, you can do magic again?"

"I thought you didn't believe in that stuff," I said.

"You spin the worst bullshit, but I do like humoring you," she said, clearly amused.

"You're a pal," I said, satisfied. It was the little victories.

Dori began chattering on about her day: she had been to see this new stylist and she was sure she could help me "put myself together," whatever that meant.

I let her talk. It was nice to hear about the mundane world after the day I'd had.

"Hey," she said. "Want to come over tonight?"

"Can't," I said. "You have no idea how tired I am. I just want a hot bath and some sleep."

I walked into my bedroom and blinked. A little vase with a single white rose in it had materialized on the dresser. The scent of very familiar magic hung in the air. "I'll call you tomorrow," I promised Dori, and I hung up.

I opened the note.

> *Ramona—*
> *Talked with F—*
> *Might have been wrong*
> *Call when you can*
> > *—Dad*

"You bastard," I said happily. It was as close to an apology as I was likely to get out of him. Maybe I wouldn't call for a couple of days. It would do him good to wait. In the meantime, there were people out there who were actually worth my time.

I called Dori.

"Hey," I said. "You know, I'm feeling a lot better. Get out the cheesy movies and the family size bag of Fritos, I'm coming over."

DEAN & TEDDY

• *Elliott DeLine*

Colin and Dean arrived at the community center around dinnertime. "Go ahead without me," Colin said. "I have to use the bathroom." He turned down the corridor to his left. "It's the seventh door on the right," he added, gesturing towards the adjacent hall. "You can't miss it."

Dean stood alone, hesitant. He took several deep breaths (in through his nose, out through his mouth) as he walked down the hall, his wingtips tapping on the linoleum tiles. He counted doors until he reached the seventh room. It sounded silent inside. Multicolored flower leis and Mardi Gras beads trimmed the entrance way. A sticker on the door proclaimed it a "Safe Zone!" It didn't make him feel any better. Still, he turned the doorknob and stepped inside.

The room was small, with several bulletin boards and posters of smiling, same-sex couples nailed to the lime green walls. Nothing surprising. The back wall featured an amateur mural: a rainbow, composed of multi-colored handprints with the word

"ACCEPTANCE" painted beneath. Dean gave it a moody glance over the rim of his glasses. He took a seat in one of the orange plastic chairs, spreading his legs and slouching. There were three other people seated across from him, all sneaking looks in his direction. Feeling self-conscious, he sat up and crossed his legs. His right foot jiggled. He avoided eye contact.

In the circle there were two transgender men and one transgender woman. The woman wore a sack dress, a cardigan, and combat boots, all in black. Rings and bracelets covered her large, boney hands and her nails were speckled with chipping black paint. She hid her face behind the curtains of her dark hair, hunching her shoulders and resembling a large bat.

The boy to her right was wearing a tie-dyed t-shirt with cargo shorts. He had dirty, beaded dreadlocks and a patch of blonde fur growing on his chin. He was listening to his iPod, bowing his head gently with the beat. He stared off into space, stoic and quite possibly stoned.

To his right sat a person who was physically androgynous but had a macho style and general aura. His red hair was shaved military-style, his ears were gauged with black plugs, and there was a tattoo of a nautical star, among many freckles, on his left forearm. His t-shirt said, "Check a Box: Male, Female, Fuck You!" Naturally, there was a check mark in the third box. He kept looking at Dean and eventually crossed the room. "Hey man, what's good?" he asked, taking a seat beside him.

Dean scratched his left sideburn. "Oh. Hi. I don't know." He bared his teeth in an attempt to smile and lowered his head like an omega wolf.

The kid nodded. "Word, word. I'm TJ. 'sup."

Dean wasn't sure if *sup* was rhetorical. "Sup," he said, hoping it functioned like *ça va* in French.

"What's your name, bro?" TJ asked.

"I'm Dean... comrade."

TJ didn't seem to pick up on the mockery. "Word, like Jimmy Dean! Cuz you're rockin' a pretty sweet pomp!

"Excuse me?"

"Hair," TJ said, reaching out his small freckled hand.

"Yes. I have hair." Dean covered his head, flinching.

"I'm basically obsessed with James Dean," TJ said, putting his hands back in his pockets. "I base my philosophy for life off of him. Live fast and die young! I should get a tattoo of that next. I watched this movie about him once, it was epic. I think I was James Dean in another life."

Dean gave him a queasy smile.

"Hey TJ!" Colin had returned from the bathroom. He strutted across the room, his hands in the pockets of his zip-up sweatshirt, his dark swoop-hair arranged perfectly. Apart from his doe eyes, most of his body parts and facial features could be described as thin and angular. His nose was especially prominent, though not bulbous. Dean always thought it gave him a majestic, bald eagle-like quality.

"Colin!" TJ said. They slapped hands, clasping and releasing. Dean couldn't help but admire their synchronized, fraternal grace.

"How've you been, man!" Colin exclaimed. "It's been ages!"

"Tell me about it," said TJ. "Hey, nice shoes!"

Colin looked down at his white high-tops. The large tongues covered the ankles of his skinny jeans. "Oh, thanks! I like yours too. And your piercings, your hair, everything! You look awesome, dude."

TJ blushed. "*You* look awesome. The hormones sure did the trick. Made you really... manly, you know?" He blushed even redder, his face nearly matching his hair. "I mean, I don't mean that in a *gay* way."

Colin laughed, patting him on the back. "I know, I know. Thanks man. It's been quite the journey. That means a lot."

Dean scowled, but no one noticed.

"So how's college?" TJ asked.

"Oh, you know, decent," Colin said. "How's high school?"

"Just finishing up. It's the shit, man."

Dean wondered if this was good or bad. He wished TJ would go away, forever.

"So you met Dean?" Colin said, placing his hand on his roommate's shoulder. Dean felt warmth spread through his body, even to the typically numb nether regions.

"Yeah! *James* Dean," said TJ. "I'm going to call him Jimmy."

"I'd rather you didn't," Dean muttered, still feeling flustered and warm as Colin took a seat beside him. He slipped off his black cardigan and rolled up his shirtsleeves.

"You even look like him!" TJ said, pointing at Dean's face. "When you came in, you were all brooding and shit. Blaze, doesn't this dude look like James Dean?"

The boy with the dreadlocks paused his iPod and gave Dean a look up and down. "Sort of," he said. "Actually, he looks more like... what's his name." He snapped his fingers repeatedly, his face scrunched up in thought.

"That's okay, don't bother." Dean mumbled. The more he tried to stop blushing, the hotter his cheeks burned. The girl in black was looking now as well.

"Robert Smith!" Blaze blurted. "That's the guy. You look like Robert Smith." He looked pleased with himself.

"No he doesn't," said the girl, not bothering to mask her disgust.

"Yes he does," Blaze said. "He looks just like him."

"No, he doesn't. Trust me, *I'd* know." She smirked. "You mean Morrissey. That's who he looks like. Sort of."

"No, I mean Robert Smith," Blaze said, "the guy from The Smiths. You know, the flaming British guy, with the crazy hairdo. No offense, dude."

"None taken," Dean said, looking at his feet. His ears were ringing. "But she's right." He pointed at the girl without looking up. "Robert Smith is from The Cure."

"Well same thing," said Blaze.

"*Not* the same thing," the girl said, narrowing her eyes.

Dean smiled at her. She looked confused and started cracking her bejeweled knuckles and chewing on a strand of her hair.

A fifth young man entered the room, closing the door behind him. "Alright, let's get started." He sat down and crossed his legs. He was dressed in sportswear, suggesting he'd come from the gym. "Welcome to TransPride," he said, nodding around. "We are a discussion group for gender-variant youth, age fourteen to twenty-two. I'm Ethan, the peer moderator." He smiled briefly, rubbing his sparse goatee. "Go ahead and sign yourself in." He handed a clipboard to Blaze. "It looks like we've got some new faces tonight, so let's do a go-around. Everyone say your name, pronoun preference, a little introduction and um... your favorite candy." He cracked his knuckles and neck. "I'll start us off. Name's Ethan. I'm twenty-two. I identify as a transgender man and I prefer male pronouns. I'm getting my degree in Physical Education, and I work at a gym. My favorite candy bar is Butterfingers." He nodded to Blaze. "Your turn, man."

Blaze nodded. "Hey. I go by Blaze. Male-pronouns. I'm in high school. I play guitar. I'm trans. Female to male, whatever. And yeah, Butterfingers are good."

"Thanks Blaze," Ethan said. "Teddy?"

The girl in black didn't smile. "Yeah, I'm Teddy. Female pronouns... if you feel the need to address me at all." She laughed a little too long at her own comment, staring at the ground. "And I dig Swedish Fish, I think. They're so much better in theory." She licked her lips, flicking lint off of her cardigan. "Such is life."

"Right," said Ethan with a forced smile. "Thanks Teddy. Next?" He turned to Colin.

Colin brushed his hair out of his eyes and then waved, slightly. "Hey, I'm Colin." The first word sounded slightly nasal and elongated. Dean noted it, as he always did. He couldn't help himself.

"I haven't been here in a few years," Colin confessed, "but I used to go as a teen. That was before I transitioned and all. Anyway, I'm twenty years old, and I'm a college student. I also play guitar, and I'm in a band. I identify as a trans guy. Male pronouns. And I really like Snickers. Especially the ice cream ones."

Dean felt his empty stomach rumble. Everyone turned towards him. He blushed, wondering if they had heard it. Then he realized it was his turn. "Oh," he said. "I'm Dean."

Everyone waited.

"I forgot the questions," he muttered.

"What did you say?" Ethan cupped a hand to his ear.

"He forgot the questions," Colin said.

"Oh," Ethan said. "Pronoun preference, identity, and favorite candy."

"Male pronouns," Dean said, sounding as if it were a shameful admission. He frowned for several seconds, staring at the mural. "I don't really like candy," he concluded.

TJ forced a skeptical cough. "You *don't* like *candy?*"

"I don't know," Dean said, adjusting his glasses. "Maybe. I like chocolate."

"That's candy!" TJ said.

"Okay."

There was silence again.

"Why don't you tell us about yourself?" Ethan said.

"I don't know," Dean said. "What do you mean?"

"Are you in college?"

"Yeah, he's my roommate," Colin said.

"What's your major?" Ethan asked.

"English," Dean said. "For now."

"And how do you identify?"

"I don't."

"Oh come on," Ethan said playfully, overlooking Dean's scowl. "Of course you do! You're queer, right?"

"No."

TJ looked confused. "You're not? So you're... straight? Wait, are you even trans?"

Colin opened his mouth but Dean gave him a deliberate glare.

"Well," he said, sitting up and smirking. "Those sure are a lot of questions, TJ. I think you ought to at *least* buy me a drink first."

"Uh..." TJ looked to Colin. "So is he a gay guy?"

"No he's trans," said Blaze, "I can tell."

"Hey," Ethan said. "That's enough, okay? If people don't want to come out, they don't have to." His voice was calm but his eyes lingered on Dean with distrust. "Let's move on. TJ, your turn."

"Okay," TJ said, shrugging. "Sup. I'm TJ. I'm a radical queer, pre-T, straightedge, vegan-anarchist trans guy. I prefer male pronouns, local music, and femme girls with tattoos." He grinned.

"Awesome," said Ethan, clapping his hands together. "Short and sweet. Alright, so. Before we move on to this week's topic, let's start by sharing two good and two bad things that happened this week. Colin and Dean, you're our guests tonight. Why don't you go first?"

The boys looked at each other. Dean shrugged passively.

Colin nodded. "Right. Well, I'll start off with the bad. I'm really stressed about final exams at school. And to make matters worse, I broke up with my girlfriend." He glanced to his right, but Dean was staring at the floor. "So that really sucked. But good news is, I've got my friend Dean here. It'll be nice to spend the weekend just hanging out at my house. And I'm gonna take him to the ocean tonight."

Dean smiled, picking at his nails. He could hardly wait to get out of this place.

"Great!" Ethan said. "Thanks Colin. And what about you Dean?"

"Oh. Um, pass."

"No, no passing!" said TJ.

Dean scowled. "Well, okay. I'll start with good things."

"Speak up!" Ethan said.

"I'll start with the good things," Dean said, not much louder. "I'm also glad to get off campus with Colin. Yes. Also, I had a good breakfast."

"What was it?" TJ asked.

"A tangerine," Dean said.

"That's all?" TJ said.

"Yeah," Dean said.

"And bad stuff?" Ethan said.

Dean stared at the mural again, thinking. "Well, that mural for starters." He laughed. Teddy snorted appreciatively, but no one else reacted.

Ethan looked around the room. "So who wants to go next?"

"Me!" said TJ, quite literally on the edge of his plastic seat. "Bad: I had to work all weekend. Super lame. Also, I haven't been passing in public places, so that's bad for my ego, if you know what I mean. But good: I got my second tattoo." He pointed to the star on his arm. "And best of all, I finally start T in a week!"

"Congratulations!" Colin, Ethan, and Blaze said at different times. Dean nodded. Teddy didn't look up from her hands.

"Yeah I'm totally stoked," TJ said.

"Well good for you, buddy!" Ethan said. "You've been waiting so long." He turned to his left. "Your turn, Blaze."

"Nothing really happened," Blaze said. "I don't know. I got this new iPod." He showed it to everyone.

"Cool!" Ethan said. "That's alright, let us know if you think of anything else. Do you want to go next, Teddy?" His voice was soft and he looked uneasy.

Teddy shrugged and sighed. "I don't mean to sound negative," she said, still looking down, "but nothing noteworthy *ever* happens to me. That's the thing. Maybe I can get some support. That's why we're here, right?" She snorted. TJ and Blaze shifted in their chairs. She continued. "No, I suppose not."

She met Dean's eyes but he quickly looked away.

"Anyway," she said "I'll try to make it... brief. I know I've been criticized in the past for ranting." She licked her lips and smirked. "So here's my issue. Like many of you, I used to read transgender memoirs, almost obsessively. I'd sneak into the Gay section when my mom was at Barnes & Noble, looking for god knows what. Anyway, I read a lot of stories. On the internet, too—message boards upon message boards, women who made their own websites—but my point is, people generally say they feel like themselves once they transition, right? That they *finally see the woman in the mirror.*" She made quotation marks with her large, white fingers. "So I've dreamed of that day since I was a kid. And I don't *regret* my decision, but I'm telling you, I've been on estrogen for almost five years now. And when I look in the mirror, I still don't see the woman I want to see. The thing is, I can't see anything. My eyes look dead, my face is unexpressive. It's like I'm wearing a mask. It's almost more mysterious to me now than it was before. It's, well, *freaky.*" She snorted again, but didn't smile. "Has anyone else experienced this?" She looked up, her pale cheeks tinged pink.

Ethan shook his head, staring down at the clipboard. Blaze was playing a game on his iPod. TJ was the first to speak. "I don't think that's normal," he said. "You should talk to a therapist—"

"Of course it's normal," Dean said, interrupting. Everyone turned, startled by his acerbic tone. He hesitated for a second, scratching his head. "I mean, I feel that way," he muttered.

Teddy pressed her palm to her forehead, grimacing. "But then what's the point?" she nearly yelled, her voice hoarse. "I was waiting for that shining moment, where I'd look in the mirror and finally see myself. I feel fucking cheated." She pounded her fist against her bare thigh.

Blaze and TJ made eye contact, trying to suppress guilty smiles.

"Yeah," Dean said, looking at Teddy's bowed head. "Yeah, that moment is a myth. I'm sorry."

"So then what the hell am I doing?" Teddy said, looking into Dean's eyes. "Why the hell am I putting myself through all this shit? Years of therapy, invasive questions, electrolysis, voice lessons, tons of medical bills, losing my family and friends?"

"I can't answer that," Dean said quietly.

Teddy attacked her tears with the back of her hand. "I guess there is no point. I'm just sick." She smirked. "They were right about me. I don't know what I want."

"*No,*" Dean said, "No. You are *not* sick."

"Then why aren't I happy like everyone else?" Teddy said, as if under attack. "Why am I so ungrateful?"

"This is getting a little heated," Ethan said. "Teddy, why don't you take a breath."

"You just can't *think* so much," Dean said. "You have to get out of your head."

"And how the hell do you do that?" Teddy asked. "Please, enlighten us all with your infinite wisdom in these matters."

Dean hesitated. "I guess, focus more on your body. Even if you hate it." He realized mid-sentence that he did not believe this at all.

Teddy glared at him. "Don't give me any Zen bullshit. Trust me, I've heard it all." She nodded at the mural on the back wall. "Acceptance? Never." She laughed. "The day I *accept what God gave me* is the day I'm dead."

There were several moments of silence. Ethan cleared his throat. "Listen Teddy, I'm really sorry you're upset, but you know you can't say things like that here. We can talk later, and there's a hotline you can always call, listed on the bulletin board. But we really need to get on with our discussion. We're running out of time."

Teddy gripped her hair with both hands.

"We're going to move on now, okay? Will you be alright?"

She nodded, not looking up. Her hair formed a curtain once more.

"Okay," Ethan said, pulling a stack of papers out from under his clipboard, "on to today's topic. I want to discuss the petition going around Facebook. Many of you have probably seen it, but in case you haven't, I'll explain. This Australian trans man was asked to take down shirtless photos of himself, because they were deemed *too graphic*. So the petition asks that all us guys pose shirtless in our profile picture, as a gesture of support. Transphobia will not be tolerated on the internet. It's time to show the world that we exist, and they just have to deal with it."

"Word!" said TJ. "I'm totally down."

Colin nodded. "Yeah, I'd do that for sure. That's really fucked up of Facebook."

"I mean, to be fair, the Facebook staff apologized," Ethan said, "and they let the guy repost his photos. But I still think we need to make a point."

Blaze nodded.

Dean didn't say anything. He was still looking at Teddy. "I'm not saying you shouldn't struggle," he said.

"What?" Ethan said.

Teddy looked up from her lap. "Then what are you saying?"

"Oh God, we're back on this?" Blaze said.

Ethan sighed. "Like I said, we're running out of time, so I'd appreciate it if we—"

"I guess you should keep struggling anyway." Dean said. "But fuck those books. Fuck the internet. The whole transgender cult is stupid. What do they know about you or me?"

"Jesus Christ," Blaze said. "Let me know when this is over." He put his headphones back on.

Colin cringed. "Dean," he said, "you're getting really intense, man. This is how you end up offending people."

Dean looked at him, tense. "I'm sorry," he said. "I'm sorry, I'm sorry."

"It's alright," Colin said. "Just, like, think before you speak. You know?"

Dean felt his throat tighten. "I'm sorry." He folded his arms across his chest and hunched his shoulders.

"Well maybe I'm just too *stupid*," Blaze said, taking off his headphones. "But I'm pleased with my reflection, and it's all thanks to testosterone. I'm a proud transgender man, and I'm proud to be queer. Is that wrong or something?"

"Have you had surgery yet?" TJ asked, turning to Teddy. "It can do wonders. Sure helped me. There are lots of ways to earn the cash. My friend started a website so people could donate to him."

"See, just takes a good old fashion work ethic," Ethan said. "If you want it enough, you'll find a way. In the meanwhile, just hang in there, Teddy."

Teddy ignored them both. She nodded to Dean. "Hey," she said softly. "I'm sorry I yelled. Don't feel bad. I appreciate your honesty."

"I'm sorry," Dean said.

Colin stuck around for a while after the group ended. TJ had discovered a new website for sex toy reviews, and he wanted to share it with the other men. Dean felt awful, so he went outside for air.

The sun was setting and the lights in the parking lot were illuminated. The sky was streaked with orange and purple strati, and birds were singing their last songs of the evening. It was a cool night in early May, and the air was still. Teddy was standing

alone against the brick wall, hunched over in a leather jacket
and sucking on a cigarette. Dean approached her, thinking that
she resembled a cross between Patti Smith, Joey Ramone, and
a Halloween witch.

"I don't know why I bother," Teddy said before Dean could
open his mouth to say hello. "I'm not like other trans people.
They all think I'm a crazy cat-lady before I even speak."

Dean sighed. "I'm sorry."

"Stop saying that!" Teddy said. "Look at me, kid."

Dean looked up at her. She was almost six feet tall, with heavy
eyebrows and a sculpted, angry jaw. Her eyes were large and
black, so the irises looked like two giant pupils. Her lips were
raw and chapped, bloody red. "Don't ever be sorry," she said.

Dean could smell alcohol on her breath. He looked away, shy.

Teddy exhaled smoke, sighing. "Don't start thinking it's a guy
thing, either. It's no different when trans women show up. Getting
their hair done, facial reconstructions, breast implants—that's all
they ever talk about. And sure, I'm a hypocrite. I mean, hey, I've
changed my body with pills and what not. But I've never tried
that hard to *be* anything. I just am. So people look at me with
pity because I don't pass and don't have the cash for surgery."
She snorted. "Well, that's the best case scenario. This girl Jen
posted about me on her blog, knowing I'd read it. She said I'm
a *fetishist*, not a *real* trans woman. I mean, are you kidding me?
What does that even mean? They think I masturbate in high
heels or something? And so what if I did? What does that have
to do with who *I am*?"

Dean said nothing. He was suddenly very tired.

Teddy ashed her cigarette with a violent flick. "It gets so you
don't trust anybody," she said. "People who call themselves
radical-sex-positive-queer-feminists still hold me up to this plastic
ideal. They think I don't *know* I look like a guy in a wig? They
think I haven't tried?" She laughed aggressively. "Well, I don't

give a fuck anymore. I wasn't meant to blend in. If I cared about that, I wouldn't have started transitioning in the first place. Half the time I wish I didn't. Back then I wasn't expected to belong to some stupid-ass community. At least back then I was invisible."

Dean stuck his hands in his jean pockets and leaned against the wall beside her. There were several centimeters between their shoulders, but he sensed her body seizing up. He sympathized, and took a step to his left. Looking at the sky, he said, "Oscar Wilde said that when the gods wish to punish us, they answer our prayers."

Teddy smirked. "That fat pedophile had an answer for everything, didn't he?"

"Sometimes I really think so."

Teddy smirked and blew smoke through her nostrils. "Listen Dean," she said, "you're a real snob. But so am I. We should keep in touch." She unearthed a crumpled receipt and a pen from the deep pocket of her jumper and scribbled a few lines. "I don't use the internet anymore, and I definitely don't do phone calls. But take my home address." She handed him the receipt. "Write me sometime. I've always wanted a pen pal."

"I will," Dean said, folding the paper. "I definitely will. Thanks Teddy. You're pretty alright yourself."

Teddy took a silver flask out of her pocket. "If you say so, kid." She snorted, and took a big swig of liquor. As she wiped her mouth on her sleeve, she glanced down at the top of Dean's hair. It was dark and voluminous, much like hers, but because it was cropped, it stood straight up, leaving his face exposed. Still, one could get lost in such things.

Dean felt her stare, but he didn't mind. He wondered if she preferred The Cure or The Smiths, but couldn't bring himself to ask. He kept his head bowed, toying with the buttons on his cardigan. They stood still for several moments, listening to the birds in meditative silence, until Blaze and Ethan came bursting out the door. Colin and TJ followed soon after, arm-in-arm and discussing testosterone injections. "You probably won't see changes for a few months," Colin said, "Except after a few weeks you'll get *a lot* hornier."

"Fuck yeah!" said TJ, pointing his left finger like a gun. "Look out ladies!"

Colin laughed. "Yeah, eventually you'll learn to control it. But for awhile, you'll want to fuck every chick in sight." His eyes flicked towards Dean, as if daring him to speak. Dean hardly noticed. He'd just seen a bat dart across the sky.

"Unless it makes me want dudes!" TJ said. "It can do that to some guys, did you know that? T turns them gay!" He laughed at the absurdity of it all.

Dean and Teddy met eyes, their expressions equally dour. Despite himself, Dean started to grin. Teddy couldn't help it. Behind her hair, she smiled as well.

MALEDICTION AND PEE PLAY
 • *Sherilyn Connelly*

I. FREE AMONG THE DEAD

In mid-October, my girlfriend Vash responded to a Craigslist ad. She and I had both written and responded to a few ads over the past several months as we finally began to explore the "open" part of what was always intended to be an open relationship. The results had been decidedly mixed, at least from my perspective. Vash had found a new partner by the name of Dietrich, and they were falling in love, while my efforts at extracurricular dating had largely been non-starters. It didn't help that I was a trans woman who was only attracted to women, since women who were attracted to trans women were in surprisingly short supply—even in San Francisco.

This particular ad was different, though. As Vash explained: "It's a guy who's looking for a woman to dress as a nun and pee into a bucket at a Black Mass. A Satanic thing. I don't think it pays, and the event itself is free. I just want to do it because it's weird."

I could certainly appreciate that, since being a writer and performer myself, I knew the best gigs were usually the ones that only paid in experience and fond memories. Nor was I put off by the "Satanic" aspect. I was friends with The Reverend Steven Johnson Leyba, a painter and performance artist who was one of the last priests to be personally ordained into The Church of Satan by ol' Anton LaVey himself, and I'd even gone on a date with one of LaVey's daughters—that very date was one of the aforementioned non-starters, unfortunately. The Mass itself was going to be performed according to LaVey's specifications in the *The Satanic Bible*.

Being raised Catholic and now identifying as atheist—not to mention being someone who never quite outgrew their goth phase and still dressed in all black, mostly for its slimming effect—I was in the prime demographic to become a card-carrying Satanist. But I never officially joined. I'm not a joiner by nature, which, on a Groucho Marx level of irony, makes me all the more qualified to join.

I did appreciate the self-awareness of Satanism. Anton LaVey had been a showman first and foremost, and he considered organized religion to be hucksterism writ large. Then there was the fact that unlike pretty much every other religion in the history of ever, it did not require any sort of belief in the supernatural. In Satanism, there was no actual Satan, or God, or any other invisible being used to scare people into behaving. Instead, Satan represented humanity at its best and worst, just another animal, ultimately no better than the ones on four legs. It made me think of Buddhism, with a strong undercurrent of "Life is short, so enjoy it while you can. Just so long as you don't hurt anyone else." That was a philosophy I could get behind, and one I'd been trying to follow with varying degrees of success over the past year since breaking up with Maddy, my second long-term girlfriend. It was essentially why Vash and I had an open relationship, and why I'd become a regular at The Power Exchange, a disreputable sex club. I went on that nights that Vash was with Dietrich, which meant at least once per weekend, but I did little more than just hang out with friends. Nobody was selling what I was buying, and vice versa.

Whatever my history with Satanism, this was Vash's thing, not mine. But I fully supported her, and I came along when she met the fellow who was going to perform the Mass, a student at the College of Creative Arts who went by the self-consciously ironic name of Peaches Pendragon Partridge. He had long hair, glasses, a goatee, a fondness for priest's collars, and—like nearly every other Satanist I'd ever met—a cheerfulness that bordered on the goofy. Scheduled for the night before Halloween—Devil's Night—the mass was going to be his final project before graduating. And, since the world of Satanists was as small as any other, Steven Leyba was going to be in the Mass as well.

The first rehearsal was a few days later, in a room at the College which was normally used as an art studio. A few of Peaches' paintings were around. The primary motif was a mix of oppressive cuteness in the vein of H.R. Pufnstuff alongside overtly controversial imagery—say, H.R. Pufnstuff wearing a Nazi uniform with Hitler's hair and moustache. One of Peaches's friends in the Mass also wore a Nazi uniform, which had nothing to do with his actual job of banging a gong every now and then. I found it almost charming, since Nazi imagery for shock value is borderline rote. Steven Leyba, whom Peaches idolized, frequently used swastikas in his paintings, though his stated goal was to reclaim the design on behalf of the countless ancient cultures, including his own Apache ancestors, which had used the symbol before Hitler came along and ruined it for everyone. But Leyba didn't mind the shock value, either. When the gong-banger mentioned in passing that he was Jewish, I began to wonder if Mel Brooks was behind all this.

By the end of the evening, though, I was considering not attending the Mass itself. For starters, I didn't feel especially comfortable at the rehearsal. Not *unwelcome*, exactly, but I felt as if I were intruding on Vash's other life, even though she'd invited me to come along. Early in the evening I'd made an offer to help with the Mass which was essentially shrugged off, and it was forgotten entirely when Peaches commented later in the evening that they were probably going to need someone else, and that I should ask my friends to find out if anyone wanted to help. That told me everything I needed to know. Then there was the fact that the Mass was the following Monday, barely a week away. We already had plans for three of the nights in the meantime, and I was worried that if Vash and I spent more time together than apart...

Earlier in the month, we went on an overnight trip to attend the wedding of one of her coworkers. When we got back to my place, Vash sat me down and said she'd been spending too much time with me. I was startled. Had I monopolized her time without realizing it? Sure, we'd spent the last forty-eight hours together, but that had been *her* idea. I hadn't twisted her arm and forced her to take me to the wedding of a stranger. I didn't even like weddings. But Vash had asked me to come along, and I never declined an opportunity to spend time with her.

She had also pointed out that we never defined what it meant to be in a relationship, open or otherwise. The words were chilling, but true. What she needed now was space to feel like her own person, so I gave it to her. What else could I do? The old maxim about setting free something you love has been ruined from overexposure on inspirational posters and kitchen magnets, but that doesn't make it any less true. I resolved to not call or email or otherwise contact her, or to invite her to shows or any of the things we used to do.

So just because she said she wanted me to attend the Mass didn't mean that she wouldn't be tired of me again by the end of it, and my heart wasn't ready to be pushed around again.

Besides, it solved perhaps the most important issue: whether or not Dietrich could be at the Mass. When Vash originally asked me how I felt about Dietrich attending, I took the high road—that is, I lied—and said I was fine with it. Though I was sure that Dietrich was a perfectly nice person whom I'd like if I got to know, I was *terrified* of meeting or even being in the same room with the woman who had been stealing Vash's heart away for the past three months. But what was the high road if not going against one's heart in the pursuit of some greater good?

No fool she, Vash could tell I wasn't remotely comfortable with the idea, and she said I could think about it some more. I appreciated that, but the more I thought about it, the more I realized the only real solution was for me not to attend. Hell, the College was practically within walking distance of Dietrich's house. They could show up together, leave together, do whatever, all without me being in the way.

It wasn't quite the high road, and it wasn't really the low road, either. It was just the road I usually wound up on, whether I wanted to or not.

II. The Saint of the Pit

The next day, I learned about a fetish dance party happening that Saturday called the Feast of Souls. It was going to be held at the Porn Palace, the aptly named and painfully hip studio of the website Kink.com. Peaches didn't know yet if they were going to rehearse on Saturday night, so in spite of my resolve to not ask Vash out so often, I invited her to come with me to the Feast.

Vash replied: "I'm already going out with Dietrich on Saturday whether Mass rehearsal happens or not, *Gato.*" It was short for *gatocita,* broken Spanish for "little cat," a term of endearment which was beginning to sting a little. She continued: "The Feast sounds interesting, though. I wish I'd heard about it sooner so Dietrich and I could have made plans to go."

That right there: that was at the heart of my issues with her and Dietrich, and the Mass, and everything else. Vash and I had always been very rough and intense with each other—what the rest of the world generally referred to as "kinky." Spending our first evening together making a spectacle of ourselves in public before returning to my apartment where we fucked and bit and laughed and scratched and clawed until the wee hours of the morning, sexual endorphin junkies who had finally met their match. There were countless things we wanted to do and explore together. We did some of them at the Power Exchange and elsewhere—most illicitly at the San Francisco Opera. Still, there were many unchecked boxes on the list when my brief, unexpected fling with a girl named Ryder fractured our devotion and sent Vash on the path to Dietrich, who—if I was honest with myself—was not only much more Vash's type than I'd ever been, but was experienced in so many things that I wasn't. The cold hard truth was that Vash didn't want to do much of anything with me anymore, not when she had Dietrich, who could do things *right* and even teach her new things, which I couldn't. Where I had just left bites and scratches on Vash's body, Dietrich left bruises that I couldn't even begin to identify, let alone replicate. And Vash loved her for it. All the adventures they had together, adventures she didn't particularly care to have with me anymore. Mostly we just cuddled and held hands and kissed hello and goodbye, and little more.

"The Feast doesn't close until three in the morning, so even with rehearsal, you and Dietrich can still go. I'll just be somewhere else," I said to Vash.

That somewhere else would most likely be the Power Exchange. There was a good chance I'd end up there either way. The last few times I'd gone, my friend Marc, one of the most regular of the regulars, kept nudging me and saying, "You're going to be here for Halloween, right? Right?" Being wanted is a powerful thing, as is the sense of adventure, which is what was drawing me to the Feast of Souls.

Vash replied, "I would never go to a party *you'd* invited me to, only to have you leave so I can play with someone else."

"Nah, I just won't go at all. You wouldn't have to worry about me."

"That's very sweet of you, *Gato*, and it *is* something I would have wanted to go to with you, if it were another time."

Another time. To the best of my knowledge, there was no other time. Never had been, never would be. There was only now.

Dressed in my standard club attire—a short black velvet dress, red-and-black stripey tights and my tall black Fluevog boots—I went on my own to the Feast of Souls. Though held in the beautiful Porn Palace, ultimately it looked like a goth club I'd been to dozens of times before: with its faux-stone floors and moodily-lit hallways that housed all manner of fetish implements on display behind a wire mesh. There were scenes of light bondage and BDSM happening here and there, nothing more intense than the weekly happenings at Bondage-A-Go-Go or the Power Exchange itself. The only scene that really interested me at all was a woman who was having multicolored candle wax dripped onto her, and that was mostly because it reminded me of the last time Vash and I had really played with each other—candle wax, the Fourth of July, post-Ryder but pre-Dietrich. It was a memory that I held onto, probably stronger than I should have, and probably because Vash and I never got around to exploring play piercings, and I knew now that we never would.

The DJ's obvious fondness for Marilyn Manson kept me dancing, but barely anyone else. After a few hours I grew bored and was ready to relocate. I needed to be social, and that wasn't going to happen at the Feast.

As a rule, the Saturday before Halloween is typically the biggest party night in San Francisco, more so than Halloween itself or even New Year's Eve. The City was abuzz as I rode the crowded, drunk-filled Muni to The Power Exchange. I decided I was the Modern and Decidedly Sober Urban Warrior, riding the currents, reveling in the freedom of movement and the ability to choose my own direction. I figured I might as well revel in it, since I was alone either way.

All of my destinations were within walking distance. During the day I would have done it on foot, but it involved some areas which were incredibly sketchy by daylight, let alone at half-past one in the morning. As I walked from the bus stop to The Power Exchange, a guy whom I couldn't see in the shadows said: "Hey, cutie, wanna suck my dick?" It was that sort of night.

Women usually got in free at the Power Exchange, but since tonight was their big Halloween Fetish Ball, it cost me ten dollars. This offended my sense of personal entitlement, since *I* wasn't supposed to have to pay to get in. But I paid anyway. On the plus side, it was also the night of the time change, and I arrived just as the clocks were falling back. A whole free hour!

It was the busiest night I'd ever seen there, especially downstairs in the Dungeon. In the middle of the Dungeon was the Cage, reserved for regulars such as myself and those who were actually playing, and tonight the space outside the Cage was packed with new faces enthused by the Halloween spirit and hungry to see something *really out there*. My transvestite friend Rhonda was her usual sex-carny self, standing at the gate, tying to lure people into the Cage to play. Sometimes it worked, mostly it didn't, but she always made the effort. On this night there were a lot more people to try.

One who did enter the cage was Amphon, a tiny, beautiful Asian girl in a nurse's uniform. She said she wanted to be a dominatrix. With that certain look in her eye, Rhonda asked

Amphon if she had ever tied anyone up. I thought again of the alien bruises on Vash's body, many of which I at least gathered were from rope. Rope, and bondage in general, was something else Vash and I planned on exploring together, and which was abandoned when she met Dietrich.

Amphon said that no, she hadn't ever tied anyone up, but she wanted to learn. Rhonda then reasoned that if Amphon was going to tie people up, it was only right that Amphon herself first experience being tied up, yes?

Uncertain, Amphon pointed at me and said: "Why don't you tie *her* up?"

All eyes remained on Amphon. Neither Rhonda nor anybody else acknowledged Amphon's suggestion, or even my presence. At that moment, I did not exist. It was obviously a ruse, after all. Besides, why would they want to tie up a six-foot simulacrum of sexiness like me when they had a petite, genuinely sexy thing like Amphon? They wouldn't, and didn't. I drifted away and said nothing more.

iii. You Must Be Certain of the Devil

Controversial stuff is controversial. That's why one of the Deans at the College pulled the plug on the Black Mass. Never mind the *Springtime for Hitler* Nazi stuff—it was the "Satanic" aspect, pure and simple. It blew my mind that people were still afraid of Satanism in this day and age, but of course I was unusually familiar with it, and the average person still associated it with urban legends about animal sacrifices and such. Which was patently untrue: I would have given it a wide berth if there *was* any animal cruelty involved.

Vash was disappointed, though it had given her the excuse she'd been looking for to buy a nun's habit. Sister Vashita Inferni, she called herself. I was disappointed for her, but also felt a bit like I'd dodged a bullet, since I had finally forced myself onto the stupid high road, having said I was okay with Dietrich attending the Mass. My friend Embeth was going to attend as well to provide me with moral support, but it still sounded hellish. In a bad way.

Peaches and Vash didn't give up, Vash the more determined of the two. She was beginning to love the idea of her favorite bodily fluid being part of a religious ceremony, and she wasn't about to let this opportunity slip through her fingers. They spent much of November trying to find a new venue. Peaches even rewrote the script, making it less of a straight rendition of the Mass and more of a composite, bringing in bits of text from Sade as well as a bunch of authors I'd never heard of. He also removed quite a lot of the Latin, since the previous rehearsals had made it clear that it was a bit much for native English speakers. Perhaps most importantly, he changed the use of his semen to the use of his blood, therefore making the ceremony less pornographic and more Catholic.

Venue-wise, he was somehow able to convince the Dean to let him perform the Mass as part of a group show in mid-December. Whatever happens only happens once, even the things that never happen at all. Whatever the Mass might have been in October, it was going to be different now. Certainly the date was nowhere near as exciting; it had gone from Devil's Night, to the 15th of December. It wasn't even the Ides or anything.

It was, however, a date that Dietrich was going to be out of town. Embeth couldn't make it that night either, but that felt less important now.

Not only was the potential audience reduced by two, some of the participants had to drop out, including the guy in the Nazi uniform and the Deacon. Vash lobbied Peaches to make me the Deacon, saying: "Watching her perform on stage is what gave me such a huge crush on her in the first place. She'll be perfect." That was the kind of little thing that kept me going, and reminded me that Vash still loved me, even if it wasn't the way it once was, and never would be again.

Peaches was happy to bring me on board. Since he'd already been making changes to the ceremony, he had no problem with my primary request: that I would get to hold the nun's piddle-basin. It was technically the Sub-Deacon's job, but hey, the nun was *my* girlfriend, so I called dibs.

We only had time for one rehearsal before the event. The prose was certainly purpler than I was used to, and the remaining bits of Latin were going to take a bit of practice, but I remained confident that it would go fine. Vash and I also worked out some new stage business for each other—specifically during her big moment of piddling into the basin. Something to make it a little more special, *personal*.

On the night of the Mass, I wore shiny black PVC pants, my Fluevogs, and a black baby tee I'd recently acquired from the Power Exchange. I wore my bleached-blonde hair up in pigtails, and pale foundation with a black band of makeup over my eyes from temple to temple completed my look—a conscious replication of Darryl Hannah's look as Pris in *Blade Runner*. Whatever else I might be, I knew I would be striking.

Not that I was the only one in the Mass wearing black, of course. Except for Vash, everyone involved tended to wear black on a daily basis anyway. For some of them, like Leyba or his girlfriend the Sub-Deacon, their street clothes worked just fine. Peaches wore black with his ever-present priest's collar, and Vash proudly wore her new habit, in full-on Sister Vashita Inferni mode.

Only one of us not wearing black, because she wasn't wearing anything at all: the Altar, a beautiful brunette atop a five-foot platform covered with black fabric. This was, of course, entirely faithful to LaVey's Mass. Accordingly, throughout the ceremony she would writhe seductively and do obscene things with a plastic Jesus.

Hanging on the wall directly behind her were three large black-on-red pentagram tapestries. In front of her was a table draped in red velvet, on which sat all the baubles and doodads for the ceremony: a sword, a bell, a skull—the usual. Other than a single red light overhead, the majority of the room's illumination came from dozens of black candles. It *felt* Satanic. I was pleasantly shocked by how Peaches had managed to transform the otherwise banal art studio into a dark chapel, if only for this one night.

I took the time before the doors were opened to prepare myself for the performance. Even though I was going to be reading them directly from a hymnal, I knew I needed to practice. I asked Steven Leyba if I was pronouncing *"Ave Maria ad micturiendum es"* correctly. It was my big solo Latin line, and I didn't want to mangle it.

"It doesn't matter if you pronounce it correctly or not," he replied. "The words don't actually mean anything. What matters is that you say them with conviction. Just be present and in the moment, and you'll be fine."

It sounded like good advice in any context.

The doors finally opened, and the audience filed in. Much to my surprise, the room was soon packed. Even more to my surprise, the audience seemed *deadly* serious. I expected that most people would be there ironically, as even *I* was on some level, but no—they were quite earnest. And when the Mass began, I expected there to at least be chuckling now and again because heaven knew parts of it were pretty silly, and modern audiences tend to treat *The Exorcist* like it's a comedy, for Pete's sake. But the crowd watched in hushed, rapt silence.

The Sub-Deacon and I stood on either side of Peaches, with Sister Vashita on the far side of the Sub-Deacon. As much as my inherently needy nature wished she was closer, I also realized that our distance would make our big moment together all the more dramatic, as I would have to cross both Peaches and the Sub-Deacon to get to her. All eyes would surely be on us.

Until our big moment, all of my lines were spoken in unison with Peaches and the Sub-Deacon. Indeed, both Sister Vashita and I would be soloing at the same time. So much the better.

Finally, Peaches said: "Enlightened sister, we ask a blessing."

I took the basin from the table, walked over to Sister Vashita, and placed the basin beneath her. She lifted her habit and urinated. Though the text of the Mass merely required her to "smile beatifically," she instead writhed and moaned, giving the Altar heavy competition for the Best Simulated Orgasm Award. I stood close, running a hand over Sister Vashita's body, reading my lines from my hymnal. Though they were not my words and it was someone else's party, I gave it my all:

In the name of Mary, She maketh the font resound
with the waters of mercy. She giveth the showers of blessing
and pourest forth the tears of her shame.
She suffereth long, and her humiliation is great,
and she doth pour upon the Earth with the joy of her mortification.
The waters of her shame become a shower of blessing in the
tabernacle of Satan, for that which hath been withheld pourest
forth—and with it, her piety.
The great Baphomet, who is in the midst of the throne,
shall sustain her. For she is a living fountain of water.
Her cup runneth over, and her water is sublime.
Ave Maria ad micturiendum est.

And runneth over she did, since Sister Vashita drank two liters of water before the ceremony. As I said the tricky line *"Ave Maria ad micturiendum est,"* she dipped her hand into the urine stream, then spread it over my lips and into my mouth. It tasted like slightly tart water. She'd been experimenting for the past few weeks with different foods to see what gave her pee the most distinctive, tasty flavor, and pineapple was the best. This bit of business also gave me a chance to turn the page of the hymnal so I could read my final lines:

And the Dark Lord shall wipe all tears from her eyes,
for He said unto me: It is done.
I am Alpha and Omega, the beginning and the end.
I will give freely unto him that is athirst of the fountain
of the water of life.

Sister Vashita spread another handful of urine on her lips and kissed me more passionately than she had in months. As we made out,her pee smeared our makeup and swished around in our mouths and mixed with our saliva. I then felt a genuine connection between us—a renewed sense of adventure, love, and finally, *hope* for our relationship.

I took the basin to Peaches. He dipped a dildo into it, performed a blessing, then offered the dildo to the Sub-Deacon and I to kiss. The dildo was dry, since not a lot of the pee actually went into the basin, and what little did make it onto the dildo had immediately dripped back off. Oh well. It would have been anticlimactic for me.

As is usually the case, toward the end of the Mass was Communion. A lot of people took it, including myself. First time I'd done it in years. As is *not* usually the case, the Mass closed with the Deacon—*me!*—picking up the sword and leading the processional out of the room.

I reflected on what Leyba had told me earlier in the evening: *to be present, to be in the moment.* Holding the sword at the front of the processional, still glowing and moist from Vash's love, I hadn't felt so present in a long, long time.

WAR WITH WAKING UP
• *Noel Arthur Heimpel*

I've been dreaming such a long time.

"Birdy. Hey, hey Birdy."

Close your eyes before the—

Dawn-light breaks.

I toss an arm over my eyes as a shield. "What the fuck, Melissa? You said you wouldn't come here anymore," I grumble.

"Yeah, well, I dreamt about you last night."

"You can't dream, Lissa."

"Says you," she says, and pulls my arm off of my face. The morning sun pouring through the window forces me to squint, but that only makes her easier to see. Rather than becoming a blur of color and shadow, Melissa's face comes into focus: skin like milky coffee, brown doe-eyes, a beauty mark on her left cheek and lips that—

Are far too soft on mine. What a way to wake up. Her grip on my wrist is so tight that she may as well have tied me to the bed. The blood rushes through my arteries, a peculiar and frightening sensation I've never quite gotten used to.

"What exactly did this dream entail?" I ask when she releases the lock on my lips.

She smirks. "You're expecting me to say we were screwing, but we weren't. It was about when we first met, except the roles were reversed. I got to see your *insides*," she says. "I got to cut you."

"And you get off on that? You're sick," I say, sitting up. A glance at Nikki's side of the room confirms that she never came back last night, probably passed out drunk at a friend's place. Good. She doesn't need to see this. "Also, don't call me Birdy."

Melissa laughs and smooths her shiny black hair. "You're the one fantasizing about a cadaver, *Haruki*, not me." She purses her lips when she says my name and draws out the *eee* sound at the end. God, she's beautiful when she does that.

"If you're just a fantasy, then how can you dream?"

"Maybe you're fantasizing that I dream about you. That's pretty messed up, considering."

"Huh. Whatever."

Ignoring her, I slip out of bed and into the bathroom, locking the door behind me. That probably won't deter her, but I feel safer. If my suitemates hear me talking to someone in the bathroom, they might get curious. I turn the water as hot as it will go and scrub my skin red.

From the other side of the shower curtain, Melissa says, "Keep that up and you're going to faint."

She watches me dress and comb my hair, making comments all the while. I answer as little as possible, even though some of the things she says are rather provoking. You should wear baggier jeans to hide your chicken legs. You know how hot it gets in Linthicum, so why are you wearing long sleeves, especially with that binder thing underneath? You stink when you sweat, although I kinda like it. Are you going prematurely gray or is that a shitload of dandruff?

"If you're a fantasy, you should be praising me seven ways to heaven," I mutter as she follows me to class.

"Not necessarily. You could be a masochist."

In the sun, her skin shimmers. It didn't look that way under the harsh fluorescent lights of the classroom. She'd looked slightly pickled, a jarred specimen saved for frightened and curious minds like mine.

Melissa Jacquelyn Phelps, aged nineteen. African-American. Cause of death:—

That's as far as I got into the file on Dr. Hanson's desk when he turned around.

I'd gone back to Tower A feeling flustered beyond belief.

Haru, what are you doing? What is that?
A dead bird.
Ew! Why are you touching it? That's gross!
It's not gross, it's... it's pretty.

I'd dreamed of her. There on the stainless steel table, she opened her eyes and smiled at me as I reached into her open chest cavity and touched her (beating) heart with my bare hand. I'd wandered to the bathroom in a daze and thrown up in joy and horror.

There was a girl in my bed when I woke. Her body was pressed against mine and undoubtedly nubile, though at the moment I was looking into her eyes and nothing else. They were six feet deep in color.
"Hi," she said in a honeyed voice. "Remember me?"
With a pink-palmed hand she traced the Y-incision that spliced her chest. Yesterday she had been broken open for all to see, but today she was stitched up, nothing but a crust of dried blood remaining. I touched the dark, raised line and she jumped slightly.
"Hey, that does hurt, you know."
"Are you... alive? Or are you dead?"

"Which do you want me to be?"
"I... don't know."

I feel slightly nauseated thinking about it now.

After class, we head into town. Towson is a pleasant city with a gritty tinge from neighboring Baltimore. Slightly up-town, but with a noticeable underside.

Prospect Hill Cemetery is one of the city's hidden treasures. When I stumbled by its sign—the only thing visible behind trees and concrete walls—on a chance walk down York Road, I had no choice but to change direction and take a look. The view was startling—from the top of that hill, I swore I could see all the way to Pennsylvania.

"It's so green," Melissa says, surveying the land. I'm sitting and she's standing on the low wall which surrounds the family grave of one of the Grand Master Masons, or someone mysterious and important like that. We don't sit or stand on the actual graves unless the occupant is willing to converse, and today everyone is silent.

"Yeah, well, if you drove up there you'd hit cities."

"I know that. I grew up in Dundalk."

"Oh."

She tears her gaze away from the horizon, frowning. The top arms of the Y-incision are visible above the collar of her t-shirt. "Oh? What's that mean? I know the poop-plants are there and all, so it doesn't smell that great sometimes—"

"I just... is that true, or did I make that up? That you come from Dundalk, which, by the way, I've never been to," I say, my momentary peace interrupted. This morning's unease worms its way into my belly and wiggles there uncomfortably.

"You think too much," she says, "especially about me."

I shake my head. "Well, it's kind of important for me to know if you're real or if you're a hallucination."

If she's not real, I'll kill myself.

Melissa squats down beside me, balanced precariously on the balls of her feet. The drop beside us isn't a short one. She cups my chin with her hand. "What exactly do you consider 'real' anyway? You're always saying you're a *real* boy, that your gender's in your head and not in your pants," she says, glancing down at my hips, birthing hips, something I'll never get rid of. "So even if I'm all in your head, why can't I be real, too?"

> *"Your silence betrays you," I said, when she couldn't answer my question. She made a face.*
> *"How tragically poetic of you. Has it occurred to you that I didn't answer because I don't know myself?"*
> *"But you should know."*

As a kid, I asked my dad why the sky was blue, and he told me it was the way light reflects off of the elements in the atmosphere. I was eight, and that's when the disillusionment began. For most people, it starts around puberty—this loss of childhood magic—but I started losing my inherent faith in the workings of the world at eight. Puberty was a whole other ball game.

"So, Haruka, your survey says you're here because you're worried about... hallucinations?"

I shift around in the oversized leather armchair, trying to avoid the psychologist's concerned and questioning stare. The school's counseling center is an old white Victorian, completely out of place among buildings and walkways of dark red brick, of new glassy structures that gleam in the sunlight. Its rooms are cramped and homey, comforting... for a doctor's office. I hate doctors' offices.

"Oh! I'm so sorry, Haru-*ki*. I didn't see that you had marked down a different preferred name. They're so similar."

"Mm-hmm."

"Sorry for being blunt, but have you been on, or are you currently on any hallucinogenic drugs?"

"No."

"You can tell me if you are. Everything you say here is completely confidential."

"I'm not." Or I wouldn't be here.

"Okay." Her voice is soft and soothing, low for a woman, which only makes me more restless. "You also marked that you identify as transgender. Do these hallucinations have anything to do with that?"

"No."

"Have you been to a gender therapist, or diagnosed with Gender Identity Disorder?"

My scalp itches. This isn't what I'm here to talk about. "Yes and yes. I've been on testosterone for three months now."

"When did the hallucinations start? Around that same time?"

"I *really* don't think that's the reason—"

She crosses her legs and presses her lips together. "You should bring it up with your primary physician, or whoever's prescribing you the hormones. Are you still seeing your gender therapist? Is there a reason you're here and not with him or her?"

"My next appointment isn't for two weeks and they're booked up," I say as a bubble of anger rises in my chest. "I didn't come here to talk about that."

She looks down at her clipboard. "You indicated that you were feeling suicidal. What kind of thoughts do you mean, exactly? Do you have a plan, or—"

"Like how I would do it?"

"Yes."

"*Yes.*"

"Do you think you're in danger of—"

"That's not really why I'm here either," I blurt out, my agitation growing. Melissa hasn't come around at all today. I stare at the psychology books lining a nearby shelf, but I can't read the titles. I have perfect vision, *but I can't read them.* The fact that she used my *old* name doesn't help. It's only one letter different, but it brings up a whole different me—namely, someone who isn't me.

What does that even mean anymore? The chair has metal buttons. I pick at one of them. My fingernails are getting too long for a guy. Small detail, you'd think, but people notice.

She pauses and flips a page over the clipboard. Slowly, she says, "I'd like you to describe these hallucinations to me, if you're comfortable doing so."

The next day, I find Melissa at Newell (the good dining hall), seated in an empty booth. She has an untouched glass of root beer and watches me reproachfully as I sit down with my tray. All I can stomach at the moment is salad without any dressing. Everything else is too heavy, and made of dead things.

She watches me eat.

"You told someone."

"Yeah, so?" I try to sound as if it's no big deal.

"You went to a shrink," she says. When I look up, I find her eyes as accusing as her voice.

Setting my fork down and straightening up, I say, "Yes. Yes, I did. I'm sorry, but I have to know."

"Can't you just believe? What happened to faith?" she says, spreading her palms before her.

"The world doesn't work that way." I can't stand her pleading tone, so I go back to my food. Maybe I can drown her out in the crunch of my cucumbers.

"Goddamn science-minded atheists," she says derisively. "You think everything works under the same rules."

She suddenly stands and knocks over both of our glasses. Rivers of caramel color and corn syrup race across the table as adrenaline and surprise race through my body. Several people turn around for the source of the clatter. Did that happen? Did they hear her? Do they see her?

Flustered and embarrassed, I turn back around to clean up the mess. But when I reach for the napkin basket, I see that only one of the glasses has been overturned: hers.

I am lying on a cold metal table. Smooth. Flawless.
(not me, the table)
Melissa is lying next to me, her arm just barely touching mine. In fact, our arms may not be touching at all. We may be so inestimably close that my mind is creating the sensation, knowing that at any second it's what I should be feeling. Above us there's a ladybug caught in one of the light fixtures. It's still alive.
Melissa rolls over and props herself up on one elbow. She's naked except for a pair of pink briefs. Pink with blue polka dots, and a little blue bow. I'm naked, too, which makes me squirm uncomfortably. My parts mirror hers, and I wish they didn't. Maybe while I'm on the table they'll change that for me.
"I won't lie: I'm thinking of eating you," she says with a small smile.
"That's okay," I reply, "I'm thinking of eating you, too."
This seems to disturb her. Her eyes widen and her body grows still. She stares at me, lips parting, and I turn to stare at the ladybug in the light fixture. I'm actually thinking about birds.

"Poor thing. I wonder what it died of."

"I don't know."

We've stopped on our way back from the cemetery to observe a small gray bird on the sidewalk. Normal people will pass by it—just another street-side casualty—but not us. Not my dead lover (can I call her that?) and not me.

What kind of bird is it, Mom?
A mourning dove.
But it's afternoon.
The word is m–o–u–r–n–i–n–g. It's what we do when things we love die, and it makes us sad.
Why? Why should we be sad?

"Are you all right?"

"..."

"Haruki?"

"... can I leave now?"

"Are you having a hallucination *now*? Or are you simply uncomfortable?"

"..."

"Have you ever considered that you may need, or benefit from, hospitalization? I can call an ambulance from Saint Joseph's if you need me to. They're five minutes down the street, and so is Shepherd Pratt. It's—"

"I know what it is. I don't want to go there."

"Because... Melissa might get mad at you?"

"..."

"I'll be honest, what you're describing sounds a lot like schizophrenia, which worsens with time, and which can seriously impede your ability to function normally. This is not a formal diagnosis and I can't prescribe you any medications, but I would like to write a letter to your current therapist and primary physician to explain what's going on."

"I'm not... I don't need... I can tell them myself."

"Are you sure you will?"

"Can I leave?"

"No."

"No?"

"You're insane, Birdy, and you need help. Lots of help, little (and big) pills in paper cups given to you at the same time each night from a doctor who won't let you even have shoelaces because you could strangle yourself with them, or sharp pencils because you could stab someone. You like blood, don't you? You know you do. You know you've thought about *doing it*. Asking her to dissect you."

"... excuse me?"

"I said, yes, you can leave. Please call me if you need anything."

After the fight in the dining hall, I remember that I have other friends. Friends who are definitely real (aren't they? *aren't they?*), around whom Melissa usually doesn't appear. I scrounge up some change and catch the number eleven bus down to Fell's Point. It takes an hour, but I welcome the time to cool down, to think.

A light breeze plays its way across my face when I step off the bus. Thinking about the sensation makes it weird, in the way that writing the same word over and over makes it look like nonsense. I have to touch my face to make sure it's still there, and even then it feels like a stranger's.

A ray of sinking sunlight blinds me as I walk past a glassy building; in the instant after, I suddenly feel released. Free. Stopping mid-stride, I stare stupidly at the street, struck by shivers and a realization.

Then the feeling passes, and I'm left grasping for the beautiful (peace)(understanding)(reality) I held moments before. What can I do? I keep going.

"Ruki!" Winter exclaims cheerfully when she spots me entering the restaurant. She jumps up from her chair, long black hair swinging, and throws her arms around me. She smells like incense and patchouli.

320

Winter is the only person in the world who can get away with calling me "Ruki." It's always sounded like a girl's name to me, almost as bad as my birth name. Maybe one day I won't cringe at being seen as feminine. One day when I have a *beard*, like most guys my age.

I can't blame Winter, though; she's too sweet.

"You're late," Lorna says as the two of us approach the table and take our seats. She is, as expected, rubbing her elbow in annoyance, but then she smiles with her perfectly straight and white teeth. "We already ordered."

"Yeah, if you can call this stuff *food*," mutters Brian. He sips his coffee and eyes the juice bar concoction the girls are sharing. "I am a carnivore. I do not belong in a vegetarian restaurant."

"Too bad, T-Rex. Liquid Earth is Ruki's and my favorite, isn't it?" Winter musses his red hair affectionately (as if it's not already mussed) and kisses his stubbly cheek. Brian rolls his eyes and then directs them at me.

"So how's things? Haven't seen you in a while."

I open my mouth to say I'm fine, but that would be a lie. Instead what comes out is, "Eh, I dunno. Been feeling... odd lately."

"Odd how?" Lorna asks.

"Can I have a sip of that? Thanks. I'm not sure how to describe it," I say, after wetting my dry throat on their juice, which tastes strongly of ginger and honey. Very potent. A warm feeling spreads through my chest.

And immediately turns cold. Melissa walks past our table and seats herself at one nearby. She looks perfectly at home under the warm track lighting, her feigned interest in the paintings on the wall almost believable.

"Try us," Brian says. Behind him, Melissa is now looking at a menu. I didn't see the waiter bring her one, but he might have in the minute I looked away.

"Do you believe in ghosts? Or at least, something that comes back after death?"

Everyone looks at me, including Melissa.

Winter nods, suddenly serious. Lorna says, slowly, "Yeah, I suppose so," while Brian puts his glass down with a heavy clunk and clatter of ice.

"Yes," he says curtly. "Why?"

I was not expecting this kind of reaction. Waves of relief replace the tension that's been building up in my body all day. "You know my girlfriend you've never met? Lissa? She's dead."

Lorna's naturally stern face softens, and she places her hand over mine. "I'm so sorry," she says, then frowns when I pull away.

"No, that's not what I mean. I mean she was dead when I met her."

"That's what I thought you meant," says Winter, wide-eyed. Leave it to Winter to understand the situation.

"You... still believe me? Because I'm not sure I believe me," I say, and when I place my hand on my chest I can feel my heart pounding. The binder keeping my breasts flat doesn't help. If anything, the constriction makes it worse. I can hear my bones straining against the tight fabric. "We don't... I always thought that when we die, we die, you know? And that's it. There's nothing after."

"Well, I know for a fact that sometimes there is," Brian says. "What can we do to help?"

"You can stay out of our business!"

Melissa appears behind Brian with a look of absolute rage on her face. She glares at my friends and then at me. Our eyes lock. Her eyes are so dark. Her hair is full of dark feathers now, all feathers, not hair...

I'm falling.

The room spins and goes dark.

Sometime later, a voice in the darkness says:

"She doesn't have much longer."
My heart has slowed from its crazy tattoo, but now it
feels too slow. So slow, too slow. There is a tube down
my throat and I don't like it. How did I even get here?
"I don't understand. This is so sudden."
Lips are dry, but the tube stops me from licking them.
I do seem to be in a hospital. The walls are buttercream
with bright butterflies painted here and there. What
is this, the children's ward? I'm not a child. There's a
teenager in the bed next to mine. That doesn't help me
figure out where I am.
"Yes, we know. But at this point, even surgery—"
My chest hurts. There are wires stuck to me and
machines going beep—beep—beep.
"How is it no one knew?"
These sheets are too starchy.
"..."
At least there are windows. They alleviate the glare of
hard fluorescent lighting and there's a little bird on the
ledge, staring at me. A mourning dove, warm gray and
probably so soft if I could hold her between my fingers...
"Doctor?"
Another bird is headed this way. A little blackbird on
the wing. But he doesn't stop—doesn't slow down—my
heart speeds up, painfully—
"I'm sorry."
«thud»

"How did she die, Haruki?"

I open my eyes to Brian's scruffy face. I'm on the floor of the restaurant, the girls and our waiter hovering nearby.

"I don't know. She was the cadaver we were using in class..."

Lorna slaps a hand over her mouth and turns away.

"What happened?" My back and head are sore. Brian and Winter both lend me a hand getting to my feet while Lorna picks up my overturned chair. So I didn't *just* fall.

Winter points at the table, where everyone's drinks have been knocked over except mine. The saltshaker has also been emptied, and written in the resulting mess the words: *Bye-bye Blackbird.*

"Did you see anyone?" I hear myself ask the all-important question, but my mind is elsewhere. Back in the darkness, in that peculiar dream or memory, whatever it was. I lick my lips but only taste blood. I seem to have bit down on my tongue.

My friends are silent. The waiter sidles away.

"Er, Ruki," says Winter, but she lets her voice trail off.

Lorna picks up for her, in a much less sympathetic voice: "It was you."

> *close your eyes*
> *before daylight*
> *breaks*

"Do you want me to call your parents? Your sister?"

I shake my head. No, I don't want to talk to them. I don't want to see them and I don't want them to see me like this. Bad enough Winter had to see me cry. She's still sitting on the bed, trying to comfort me. Her presence is about the only one I can stand right now, and definitely the only thing keeping me from figuring out how to get onto the roof of this sixteen-floor building.

"You could stop stroking my hair, please," I mumble through snot and tear residue.

After a moment, she says uncertainly, "I haven't touched you."

Damnit, Melissa. I pull the covers over my head, which forces her to stop. Wherever she is... in whatever form. In my mind?

"Winter?"

"Yes?"

"Do you think I should be in a hospital?"

"Only if you were really sick."

"Isn't that obvious?"

"She could have possessed you, if she really is a ghost."

I can't help it. I laugh. I laugh and laugh and laugh and can't stop.

Winter waits until I'm choking on the last few chuckles to say, "If you want, I'll stay here with you tonight. If you think Nikki won't mind me sleeping in her bed, of course. She's almost never here. Are you sure your roomie's not a ghost?"

She means it as a jest but the notion gets my brain going. What's real and what isn't? Who's dead and who's alive? How do I tell? What if I don't actually have a roommate?

What if Melissa's just some fragment of myself? Maybe when I rejected the body I was born with and threw away the dresses from my childhood, I also threw out a piece of a person. Suddenly I'm terrified that my being transgender is what spawned Melissa, and her appearance is a sign that I'm not really a boy, that I'm just very, very sick. Just like all the conservatives say—I'm confused, a liar, a fake.

What if?

Winter clears her throat. "I think I'll stay. We can think clearer and sort this out in the morning, okay?"

> The light is blinding. Harsh. My fingers twitch and scrabble against cold steel—on the operating table again, yes?
> "Yes."
> I turn my head and Melissa is there. Of course she's there. Her curves are hidden by a long white coat, starched and without a stain.
> Scalpels gleam.

I feel exposed.

"Let me show you how I died," she says. The gleam is in her hand now. My skin prickles with goosebumps, every hair standing on end in a miracle reaction of stimuli and electrical impulses. I can feel the currents racing along the synapses in my brain.

Don't touch me with that, what are you doing?

Wait, that's going to—

Pain. How fine an edge, how sterling, to cut through flesh and blood so easily. Her stroke is effortless and soft, a cold line followed by flooding warmth. Under the lamp the blood—my blood—is bright and beautiful. Water and plasma, the same state of matter attributed to fire and lightning.

The fire spreads through my chest and the lightning pours out onto the table.

"I thought you'd cry, but you're silent. That's good. I don't like hearing you cry." Melissa leans over and kisses the incision before kissing me on the lips and the forehead, leaving sticky patterns of warmth behind. Then she takes her fingers and—Oh, no.

"Hey, don't!"

The sharp crack of my own bones sends me into shudders. I opened my heart to you but now you've opened it yourself in a much different way—how different? I should have passed out, or I should be dead. My ribs stick up before me like a bizarre basket filled with blood and innards. I reach up and touch one. It's smooth. Let me show you how I died.

Cold air touches me in places it was never meant to, stark contrast to Melissa's ungloved hands. She traces arteries with her fingertips, tracing a child's maze puzzle to the end. To my—

"—heart. That's how she died, something was wrong with her heart."

Winter sits up and squints at me sleepily from across the room. She rubs her eyes and looks at the clock. Five thirty-six in the morning. The first rays of pre-dawn are just creeping over our edge of the Earth and coloring the campus gray.

"Like, figuratively, or literally?" she says with a huge yawn.

I wipe the sweat from my brow and push back the covers. I won't be sleeping any more this morning, much as I... much as I would have liked that dream to continue. Instinctively, my hand goes to my chest.

There's a bruise over the place my heart should rest. Deep purple spreading beneath pale skin. I touch it lightly and wince. It'll be sports bras instead of the binder for a few days.

"I don't know. I meant it literally, but maybe... maybe both."

Dawn breaks behind a wall of clouds, the kind that keep the light soft and silver all day long. The world has been sapped of color, reduced to something pallid and somber. I head for the cemetery despite the threat of rain.

The light doesn't seem to affect Melissa, who appears dark and intense as ever. Her eyes are downcast and she doesn't look up when I take a seat on the wall beside her. I try to sound upbeat.

"Hey Lissa."

"Hey," she replies flatly.

"Um, look. I wanted to say... I'm sorry."

She shrugs.

"Really. I just want things back to how they used to be between us. How they were at first. You know," I plead. She sighs and rolls her eyes. They land on me, six-feet-deep as always.

"And how was that?"

I take her hands in mine. They're cold. Once they were warm and life coursed through them, but now they're always cold. They have been since we met that dreary day in the science lab. Met in death. Sometimes, though she is ten times more beautiful in this "live" apparition, I think I preferred her on the table, open and broken.

"Wonderful, that's what it was. I didn't care what you were, just that you were there. You're still here, aren't you? So be here for me."

"Promise me that you won't go running to that shrink or your friends again?" she says. Her expression is still mistrustful, and her lips pressed into a strange shape.

"I promise," I say, and the lie is bitter on my lips, but her kisses taste so sweet.

> *I love you I love you I love you I love you I love you I love*
> *you I love you I love you I love you I love you I love you*
> *I love you I love you I love you I love you I love you I love*
> *you I love you I love—*
> *desperately need you*
> *Mel–Haruki–ssa.*
> *Kiss me.*

At least she's warm. We lay in bed, touching, only touching. Thinking back to my theory that she's my femaleness cast out, does this mean I'm getting "in touch" with my feminine side? Not only is that a terrible pun, but it feels wrong. I'm me and she's her, right? If only I could be sure of that.

She's been quiet for a while now, and I break—no, *shatter* the silence with:

"What's dying like?"

Melissa stiffens. Her eyes flutter open and she rubs at the beauty mark on her face.

"Like being born, I guess. You know it happened but hell if you can remember," she says slowly, and then laughs. It's a nervous sort of laugh, with none of her usual confidence.

"Oh."

"Yeah."

I should get out of bed, but I don't want to leave her or her warmth. I think it might hurt if we stopped *touching*.

"How... how did you die?"

She doesn't answer. I glance at my cell phone: I'm going to be late for class if I don't get up and start getting ready. I linger a bit longer before rolling out of bed. Brushing my teeth, my hair. Throwing some clothes on (not particularly matched). It should feel so normal, but it doesn't. Feels like the old days, before I came out and started being the real me.

The *real me?* Yes. I'm me and she's her. I'm a little more sure of that now.

As I straighten up from buttoning my jeans, a sudden pang of longing hits me. Longing for what, I'm not sure. The feeling is similar to the one I had down in Fell's Point, a rush to the senses and to the spirit, as though I've grown too large for my skin. I throw the curtains back and the sunlight streams in, blinding and beautiful.

Melissa says, "He broke my heart."

close your eyes before

Breathe in, breathe out. Breathe in, breathe out. This is the end of the world—the end of my world, at least, of *a* world. Winter's hand is small but warm in mine; Lorna stands stiffly, counting under her breath as she is wont to do. Brian stares sullenly at the door.

"What if it's just me? What if I'm really just insane?"

Brian shrugs and says, "Then we'll take you to a hospital."

The bottom of my stomach drops out.

"Eh," says Lorna, now chewing on her nails and rubbing her elbow (so often rubbed that it cracks and peels), "hospitals don't necessarily do any good."

"Obsessive-compulsive disorder is different than having schizophrenia."

"I *know* that, but it really doesn't change much. Plus it's damn expensive."

"Shh!" Winter hushes both of them, removing her finger from her lips, and points.

There, in the slinky white t-shirt dress. Just enough drape, just enough cling, in just the right places. Hair sleek and shiny in the lamp-light, in the polluted city-light, undoubled by a reflection in the glass of the Glen dining hall beside her, like a piece of modern art. She could never be something *I* cast off. My femininity was clunky and childish, nothing so—

So perfect, I'm sorry.

I throw my gaze towards the sky. I want to be on top of these fourteen-floor buildings, not down on the ground. Somewhere I can jump from if everything goes wrong. I am sick with the essence of my own betrayal. Have I really done this to myself? Something in the depths of my chest screams *no, no, you've always been a real boy*, but the doubt lingers.

My friends slink into the shadows, and Melissa approaches. The serious face turns into a bright smile. Can hearts be broken twice? Or are they never repaired after the first crack?

Words leave my lips and—

"Lissa, I love you, but—"

> "I love you, but I have to end it."
> So cold, I feel so cold and yet my chest... a burning core
> of heat, of thudding bass, a tempo set to burst through
> flesh and bone and skin.
> "It? You mean us. End us. How could you?"
> Never felt quite this bad before, sure, similar times
> before, always when upset, but then I've never been

this upset so
"Look, baby, it's just not working. You have to see that."
Somewhere, a mourning dove calls solemnly.
Appropriate? But no one has died.
"I don't. I don't see it at all. I thought we were gonna
be together forever! I thought... but... how..."
Yet.
"Lissa? You okay baby? I know this is hard, but—Lissa?
Melissa! Answer me—
«thud–thud–thud–thud–thud»
bye bye blackbird bye bye
away
you
fly

"I love you, too, Haruki, can't you see that? That's why I picked
you, because you picked me that day in the lab. Your love was
so strong that I just *had* to come. I *had* to.

"You were so beautiful and new, with the right chemicals finally
rushing through your veins... the excitement of that first needle
lingering on your skin. You were strong and ready. I needed
that. I needed you."

So much blood, everywhere.

Her heart was defective from the start
No wonder it was broken so easily
Should have had a sticker
Handle with care.

It's on my hands and hers, too. Mine but not mine and not
hers. Oh BrianLornaWinter, I'm so sorry I brought you into this.
Don't die. One ghost is enough of a haunting for me, thanks.

> *You guys believed me awful quickly. And even after I...*
> *went crazy and all at the restaurant.*
> *Yeah well, we've seen a few things ourselves. Things*
> *that make us instant believers, as it were.*
> *Like what?*
> *Can't talk about it.*
> *Sorry.*
> *All my fault, too.*
> *Brian—*
> *No, really, it is. Don't say it's not, Win.*
> *What they mean is, we'll help you.*
> *Yes. And we have a plan...*
> *A plan for what?*
> *For getting rid of your stalker.*
> *But I...*
> *It's not healthy and you know it.*
> *But*
> *(if not for you, do it for her, Ruki, do it for her)*
> *But*
> *Okay.*

Where did the scalpels come from? Surely I didn't have those tucked into my pockets, did I?

"If you hurt anyone, it should be me. Not them," I whisper. The crowds of sparkling girls have disappeared; the eyes of the Towers are shut and dark, as if we're the only ones awake, the only ones left. Plunged into darkness and yet not darkness. In the city there is never really true darkness, except perhaps of the heart. My heart is bright, though.

Blood on the bricks. Blood on the bench.

"True enough," Melissa says. Her inky feathers ruffle in the breeze. She raises her fist, where sharp metal gleams. My arm raises, too, a mirror image; I am the reflection she lacks, the shadow she never casts. Or is she mine? Is she trembling the way I'm trembling? Earthquakes in my soul. I know it now: she's mine but she is not *me*.

Relief, and then—

"Let me show you how I died."

And there it is—there *I* am—parts of me never exposed to daylight now under the moon and city-light. Our hearts beat frantically, terrified of such exposure. Oh, but wearing your heart on your sleeve *does* always lead to breaking, doesn't it? Such fragile things, some more than others. Melissa's heart is dark and swollen.

She raises the scalpel. I do the only thing I can think of. I touch her heart.

"You really do love me."
"Of course I do. I wouldn't lie about that."
Flesh and blood and bone entwined, arteries arching and looping through tangles of capillaries and tendons, we are one and that is all that matters. The ultimate embrace, beyond any intimacy I've ever indulged in before.
All in utter, still calm.
No heartbeats.
"I'm sorry I had to do that."
"How did you know I would react that way?"
A nod, her forehead bumping into mine lightly. Our toenails grow into the ground.
"Some part of you needed me."
"All of me needs you."
"But now I have to go."
"I know."

"Thank you for fixing me."
One more kiss, one more light brush of lips and fingers,
wisps of hair tickling cheeks and noses.

"Now wake up, Haruki."

I open my eyes and daylight breaks. My heart beats slowly behind my ribs, my unbroken ribs, which still hurt when I run my fingers along them. I peer down the front of my hospital gown and find, unsurprisingly, a wealth of purple bruises.

"Mind telling us what happened out there? You suddenly dying and coming back to life and all?" Brian says during his visit later. His presence, and those of the girls, is cheering in this white-washed hospital setting. Shepherd Pratt is practically on campus, but I feel a world away.

They have no injuries, no bloody bandages that I can see. Strange, but unimportant.

I smile.

"You tell *me*."

The bruises appear to be in a random pattern only until I look in the mirror later and find they're in the shape of wings.

Bye bye, blackbird, your dove will miss you.

It's a brand new day.

CURSED

• *Everett Maroon*

It wasn't out of concern that he told me I'd never have a boy phase—it was spite that pushed the nasty sentiment out of his mouth. I considered countering it with a quantity of my own meanness, but Alex wore me out in a way that tended to tangle up my responses. At that point my only option was to curl up a couple of fists and flood the capillaries in my face with blood before storming off.

—Thanks for your support, I said, which was all I could manage before letting the screen door clang behind me. He called out after me, his voice froggy from three months of hormones, his version of the boy phase. I knew what he thought of me: I was a copycat, a weak imitation, a butch who had aspirations to leap to his more hip plane of transfolkitude. He wished me lots of sex with myself as I took long steps across the street to the next corner, even though the blinking orange-red hand warded off pedestrians and the police were on their late-month vigilance against jaywalking. *Hit me with your $5 fine, assholes. I didn't even have a boy phase ahead of me. I will not pass GO and I will not collect anything but fakery.*

To my frustration, he turned out to be right. Five-foot-eleven people don't have much in the way of waiflike boyishness before the hormones go to work, much less afterward. I had progressed quickly, feeling my muscles consume the T like hyenas. I broke out as beard hairs emerged, and I catapulted over the squeaky adolescent voice, careening directly into baritone range. It wasn't that I wanted to avoid a second puberty—I just didn't want to see Alex be right about anything.

Actually I was thrilled to see my face in the mirror, reflecting back not only myself, but my life after all of the tumult with Alex. Two years after the summer mosquitoes and my own worries tried to eat me alive, I found myself commuting as a stealth trans man to my job on the other side of the city. On the subway I blended in with the other artists, computer nerds, and professional wonks—relishing the regular vibration from the train track and looking forward to popping out into the morning sunlight on my short walk to work.

I caught a glance from a man in the single seat across from the driver. He'd been on my commute since late last week. New job, in town for a conference, or—less probable—the stalker of someone else far more interesting than me. I had another sensation of being watched, and this time he noticed me noticing him. He beamed over a quick smile. Reflexively, I did the same. If given the opportunity to hold a poker face or make eye contact, I would have chosen a blank expression, but another part of me craved attention and, even though it was known only to me, the validation that I passed as the man he presumed I was.

The sing-song of the door jingle took me out of the book I was reading. I stood up and juggled it with my bag while also fumbling to locate my speed pass, the fourth I'd had in a year.

It seemed to be a purposeful policy at the subway management office to make the reusable cards as flimsy as possible so that they would suddenly crack into eighteen pieces and float down to the floor like so many maple tree seeds. This bit of plastic was only a couple of weeks old, and already it was showing signs of wear, with the transparent membrane beginning to curl back from the rounded edges on two sides. I cursed at it and twisted it around my fingers to hold it near enough to the scanner to let myself out into the humid sunlight of a Tuesday morning.

—It can't be that bad a day already, said a voice behind me, Mr. Glance.

—I don't see why it can't, I said. Great. I was arguing with him and using double negatives. I should just make the international sign for not talking, but my hands were full, as already noted. Besides, there is no such thing as an international sign for not talking. I kept moving along to the start of the towering escalator.

—Well, maybe your day will improve from here, he said, stepping into place next to me on the stair. It was a three minute ride to the surface. A glance on a crowded subway car was one thing, but now he was next to me. I could study the fine stitching of his Ben Sherman dress shirt and smell his cologne, a surprising mix of musky and crisp.

—Maybe it will, I said. Again, without meaning to, my body reacted without my approval. I had flashed him a smile. Out from his pocket he snagged a white business card, holding it out to me and then tucking into the pages of my book. He suggested quietly that I call him sometime. I nodded to say that I would, though I doubted my ability to dial his number.

Free of him and back on my solitary commute, a four-block walk to my office. Along the way I replayed our brief conversation. My mind presented close-ups of the corners of his mouth as he talked, surrounded by a lush, brown beard. The kind of beard trans men whine about not having, myself included.

Of course I couldn't call him. He was expecting a gay man with no surprises, or at least nothing really out of the ordinary. I was nothing if not 207 miles away from ordinary. Sure, I hadn't gone through a boyish phase. I would never be teen heartthrob material, and I was okay with that. But I didn't know how to respond to people who made assumptions about my status or rather, my body. I ignored the slice of cardstock that peeked out from the middle of the pulp novel, even though it distinguished itself from the pages by virtue of being stark white and smelling notably better than old mass market paperbacks ever manage, even when new.

I took phone calls. I argued with suppliers and scarfed down an overpriced grilled vegetable sandwich. I went so far as to turn the book around, leaving the card to harass the other side of my small office. But it kept its place in the forefront of my mind, bugging me like the dead guy in that Edgar Allen Poe story. I considered throwing the whole book in the trash, allowing that it wasn't a very good story anyway and that I had other things to read. I was fooling myself that Mr. Well Dressed would ever take me seriously.

Back on the subway my route traveled in reverse, an unraveling of the morning commute. I shoved the card deep into the binding, 200 pages from where I was reading so it would be mashed into the curve as I held the book open. I scratched at my afternoon scruff and hoped for a good climax. Racing through to the end, I was left with a decent experience, but it was a story I'd forget soon enough. Like the pain of my relationship with Alex.

On Wednesday, Thursday, and Friday morning I thumbed through a boring true crime book, skimming to the middle glut of pictures showing murderers and their victims. I'd almost forgotten about the man with the business card.

I let myself be talked into happy hour at a local pub, intending to meet up with some friends I hadn't seen in a few months. Three feet inside the door stood the bar, not wanting to give patrons too much time to reconsider their entrance to the establishment. I'd never been here before. It was dark enough inside to help hide a person's least attractive features, but bright enough to preclude people stumbling into the walls.

Before my pupils could dilate enough for me to comprehend what beers they had on tap, I felt him right behind me, that same cologne sneaking into my nostrils. He pressed himself into me, all gentlemanliness evaporated with the outside light. He was hard. In the space of one second I considered pushing him away, but my own T-modified dick had followed suit with his. I leaned into him and said hello.

He took my response as a cue to grapple with me, placing his hands on the bar and forcing me into it. Instead of haranguing him for his breach of boundaries I groaned, hearing my vocal chords reach into the nadir of my range.

—You didn't call me, he accused.

—I'm a very stupid man, I said.

—I don't think so. You're a very hot man, and smart, and lacking confidence.

—That's not all I lack, I said, feeling my boxers get damp and steamy.

—I know, he said as he continued to grind into me, his erection becoming impossibly hard.

I found enough space to turn around and face him, inhaling his real scent from underneath the expensive perfume. Now he would know my motivation for reticence. Now is when he would walk away and curse me for not wearing a neon sign over my head.

—I've ridden the subway with you for three years, he said, catching his breath momentarily.

—You have?

He nodded and planted his hands on the pointy parts of my hips. His mouth hung open a little, rosy full lips revealing shiny teeth.

—So you know. About me.

Another nod, and he came forward, kissing me. I could feel the length of him throbbing. I'd missed boyhood and adolescence completely, and I did not care.

BIRTHRIGHTS

• *M. Robin Cook*

CJ's not due home from the dealership for another three hours, so imagine my shock when the little weasel walks in. There I stand, fumbling at my brassiere half in the dark because the drapes are all drawn shut. They're these horrid brown paisley things that CJ had picked out the day we closed on the house. We had argued about some insignificant thing or another after leaving the realtor, and by the time we got to the mall I hadn't felt like fighting over curtains. I had been pondering my face in the mirror, a full-length oval thing rimmed with a garish, gold-colored frame, when I heard the rattling of the door latch. The mirror had belonged to CJ's grandmother. I guess they liked gaudier things back in the day. I had been wondering if I would ever get good at putting on my own make-up.

The restrained light is flattering, but only a little. At my very best I am nearly passable, or so I had come to believe, but moods and lighting, with just a few ticks of the twilight clock, can change so quickly. At those times I wondered if I had succeeded only in creating a horrific chimera. Oh what the hell, I do the best I can with the raw materials on hand. At least I go with the mirror. And that's what I'm thinking until the door opens, that I've somehow come to terms with my own shortcomings, after many years of trying on this or that shade of rouge, this or that shoe or dress style, and a surfeit of false perceptions, like an assortment of kitschy accessories that had swelled to a watershed.

As CJ and I stare at one another across the room, my inner monologue feels so sudden and immediate that I have to clamp my jaw down hard to keep from saying out loud, this will change everything. I'll remember this moment, I'm thinking. I had always believed it inevitable, but it had been so long in coming that I guess I had fallen into denial about it. And that kind of unconscious disregard can chip away at all kinds of faith, until the only thing left is, I suppose, the belief that nothing at all will happen. And so it is that this revelation I've imagined often, sometimes in hopeful dreams, sometimes in sable nightmares, since I was a kid, since CJ was a far-off concept with no face or name, shocks me in a way that feels tantamount to clawing my way from the depths of a heavy sleep. Secrecy and subversion, they are twin demons, heralds of ecstasy and castigation. Who can say, until the last card is turned, which way the deck was stacked?

I want to say something, anything to shatter this onerous silence, but I won't. Not yet. I think, *it's your move, Weas.* I feel riveted to the floor with CJ sizing me up like this. It's as if the spot where I'm standing has suddenly become my sole place in the universe, with borders so close I understand claustrophobia for the first time. It's not what I expect, not like the room is shrinking. It's more like my world has lost the ability to expand beyond me, like I've given up any chance for my life to encompass this space, the house and its possessions, CJ. The scent of the perfume I'm wearing—*Curve*—and the lingering smoke from the cigarette I just stubbed out are a combination suddenly acrid and overwhelming. This anticipation (it has, after so many years, grown to feel like the company of an old friend), this excitement I had been feeling, plummets from my head to my stomach and settles there as nausea, and I am amazed at just how fast human physiology can change. In a moment, in the twinkling of a lined eye.

CJ's staring is beginning to feel interminable, like tedious dialogue in a poorly-written fiction. It's the kind of thing you say no one talks like this or it doesn't seem real about, and you know immediately that you can't be right because the evidence is clear, right there in plain black and white. If you were to read it out loud your critique would crumble. you'd author the very exception you claim doesn't exist. Imitations are not copies. They proscribe any such possibility. Their substances, their borders, are their own. Were my ersatz shamming personified it would be screaming bloody awful murder right now. I suddenly feel like a clever fake whose flaws stand in relief when held beside the real thing. CJ knows this, I suspect, but doesn't show it. The Weas just stares.

CJ shuts the door and takes a step toward me. I look squarely into those steel blue eyes, hoping to find something telling there, but I find nothing palpable, nothing to grasp. Then I have what should be, I suppose, a most laughable thought. Or rather it *could be* laughable if I were capable of levity, even the nervous kind. Maybe CJ doesn't recognize me. Would that make me a stranger in my own house? Gall rises in my chest as I think, I can't read you (I was always so good at reading CJ's moods). For the first time that I ever remember I can't read you, and I'll bet you're thinking the same thing. I'm beginning to feel trapped, so I lower my eyes and examine some nail polish that is still drying on a run in my pantyhose.

Is that my bra, CJ says, finally.

I say, I guess my secret is out, and it feels like vomiting. No, I say, it's mine. I borrowed some eye shadow is all.

Cups are a bit big for you, CJ says.

I quip, yea, I guess my tits are too small. I am trying to smile—trying to *hope*—but still I just stare down at my pantyhose.

Don't call them *tits*, CJ says. I bet you don't even know how much I hate that, do you. They're *breasts*. Or even *boobs* is better. If you're going to go traveling in a foreign country, learn the language.

I look up then, searching, but those features are rock hard, impossible to penetrate. Boobs, I say. Sorry, my boobs are too small.

Well, not everyone can have these, CJ says, touching those breasts that have so often filled me with a longing so deep some would label it *exquisite anguish*. Well, there's always surgery, CJ adds, and I think I hear a small crack open in that steady voice. I look hard for something more, but the soft curve of CJ's face and the lax line of those lips are as flat and mute as a sheet of opaque glass.

CJ looks toward the mirror and says, is this what you do—look at yourself?

I stare into the vanity; we are framed there together. CJ's eyes hold mine in the reflection. Yes, I say, wondering why I love this person, wondering how this system, this way of talking that has grown up between us *really* works, how I can *say* a thing and CJ *becomes* the thing I speak. It's like the craft of Emerson's artist, who has "dissolved a solid-seeming block of matter by a thought." He thought it was beautiful, this métier of poets and philosophers. But it sounds like rape to me. Once a person becomes trapped like that, encoded like a wartime secret in our languages of love and desire, can they ever be understood any other way again? Do dark ladies ever glow again? *Wives* and *husbands, significant others* and *life partners*—the names we give one another are like seating assignments in a room where all the chairs face outward. How terrifying that the puerile silliness of notes passed between schoolchildren at recess, meaningless scraps of paper inscribed with little X's and O's, might someday mutate like a runaway experiment in a horror film to a bloated and empty "X." Bobby's my "X." Billy is my "X." Bev is my "X." That rotten bastard is my "X." I'm thinking, I cannot decipher you, CJ. How do I love you—by desiring you or desiring to *be* you?

I laugh out loud. Who's really the weasel here? Whose, I think, is the bigger lie? And without warning a fury so intense I would almost call it murderous pulses through my half-dressed and breastless body. I know it's just a reaction to the impetuous onset of guilt against which I am powerless to brace my *self*. Instead, my thoughts derail with the precipitance of a slamming trip hammer. They careen and I'm thinking, suddenly, *you sell cars*.

You sell used fucking cars, I say. What the hell is that all about, I say. You spend your days taking people for rides, and then you come home and tell me all about how happy you made some guy and his wife today. About what a perfect fucking couple they were. How satisfied they were as they drove off in their practically new Aveo (CJ sells a lot of Aveos) and how relieved they were to be rid of that old clunker with no room for the new fucking baby. What is that, anyway, I say. My chest feels clamped in a vise, and I barely spit out, you were supposed to be gone for another three hours.

I took off early, CJ says, unflinching. I thought we might do something this afternoon.

Well I had other plans, I say.

Obviously, CJ says.

I want to die. Just fucking die and get it over with. You want a reason, I think, and I haven't got one. There is no reason. Reason is just window dressing for the raw sewage of emotion leeching to the surface here, now. This is archetypal, elemental. This is anima.

I can't keep from focusing on a smudge on the mirror which covers the reflection of my right eye, blurring it. The visual paradox is disconcerting, and the consternation which accompanies the sight robs me of my rage. It drains from me furtively, as if an emotion could jump ship like a rat escaping an onboard fire. I am exhausted, like I haven't slept in days. I say, guess this isn't what you had in mind, was it.

I am surprised at how little defensive energy I had when the time came, having hoarded it for what seemed like every day of my life. I have rehearsed every argument, imagined every possible feint, constructed my case line upon line, precept upon precept. But I realize that it's just gone. Expended in a speech about salesmanship, a red herring and not even a good one. Or maybe, I think with a chill, there's nothing here to defend.

What I had in mind was to come home, CJ is saying. You know, home. I wanted to relax a little. You can't hardly do it at work, and I get tired of it. But home is different. I can always be me here. I have a right to do that, haven't I. At least I've earned that. I should've known, sooner or later. You're always taking things. Why don't you buy your own goddamn eye shadow.

I bought some, I say, but the color doesn't look very good on me.

And you think mine does! CJ snaps and I wince.

Well, I like it. I'm sorry, I guess I shouldn't. Like it, I mean.

No, CJ says. So, is that what you want.

Is what I want, I say.

Surgery. To have surgery. Is that what you're going to want.

Real ti—I mean, boobs—would be nice. I don't know about the rest.

CJ walks toward me, eyes still intent on my reflection, places a hand on my shoulder and leads me to the dresser. It's not coming out of our regular money, you know, CJ says. You'll get a second job to pay for it. CJ struggles to close the snaps on my bra from behind. This is too small for you, CJ says.

I guessed at the size, I say. I've always had to guess. It's not like I ever had a mother or big sister to show me, you know.

We'll go bra shopping, CJ says, and I feel the muscles in my neck and shoulders relax a little.

CJ removes two pairs of balled-up, white tube socks from the top drawer and places them, hands over my shoulders, in the bra cups, molding them with manicured fingers. There you go, CJ says. Boobs. My eyes dart from the reflection of CJ's distant features to the mounds of cotton on my chest. The power of it is stifling, and my breath hitches.

Look at me, I say.

I am looking at you, CJ says, staring at me in the old mirror.

No, look at me, here, I say, pointing to myself.

I am looking at you, CJ says. You look different.

But what do you think.

What do *I* think? There aren't any words for *this*. But that's not it *exactly*, is it. Maybe it's just time for a change. Yes, CJ's voice drifts. That's it: a change.

What are we changing, I say. I mean, you know, beside the obvious. My throat feels tight.

I quit my job today, CJ says, hammering at the word *quit*.

I thought you took off early, I say.

I did, but I'm not going back, CJ says. I haven't told them yet, but I've decided I'm not going back.

What will you do, I say.

I don't know. I haven't sold anything in two weeks, CJ says, they'll most likely fire me anyway. I can't sell anything. I feel like such a hypocrite. The cars are shit. They do whatever it takes to dress them up on the outside, but they're just junk. And the shittier they are, the more we have to push them. I'm a liar. I get paid to lie.

I can't decide whether I feel sorrier for myself or CJ. I'm sorry, I say. I thought you liked your job.

Well, I don't, CJ says. You don't *know* everything.

No, I suppose not.

What will your mom and dad say, CJ says.

They'll say *do what you have to do.*

About you, I mean, CJ says.

I know what you mean. They don't have to know, do they. Maybe someday, but not now.

People will know, CJ says, they'll notice something's different.

Not unless I want them to, I say, choking back an urge to scream, not wanting to break my verbal cadence. They'll be just like your customers. They want to believe it's a good car they're buying, blah, blah. They'll kick the tires and honk the horn and wonder if it's ever been in an accident, yada yada yada. But in the end they'll believe what makes them feel good about themselves.

Is that what you're doing, CJ says, feeling good about yourself.

It's more like trying not to feel bad all the time, I say.

I didn't know you felt bad, CJ says.

I feel like, you know, wrong. But you never look, I say. Just like you're not looking now.

I'm looking right at you, CJ says.

Sooner or later you have to take your eyes off the mirror, I say. It's not really me in there. It's not really you. You can get caught up really easy in there. It's almost like you're looking at another person, but you aren't. When you realize that person is you, then you're free. Believe me. I've had a lifetime to think about it.

I don't know what the hell you're talking about, CJ says. You're too damned philosophical. Besides, I can't believe you're the one lecturing me.

I resist the urge to roll my eyes. Sorry, I say. I should try to dumb it down more. The arrogance of the remark shocks me, and I am suddenly sorry for having said anything. I can't tell if CJ is angered or hurt. Goddamn stone.

Without skipping a beat, CJ says, maybe I'll go back to school, finish my Masters.

I think that's a good idea, I say, wincing. I think, this is getting fucking impossible. I mean, I say, it's something you've always wanted to do.

Maybe I'll teach, CJ says.

I say, I've always thought you'd be a good teacher.

Obviously, I could teach you a thing or two, CJ says, those flat and penetrating eyes dissecting my reflection with surgical precision.

Touché, I think. It's like getting punched in the stomach.

So, teach me something, I say. Pretend I'm your newest mark and you're peddling your wares. Stun me with your wiles. Look at me. You'll never find an easier sell.

Sorry, some things can't be bought, CJ says. You either have them or you don't—either you're born with them or you're not.

How would you know. Modern technology is pretty amazing.

I notice how my reflection cuts me off at the waist, and I can't help but wonder if there is an implication to such a disembodiment, something important I'm missing. I chuckle at the corny metaphor.

I know *you*, CJ says. What's so goddamned funny, anyway.

Apparently not, I say flatly, and I think CJ winces a little. And anything can be bought, I add, for the right amount.

I don't resist as CJ gently grabs my shoulders, turning me toward my profile in the mirror, still intent on my reflection. I study my new points. I can't, CJ says, I'm quitting.

You can't what, I say.

Teach you anything, CJ says. You already know, anyway. Everything that isn't you, that's what you want. That's what you're looking for, just fill in the blanks.

Sounds like you have a pretty low opinion of yourself, I say.

I see the way the other guys at the dealership look at me, CJ says. Those guys pawn the biggest piece of shit on the lot off to the toughest customer and they are great salesmen. I do it and feel like a whore, a lying whore. They pat me on the back and say good job, but it's there, in their eyes, like they're accusing me. They don't need to say it. I've heard it my whole life. They can't imagine I could sell anything without flashing some leg. Then, as an afterthought, CJ adds, you have no fucking idea what you're getting into.

You are not a whore, I say, but you're probably right, about me being clueless I mean.

No, I'm goddamn well not a whore, CJ says. I'm *quitting*. I'm doing the right thing. Giving up. Just like you.

I am not giving up, I say. I'm trying to move on.

You have no idea, do you, CJ says. No clue that you're letting go of everything. Every. Fucking. Thing.

You sound like you think being me is a picnic, I say.

I know power when I see it, CJ says.

Then look at me, I say.

I am looking at you, CJ says, holding my gaze in the reflection. I can't stop looking at you.

RIDE HOME UNDER A THUNDERSTORM

• Oliver Pickle

Tonight I ride home under a thunderstorm to windows and doors flung open in the house and no one home. It's just after midnight and the others went to karaoke, most of them getting there before the rain started and the cheap drinks ended.

"But last summer you didn't care about me," he said.

The first time I went to his house we turned in circles under his small comforter and he put us side by side like shoes, like the main difference was left and right, not girl and boy. We spend more nights together now, as fags, jarred in the morning by light throbbing through the thin curtains, and again by the world outside of ourselves at the café down the block with the strongest coffee in Montreal. When he's not there they ask me, "Where is the other girl?" Days like that, my stomach drops and distress simmers up from where it rests, latent, in his presence.

In the morning I fold myself in three and breathe into the sheets. They smell like cum and the air in the back alley where I hung them to dry. They smell like his hands. There's grit from the hallway that nobody sweeps.

For a lot of the days before he left the heat was so thick that the sheets were saturated with inertia and sex even though touching made sweat stream and humidity makes me whine. I should change them.

The pain is getting stronger. I imagine him over the Atlantic stepping offstage and flipping open his phone in the corner, organizing his ride home from the bar as his eyes flit down to the screen. The emergency room, or worse. It doesn't really matter; I've gone through the list of possibilities in nightmares. Getting on my bike, kneading my abdomen, asking the surgeon if they'll be using anaesthetic and not caring they're replying with a name I don't use anymore. I picture his face, small like a baby's but thin like a man's, working through a heap of emotions so briefly you would miss it if you sneezed, then wrapping them up and slamming them into a corner of his gut, unfindable until years later.

I imagine the call. Him getting on stage four days afterwards, sleeping in someone's bed closed off to the weight and the swing of grief that will eventually knock him down. One time he said this in the night:

"That park in London was a mass grave."

"Oh yeah you told me you had to call someone the night you walked across it but actually lots of people get their phones stolen there."

"Yeah but it was him I was talking to."

"Oh."

"I fell off the wagon on that trip after I'd seen him in the street."

It was the last time they saw each other.

The day after he told me I didn't want to leave the house for fear of dying too. I pictured the standard series of near misses: the click of a car door and my swerve, the lean on a horn as someone runs the red way too late. The pedestrian's shoe flung into my path while they look the other way. White back-up lights racing down the lane the wrong way. So fast and nowhere to go. His first two trans boyfriends, and the repetition would ruin him.

His story was so taut, he lay on his back and I gripped at his shoulder. I held the tiny bone beside the seam of his undershirt, which kept still as the words emerged.

///////

Today I wake earlier than I ever do on my own and it's because of panic. He'd died in my dream. I might have expected it yesterday but not after such a long conversation last night, the camera on his computer making a dull pink glow, our tongues poking out in jest. The dream lag, I guess. No one can keep track of anyone all the time, and I don't want to.

It was 3 am where he was and the conversation turned to types. It was late enough that we tried on ideas we didn't fully believe about masculinity, femmes, sex. The usual. How things change over time, sometimes to match a new lover. Because of the bulk of what I've wrapped this person in, the largest part of our attention for so long has been on examining my gender.

353

Dragging it through the eye of the needle of his, biting both of them off and placing them in between us, a translucent shield.

I imagine the train. Fast first class, closed inside a four-seat compartment to himself. Looking like a wayward teenage boy, arm tight to his face, body as small as a fist. The collision. When they would call. If they would. I look for his words online, finding the most recent ones to prove in that digital way that he's still around and alert.

This morning the moon's still pale like a cirrus next to the clouds, bumped up above the poplar at its peak. The cicadas are out but probably not for much longer. Last night it went down to 15°C and August breezes sometimes foreshadow fall. He's not alone but he is far away and I couldn't do anything even if I wanted to.

I've stopped wearing a binder that pulls tight over my gut to my hipbones, increasing the bloating and fear. I've visited doctors, asked for a ride, eaten prunes and greens. I've hyperventilated at the head of the table at the cottage, physically certain that some family friend's sudden death would be mine that night.

In the past couple of days there's been no calls, no writing; not that long but long enough that I do the exact thing I'm not supposed to do, which is to wonder about him when I'm otherwise occupied. It's part of our pact to not use up anxious mental space on each other when we're not together, when there's effectively no need.

I'm succumbing to the exhaustion from trying to work out homeostasis in my sleep, adrenaline building and waking me up, keeping me up with worries. Later I know that I have a problem, but it's not a tragedy. Just something to work on and work out. Like my mom's arm. Like my gut. Like my heart and how it can stretch over the ocean if I let it. Like letting people go when they're over the ocean.

It's wanting him. Needing stability in the form of constant tension that's not so hot that it burns. Wanting so many things, but none of them things. Wanting big pieces. Unmanageable changes. Loud shouting, hard biting, quiet quiet quiet. Wanting it to work so that everything fits itself back together in our bodies, our lives. A quality of completion found in beginnings. Fulfilled and blissful as shit.

It didn't rain today, even though the warnings were high. He left a water bottle at my house; he does after every trip.

I've been defensive. When I'm like that it comes out like yelling.

I say "You suggested we spend less time together and then you—"

"You have to trust that I don't want to hurt you," he says.

My life has been folding in on itself, though. Not enough that I can't see how a small breath might make something bigger than I've ever had out of what now feels crumpled and deflated, but enough that the words cut. I'm learning to take up space and ask to be seen how I want to be, pushing the walls outwards. I need so much.

As the plane landed and he moved through customs, passing as a lady for the officer, the pain came back—sharper than it has been. I pictured taping the note to the door, trying to text his phone with no credit, calling my friend downtown to come meet me at the hospital. Instead I lay on the bed, breathing. I pleaded with each section of my body for it to melt into the mattress, for it to puddle down and let the pain dilute itself in the liquid, let it keep me together.

I rolled a cigarette and had taken a third drag when he tapped down the street with luggage from an unexpected direction. He threw the guitar case on the wet ground and dragged the suitcase up the steps, one at a time, cursing.

"I'm so happy to see you," I said, after he'd taken off my shirt and I had grabbed his sweaty rib cage in my hands, the pain sliding past the limits of my skin, forgotten.

///////

What did we say?

> I want to live with you.
> I didn't notice I wasn't happy 'til I saw you.
> I wanted you to be there.
> You're so pretty. The prettiest boy.

This can't be timid, it has to be big: moving in but not keeping track of each other. Vegetables in the fridge. Private rage. Shiny matching shoes, different sizes. The shivering vulnerability of asking for help. Pulling what's best and hidden out of each other.

Too perfect and we'd both decline, setting up separate spaces. Perhaps close to each other, but not shared. Two years later and it's still the struggle that keeps it possible, the bred contrariness, the banter:

"Ew I thought you were suggesting we should be monogamous!"

"I know I take forever to talk but you have to wait or else I'll never say it."

"You have to tell your mom to call you that."

And the sense of duty that backs the feeling when he says he will take care of me if this health situation gets worse is a powerful determinant.

"But last summer you didn't care about me," he says.
"Yes I did."
"But the way it felt and the structure we'd built didn't match up—"
"Yes they did!"
"But you never told me you loved me!"

A sense of self-worth can't come entirely from external sources, but it can be nurtured there, bathed and polished and embraced. We can do this over the ocean. We can do it from the keyboard and through the rising pitch of our alarmingly high voices.

Frequent enough to sate me. Potent enough for hope.

ENTRIES

• *Riley Calais Harris*

One of my earliest childhood memories that I can't attribute to a movie I saw is from when I was six. Right? That sounds close. Anyway, I got to kiss one of the girls in class. Not while we were in class, she was in the same class as me. We were out in the field behind her parents' house. I think she called it "mouth dancing," and I didn't know what that meant. I knew what dancing was, and I knew what mouths were, but I wasn't very creative when it came to putting things like that together back then. I don't think my classmate was either, as it doesn't strike me as a particularly romantic memory. I just think it's funny that it's my earliest. I mean, you'd think that would just be like, pooping or something, right? Like, I imagine when your long-term memory is testing itself out, it would just go with whatever is going on at the time, and people spend a lot of time pooping, so everyone's earliest memory should just be pooping. That girl and I didn't keep in touch.

There isn't much else to report from my childhood. It was a blend of video games, action figures, a little bit of pink, and more birthday cake than is probably healthy, although certainly not more than is normal. I try not to remember much from when I was actually going through puberty. Which I imagine is also normal. There was some mild childhood depression, but no one is very comfortable in their skin at that point.

Toward the end of puberty I wound up pretty short, which I don't mind anymore, but despised at the time since it kept me off the basketball team. I joined the swim team instead. I didn't particularly like being in water, but I figured I'd like it more than being one of those kids who does nothing and has no identity. Back then I didn't think there was any more to identity than one's extra-curricular activities. I'm still not sure if that was just my perception at the time, or if it's really true for suburban high schoolers. Like, when you graduate, the actual definition of identity changes retroactively. Also, have you ever noticed that people seem to be best at things they don't like to do? I got to state semi-finals my junior year, and I didn't even swim my senior year.

After practice one day a teammate asked me if I knew how cute I was when I swam. My shaky, hormone-addled voice replied, "Um, no?"

She started to fill me in, and while I was hoping she would say something like, "So anyway, my brother wants to make out with you, no strings attached, in the back of his car," she dashed my hopes against the jagged reality of her mouth dancing, and I made out with her instead. "Jagged" isn't fair, though, she was all right.

I think I had always expected bisexuality, but didn't think it would ever really be relevant. I just thought it would be something I would identify with for the political association, and would leave it at that. Oh well. Some are born gay, some achieve gayness, and some have gayness thrust upon them. That's probably not true, but it would make a good bumper sticker.

My teammate and I probably would have dated if things had gone differently. Well, if one thing had gone differently. After practice, while the two of us were connecting in her childhood-ridden bedroom, she leaned in to my ear and whispered, "I want to do it so skanky. Take this dirty piece of luggage to town." Which honestly wasn't the problem at all, I would have been happy to be her number one bellboy. The problem was that I started giggling, even though she was very serious about the whole thing. I went home and played video games until I forgot how bewildered I was. Sometimes I think teenagers have acne as a sort of external manifestation of how smooth they are.

The Incident happened a few days after I graduated. It only gets capitalized as a joke, it really wasn't that big a deal. I was in a car accident, and now it's a little harder to go jogging. On the other hand, I can get Vicodin whenever I want, which isn't very often, but I sound cool when I mention it at parties. And really, what's a minor disability in exchange for street cred, am I right? Not that I get to bring it up that often, either, though. The kinds of people who would get genuinely excited about the prospect of a friend who can provide free prescription painkillers usually aren't the kinds of people I get excited about spending a lot of time with. It's sort of like when I was a swimmer in high school: I would be really good at making friends with people I don't even want to be friends with.

Anyway, there were a few important things that came out of The Incident. The first was Cheryl, the physical therapist I had for three weeks. And yeah, I still remember her name. We didn't talk a lot, and the conversations we did have usually centered around my knee, but she was the first real butch I think I ever met, so she deserves a milestone in the road of my life. Even when I had questioned my sexuality in the past, I had never met someone I was genuinely surprised to be attracted to. I think at first I didn't even realize I was attracted to her. I wasn't particularly femme at that point, and butch-on-butch lovin' wasn't a part of my eighteen-year-old understanding of the universe. I played it cool, though. She probably thought I was so wide-eyed because of all the pain and instructions I was going through.

The other big result of The Incident was the other therapy it led me to. After I graduated, my childhood depression matured into a full-fledged identity crisis. I went from suburban, teenage malaise to hopeless, getting-out-of-bed-is-an-accomplishment, dejected sorrow. Oddly enough, though, I'm almost glad it happened now that I'm through it. I'd say it was a "catalyst for change," but I don't want to be the kind of person who says things like that. It started when I didn't get into college. I had the grades, and some decent extra-curricular activities to pad my resume, but I just had no real motivation or goals for college, and I think the admissions folks could tell. Between that and never finding a Plan B school, my fall schedule was pretty open. I had a job lined up through a friend of my dad's, but I was unable to work for a few weeks after The Incident, and by the time I was better the company was in dire financial straits, so I spent a summer limping around my parents' house, looking for whatever job I could get. By the time I was desperate enough for fast food, all those jobs had been grabbed by the college kids home for the summer, and the high schoolers who had been working since February. My friends all wound up working or traveling that summer, so I was in a pretty miserable spot. When I asked my mom if our insurance would cover a psychologist, she was so relieved she practically shouted her "yes" at me.

I started telling my deepest secrets to a femme Klaus Nomi. Well, a female-identified Klaus Nomi. Less forehead was the only major difference. I talked a lot about feeling trapped. At some point I even said the cliché "trapped in a man's body" line.

I probably mumbled it, too, in a reluctant boy voice. I mean, whatever voice-body combination you want to go with is great, but you have to admit, it's a little tragic when someone's gender expression becomes reluctant. It's like a deer in headlights, if the deer were self-conscious about the whole thing.

In my defense, she wasn't cool, either. The first thing she asked me after I mentioned the trans thing was, "How long have you felt like a woman?" Maybe it's just me, but that seems like the worst way to ask that question. It just sounds so awkward. It's like we're talking about menstruation. And in this case, it was like talking about menstruation with someone else's grandmother. What's wrong with, "How long have you identified as trans?" or, "How long have you wanted your chest lumpier?"

When I was able to spend a day on my feet, I got a job at a day spa. It was called "Waves." I still don't know why. Honestly, I think someone just thought the word sounded pretty and relaxing. Most of my time was spent moving towels and heating rocks. It was the perfect place for someone who isn't suicidal, only because her depression keeps her from being proactive at all. According to my memory, I spent every moment of a whole year wide-eyed and furrow-browed. I don't know that I trust my memory, but I know it is based in truth.

I got my job at Waves thanks to a friend of my mom's, who made it a point to tell us that the spa wouldn't be closing anytime soon. We all chuckled, even though none of us thought it was funny. My dad was visibly upset, but he waited until later to share that he felt like I was siding with my mother. It doesn't take a marriage counselor to know that when someone is upset at their spouse because their child accepted a job, it's an indication of deeper dissatisfaction in a marriage. Recently he said he was just being overly dramatic because he was going through a rough spot at the time. I didn't care why he said it at the time, and honestly I still don't. The only thing that bothered me is how catty and childish they became before they actually broke up. It was like all those social rules they taught me as a kid, all that stuff about honesty, just stopped existing. I loved spending time with them when I was younger, and I love spending time with them now, but between their marital bliss and their marital conclusion? Good lord. It was like the worst of the worst teen dramas. At one point I went to a friend's house for an inebriation break, and after I vented about how ridiculous it all was we discussed the possibility that it was all a conspiracy to make me feel like an adult so I could finally get over my depression. I woke up the next morning with a note on the back of my hand that read, "The Incident: Part 2." I took a picture. And I don't smoke with that friend anymore.

I tell people I went to massage school because I like taking care of people but I didn't have the stomach to become a nurse. The truth is that the massage therapists at Waves told me I could have a decent paycheck, and I might get free electrolysis if I worked at a place that did both. Seriously, if you're ever plotting to blackmail a trans woman, don't. Just offer to pay her transition costs for her. It's way more effective, and everybody wins. I never got any free electrolysis.

I never really needed a lot, either. I was never able to grow much more than a hipster 'stache and some patchy neck beard. I also had a little bit of belly fuzz, but by the time I was through with the electrolysis around my face I felt pretty empowered by my happy trail. It's weird how your mind works, sometimes. In high school I was totally fine with my hair. It would have looked gross so I didn't grow it out, but it didn't bother me that I had it. When I first came out I couldn't wait to get electrolysis on my face, and my belly, and even my legs and everything sounded pretty nice. I even thought about how nice it would be to just get my eyebrows zapped and be done with it. Anyway, I'm glad I got the electrolysis I got, but it just seems like the least significant thing to me now. It's like when you get to high school and all the problems you had in middle school seem insignificant. I guess that happens with high school, too. Okay, how about this: after you get out of whatever station in life you were just at, the problems of that previous station look insignificant in retrospect. Something like that. I shave my legs every morning, but I don't really know why. I only ever wear pants. I think it might just be habit leftover from my days as a swimmer.

I dated this radical activist for a while. Zie was this gorgeous handsome gender fucker, and I always felt way out of my league. I don't mean that in a shallow zie's-more-attractive-than-me way. Well, I don't only mean it in that way. Mostly I felt out of my league in terms of my queer-feminism experience level. My partner always knew about the latest forms of oppression, and why people should be concerned about them, and usually already had plans for some kind of sit-in or something. Looking back I think it was just because zie was a news junky. And zie read the right news. I always felt like I had this great opportunity to be a part of some huge, important political movement. I think we broke up because zie was waiting for me to see the light and stop shaving my legs, and I was waiting to see the light and stop wanting to shave my legs. Neither of those happened, so after a while we told each other things like, "I think our lives are just on different paths, you know?" I think I was excited to date hir because zie seemed like the right person for me to date. Like, I met hir and then thought, *yeah, this is probably the person of my dreams.* Do you ever feel like you decided to be attracted to someone? I'm not sure if it's sad or if it's like, a sign of supreme agency. Like, you aren't even at the whim of your own instincts, you can just determine your own attraction however you want, you know?

Then I had a couple of dates with this adorable femme lady. It went well, but we were both terrified of it going well. I'm the first trans lady she dated, and she's the first femme I've dated as a femme, and I think that made us both nervous. It's exciting and empowering, though: I can date someone who is girly, and someone is dating me for being girly. It's like I feel like I belong. Like, not only did I have my official membership to an exclusive club, but that the veteran members of the club accepted me as one of their own. Wait, is that a thing that happens? Maybe it just happens in movies. I was just giddy that those dimples like me back.

I started getting involved with a lot of pride events in town. I felt a need for more community, and there are always plenty of volunteer opportunities where I live. I started marching in parades, going to film festivals. I was at a resource fair one day, and I traded contact information with a person who was excited to have another queer friendly massage therapist to recommend to folks. That contact has gotten me a number of new clients, one of whom shared an interest in making massage therapy more communal. We met a couple times to discuss the idea of group sessions, and when that idea sounded terrible we discussed the idea of educational workshops, and when we realized that idea required a lot of resources neither of us had we discussed the idea of me lending my skills to the atmosphere of a play party. Well, by "discussed" I mean she invited me to a play party. Of course, I had to ask the naïve twenty-something question, "Play party? What do you play?" And being cool enough to ask a girl like me to a play party, she just smiled and replied, "Each other." I probably still have some residual blush. It was like my high school swim mate was all grown up and still one step ahead of me on the path of awesome sex. She assured me I would have final say in terms of audience, amount of my participation in other events, and number of tits I would see. She also assured me the same assurance went for all other attendees as well. I'm still not sure if that makes me feel better or worse about the situation. She told me her vision was just to have a room where people could get a quick shoulder rub, or calm down in or after subspace, or watch other people get massages (if that was cool with me). The list went on and on, it didn't help with the blushing. She even offered to pay me and said I could totally have a tip jar at the ready, since I'd be giving out free a service I normally charge for. It took some sputtering, but I finally accepted the invitation.

I put up a lot of boundaries for the first party, including the no tits rule, which was of course expanded to all genitalia as well. I got my own room to set up in, and I got to make sure that the music wouldn't be too loud in my room. I had my own safe word that everyone knew in case I needed to be alone and clear my head. I had a "busy" sign so I could limit the number of people I was dealing with. I got all my nice oils and lotions lined up, and I had a nondescript tip jar set up, and then I wound up sitting in my room without a visitor for about an hour and a half until I finally worked up the courage to walk downstairs. I think I was expecting the living room to be an incoherent mass of naked, writhing bodies, with only a strobe light and dim candles to light my path, all to the heavy beat of what I would assume to be techno music. It turns out the naked part was only half true, but the rest was just in my head. It was really just a pleasant, quiet gathering among friends. The last party I went to I didn't even bring a table, I just sat in the living room the entire time, rubbing half to completely naked folks' shoulders, and enjoying the silly conversation and occasional show. I didn't call myself a voyeur, but I still really like it. It's like a movie night with friends, but more buttsex. And just being able to be around and a part of so much love is really empowering. It feels so good to have the agency to enjoy whatever I might enjoy.

Oh, you know what? That's probably why I shave my legs.

POWER OUT

• *Adam Halwitz*

I don't know whether I suffer from garden-variety neurosis or a special trans neurosis—probably a big chunk of both. It comes out as a tendency towards resigning myself. The way I deal with inconvenience is to raise my eyebrows and pull at the cuffs of my shirt. Transition's riddled with stuff to complain about, but it's rare I've had enough chutzpah to manage making a real clamor. I am not the kind of person who makes eye contact with the eye of the storm. I think I was born with a chutzpah deficiency.

So the incident at Kenner's, that small and rare and wonderful attack of *Listen-up-cis-people!* rage, is something I still can't get my head around. Mona says it's just a tiny breakthrough in my personality. I'm not sure.

It wasn't long after chest surgery—*The Surgery*, as my mom portentously called it. She said this like you'd say "The Accident" to refer to somebody's stroke, or "The City" for New York. I didn't think The Surgery was as important as that, but I'd had some complications and I still ached all over. Falling and staying asleep seemed like enormous hurdles.

My landlord, after having taken care of me for a couple of awful days, was rewarding herself with alcohol that week. Mona liked to get drunk. She'd gaze right into your eyes and give you a lot of real, sincere compliments on which her voice would crack with earnestness. Sometimes she'd try to stare down our cat or clasp him round the neck. He would always thump away down the hall like he was worried that Mona might spring. It was amazing how much noise a cat can make on a wooden floor.

This was what I thought woke me up on the night of the thirtieth. Once I was conscious, I realized after about four seconds how much pain I was in. Even my mouth hurt. I'd gotten dehydrated after sleeping for too long. The cat was zooming around somewhere, and Mona crooned at him to stop.

A tremendous thunderstorm was in full burst. It wasn't really ideal as a traumatic-surgery-recovery environment. I was in bed, wedged in a nest of pillows and thinking about this, when my yellow moon night-light went dim. My clock radio shifted from 3:48am to a blinking, battery-powered 12:00.

There was a noise of thunder: not a rumble but a bang.

Mona, maybe at the bottom of the stairs, was dialing the Weather Service with a loud ancient cellphone. She will inevitably dial the Weather Service at the first sign of trouble. It's not as though they're very helpful—if there's snow up to your windows, what they say is "Probably try not to go out," and things like that. Mona says she finds it comforting. She says she has a love and trust for authority that's left over from her upbringing. I haven't been able to tell whether she's serious, but it's reflected in her behavior. Sometimes.

Her voice was softer than the blare of the phone. She hung up.

By then it must have been about four o'clock, late enough for the sky to be luminous gray, and Mona was at least aware enough to be talking quietly. I heard the cat stop thumping and skitter on the thin rug toward his bed.

"Mona?" I called, not very loudly.

She didn't hear. There was thunderstormy gray light coming from the crack near the top of the windows where the curtains had not been pulled shut.

"Mona?" I called out again. The cat came to my door, butted his head against it, and started to scratch—*Scrit-scrit-scrit.*

I got up, which took me about forty seconds, and opened the door to let him in.

It had been Mona raking her fingernails on the wood. She laughed at my expression.

"The storm's knocked down one of the cedars," she told me, "and the electricity is out."

"*That* was the noise? I thought it was the cat running away from you."

"You slept through a tree crashing, but a running animal woke you up." She laughed again, about twice as hard.

Even bent and tired like this, her big head, with lots of thick black hair piled on top, stuck out in a lovely profile in front of the dim hallway. The flashlight made her hair gleam. She sat right in the middle of the floor.

"Well," I said. "How about the Internet?"

"Goes down when the electricity's down."

"I need some Internet access," I said. I sank down next to her.

"Any special reason? Besides dependence?"

"I have a video chat appointment."

"An '*appointment*,' huh?"

"With the dude from the surgeon's office, the nurse. He wants to look at me and make sure that pieces of flesh aren't going to fall off."

She sat up a little straighter. "When's that supposed to be? Maybe everything will be back to normal."

"4:40 a.m.," I said. "He's in a different time zone. And on Wednesdays I usually go to the bakery early anyway."

"Can't you call to reschedule?"

"Right before the appointment?"

"It's his job to take care of you."

"It'd be a big deal," I said. "It'd be a pain."

"I could call him for you."

"Oh *God*."

She shrugged. "Then you're going to have to get somewhere with access to electricity. With actual lights on, and Internet."

I couldn't think of anything funny to throw back at her. I think I might actually have moaned.

"Which," she said, "could be done. It would require a drive."

"To the bakery?"

"Since when have they broken out of the 90s and acquired wi-fi?"

The answer was "Never." I said so. I felt justified in my error. Nobody could think straight with Mona staring at them under the bottoms of her too-strong glasses, pushing back her hair.

"To somebody's house?" I added, trying to think.

"Are you out to anybody who would be awake now?"

I shook my head.

"This is the modern age. Only Green Light Bakery has disregarded that fact," Mona said. "You can go to a private part of a public place. Everywhere else has wi-fi. Starbucks has wi-fi. The Two Months Free Storage place has wi-fi. I think Kenner's must, and that's open 24/7."

"I can't expose my nipples to all those butch guys at Kenner's," I said. "Not even in the windowless basement part."

"So do it at Starbucks, in the bathroom."

"No! And are they even open? No."

"I thought you wanted to get this over with," Mona said, fiddling with the tap in the kitchen sink. "You keep horrible hours. I'm so glad I don't have to sleep like you. I hope you're in good enough shape to drive."

"*I'm* driving?"

"Isn't that what I said?"

"You said it was '*a drive.*'"

"I didn't think I would have to tow you anywhere. The thunder woke me up. You were asleep. I got bored and had some drinks."

"You're coming with me?" I asked.

"You've had major surgery—I can't just let you drive alone."

"But you can let me drive."

"Shut up," she said, with a kind of briskness that made me wonder how tired she really was.

It stung me into silence for at least five more minutes, which I don't think Mona minded. I took another full forty seconds to get into the car. Once I had gotten there, I found myself feeling all right. The sun was coming up and the clouds were black, wetly heavy. They made everything else seem a lot brighter by contrast.

Mona rolled down the window. I've been to a couple of aquariums, and the air was like that: warm and steamy, with a wild, animal smell to it, not like a steamy bathroom after a shower. The sky was pink but dark, the sun rising slowly. I kept thinking about trans shit, and I looked to the side, on and off, at Mona.

I wondered if there were any trans people driving in the lane beside us, or even within a radius of ten miles. Fifteen miles? Were there any at Kenner's? I thought about the shape of my body, the way it took up the car's space, what it looked like to the other drivers. Maybe they were turning their heads. *That dude's really small-framed*, they could have been saying to themselves. *His face is really round.* Doing a double take. They weren't. But my chest itched and prickled; when I switched gears, it'd pull a little bit, and I couldn't reach back to the cup holder.

"Did you make K drive after ey had surgery?" I asked Mona. We streamed toward the Fast Lane, watching trucks inch through the toll booths.

"Ey couldn't *see*," Mona said. "Eir face was that blown up."

"That happens?"

"With facial feminization? Are you kidding? Yes." She shut the window. "Ey wouldn't let me take any pictures."

"It happen to you? Did your face swell up?"

"What do you think?"

"No pictures?" I said.

"Fuck off." Mona tapped the bridge of her nose. "Tell me about *your* stuff. Do you think you're a real man now?"

I started to laugh so hard I coughed.

"This is an emergency," she said. "You have to get there on time."

I said, "I have padding and shit taped to my chest. I'm crinkling."

"Goo's all oozing out of you," she agreed. "At least you smell like thunderstorms. It's just seven more miles. You're a trooper."

There was one guy behind the counter at Kenner's. He'd propped his jaw on his hand and was playing Solitaire on his phone. I looked over his shoulder. He wasn't very good. Probably out of boredom, he had turned the CD player's volume almost as high as it would go. The instruments throbbed. Vibrations went through the floor. I hitched the strap of my laptop bag a little tighter.

"Can I do something for you?" he asked through some crashing piano.

"Do you have Internet access? Maybe even in the back room?"

"You mean the function room?"

There were about three people eating fish and chips in the front part of the restaurant. It seemed like they'd strategically chosen the spot furthest from the sound system. A couple of them looked up.

"I promise we're not having a function at 4:30," I said. "But the power's down, starting a ways north of here, and so's our Internet. I have this video chat that I urgently need to complete."

Mona poked me in the back. "In private," I said.

"In *private?*" he echoed. "There's nobody in the function room."

"Could I go in there with the door shut? I can get something to eat if you want."

He only looked amused. "No problem either way."

"Can I have some fries? With barbecue sauce."

The fish-and-chips-eaters lost interest at this point; they turned back to scraping some remaining fries in the little saucer of mustard. I didn't hear what Mona ordered. I got up and nearly limped to the function room. But I heard her voice, and the clank of change, as I opened and booted my computer. She joined me with a steaming mug of something.

"Did you ask him for the wi-fi password?" I said. "You might not want to watch this, unless you're interested in gross nipples."

"I've already seen your gross nipples. It's 'KENNER1234'—they're not security freaks."

"Yeah, that guy at the counter didn't ask me if I was conducting a drug deal."

Mona took a big sip. "You don't look scary enough."

"I'd be scary if I showed him my chest."

"You know what *you* think is scary? Annoying some cis nurse in California. '*I can't reschedule! It's so-o-o rude!*' You could have just gone back to bed."

"I don't have the energy to deal with pissing him off."

"Fine," she said. "Pick your battles."

"Hi, Mark," the nurse began.

It was 4:43. The video quality was pretty good.

The nurse was clean-shaven, but his beard shadow was so dense that it darkened his face right up to below the cheekbones. His eyes shifted around—looking not just at me, but at everything in view around me. I was sitting at a booth. There were salt and pepper shakers just by me, and a neon sign that sparkled the word CORONA above my head. The classical music was still blasting away.

To his credit, he did not ask the obvious question of "Are you in a restaurant?" He didn't even ask the more intriguing "*Why* are you in a restaurant?" Instead he said, "I know it's 4 o'something your time; I know it's horribly early."

"I was the one who picked the time," I said. "I work for a bakery."

"I see." He still didn't ask. He didn't launch into any kind of medical-speak, either, for a few seconds.

"Do you want me to take my shirt off?" I offered.

"It looks like you're in a public place," he said. "I was hoping I'd be able to see it quickly, just to make sure no tissue's dying or about to fall off, but I probably didn't make myself quite clear—"

I said, "It's fine."

I stripped off the layers. There was the thin button-down to ward off the morning chill, then the t-shirt I'd slept in. Then the post-surgical binder, clipped and zippered up. It had dug grooves into my skin—deep red scallops of pressed-down flesh in my shoulders and at the back of my neck. Ridiculous how deep they were. Like linoleum carved for printmaking. Underneath my binder were white bandages, themselves grooved by the lines of my clothes, which I'd stuck down with paper tape.

Mona was not looking. Even the nurse, artfully, was not looking. He could look at someone naked but not someone getting naked.

I said as I unpeeled the tape, "I had a pretty awful time getting here."

"The complications," the nurse said, "will resolve." He leaned forward, peering. "In simpler terms: nothing's dying. That's virtually all I needed to know. Just a very quick look. As long as it's not hot around the incision sites, or gross—"

He waited for me to shake my head No.

I wanted to say, *That's not what I meant by "an awful time."*

I didn't say anything.

"I know it's important to you that your chest looks biologically male," he said. "I think it will, when it heals."

I thought about this phrase "biologically male" and wondered whether or not to say something. I thought about it for so long that, when I looked up and met the nurse's eyes, he was staring.

"I remembered you saying it was important," he said. "It's not important?"

"I mean, I didn't put it like that, I didn't say 'biologically male.'"

"But that is what you wanted, what you prioritized, I mean?"

He was going to say the word "important" again, or the phrase "biologically male," or maybe both in the same sentence. He was opening his mouth to speak.

I wish I could say that a big gust of wind came just then, rattling the trees I could see through the frosted window, or a big bolt of lightning. I could've leveled with the nurse's gaze and told him off. All that booming music was pretty theatrical in itself.

Instead what I said was, "You said my chest would look *'biologically male'*?" Neutrally, but at least not meekly. I hoped I was pronouncing those quotation marks.

The nurse skated over them. "You might not retain all feeling—"

"That's not—it's just—a lot of people don't use that phrase anymore, *'biological.'* Because if you say *I'm* not, that implies, like—"

The words wouldn't come.

I could feel Mona's eyebrows raise even if I couldn't see them. I could feel her tiny grin. I glanced back at her for just a second.

"—that I'm like a *robot* or something. That I'm not a living person. It doesn't make sense."

I only heard silence, not even breathing, though the sound wasn't turned up high. The nurse's face stayed professional, unaffected.

I said, "A lot of people use another word: 'cis.' It's the opposite of 'trans.' It's the parallel word to 'trans.'"

"The guy we operated on yesterday," the nurse said, "used 'biological.'"

"Some people, yeah, some trans people do."

"I'm sorry if I've offended you."

"I'm glad my chest is all right," I said. I ate the last French fry, then sucked my breath in hard. "But listen: I haven't been able to sleep. I had to pay for this thing from my own credit card. I'd like you to use this word 'cis.' I really, really would."

"Well," the nurse said, "I don't think I'll have to see you again—I hope. But thank you for the tip, Mark."

"I would have offered you a fry," I said, "but I don't think food works that way."

When I shut the lid of the laptop, Mona told me, "You sure had enough energy."

"To correct that nurse?"

"To deal with his shit. You had enough."

But I was glad, gladder than I've ever been about anything, when I walked out of Kenner's—past those three people eating fish and chips, past the guy playing Solitaire at the counter—knowing that they would never have to know how close I came to having a nipple almost fall off. Probably they didn't give a damn about my biology, but they wouldn't ever know, because I wouldn't ever tell them. I didn't want to. I was surprised by the force of how actively I didn't want to.

I'd run out of chutzpah, and my sides under the binder were itching and prickling again.

THE AUTHORS

SUSAN JANE BIGELOW is a transgender woman, reference librarian, political commentator, and SF/fantasy author from Connecticut. Her debut novel *BROKEN* (Candlemark & Gleam, 2011) was called an "unusual and heartfelt take on superheroes" in a starred review by Publishers Weekly. She ran the state-focused political blog Connecticut Local Politics from 2005-2010. She is currently a contributing columnist at CTnewsjunkie.com.

ELLIOTT DELINE was born in Syracuse, NY in 1988. He studied literature at SUNY Purchase and Syracuse University. His first book, *Refuse*, was a finalist in the LGBT Rainbow Awards for Best Debut Transgender/Bisexual Novel in 2011. His work has been featured in several publications, including the Modern Love essay series of The New York Times as well as his blog on Original Plumbing's website. He currently lives with his family and cat in Syracuse, where he writes and works at a library.

IMOGEN BINNIE is the author of the zines *The Fact That It's Funny Doesn't Make It A Joke* and *Stereotype Threat*. She is currently a monthly contributor to *Maximum Rocknroll* and has previously written for *Aorta Magazine*, *The Skinny*, and PrettyQueer.com. She writes about books at keepyourbridgesburning.com and performs in the queer doom metal band Correspondences. Her first novel, *Nevada*, is forthcoming from Topside Press in 2013.

TERENCE DIAMOND is a playwright, journalist, and short story editor whose work has been listed in *Gay and Lesbian American Plays*. He is formerly an assistant professor of English at Long Island University and a member of the Dramatists Guild. Terence teaches grant writing to artists at 3rd Ward Education in Brooklyn, contributes to PrettyQueer.com and *Curve Magazine*. Terence worked on the novel *Big Pink Meat*, from which his story is excerpted, at the PAF residency in France.

EVERETT MAROON is a memoirist, humorist, pop culture commentator, and fiction writer. He holds a B.A. in English from Syracuse University and went through the MA program there as well. He is a member of the Pacific Northwest Writers' Association and was a finalist in their 2010 literary contest for memoir. He is the author of a memoir, *Bumbling into Body Hair*, and has written for *SPLIT Quarterly, Twisted Dreams Magazine, Bitch Magazine*, GayYA.org, I Fry Mine in Butter.com, *RH RealityCheck*, and *Remedy Quarterly*. In 2012 he will begin writing for *Original Plumbing* on popular culture and trans civil rights.

CALVIN GIMPELEVICH spends most of his time in a small, ill-lit room researching his obsessions. He lives in Seattle, having bounced through Berlin, San Francisco, and Santa Cruz in the past few years. His current goals include visiting every queer city.

K. TAIT JARBOE is a sound and new media artist from the Boston area. They graduated with honors from the Massachusetts College of Art and Design and are currently engaged in a service year at a local high school as a media arts coordinator. They are working on a novel, and blog at toomanyfeelings.com. This is their first publication.

OLIVER PICKLE is a trans writer based in Montreal. They recently released a collection of vignettes called *Gays in the Workplace* and are working on a book of short stories.

SHERILYN CONNELLY is a San Francisco-based writer. Her words can be found in anthologies such as *Gender Outlaws: The Next Generation, It's So You: 35 Women Write About Personal Expression Through Fashion and Style*, and *Unthology No. 1*. She also writes for *The Village Voice* and *SF Weekly*.

RJ EDWARDS lives in Rhode Island and is a writer, cartoonist, and creator of *Riot Nrrd*—a webcomic at the crossroads of geek culture, social justice, and queer romance. They are a founding member of The Ever Eccentric Unfactory, a collective of transgender comic creators. Their other projects include *Child Friend Kin Queer*, a collection of writings and resources on coming out as non-binary, and *SUPER*, a zine series imagining and illustrating one hundred original superheroes.

CYD NOVA is a community organizer who runs an HIV prevention program in San Francisco. He has written many, many zines of varying quality. You can find his writing on PrettyQueer.com and HIVandHepatitis.com.

NOEL ARTHUR HEIMPEL is a lifelong artist and writer whose works focus on queer college kids in surreal situations. He is working on a degree in painting at Towson University in Maryland, and running a twice-a-week webcomic called *Ignition Zero*.

CARTER SICKELS is the author of the novel *The Evening Hour* (Bloomsbury, 2012). He has been awarded scholarships to Bread Loaf Writers' Conference, the Sewanee Writers' Conference, the MacDowell Colony, and VCCA. Carter received his MFA in Fiction at Penn State and a MA in Folklore at UNC-Chapel Hill. He has taught creative writing classes at IPRC, Gotham Writers' Workshop, and Hugo House. Carter lives in Portland, Oregon.

KATHERINE SCOTT NELSON is a writer living in Chicago. Hir first novel, *Have You Seen Me*, was a finalist for the 2011 Lambda Literary Awards. A mainstream literary magazine once rejected "Winning the Tiger" for being "too aggressive."

RILEY CALAIS HARRIS An Oregon native, Riley is now a software engineer at an Electronic Health Record company in Wisconsin. This is her first published piece.

ADAM HALWITZ is a student and writing tutor at Marlboro College in Marlboro, VT, and an occasional editor for the magazine *Teen Ink*. "Power Out" is his first piece of published fiction.

M. ROBIN COOK is a writer living in Ohio. Ze is heavily influenced by the work of Kate Bornstein and Leslie Fienberg.

RYKA AOKI is a writer, performer, and educator who has been honored by the California State Senate for her "extraordinary commitment to free speech and artistic expression, as well as the visibility and well-being of Transgender people." Ryka appears in the recent trans documentaries *Diagnosing Difference* and *Riot Acts*, as well as the anthologies *Gender Outlaws: The Next Generation* (Seal Press), and *Transfeminist Perspectives* (Temple University). Ryka has an MFA in Creative Writing from Cornell University and is the recipient of a University Award from the Academy of American Poets. Her chapbook, *Sometimes Too Hot the Eye of Heaven Shines*, won the RADAR's 2010 Eli Coppola Chapbook Contest. Her first full-length volume, *Seasonal Velocities*, was released this year by Trans-Genre Press, the first press operated by and for trans people in the United States. Ryka was the inaugural performer for San Francisco's first ever Transgender Stage at San Francisco Pride 2005, and has performed in venues including the San Francisco Pride Main Stage, the Columbus National Gay and Lesbian Theatre Festival, the National Queer Arts Festival, Ladyfest South, Atlanta Pride, UCLA's OutCRY, Santa Cruz Pride, and Emory University's Pride Week. Ryka was keynote speaker at UC Santa Barbara's 2005 Pride Week, GenderFusions 2008 at Columbia College, and UW Madison's Trans Awareness Week 2009. She is a professor of English at Santa Monica College.

MJ KAUFMAN is primarily a playwright, currently studying at Yale School of Drama. MJ has received awards and commissions from the Huntington Theater, the Program for Women in Theater, the Playwrights' Foundation, the National Foundation for Advancement in the Arts, and Young Playwrights Inc. MJ's play *A Live Dress* was awarded the Jane Chambers Prize for Feminist Theater in 2010.

CASEY PLETT grew up a kid in Southern Manitoba, Canada, and a teenager in Eugene, Oregon. She was the author of "Balls Out," a column about her first year of transition, for *McSweeney's Internet Tendency*, and has published essays in *Line Zero, Anomalous Press*, and *Cavalier Literary Couture*. She is currently at work on a memoir and other pieces of short fiction.

MIKKI WHITWORTH is a disabled veteran and student pursuing a Bachelor's Degree in English with an emphasis on Creative Writing. She is a three time medalist in the VA Creative Arts Festival's National Competition. She serves on the editorial staff of *ellipsis... literature & art* and occasionally writes for *Q Salt Lake*, Salt Lake City's LGBT magazine. "Masks of a Superhero" is her first piece of fiction to be published.

DONNA OSTROWSKY was born and raised in Boston's western suburbs and received a BFA in Dramatic Writing from NYU. She has collaborated with the Internets Celebrities as a video editor and directed their hit mini-documentary *Bodega Cats*. Donna resides in Brooklyn. "The Queer Experiment" is her first published short fiction.

ALICE DOYLE is a writer and artist from Mississippi whose work has been seen on PrettyQueer.com. She is currently completing a degree in art and literature at the University of Southern Mississippi. This is her first major publication.

MADISON LYNN MCEVILLY is a writer, musician and performance artist from Hamtramck, Michigan. She has worked extensively both on and off stage as monologuist, playwright, and music director. She has toured U.S. and Canada with her one-woman shows *I'd Like to Bash Back Please if That's Okay With Everyone* and *Alecto*. Her most recent piece, "Objects, Rooms," was featured in BoxFest Detroit, a theatre festival dedicated to giving opportunities and exposure to women directors and performers. Madison is also an accomplished session and bluegrass musician who plays a range of instruments but specializes in the singing saw. A collection of her poetry is available from [sic] Detroit in the 2012 anthology *THUS!*

STEPHEN IRA is a writer and activist. His writing—fiction, non-fiction prose, and poetry—can be found in *Spot Lit Mag*, *365 Tomorrows*, and *LGBTQ Nation*. Some of his poems are forthcoming online in *EOAGH: A Journal of the Arts*, where they will be featured as a part of the *Trans Poetry Anthology*, ed. TC Tolbert and Tim Trace Peterson. Stephen also blogs both at his personal website, Super Mattachine, and for Original Plumbing. He is currently pursuing a BA in Writing, Literature, and Anthropology at Sarah Lawrence College.

RED DURKIN is the managing editor of PrettyQueer.com. She is a writer, comedian, and vlogger. She has toured extensively as part of the Tranny Roadshow, performed at Camp Trans and the Transgender Leadership Summit, and was a member of the Fully Functional Cabaret. She has written nine zines and was featured in the final issue of *Punk Planet* magazine. Her work on Youtube has been shown in college classrooms, played at various events internationally, and translated into German. Red's first novel *Ready, Amy, Fire* will be published by Topside Press in Summer 2013.

A. RAYMOND JOHNSON is a writer, shiatsuist, DJ, and karaoke aficionado. He received his MFA in Fiction from Antioch University in Los Angeles and has been awarded writing residencies at Ragdale and Millay Colony for his novels-in-progress. He has blogged since 2000, including at Out Magazine's Popnography and I Fry Mine In Butter.

R. DREW is a transgender writer and artist currently living in Germantown, Philadelphia. R. uses writing as as a subversive activist tool to further the understanding and discussion of transgender identities and experiences. R. Drew is a graduate of The University of the Arts.

ABOUT THE EDITORS

Tom Léger and Riley MacLeod have been writing together and fostering space for transgender artists for over 10 years. Their plays have been seen at HERE Arts Center, WOW Cafe Theater, Clemente Soto Velez Cultural Center, and included 9 sold-out episodes of their serial comedy *Butch McCloud: Your Friendly Neighborhood Lesbian Superhero* which delighted audiences in New York for more than a year. Léger and MacLeod wrote the screenplay for the celebrated short film *F. Scott Fitzgerald Slept Here* (2007, dir. Jules Rosskam) which EMRO noted was "surprisingly blunt and humorous" and also "quite amazing". The two also co-produced STAGES, the first international transgender theater festival, in New York City in 2003. *The Collection* is their first book project.

KNOW THY WORK
• *A Note from the Publisher*

In 1843, Thomas Carlyle wrote a book entitled *Past and Present* and with respect to labor, he tells us, "know thy work and do it," a reaction to the ancient Greek aphorism, γνῶθι σεαυτόν, usually translated as "know thyself."

Carlyle is writing at a time of economic collapse, of great technological advancements, and massive transformations in the cultural and political structures that connected humans to one another. In other words, at a time that bore strong resemblance to our own.

"Long enough has that poor 'self' of thine tormented thee," he says, "thou wilt never get to 'know' it, I believe!"

Carlyle was, obviously, not referring specifically to trans people and art, but his advice to place one's faith in labor rather than introspection and identity has been a guide to us while compiling the book you hold today. What the authors of *The Collection* have done is an act of labor as much as it is an act of art.

In the nearly 400 pages of this book, twenty-eight authors from the US and Canada have produced a body of literature that has never been seen or conceived of before—and they have done it not through the search for self but the will to work. The texts they produced are not a catalog of identities and facts but the beginnings of an investigation into a new world of thought. Carlyle's work was a method of building the British nation state, but our work builds something that is less physical, the borders not oceans and walls but instead porous and transitory, more like the membrane of a cell than the walls of a prison.

As readers, we have suffered through literally decades of coming out memoirs, political tracts, and even medical texts in an attempt to discover and define ourselves. These factual and objective texts do record and disseminate truth, but wholly neglect the Truths that literature elucidates. These factual texts are about answers, about certainty with knowing one's tormented self with an incredible clarity. With this book, we have attempted to put together a collection of work, of the literal struggle to know, if not the answer, then the question.

In some ways, this book is a response to what so many professors of English language literature ask their students to consider at the start of each semester: Why literature? What does literature accomplish? To these Freshman, a assignment after reading this book might be an essay on "What it's like to be a transgender person" or an essay on their own gender and the complexities that these stories bring to light for them. However, a talented professor will push them beyond this interpretation, beyond a reading of any book that isolates the work into a comfortable bubble, discrete from the decisions they make in the "real" world.

By midterms, the cleverest students may suspect that their job is to consider and reconsider what it means to be human, and how literature shapes their point of view. However, the luckiest students are those whose professors force them to ask "What do I want the world I live in to look like?" and "What can I do to realize that world?" It is perhaps for this reason that transgender literature is such a vital part of the literary mosaic. Literature represents a contribution to transfeminist political movements only when trans characters are forced to be considered not as the object but as the subject of the narrative. The works in this volume are some of the first make it clear that it is possible for trans characters to not simply exist as an obstacle for the protagonist to happen upon, to learn from, to overcome.

In curating this work, we did not seek to find so-called "positive" representations of trans people, or sympathetic protagonists, or perpetrate some other manipulation to correct a perceived imbalance. (Certain political advocacy organizations advocate for more positive images of trans people, but these portrayals are uniformly too boring to suffer.) We also did not police the genders of the authors themselves, and as of the date of publication have not formally inquired about their chromosomes, their genitals or how many trucks/dresses they own.

Instead, we sought authors with an interest in seeing trans characters as agents of their own destiny. This feat alone is so difficult that most writers—trans or not trans—are unable to conceptualize it. To argue that only actual trans people can write authentic trans narratives is to argue (1) that there is a way of being "actually trans" and (2) that readers who are not trans can not possibly understand narratives of transgender characters, two statements which must be categorically rejected on feminist grounds. As the fiction in this volume begins to inspire artists and thinkers to take trans art to its next iteration, it will be a credit to the thousands of hours of physical and intellectual labor that the authors have put into their craft, not the labels they claimed or invented for themselves.

Likewise, readers who choose this volume to find truths about gender, normative or otherwise, are likely to find themselves disappointed. Of course, as trans writers all of us engage the complex ways that trans people both challenge and reify boundaries of gender. Are the second wave feminists correct, are trans people by our very nature responsible for rebuilding the patriarchy and the oppression of women? Or are the radical gender faeries on the right track with arguments that the trans and genderqueer communities work toward building a world of true gender equity, a post-gender landscape of prelapsarian bliss?

The truths lie somewhere beyond, and we are so far from the answer that we have yet to begin to really ask the right questions. We can not and should not attempt to represent the work of these writers as a sample or snapshot of living culture, or the writers themselves as the best, the brightest, or the only writers working in this genre and struggling with these questions. Rather than attempt to synthesize a conclusion based on a survey of the texts, the wisest reader may be the one who asks, "What's next?"

In this way, perhaps the works can be better conceived of as a catechism, an endless series of inquiries, a contribution to the beginning of a new age of queer and feminist thought and art.

With that, I will leave you to consider the literature. You may catch yourself enjoying it, but resist this impulse. The word *enjoy* implies a level of sufficiency and satisfaction that we all should be uncomfortable with accepting. Your readership more complex, your time more valuable. Enjoy your dessert, enjoy a sexual encounter, but for these authors, at this time, enjoyment isn't enough. We hope you read the book, and we hope it moves you: to write, to act, to *work*.

—T.L.

THE COLLECTION

WAS DESIGNED BY JULIE BLAIR IN BROOKLYN, NEW YORK. THIS BOOK IS SET IN SCALA—A TYPEFACE DESIGNED AT THE END OF THE EIGHTIES BY MARTIN MAJOOR. *The Collection* uses Scala's serif and sans-serif faces with customized ligatures made by Julie Blair. Titles in this book are set in several weights of KNOCKOUT, an unavoidable type family by Hoefler & Frere-Jones. Letterforms for the cover and logo were created especially for use in *The Collection*, and only the necessary letterforms exist.

NEVADA
a novel by *Imogen Binnie* • March 2013

Nevada is the darkly comedic story of Maria Griffiths, a young trans woman living in New York City and trying to stay true to her punk values while working retail. When she finds out her girlfriend has lied to her, the world she thought she'd carefully built for herself begins to unravel, and Maria sets out on a journey that will most certainly change her forever.

READY, AMY, FIRE
a novel by *Red Durkin* • Summer 2013

Hans Tronsmon is an average 20 year-old transgender man. He's the popular chair of the transmasculine caucus at his women's college and the first draft of his memoir is almost finished. But his world is turned upside down when his happily married gay dads decide to stop paying for his off-campus apartment and start saving for retirement. Hans must learn to navigate the world of part-time jobs, publishing, and packers if he wants to survive. *Ready, Amy, Fire* is the harrowing tale of one man's courageous journey into boyhood.

More information at www.topsidepress.com

TOPSIDE SIGNATURE
QUEER AND FEMINIST BOOKS OF EXTRAORDINARY LITERARY SIGNIFICANCE

MY AWESOME PLACE
THE AUTOBIOGRAPHY OF CHERYL B

written by Cheryl Burke
$25.95 (hardcover) / $15.95 (paperback)
ISBN: 978-0-9832422-4-6 (hc)
978-0-9832422-5-3 (pb)

A rare authentic glimpse into the electrifying arts scene of New York City's East Village during the vibrant 1990s, *My Awesome Place* is the chronicle of a movement through the eyes of one young woman working to cultivate her voice while making peace with her difficult, often abusive, family.

An unlikely story for someone whose guidance counselor recommended a career as a toll taker on the New Jersey Turnpike, Burke was determined to escape her circumstances by any means available—physical, intellectual or psychotropic. Her rise to prominence as the spoken word artist known as Cheryl B brought with it a series of destructive girlfriends and boyfriends and a dependence on drugs and alcohol that would take nearly a decade to shake.

"Bracingly honest and insightful throughout, particularly about family relationships and what it felt like to be young in NYC in the '90s."
– KIRKUS REVIEWS

For more information, visit: www.topsidesignature.com

CPSIA information can be obtained at www.ICGtesting.com
Printed in the USA
LVOW10s0332140813

347797LV00008B/104/P

9 780983 242215